The Urbana Free Library

To renew materials call
217-367-4057

TALKING
to the
MOO

D1506584

Го- 8

TALKING
to the
MOON

A NOVEL

Noël Alumit

CARROLL & GRAF PUBLISHERS
NEW YORK

TALKING TO THE MOON

Carroll & Graf Publishers
An Imprint of Avalon Publishing Group, Inc.
245 West 17th Street • 11th Floor
New York, NY 10011

AVALON
publishing group incorporated

Copyright © 2007 by Noël Alumit

First Carroll & Graf edition 2007

Library of Congress Cataloging-in-Publication Data is available.

ISBN-13: 978-0-78671-629-6
ISBN-10: 0-78671-629-0

9 8 7 6 5 4 3 2 1

Designed by Pauline Neuwirth, Neuwirth & Associates, Inc.

Printed in the United States of America
Distributed by Publishers Group West

FOR MY DAD,

Angel Alumit

Takalajo, amud tan kalaching, jun kaapoapo. Kalajo, panookobantayo
ja kuchil tan tapuy. Ispaispayo bakanangjo, ispaispayyo kapadadjo; say
guaray kapalpaltakanjo ni katagual katagualanjo moan. Takalajo.

Come, souls of our near relatives and souls of our great. Come,
let us eat and drink together hog and rice wine. Grant us riches,
grant us long life, so that there may be ceremonies of calling
you again. Come.

A PRAYER
Benquet Province, the Philippines

The soul will not know either deformity or pain.

Ag amtaan ni adia e balsharo uno ansakit.

SPIRITUAL LAWS
by Ralph Waldo Emerson

TALKING
to the
MOON

———

OCTOBER
1999

JORY

$\mathscr{S}$OMETHING HE KNEW: most people
don't die sensationally. Most deaths don't make the evening news.
Not everyone dies in a war or is killed in a driving accident. Most
people die quietly, perhaps in the night. "She went in her sleep,"
someone might say, as if her soul had attached itself onto the tail
of a dream.

Jory thought his life would end this way. He would close his
eyes, the back of his wife's head the last thing he'd see, then wake
up elsewhere—perhaps on the Moon. It should have happened
this way.

Instead . . .

Jory stared down the barrel of a gun. A man in a dark Toyota
Solara drove up and asked him for directions. The driver, a pink,
balding man, asked Jory where Victory Boulevard was. Jory
adjusted the mail bag on his shoulder, pointed with his left hand
down the road, looking in that same direction.

"Go this way. You have to go straight," Jory said. "Go three blocks and you'll hit—" He turned to address the driver and found a gun in his face.

Jory dropped his mailbag, letters spilling into the street.

"Victory is that way," Jory whispered. The gunman remained silent, keeping the black metal gun still.

Jory saw the hand that held the gun. It was a hairy hand with peeling knuckles. He saw an arm with lightning bolts tattooed onto it. When Jory saw lightning, he thought of snakes, which led him to think about Adam and Eve. Jory didn't want to be as stupid as they were, human beings who didn't know how to properly handle a snake, leaving empty, naked, and riddled with shame. Jory didn't want to leave anywhere feeling like that.

He latched onto the gun with both hands, turning it immediately away from him. He wrestled with the arm, using whatever strength he had to push the barrel away, maybe grab it himself.

Jory's grip was strong enough that he saw the gun tilt downward. It might fall. If it did, Jory would kick it out of the way. Even better, he would grab the gun, aim it at the gunman, and yell for help. Or the gunman, shocked at the old mailman's nerve, would withdraw the gun and simply drive away. There were a million endings to this situation. Jory had lived long enough to know the ending is never what we wish it to be.

Another hand reached out from the window and grabbed onto Jory's shirt. Jory felt a strong tug, and he was almost pulled into the Solara, his face slamming against the top of the car. His cheek burned, and he shut his eyes in pain.

He heard a bang, then felt a velocity push him away. He opened his eyes and saw his mail truck. The velocity had turned him completely around. He looked down and saw a juicy red spot on his shirt, just to the side of his navel.

All he could think to do was get away. I should have worn

bone, Jory thought, a piece of a snake's vertebrae to protect me. He had such a thing at home. He wore it on rainy days to ensure protection against lightning. Today was beautiful, the sky clear.

He saw his white truck with the blue eagle on the side. *Fly. Just fly,* he thought. He would get inside somehow and drive away. He would drive to a house, clutching his bleeding stomach, and someone would call an ambulance. The medic would say, Don't worry, it's only a flesh wound; you'll live.

Belen, he thought, *you wouldn't believe what happened today. Emerson, I was shot today. I got away. Do you want to see where he shot me?*

He would call the post office and tell his supervisor about the nut he encountered. His supervisor—being the asshole that he is—would have no sympathy and tell him that he would have to get back to work as soon as he was bandaged up. However, his fellow postal workers would sympathize, and his story would go down with the other hazards of the business like being attacked by dogs.

He was eight feet from his truck when he heard a pop, a loud pop. It sounded like a balloon bursting. He thought of a child's birthday party and some of the children getting hold of the string of balloons hanging from the ceiling, choosing to stomp on them to hear the noise they'd make.

Jory felt little explosions on his body like firecrackers going off at his right arm, near his waist. Although he sensed the pressure of the bullets hitting him, he didn't feel them. His body was going into shock, he knew. When his oldest son Jun-Jun was in the hospital, the first question Jory asked the doctor was if his son suffered, felt any pain. The doctor told him that the body goes into shock, a severe numbness, when it is being traumatized.

He heard one last pop. He felt a thud in his back like someone had just slapped him there. He fell forward, hearing his body hit the ground, hearing himself exhale a small groan. He felt the hot asphalt against his cheek and saw the vertical yellow lines imprinted into the black road. He felt his body twitching. He tasted blood coming from the back of his throat. He coughed. Red spittle flew from his mouth. He would be the second person in his family with blood on the street. He felt himself drifting away, his eyelids falling, dying.

Jory had no choice about his beginning, but he would certainly have something to say about his end. He willed his eyes to remain open, seeing his blood ooze onto the yellow lines on the road.

BELEN

*B*ELEN WAS SURE that Mr. Addison would try to seduce her. Male nurses were usually assigned to him, but today men were not staffed. A coin was flipped, and she lost. She looked at her watch, waiting for the Addison family to arrive. They came once a month, all the way from Riverside, to bring zucchini bread. They were late, and she dreaded the thought of having to feed Mr. Addison herself.

She picked up the tray from the cart and headed into his room, a luxury suite, one of the best ones A Place of Rest had to offer. The room had hardwood floors, floral curtains, and two hospital beds pushed together to make a queen.

Mr. Addison sat by the window in his wheelchair. His cane against the wall. He was eighty-two years old and as energetic as a toddler. "Hi there, snookums."

She rolled her eyes and asked, "Where do you want to eat? There by the window or at the table?"

"Oh, here will do. Any sign of my daughters?"

"No, not yet. Why don't you eat at the table? I'll leave the food right here."

"No, no. Bring it here. Come closer to me."

Belen took a deep breath, approached the old man with a tray of warm, unsalted food like the nutritionist had ordered. She was two feet away from him when she saw him pick up his cane.

"Now, Mr. Addison, put that down."

"I'm not gonna hurt you. Put the food down right here on my lap."

"You don't need your cane to eat."

Mr. Addison grinned; his spotted fingers gripped that long piece of shellacked wood. "C'mon closer, I'm not gonna hurt ya."

She looked at the old man's dentured smile, shrugged her shoulders, and decided to just get it over with. She put the tray on his lap, undid the cloth napkin, letting the silver flatware fall onto the tray, preparing to place the napkin bib-style around his neck.

"See, I'm not going to hurt ya," he said.

Belen felt the tip of his cane rub against her calf.

"You like that?" he said.

Yes, she thought, *that's exactly what I need. A man who uses his cane to substitute a part of himself made useless from age and testicular cancer.* "Now, Mr. Addison, you know the rules." She felt the cane rise up to her knee.

"Rules? Do you think I can afford the nicest suite at this place by playing by the rules?"

Blessed Lady, Belen prayed, *help me or I'm going to strangle him.*

"You know," he said. "I've had Oriental women before. When I was stationed in Korea."

I'm going to wrap this napkin around his neck and pull, she thought. Murder was a sin, Belen knew. *Thinking about murder was not,* the Virgin once whispered to her. She chose to step back. She was two feet away from Mr. Addison, and he still had his cane between her legs.

"Will you feed me?" he asked.

"You can feed yourself."

"I don't pay an arm and a leg here to feed myself. I pay to have someone pretty and young, like you, to feed me."

Belen put her hands on her hips and smiled. She lowered her head and shook it. To a shriveled man in his eighties, she supposed a woman in her fifties looked pretty good. *Be kind, be patient. He is old,* she thought.

"Pop, I hope you're not giving the nurses hell again," Belen heard from behind her.

Thank the Virgin, she thought. Before she turned, she knew his daughters would be there, Ava and Lana, named after the two most beautiful actresses Mr. Addison said had ever lived. The twins Ava and Lana were probably attractive women at one point in their lives. She saw it in their proud faces. They both had thick liner coated around their eyes, Egyptian-style, the way it once was popular in the sixties.

"I hope he's not being a pain," Ava said.

"No," Belen said, "just his usual self."

"So, he is being a pain," Lana said.

Belen laughed. "You're just in time for feeding."

"I'll do the honors," Ava said, picking up a spoon.

"No way," Mr. Addison protested. "I want her to feed me." He pointed his cane at Belen.

"Pop, you gotta leave the women alone," Ava said. "That's why God took away one of your gonads. The Man Upstairs had enough of you chasing women. I probably have siblings I am not aware of. God sees fit to take care of such things."

Belen closed her eyes briefly, knowing full well what God is capable of.

"You know," Lana said, "it was Pop's running around that drove Mama away. Divorced him like that. Just had his pants below his knees way too much, right, Pop? His trousers went up and down more times than an elevator."

Belen blushed and turned to leave the room. She heard Ava say, "Enough talk about women. Eat your dinner. Later we can have some zucchini bread."

"Women keep me alive," Mr. Addison said. "Without them, I might as well die. I wonder if Viagra will do anything for me."

"Oh, Lord," said Ava and Lana simultaneously.

EMERSON

Rrrrrrrrrrrring.

—Hello, Emerson said into the phone. He quickly closed his office door.

—Hey, Emmy.

—I told you not to call me at work.

—I would have called you on your cell, but you don't have one.

—That's because I don't want you buggin' me all the time.

—Is that the way you see it?

—No, of course not. You know that. But how do you think people would react if they knew I talk to my dead brother?

—Something told me you needed a call. Are you busy now?

—No, but I get busy . . . I'm just . . . you know.

—He hasn't called.

—No.

—What you did was pretty crappy, Emmy. Crappy, scrappy.

—Can you be a little more supportive? Just a little? I don't need this from you right now.

—You gotta let some time pass. It's only been a month.

—Is this what you learn when you're a corpse?

—This stuff takes time. I'm sure Michael will call when he's good and ready. Even if Michael doesn't call—

—Don't say that.

—Even if Michael doesn't call, you'll be all right.

—I don't know. Something's different now. He was like no one I'd ever dated.

—Anyone you date is like no one you've ever dated, Emmy. That's your problem. You didn't see him as a guy with a life. You saw him as the guy in front of you, nothing behind him. You liked what you saw, but didn't go deeper. You've had this problem before.

—That's not true.

—It is true! You purposely choose guys you can't properly speak to, hold a decent conversation with. Nobu, Chi-Wai, Pak, Pedro—

—All right.

—Not everyone is going to be like Doug.

—Don't ever mention his name. You know how I feel about that.

—Sorry. I knew one of these days a guy would figure you out and give you what you deserve. Ha-ha. Michael gave it to you. Gave it to you big time. Who knew that Taiwanese boy had it in him.

—He was pretty mad. Never seen him so mad.

—I was proud of him myself.

—You don't have to take his side.

—Hey, I'm always behind you, but Michael let you have it.

—Okay, he let me have it. The fun is over. Why can't he call? Just one call.

—He probably wants you to feel it. Feel it real good. Feel it so you'll never forget.

—I feel it already. Enough is enough. I'm gonna call him again.

—What's the use? He's not going to pick up. Just chill.

—Look, I always feel weird talking to you at work. Call me at home. And only at home.

—Time, Emmy. Remember: give it time.

JORY

"*H*ELLO, BUDDY."

I am not your buddy, Jory thought. He felt his chest pushing against the ground as he tried to breathe.

"I'm gonna put this needle into your arm. And it'll make you feel real good," Ambulance Man said.

I don't need a needle, idiot. I don't feel anything already.

"Okay, here we go."

Jory didn't feel the needle break his skin, but he could feel the serum flow into his arm.

"Boy, you got banged up pretty bad."

Why are you talking to me like a child?

"We're going to have to turn you over. You're doing fine, just fine. We're going to put our hands under you and put you on the stretcher. Okay, guys, on the count of three. One, two—"

Jory didn't hear the word *three* when hands lifted him into the air, slowly turning him over, and resting him on his back. He looked up and saw at least four people standing around him. Where did they come from? Three men and a woman. He saw a clear mask go over his face and clamp down on his jaw.

"All right, buddy, just rest. We're going to have to put this on you."

A plastic collar was placed around his neck, keeping his head still.

"We're gonna take you away. Conserve your energy. We'll take care of you. We're taking you someplace safe."

Take me to the Moon, Jory thought as he was lifted into the ambulance. *That's where I'm going, you know. I come from wood,* he wanted to say. *I was found inside the trunk of a tree just before the beginning of World War II. Villagers passed the tree and almost didn't notice me.* Jory was brown like the bark and easily blended into the branches. It wasn't until one of the villagers saw the tree move that a baby wearing nothing but rags was discovered nestled in the trunk.

"We're taking you to St. Joan's," Ambulance Man said.

I was brought to St. Teresa's in the Philippines, Jory thought. St. Teresa's: a church that also doubled as an orphanage. He was delivered on the feast day for St. Joseph. Father Ryan, an American priest, received him. He was quickly baptized Joseph but the Filipina nuns gave him the nickname Jory, a hybrid name of the saint whose feast day he was delivered on and the priest who took him in.

Lying on the stretcher, looking up at the ceiling of the ambulance, Jory saw a fly. He was reminded of the orphan boys who slept on floor mats in the back house of St. Teresa's, an old, dilapidated Spanish-style building with brown walls, located on the northernmost part of Luzon Island in a province called Cagayan. The church's dilapidation looked romantic and charming to passersby, but the locals knew it to be a rundown place with lizards that ran up and down the walls and mosquitoes that hovered by the ceiling.

The one redeeming quality of the church was the stained glass windows colored deep red and dark blue. There were six windows, and each window had a crucifix worked into the glass. The glory of the church was the fifteen-foot stained glass window of St. Teresa of Avila, wearing a habit with a dove hovering by her head, located above the altar. When the sun came through the window of St. Teresa, the dull walls of the church took on the hues of the stained glass, transforming itself into a jewelry box with parishioners imbedded in rubies and sapphires.

Jory shifted his gaze from the ceiling of the ambulance to the window. There were orange letters that he couldn't read because his head was restrained by the collar. The windows at St. Teresa's had lettering, too. They were in Latin. Those windows were always properly maintained, cleaned on a regular basis. If it rained, Father Ryan made sure tarps were put over the glass to protect it and decreed sports involving the throwing, hitting, and kicking of balls forbidden on the property.

"It was those windows," Father Ryan once said, "that saved the building from being damaged or looted by the Japs. Those Japs may have been our enemies, but they knew art when they saw it. And they respected it, too."

After the war, more parentless children were brought to Father Ryan. The boys stayed at St. Teresa's while the girls were taken to a girl's orphanage closer to Manila. The boys slept in a large room at the far end of the church grounds. The room didn't have stained glass windows; the windows didn't have glass at all. Rags, a poor attempt to keep the mosquitoes out, covered the glassless windows. Carrion still got in and more than a few of the boys had bouts of malaria caused by mosquito bites.

Some nights, when the summer evenings got too hot, and the noise of buzzing flies kept them from sleeping, the boys wondered who their parents were. Most of the boys had cinnamon-colored skin and hair the color of onyx. Some had pale skin and light, feathery hair. One boy was easily the child of an American soldier, with green eyes and reddish curls. He was one of four boys who had come down with malaria and eventually died.

Jory and the other orphans constructed a wooden box for the child to be buried in. The boy was given a pauper's funeral and buried in the corner of the village cemetery. You could tell which boys in the cemetery came from the orphanage because they didn't get granite or stone markers with phrases like "Dearly Loved" or "Sweet Son." They just got a wooden cross with the boy's first name etched in. The four orphan boys who died had small plots, no bigger that four feet long and two feet wide. Their names were Laurencio, Lazarus, Bernardo, and Andres. All of the orphaned boys had first names but no last names.

"What is your name?" someone in town might ask him.

"Jory."

"No, what is your NAME?"

Jory came to know the full meaning of that question. *What is your name?* meant who is your family? Do you come from good origins or bad? Are you related to the family who lives on the hill, where the father works hard and the mother cooks good meals? Is your mother the seamstress who repairs holes in pants so well that you never knew a hole existed there before? Are you related to the Luistro family, whose sons died in the war? Maybe you are a son of the Abaya family, notorious for having husbands who cheat on their wives? Could it be that you're a member of the Villacruz clan known for bearing beautiful but dimwitted daughters? You have the smile of the Chuas, a jovial bunch that takes to liquor on rainy days. Is your name one of those?

What is your name? became the spear that jabbed Jory in the gut. A question that made a little boy bow his head in shame.

"What's your name, buddy?" Ambulance Man asked, not

expecting an answer. Jory watched Ambulance Man adjust tubes hanging from his head.

My name is Jory. Only Jory, he thought. Everyone knew a boy with one name came from the orphanage over there, where the children were suspect. In this Philippines, where family was important and lineage traced, what must you be to have your mama give you up? A rapist's child, a whore's son, a kid with a mental defect so bad that a family refused to call him one of their own.

It was the town whispers that made Jory stay close to St. Teresa. He was safe there, doing things that kept him busy. "Remember what Ralph Waldo Emerson wrote," Father Ryan said. "'Do your work, and you shall reinforce yourself.'"

Part of a boy's duties at the orphanage was to assist Father Ryan and the nuns with the business of maintaining the church. He ran around making sure there was holy water available for the parishioners to bless themselves. He made sure the grass in the courtyard was cut. He caught the lizards that made their way into the church. He swept the dirt from the front door. He varnished the pews and polished the chalices used during Mass. He held the gold bowls that held the communion wafers representing the Body of Christ. He marched down the center aisle of the church in his altar boy robe as one of God's minions. In some cases he stood by the elderly ladies fanning them with the unused missals left on the pews. After a while, a boy became respected. Villagers saw him at church and took him as divine. It was assumed by the villagers and by Jory himself that he would serve God.

Some of the boys in the orphanage were "adopted." Everyone knew that meant the boy was recruited for servitude. An elderly couple adopted a son to make sure the house was properly kept, the floors scrubbed, the curtains drawn at certain times of the day. A boy was adopted to train as a shopkeeper's apprentice, to greet the customers, keep inventory, make sure the store windows gleamed. A boy was adopted to cultivate land, waking up early, going to bed late, smelling of mud. They became unpaid labor. In exchange, they got a name. It was that name that made becoming a slave worth it.

Jory wasn't considered for adoption. Potential parents looked him up and down, then passed him by. He was too thin. He looked like he didn't have it in him to put in long hours or carry heavy loads. Growing into his teen years, he looked like a lone sapling that would easily break in two when a strong wind blew by.

Jory was also too dark. The *mestizos* or mixed-blood boys were the ones who were adopted first. Their light hair, light skin, and pointy noses suggested better breeding. These boys could grow to be six feet tall like their fathers (it was assumed that if you were part white, you would grow to be tall). A boy like that could certainly help with manual labor.

For some, these *mestizos* were considered even more intelligent. Filipinos, even those darker than Jory, wanted the mixed-race Caucasian orphans. Those orphans could have come from drunken sailors or be the product of a rape, but they were seen by locals in the area as sons of General MacArthur, the American who worked with the Philippines to fight the Japanese.

He turned fourteen and knew he didn't have a chance at being adopted. He was too old and still as skinny as bamboo. He would be Jory, just Jory, a boy with no name, no ties to a history. He would die with a wooden cross on his plot with a single name marking his existence.

~

THE SOUND OF the ambulance siren blared in his head.

"We're almost there, buddy. Just rest. Almost there."

There. Where's There? Jory thought.

"Close your eyes and rest. Do what I say, buddy."

I don't want to close my eyes.

"Close your eyes, buddy."

Jory felt small again like a child, someone telling him what to do. Jory did what Father Ryan and the nuns told him, striving for dreams they gave him. The dreams they had for him were to be a priest. It was difficult for Jory to think of serving the Lord when he woke with an erection. He wondered about girls when the nuns who worked at the church intrigued him, wondering what they looked like underneath their habits. He knew these thoughts were blasphemous and usually spent a good hour on Sunday mornings prostrate before the image of Christ begging for forgiveness.

During Mass, he sat by the altar with a clear view of the congregation. He looked over the crowd, setting his sights on the prettiest girls in the village. He assisted Father Ryan in administering communion, following the priest with a brass plate. Congregants filed one by one to the altar, knelt, and opened his or her mouth to receive a wafer that was the Body of Christ. Father Ryan offered the Body of Christ to a churchgoer, and Jory placed the plate under the chin to catch the wafer in case it should somehow miss the mouth and land on the floor. ("The Body of Christ cannot touch the floor!" Father Ryan warned.)

It should have been an easy task, but for an adolescent boy wondering about the opposite sex, it became a disaster. A pretty girl, one with nice breasts, approached the altar; Jory saw her coming. It became overwhelmingly hot in the church, and girls often fanned themselves. He went crazy watching wisps of hair blowing away from their faces. He knew it was a sin to have an erection while administering the Body of Christ. His saving grace was that his altar boy robe hid the growing member in his trousers.

He grew weak when a girl approached the altar, kneeling before Father Ryan and himself, clasping her fingers to her chest, her hands sweetly tucked between her breasts, then looked up and opened her mouth. Oh, the thoughts that ran through his head.

One Sunday, he knew he was in trouble as six girls in a row

approached the altar, one prettier than the other. One kneeled and opened her mouth. Jory shook. By the time the fifth girl kneeled, he lowered the brass plate under her chin. He smelled her perfume, mixed in with her sweat from the heat.

"The Body of Christ," Father Ryan said.

"Amen," the girl said and opened her mouth. The oppressive warmth of the room made him dizzy. The girl sighed, and Jory got a whiff of Kalamansi juice on her breath. All was lost. His erection reacted, and he felt a rush deep inside him. Jory felt a kind of pleasure he'd never known before. He honestly believed that he was dying, and this pleasure was what it felt like to be ascending into heaven.

The temperature in the room became unbearable. Jory dropped the brass plate, his hands shaking, his knees folded. He leaned to one side, falling against Father Ryan. Father Ryan tried to support the Filipino teenager, but Jory's body was dead weight. Father Ryan fell down, the bowl of communion wafers falling from his hands, Bodies of Christ spilled onto the floor.

Jory lay on the altar, trembling. The rush of pleasure still seeping from him. He looked up and saw the stained glass of St. Teresa, convinced that his last moment on earth was coming. He imagined himself being buried with a wooden cross on his chest bearing a single name.

Father Ryan got up, looked down on the fallen altar boy, and said, "What is it? What's the matter?"

"I think I'm dying," Jory said.

The congregation surrounded the poor teenager, including the six girls that contributed to his downfall. One of the girls got on her knees, leaned forward and patted his forehead. Her breasts fell across Jory's face and Jory moaned.

"He has a fever. He's burning up," the girl said. "He might have malaria."

Jory's eyes fluttered, and he thought of the other boys who had died. No one to visit them, no one to bring flowers to their graves. There would be no one to remember them. Soon, he would join his brothers in the ground. He had no place in history. He was not born. He merely appeared, grew from the trunk of a tree. He did not come before or after a sibling. He was inserted into time like a blank page placed into the bible: there were no stories there.

Jory closed his eyes, waiting to be taken to the Kingdom of Heaven. It was coming, he knew, because the rush of pleasure was nearing its end. What he was told and what he believed was that soon he would be lifted, raised to that place where Jesus, Mary, and the saints lived, and feel loved. Indeed, a sense of peace overcame him. He stopped trembling and numbness swept over his body. He felt a hand reach under him and hoist him up. He thought it was Jesus elevating him to heaven, then he heard Father Ryan's voice say, "Can you walk, son?"

Jory opened his eyes and found himself in a sitting position. The whole church looking at him.

"Can you walk?" the priest asked again.

Jory nodded and was brought to his feet. Father Ryan walked him out of the church, into the courtyard. The fresh air sobered him up. He felt something wet and sticky ooze down his legs. Jory was placed on a bench while Father Ryan announced that Mass would resume in a few moments. People went back into the church.

Jory sat in the courtyard alone. He dried the sweat on his palms, rubbing them against his robe. He brought the hem to his face, wiping away the moisture on his forehead, cheeks, and nose. He took a deep breath, stunned at what just happened. He lifted his head, slowly realizing he would not die. He heard the final prayers of Mass being said and soon the parishioners would be milling about.

He brought himself to his feet, walked across the courtyard to the backhouse where he slept. He entered to find boys sitting and playing cards. They saw him and took note of his disheveled appearance.

"What happened to you?" one boy asked.

"I thought . . . I thought I was dying." Jory took off his robe. His T-shirt was drenched with sweat, and there was a visible stain in his crouch area.

The boys were horrified and stood up. No one dared to approach him, afraid to catch whatever disease he had. Jory turned away and undressed. He slipped off his trousers and, with his back to the other boys, he examined his pants, pondering the wetness that came from him. It did not look like urine, and Jory had some inkling of what it might be.

He heard shuffling feet, the boys approaching him. He quickly bundled up the trousers, turned around, realizing he was naked. He covered his privates with the bundled clothes. "It's perspiration," he said. He would not dare say that he peed in his pants. "It was so hot in there I sweat all over."

Before the boys could respond, he went to a curtained-off area of the room and found new clothing. He slipped into some new trousers and went to the stream to wash his clothes.

Later that evening Father Ryan asked Jory what overcame him. Jory sat with the priest in the rectory, his eyes cast to the ground. Behind Jory were two paintings: one was of the current Pope, Pius XII, and the other was of Jesus.

"Jory, you had a little problem today?"

Jory considered Father Ryan to be a kind man. He was a straight-forward person in his fifties with a sharp nose and white hair.

"I'm sorry, Father," Jory said. "I got sick. I ate something, I think."

"I thought I lost you. Maybe it was just the heat. It gets hot in that church. And a boy your age—how old are you now?"

"Fourteen."

"A boy your age has to learn how to handle such things. You're becoming a man now and have to learn to withstand anything. In the words of Emerson, 'The natural measure of this power is the resistance of circumstances.' You need to learn to overcome. Heat should be the last of your worries. Have you read the books on Mr. Ralph Waldo Emerson I gave you?"

"Yes, sir."

"Emerson fell in love with a girl when he was young. Married her, too. When she died, he was devastated. Did you read that?"

"Yes, her name was Ellen Tucker."

"Now, the death of a spouse can destroy people. Ralph Waldo Emerson rose above it."

"He learned to transcend."

"Yes, he spurred the transcendentalist movement and became one of the greatest men of letters America had ever known."

"Yes, father."

"Jesus was another man who withstood anything. You should strive to be more like him. Look up to Him and love Him."

"Yes, sir," he said, then left the room, entering the courtyard, sitting on a bench. He thought about Father Ryan's words. Jory respected Jesus, but he did not love him. Respect was dutifully taught at St. Teresa's. He was told to let the girl enter the room first. Stand when a teacher enters the room. Lower your head when those older are speaking to you. Accept a gift offered to you and say, "Thank you." Shake a man's hand firmly. Do what the priests and nuns say—always. All of these things were acts of respect. But love? None of that was taught. No one certainly said it. Jory never said it. No one ever said it to Jory. Here was a teenage boy who knew nothing about love.

Except love for Jesus. He was told you show love to Jesus by attending Mass, by honoring Him. Jory had done that every day of his life. It was a duty. If this is what love feels like, it can best be described as bland.

He was told that Jesus loved him. There were times he prayed, waiting for God's love to happen. He stayed on his knees, waiting to be loved. Every time he bowed his head, and brought his hands together, he hoped he would leave the experience feeling loved. He opened his eyes, lifted his head, and felt nothing around him.

The only time he witnessed anything that would be considered love was when he saw kids with their parents. He'd watch a mother bring a babe to her breast and knew that she loved that child. When a father patted his son's head, making the standing hairs lie down, that was love, too. *Those* children were loved. Jory knew none of that.

He entered the courtyard thinking about his near death experience, feeling something he'd never felt before. Maybe what he felt was love also, and he felt it toward a girl. This was a new feeling. What other things needed to be felt? For the first time in his life, he began to have dreams of his own.

Jory graduated at sixteen and immediately started seminary school at the same church. Jory was told that entering the seminary was a testing period, to see if serving God was his true vocation. He was told a young man can leave at any time, but he knew he was expected to stay. Two orphans, Mariano and Joseph, chose to leave the seminary after six months of study and they were ostracized. They were considered unmarriageable. The locals knew that they didn't choose God, and they believed that surely He would remember that decision some day, bringing havoc upon the young men.

Even those who didn't believe such things, who didn't give God that much attention, usually families engaging in commerce, couldn't see marrying a daughter off to Mariano or Joseph. They may look all right on the outside, but they might have some sickness or insanity lurking deep within their genes. Fortunately, Mariano and Joseph didn't want to get married. Jory noticed how they chose to sleep side by side, nestled against each other sometimes. Watching them, Jory knew they were not like the other orphans who grew up alone. They had found each other as boys, eating together, playing together, comforting each other when a nun slapped one of them.

Mariano was considered for adoption, but would not leave without Joseph. Mariano thrashed about, yelling like he was possessed when he found out he would leave Joseph behind. Joseph took to bed and would not rise believing that Mariano would be taken away. Finally, Father Ryan relented and decided to keep the boys together. The couple who wanted Mariano could not afford to feed two boys, thus adopted someone else.

Jory knew there was something else that Mariano and Joseph felt for each other, something more important than a coveted last name. The last Jory had heard of the two men were that they were working as field hands, hoping to save enough money to leave and start new somewhere.

What made orphan boys good candidates for priesthood is that they knew no family life and, therefore, wouldn't know what they were missing. Taking the holy vow of poverty should come easy, considering they were raised with no money in the first place. They knew nothing of material possessions, no fancy clothes or toys to play with. The boys played with the lizards they caught crawling on the church walls.

Jory started his training for priesthood by being given a history of Christianity by the nuns who taught there. He was taught the full sequences of every form of Mass, learning Latin, reciting every necessary prayer for Easter, Christmas, and the New Year. He knew the feast days for every major saint like St. Francis or St.

Paul. He wasn't too particular about remembering feast days for the obscure saints like St. Amantius or St. Lizier. He knew the feast day of his namesake, St. Joseph.

In addition to liturgical studies, he received an education in art and literature. Father Ryan kept the books of American writers on the shelves of his room. In addition to church doctrine, Jory received lessons on the work of Stephen Crane, Robert Frost, Jack London, Edith Wharton, Walt Whitman, Harriet Beecher Stowe, Herman Melville, Henry David Thoreau, and Ralph Waldo Emerson. Filipino writers were not part of the lessons, because some of the country's most respected writers often wrote of rebellion, independence.

There were times Jory stayed up late, reading the work of these American writers, keeping the light of a candle glowing by his bed. The other orphans would get annoyed and tell him to blow out the candle.

"Gago," one boy would say. "Stupid. Enough reading! Go to bed."

"Close your eyes, buddy," Ambulance Man said. "Just sleep."

No, Jory thought.

BELEN

*S*HE DROVE HOME, wondering about the children. On the radio, the announcer said an unidentified man riddled a Jewish day care center with bullets. A child and school counselor were rushed to the hospital. Belen rolled up the window of her Chevy Nova and shook her head.

"Sweet Lady, Mother of God," Belen whispered.

The shootings, the announcer said, appeared to be a "hate crime." She always felt sorry for the Jews. Jews and blacks, what with people hating them all the time. Terrible, just terrible.

She arrived at her small two-bedroom house—a house long rumored to be haunted—and thought nothing of a message on the answering machine, left by Jory's supervisor, asking her to call him back IMMEDIATELY.

Belen rolled her eyes. She knew how Jory felt about his supervisor.

"He makes a mountain out of an ant hill," Jory once said.

"Mole hill."

"Mole hill? What is a mole—never mind. My boss always says, 'Do it immediately or suffer the consequences!'"

Belen had heard Jory complain so much about his supervisor that she despised the man without having met him. *Immediately* meant something else to Belen. It meant after she lit Jun-Jun's candle—something she had been doing religiously for over twenty years.

"How are you today, Jun?" Belen asked. "I had a so-so day."

This candle was left on a mantle next to a photo of a boy everyone called beautiful. She returned messages, paid bills, cooked dinner, took out the trash only after she paid homage to her son's spirit. She prepared a little snack, some cookies or half of a sandwich, to place next to her dead child's image.

Belen would have loved to have had a little statue, or at the very least a photo of the Blessed Lady on the mantle, but she knew how Jory felt about all things Catholic. She had to make due with a little picture card of the Virgin in her purse and a miniature pin of Mary attached to her bra.

On this same mantle was a small 2 × 2 picture of Valentino, her father, a man she wished she had known. Belen stole that photo from her mother, Ermaline Dubabang, believing that she wouldn't miss it among the other photos of her dad. With Ermaline's help, Valentino "died" during World War II. Belen placed the tiny, black-and-white picture of her father slightly behind the colorful 8 × 10 photo of her son.

On this particular afternoon, she lit the candle, placed a bowl of Doritos next to Jun's picture, then called Jory's supervisor. She was put on hold. She went to the stereo, pressed a button, and listened to an instrumental of "Love Me Tender." She knew all of Elvis's songs. Elvis was her singer of choice when she danced the night away at parties she attended a lifetime ago.

While she was on hold, she decided to undress. Emerson had given her a cordless phone for Christmas—a gift she loved—so she could wander the home and talk to all her friends. She would call her neighbor Mrs. Kim and talk and talk and talk. Even though Mrs. Kim lived right next door, Belen would call and chat, maybe decide whose car they would take to Mass, maybe talk about their children.

"You lucky," Mrs. Kim might say in her slight Korean accent, "you have son who live in Los Angeles. My children go away. My daughter Eva, sometime she call. My son Sung never call."

Belen wouldn't admit that her son Emerson rarely called or visited, even though he lived nearby. In the children department, Mrs. Kim's kids were doing far better than her son. Eva worked on computers in New Hampshire, and Sung was a successful lawyer in San Francisco. Belen wanted Mrs. Kim to believe that Emerson called often, making him good at *something*.

She kept the cordless phone in close proximity to her ear as she took off her gold earrings, well, gold-plated, and placed them on the coffee table. She hummed to the instrumental of "Love Me Tender." She put her white shoes, with the toes pointed toward the wall, near the front door.

She entered the bedroom, unzipped the back of her white uniform, letting the polyester outfit fall from her shoulders to the floor. She picked up the uniform, smelled it, and decided that she could wear it one more time before sending it to the cleaners. She slid into a green house dress, with flowers printed by the hem, stepping into black velour slippers. She loved velour. Thank the Lord for velour. It feels so good against your skin. So comfortable, yet so cheap. She went to the hamper, looked inside, and decided that yes, she would do laundry tonight.

The patients at work were not cooperative today, not cooperative at all. It wasn't just Mr. Addison. It was those who refused their pills, complained about the food, and kept buzzing her for the most trivial of things. One patient called her into his room to get him a magazine that was on his nightstand a foot away from his bed! He may have been old, but he could certainly have reached for a magazine twelve inches from his pillow.

Belen shoveled the dirty clothes out of the hamper, trying to cradle the phone between her cheek and shoulder. She threw the dirty clothes into a plastic basket she got from the 99 cents store. She loved that store. Imagine! Everything in the store for less than a dollar.

Suddenly the supervisor came on. "Bell?"

"Belen," she corrected him.

"Yes, Belen," he said. "Something happened. Jory . . . Jory was shot. He was shot, Belen."

Belen felt sweat building on her forehead. She wiped the moisture away with her forearm.

"Did you hear? Jory was shot," the supervisor repeated. "I don't know nothing else."

She looked around the room and caught the flickering light of Jun-Jun's candle. The child killed by a speeding Comet. Belen dropped the phone, dropped her basket of laundry, and fell to her knees. She found herself sobbing on a mound of dirty clothes. One article of clothing belonged to Jory. It was a shirt, part of his uniform. She had told him many times to get his work shirts dry-cleaned, but he didn't want to spend the extra money. Belen believed in dry cleaning, particularly for uniforms.

She tried to find the phone, but it was buried underneath the laundry.

Belen said, "No, not again, not again—"

"Belen? Mrs. Lalaban," the supervisor said on the phone. "Mrs. Lalaban?"

It can't be happening again, she thought.

"Mrs. Lalaban? Are you all right? Belen? Are you there? Belen?"

She heard her name. She rifled through the dirty clothes and grabbed the phone. "Yes, I'm here."

"He was shot, that's all I know. He's at St. Joan's Hospital. I'll arrange for someone to pick you up."

"No, don't do that. I know where St. Joan's is. I'll meet you there." She hung up and sighed. She tried to stand but couldn't. Her bad knees kept her down. She shook her head. As much as she loathed to admit it, she needed Emerson's help. She dialed her son at work. It was close to 7:00 P.M. and knew he would be at his job. If she had called at 10:00 P.M., he would have been there, too, she knew.

"Emerson, it's Mom."

"Yes?" He sounded weary.

"I have to tell you . . ." She lost her breath. The weight of the phone put her off balance. She took a few quick breaths and shut her eyes.

"What's up?" he said.

"Emerson . . . it's about your dad. He was shot. I need you to take me to the hospital right now."

"I'm coming right over. Stay put." He hung up.

She sighed. One thing she could depend on was that Emerson knew what to do in serious situations. That was what made him so good at his job, she supposed. Having to find food for the hungry or shelter for the homeless at the nonprofit he worked for. She loved telling her friends that Emerson helped people for a living, the only thing really worth bragging about when it came to her remaining child.

She waited for her son, picking up the laundry that she'd spilled and slowly placing it in the basket, moving with the sad sounds of the music filling the air. On her knees, she was reminded of praying. She held Jory's shirt, inhaling it. She delicately wiped her face with the sky blue cloth. She folded it, noticing a smudge on the collar. Seltzer water should help remove the stain, she thought.

She'd wondered when the Curse would return. That Curse—made up of displeased ancestors, an angry Catholic God, and a spell cast by the great Ermaline. As long as she lived It would be there. The Curse made her unable to conceive for the first years of her marriage. The Curse took away Jun-Jun. The Curse even affected Emerson, though Emerson refuses to believe it.

"Holy Mother," she whispered.

Yes, dear, Belen heard, and she calmed immediately. The Voice of the Blessed Virgin speaking to her always did that.

I never thought it would get my husband, Belen thought. *I thought the Curse was only limited to my offspring.*

Yes, dear, it was, the Voice of Mary responded.

The wistful whisper of the Mother gave her hope. *Yes, the Curse only affects my children,* she surmised, *this Curse did not apply to my husband, not to Jory.*

No, not to Jory, Mary's whisper confirmed.

With this newfound belief, she stopped crying. Oh, how Mary always came in her time of need. She straightened her back and looked around her living room, taking in her house (just three more years of mortgage payments and it would be theirs, fully theirs). She felt foolish for behaving this way. How would she explain to her son that this was a false alarm. Jory would be fine. The Blessed Virgin herself had whispered it to her.

She heard Emerson's car pull up to the driveway. Emerson entered, stopped the music, his intense eyes shooting toward her. Those eyes made her uneasy sometimes.

"Mama, you okay?" Emerson's voice was direct, sharp. There was no compassion there. She had no doubt that he cared for her well-being, but couldn't he be just a little warmer?

"The Curse doesn't affect him," she said.

"Please don't bring that up right now, okay? That's the last thing I need to hear. Which hospital is dad in?" he asked.

Sayong, *he never listens,* she thought.

"He's at St. Joan's," she said. "I don't know where that is."

"I know how to get there," he said.

She extended her arm. He lifted her up. His touch was cold, mechanical. He might as well be lifting furniture. He quickly escorted her to the driveway. He opened the right passenger side door. The door opened with a loud creak. She slid in. Her son joined her on the other side. The slam of the car door forced her to jump.

Belen didn't like the smell of her son's car. The air freshener didn't help. It was an old car, perhaps from the 1960s, that maintained the scent of all the people who had ever ridden in it. The seats of the Galaxie were hard, and there was a rip in the vinyl that snagged her dress.

Emerson, she rehearsed in her head, *your father will be fine. Emerson* . . . She wished she had something more endearing to call her son than Emerson, but a name never stuck. She tried calling him Emmy, the way Jun used to call him. It just didn't sound quite right coming from her.

The car started to move, and she stared straight ahead, every once in a while turning toward her boy. She thought of arriving at the hospital and finding her husband. She thought about Jory sitting in his hospital bed, eating a donut. Yes, he was shot, but it was nothing serious. She was a nurse. In her earlier years in America, she had worked in emergency rooms at big hospitals. She had seen people shot before. People shot in the arm or leg, even the chest and stomach. They were still lucid, able to talk. A bullet doesn't have to mean death.

Yes, that is how it will be, she thought. He will have a wound. But he will be eating a donut. And when she would enter the hospital room, Jory would look at them oddly and simply utter, "What?" She would yell at him for being careless, not being safe enough. Then Jory would groan, "Not now, I'm eating." They would bicker. She knew Emerson would roll his eyes and sigh, dismiss them as idiots. He always did. Yes, that is how it would be.

They got on the freeway. There was traffic.

"Oh, for heaven's sake. Move your ass!" Her son yelled out of the window. It amazed her that Emerson couldn't stand to speak in front of people, but could curse at them easily. Freeway traffic started briefly then came to an immediate halt. She lifted her hand, wanting to touch him, wanting to tell him that his father is really all right. Traffic. A good sign. She believed that if her husband was in bad shape she would zoom to the hospital, make it there within minutes. That's how it happened before, transported by some unseen force to the hospital, something telling her that she needed to be there quickly. She wanted to touch her son and let him know this.

She reached for her boy. She witnessed his hands tighten around the steering wheel, his forearm muscles growing taut. She chose to withdraw.

"Jeez, move," Emerson said, staring at the cars in front of him.

Yes, he's tense because of the traffic, the insane traffic. She refused to believe that his fingers gripped the wheel when he felt her touch approaching.

EMERSON

*H*E SAT IN his office and thought, *I just need one long drag of a joint—that could fix anything.* It would fix a day that's going by much too slowly, exacerbated by a headache forming at back of his skull, and a client who'd missed yet another appointment to discuss his drug regimen. Most importantly, it was another day that Michael didn't return his calls. One drag. One long, blissful drag of a joint.

He looked at the telephone, focusing all his mental energy on it. He envisioned a yellow ray of light leaving his forehead, entering the phone lines, traversing miles of land, rising into thin air, connecting to a cell phone of a steward aboard a Taiwan Air plane, somewhere between Taipei and Bangkok.

Call me, Michael, Emerson thought. *Just one call.* The phone remained quiet, and Emerson sat back and rolled his head around, trying to rid the forming of a migraine. He shifted his attention to his computer, logging onto the internet. He immediately went to the Taiwan Air Web site, fuming at how slow it took his computer to download the images of the site.

He'd visited this Web site many times since Michael left. The images appeared: first a blue sky filled the screen, then gradually a tomato-colored airplane, boxes asking to continue in English, Chinese, Japanese, Spanish, French. He didn't care what language was available. He waited for the last image to download, a picture of a happy Taiwan Air staff: two middle-aged pilots in a salute, three stewardessess carrying trays, and one beautiful steward lifting a cocktail.

There he is, Emerson thought. Michael Zhang in his uniform, a red vest over a white shirt and tie. Smiling. Emerson put one finger on the screen, outlining Michael's face. He started at the tip of Michael's head, filled with black hair, slicked back, revealing one of the most unusual aspects of Michael's face: a hairline that gathered to a tip, forming a widow's peak. He traced the line of his cheek, the bottom of his jaw, down to the gold buttons on his vest.

Fly back to me, Emerson thought. He logged off, knowing that he could have stared at that picture for hours. He had done so alone in his apartment, looking at the image of Michael, turning away, looking back again.

He massaged the back of his neck, the headache becoming worse. *Dad,* he thought. He looked at his watch and knew his father wouldn't be home for several hours. His mother would be home soon though. He would call when he knew his father was there to avoid lingering too long with his mom. Emerson had encountered many gay men who simply adored their mothers. He was not such a man. Emerson knew early on he was not the person his mother hoped him to be. He was not his brother, a playful affectionate child. He was not his father, a comforting and charming man. Emerson wasn't even attracted to girls. Having an attraction to someone of the opposite sex was the most basic aspect of human existence. Emerson couldn't get that right either.

Take it easy, he whispered to his father, imagining his father's back giving under the weight of that mailbag—he'd been lugging that thing around for thirty years.

Emerson felt a thin line of pain rush up his spine and press against his skull. He reached behind his neck and grabbed the flesh below his hairline. Something's wrong, he knew. He wanted to call home, but needed to have the phone lines open, waiting to hear a voice from across the ocean.

Ring, he thought. *Michael, please.* He looked down at the open file on his desk and tried to work. He wrote, "Client stated that he is not adhering to his regimen. He decided to take a drug 'holiday' and not take his meds. He said he is making these decisions without the supervision of his doctor. I strongly suggested therapy and referred him to psycho-social support team." He closed the file, placing it in his filing cabinet.

"Hi," he heard someone say. He looked up and saw his coworker Daisy Chan peering through his door. Her signature dyed blue hair matched the tie around her neck. She adjusted the lapel on her suit and asked, "Are you coming?"

"Where to, Duke?"

"To the vigil in West Hollywood? It's the one-year anniversary for that blond boy killed in Wyoming. You know, the one who was gay," said Daisy, a wide-faced, broad-shouldered woman, nicknamed Duke by her friends. "Some of us are going to go down there."

"Got work to do. 'Sides, I don't like crowds. You know that."

"I know, but I thought you'd want to go to this."

"No, it's not my thing."

"It'll be inspiring. The mayor will be there, maybe some celebrities."

"It'll be a mess. There'll be traffic, nowhere to park. I try to avoid places like that."

"Fine. Hey, you want to do a presentation with me? It's for our funders. They want to know what we're up to."

"Can't you find someone else? You know I just get all weirded out when I have to do stuff like that, talk in front of people. My thoughts get jumbled. I sweat."

"I know, but it's only in front of two people. It's not like you'll be in front of thousands."

"Two people, a thousand. It's all the same. I'm not good at it. You don't want the funders to see a nervous wreck." Emerson felt a surge of tension run up the back of his skull. "Hey, you got an aspirin? I got this migraine. It's killing me."

"Yeah." She dug into her pocket and shook a little white bottle. "Here. Keep it."

"You sure?"

"Please. I buy aspirin by the case. Aspirin became a way of life when I was going through law school."

Emerson lifted the red lid, dug through the white cotton, and threw back two pills. The phone rang. Emerson looked at the receiver. With Daisy in front of him, he waited for a moment to hear if it was a real ring or a ring from his brother that only he could hear.

"Aren't you gonna pick it up?" Daisy said.

Emerson grabbed the phone. "Hello? Yes, Mom? What's up? I'm coming right over. Stay put." He hung up.

"What's the matter?" Daisy asked. "Emerson?"

"My . . . dad," he uttered. "He's been shot."

"Oh, my God. Is it serious?"

"Don't know. I gotta go."

He ran out of his office. Daisy yelled after him, "Call me if you need anything, 'kay?"

He ran down the hall, past the clients in the waiting room. He got into his car, an old Galaxie, maneuvering the streets of downtown. He knew every alleyway, every shortcut, places he learned about in his youth. He pulled into his parents' driveway, stepped out of his car, and looked at the street. He sighed. He approached the front door, opened it, and saw his mother on her knees. Music emanating from the Magnavox stereo.

Not again, he thought.

⌒

IN THE CAR, his mother sat frozen by his side. She was calm, strangely calm, and he thought he detected a slight smile on her face. *She's a strange one,* Emerson thought. Then again, strangeness ran in the family. His grandmother, a woman he'd never met, was strange, too. "My mother was an evil woman," Belen once said. "She cursed me. My own mother cursed me. I thought it was a blessing what she said, but it wasn't. After all the trouble she knew I had, she still had the nerve to curse me." Emerson never asked about his relatives again.

"There," Belen said, "pull in over there."

He drove onto the parking lot of the hospital; people rushed his vehicle. He heard his name. He looked around and saw faces. He didn't know who was yelling for him. He scanned the faces of the men and women outside of his car windows, trying to connect the voice to the face. Then he heard his name, over and over again. Emerson, Emerson, Emerson, Emerson. This time it was easier to see who was calling him—all of them were.

Look at all the *people,* Emerson thought, feeling ill. All these bodies. Postal workers, well over a dozen of them. They were people he'd seen through the years, friends of his father's. As soon as he parked, someone opened the car door. He heard a phone ringing, a distinct ring, a rolling ring: rrrrrrrrrrrrrrrring. Arms reached into the vehicle firmly holding onto Emerson's arm, tugging him out of the car, pulling him like creatures from a nightmare. Emerson looked to his side and noticed someone had also opened the right passenger door and lifted his mother out of the car, too. Rrrrrrrrrrrrring. He looked around, trying to detect the sound's origin. He saw a cell phone attached to a postman's waist. He knew no one else could hear this ring. Calls from his brother were ones that only he could hear, but he never got out of the habit of checking other faces to see if they heard it, too. *That call's for me,* Emerson thought.

The hands locked onto his elbows, guiding him toward the sliding double doors of the hospital. The hands had veins almost bursting from the skin. They belonged to men in uniforms, all of whom had eagles on their chests. The men lifted Emerson and his mother into the hospital. It seemed he was being elevated, floating rather than walking. They carried him down a corridor with a yellow line on the floor.

Rrrrrrrrrrrrrring.

"We're praying for him," someone said. *Don't do that,* Emerson thought, *my father wouldn't appreciate it.* "Yes, we're praying for him." The voice came from behind. He turned to see who it was. It was a woman's voice, a black woman with tinted blonde hair. She, too, wore an eagle.

Rrrrrrrrrrrrring.

He was carried into an elevator, his mother not far behind. In the elevator, Emerson couldn't breathe. There were too many bodies, too much. He heard a barrage of voices echo within the small room: It'll be all right . . . I think he'll pull through . . . God, help us . . . Goddamnit . . . God willing . . . He's stable . . . He's critical . . . Your dad is a strong man . . . You'll see, he'll be fine . . . Yes, that's right . . . He'll be fine . . . Jory's strong, always been . . . He'll make it . . . God will take care of him.

Which God are you thinking of? Emerson wanted to ask them.

Rrrrrrrrrrrrrrring.

The little elevator seemed to be rising and rising. Emerson perspired. He did not know if the elevator was warm due to all of the bodies or if he was panicking. Rrrrrrrrrrrrrrring. He looked at the cell phone attached to the postman's belt. He almost reached for it when the elevator stopped. The doors parted, and men and women in white crisscrossed his path.

He felt himself being lifted again, through the elevator doors. Emerson took a deep breath, grateful for the new air, the space. He and his mother were carried through a hall, under what seemed to be blinding fluorescent lights bouncing off of bleached white walls. The walls reminded him of the skin of a ghost. Three pay phones came into view. They began to ring, too. Rrrrrrrrrring.

He came to an abrupt stop, left to stand in front of a hospital room. He heard the ringing of the pay phones behind him. The hospital room door opened, and a man in blue came out. On his uniform was a design of two snakes that appeared to be wrapping themselves around a pole. On his chest, just to the right, was his name, Dr. Jones.

Dr. Jones led them into the hospital room. Emerson saw his sleeping father, wearing a plastic mask, tubes ran out of the blanket covering him. Bandages were on his face, shoulder, torso. He heard his mother sigh, "Oh, no."

Rrrrrrrrrrrrrring. The white phone next to his father's bed blared. Emerson put his hands over his ears and doubled over. Anyone seeing him might guess he was overcome with sorrow.

JORY

*H*E WAS LIFTED from the ambulance and rushed through the antiseptic white walls of a hospital. He watched the fluorescent lights above him whiz by. He heard the chatter of doctors and nurses around him.

"What do we got?" one doctor said. The doctor was young, perhaps the same age as Emerson.

"Shooting," Ambulance Man said. Jory watched the two men exchange words, nodding and shaking their heads. He watched Ambulance Man leave.

"Hi. I'm Dr. Jones. We're going to take care of you."

That's what the last man said, Jory thought.

"Can you hear me?"

Jory gave one slight nod.

"Can you speak?"

Yes, Jory wanted to say. He parted his lips, but no sound came out. He exhaled a small breath.

"Can you tell me your name?"

Jory. Just Jory. At the orphanage, he wanted to be a two-name person. His plan, a plan he devised four years before when he was fourteen, was to leave and work at another church. He excelled in his studies, learning priesthood with the belief that someday he would be sent to another church in a different part of the country to work. A few months after his eighteenth birthday, he got his wish.

Father Aga, a priest in the mountainous areas of his island, requested assistance. Jory was appointed by Father Ryan to go. Jory would travel to Our Lady of Mercy in Benquet Province.

He stood in the open fields near the church and knew there was a road that went up there. He was told going up that mountain was a dangerous thing. The people who lived up there were heathens, he was told. Wild. The Igorots, or Mountain People, were known for bizarre practices. He'd heard of one tribe known for beheading people.

Every once and a while an Igorot made his way down the mountain and attended Mass at St. Teresa's. He looked fine, dressed like everyone else, but whispers soon abounded that the Igorots were seen out in the forest, wearing nothing but loincloths, partaking in some ritual ceremony that was surely sinful. Wildness. There was wildness up there, Jory believed.

One of the worst insults that you could inflict on someone was to call him Igorot. A parent might yell at her misbehaving child, "Stop acting like an Igorot." What made Igorots seem so scary was that for several centuries they lived so very far removed from the rest of the country. Roads and buildings were only constructed in the early twentieth century. The Spanish were late in eradicating any of their mystical ways. Catholicism had certainly found its way up the mountain but they were not wholly civilized yet.

Jory would have a lot of work to do. Before leaving, he walked around his village, stopping at the cemetery. He visited the small plots of the boys who had died of malaria. Dead for over ten years now. They were pretty much forgotten about as boys with one name often are. He could barely see their names on the wooden crosses. Ten years of weather had blurred the identities of the boys. Jory could still make them out though: Laurencio, Lazarus, Bernardo, and Andres. In a few years their names would be gone.

Standing there, Jory looked forward to leaving. He would choose a second name. He pondered what it would be. Something grand-sounding? Or something more simple? Reading the barely visible names of the four boys, he chose to make one up. Laurencio, Lazarus, Bernardo, and Andres. Jory combined their names, choosing only the beginning letters. A name taken to remember four soon-to-be-forgotten dead boys.

"His name is Lalaban. Jory Lalaban," a nurse said, appearing out of nowhere. In her hands was his wallet, one with a Velcro flap. Belen bought it for him at the 99 cents store.

"Mr. Lalaban," Dr. Jones said. "We're going to inject you with this."

Another needle? he thought.

"It'll relax you, make you sleep," the nurse said. "Sleep. Just sleep."

Jory slept on the bus taking him to Baguio, the big city of Benquet Province; he was ready to teach. He recognized that the very goodness of his soul was due to the church and his very well-being as an orphan was because of the kind charity of a Catholic orphanage. He was proud to be part of an institution that contributed to world art, politics, and science—indeed all of civilization for nearly two thousand years. He was raised to believe, like Catholics of his time, that the Catholic Church was the true and only form of Christianity. Catholics and only Catholics held the exclusivity on salvation, no one—certainly not the Protestants who sent their own missionaries to the Philippines—could claim otherwise.

And if it weren't for the Christians who saved the Philippines, the country and all its inhabitants were damned to hell.

"Jesus Christ!" the nurse said, raising her hands. Her fingers drenched in blood. "He's bleeding again!"

Jesus Christ, Jory thought, watching the nurses rush about. *Jesus Christ. What a character.* By 1956, Jory was eighteen and well versed on the influence of Jesus in Europe and the Americas, the rise of Christianity in the world, and how early believers of this new religion turned away from other gods like Mars and Zeus, choosing a more monotheistic approach. He recognized that other gods and goddesses were present way before Christianity, or any other religion of Abraham, made its presence on earth. The power to worship was inherent in all humans, he surmised.

Although a Jesuit by training, Jory could competently relay information on other Catholic orders like the Benedictines, Franciscans, or Augustinians. He could discuss an upstart order like the Missionaries of Charity started by a relatively young nun in India named Teresa.

What he did not know, which became problematic for a young priest in training, was the wonder and joy of knowing Jesus. He did not grasp the awe that others in religious service seemed to have. There was a serenity and a silent joy that emanated from the priests and nuns he had known. He'd examine the faces of the devout in church and see that they were being touched by God.

Even the lay people who attended Mass appeared to have more astonishment for the Lord than he. He watched them on their knees, sometimes for hours at a time, believing in the miraculous glory of Jesus, Mary, and the Community of Saints. He saw the women with modesty veils atop their heads, clutching the rosary beads for dear life, weeping, experiencing a kind of rapture.

He'd witnessed boastful, cocksure men enter the church, gen- uflect, humbly bow their heads, and leave behind any form of arrogance. These men who swaggered down the street, proud of what was between their legs, put their hands together and whispered secret prayers.

He watched rowdy children become quiet and solemn, putting away their balls and their dolls, with their eyes to the ground. He taught these children Christ's Passion and the necessary prayers needed for their first Holy Communion. Somehow these children knew that Communion was a rite of passage, accepting the Body of Jesus into their lives. Even they, these youngsters, had a reverence for God that Jory did not feel.

Jory had tried to know Jesus. Indeed, he tried. He prayed and prayed often, sitting in silent meditation, hoping to be "called" to religious life. For, as it was, he was not called into spiritual duty, but merely accepted the job because he had no other alternative for a vocation. He'd sit for hours with nothing coming to him except the need for what his next meal might be. He'd think about movies and music, wondering if he'd get the chance to catch the matinee at the theater on Session Road.

In his attempt at silent meditation, he'd hear young men bouncing a ball outside, preparing for a game. He watched them play, wanting nothing more than to join them. He saw them laugh and taunt each other with a daring move on the court. He approached them, and the men, no older than he, stopped at his presence. The sound of sport ended when he came near.

"Are we bothering you, Father?" one athlete asked. Jory was quiet because he was not a Father yet. He was a Father-in-training but he still wore his white collar and dark clothes and would be easily mistaken as such.

"No, not at all," he replied and like a child on his first day of school watching the big kids play, he wanted to join them. More than that, he wanted to be one of them. He wanted to wear T-shirts and jeans, and style his hair like Elvis. He wanted to put gobs of pomade on his scalp, knowing that doing so concerned the sin of vanity. He wanted to wear hi-top canvas shoes with laces so long that the slack had to be wrapped around the ankles.

He wanted a girlfriend like the ones who sat at a nearby bench, waiting for their boyfriends to finish playing ball. He wanted a young lady who tied her long hair with a ribbon and looked into a compact mirror to wipe away the lipstick on her teeth. He wanted a girlfriend who refused kisses then gave in with a laugh. He wanted to hold her hand, his fingers entwined with hers.

"Hold onto the sheet!" the nurse said. "Goddamnit, hurry." Other nurses appeared, surrounding Jory. They lifted the sheet under him, carrying his damaged body from the stretcher to a rolling bed. Somewhere in midair, Jory latched onto a nurse.

"He's got my hand," a nurse said. "Let go. You have to let go. We're going to take you to another room. C'mon, leggo. I know you're scared, but it'll be all right."

By the time he was eighteen, Jory had never touched a girl. He knew that surely this feeling of curiosity and wonder would certainly turn into regret one day. God made Eve because a man alone, even in the paradise known as Eden, was nothing and would breed nothing. God recognized the importance of feminine company, and indeed the greatest sacrifice a Catholic man could make is to live without the companionship of a woman.

The hospital bed rolled down the hall. He heard the rat-tat-tat of the metal bed frame shaking. A rhythmic sound. Tat-tat-tat. Tat. Tat. Tat.

"Is the sound bothering you, Father?" an athlete said, bouncing a basketball. "We can stop."

"No," Jory said. Jory looked to the ground and felt the awkwardness of the young men on the court, wondering what to make of the young man in black. "Can you teach me? Teach me to play basketball?"

The athletes looked at each other, some raising their eyebrows, most raising their shoulders, suggesting, Why not? One boy threw the ball to Jory and quickly explained the rules of the game. Within an hour, he'd been playing ball like he'd been playing it all his life.

"You play pretty good, Father," one of the boys said.

"I'm not a Father yet. Call me Jory. Jory Lalaban."

"Okay, Jory," Dr. Jones said, "You've proven to everyone that you're a tough guy. Let the medicine work and sleep."

Jory let his lids fall.

BELEN

"*O*H, NO," BELEN said, stepping into the hospital room. Jory was motionless, eyes closed, barely breathing. She wanted to speak, but she could not utter how she felt. Words like *misery* and *pain* and *turmoil* and *devastation* did not contain all of what she was feeling. A new word would have to be invented to fully comprehend the depth of her sorrow.

Belen approached the hospital bed. Jory looked bad, real bad. Her instincts were to check the bandages, which she did. They were properly installed; the nurses at this hospital appeared to be competent.

The Blessed Mother had led me to believe that you were okay, she thought.

He is okay, Belen, dear. At least for now. She heard the voice of Mary speak to her. *I had to provide you with a little hope, or else you wouldn't have been able to leave the house. You would have sat there and not moved. Emerson would have had to push you out the door. You didn't*

*want him to do that, did you? You know how strained your relationship
with Emerson is already. This way, you were able to leave the home quite
calmly and be here with Jory. Be with the husband that needs you now.
You understand, don't you, dear? I had to make you believe those things
to get you here. You understand, don't you?*

Belen nodded her head.

She kissed her index finger and placed it on her husband's forehead. She would have placed it on his lips, but a plastic mask covered it. She pushed the hair back onto his head. He was in critical
condition. No one had to tell her this. She could tell from his
body and from the machines attached to him that, yes, he was
critical and may not make it.

"You're supposed to be eating a donut," she whispered.

"The X-rays should tell us a lot," someone said. Belen turned.
It was Dr. Jones. "Maybe we can talk in the hallway."

Dr. Jones was young, she noticed. Too young to understand
bedside manner. She had been a nurse for too long not to know
when a doctor is good with patients and when one is not. There
were brilliant doctors, and there were caring ones. Belen noticed
the Ivy League ring on his finger. He was not good with patients,
she decided. You do not pull a wife away from her injured husband to talk business, especially since she had been in the room
for no more than five minutes.

"Maybe we can talk outside," Dr. Jones said again.

"May I have a few more minutes with my husband?"

An hour later, Belen joined Dr. Jones in the hallway. Emerson
followed them. The hallway was full of people, postal workers
mainly.

"You all have to leave," Dr. Jones said to the crowd. "You can't
loiter around here. This is a hospital, for heaven's sake."

"We just want to be here," someone whom Belen did not recognize said, "to lend, you know, support or something."

Dr. Jones went on, "We can't have you blocking the hallway. Besides, only family is allowed up here."

Say something, Emerson, Belen thought. *Tell the crowd to leave.* He didn't, wouldn't. Even in this time of need, Emerson couldn't find the strength necessary to overcome his stage fright.

"You have to go," Dr. Jones said. The crowd dispersed, taking the elevator down to the lobby. In the now quiet, now-deserted hallway, Belen noticed how Dr. Jones did not look at her. Nope, not good with patients at all, she reconfirmed. He chose to look at Emerson, and she wondered why men did that? They looked at each other, as if Emerson would better understand him.

"He's in bad shape," Dr. Jones said again. "We took out two bullets, but there are two more that we're going to wait on."

We're supposed to be at home, Belen thought. *Right now. Not here.*

"Two more?" Emerson said. "Jesus."

"They don't pose an immediate threat. We'll get them out when he is a little more stable."

Belen looked up and noticed that Dr. Jones was taller than she. Of course, most everyone was taller than Belen. He was slightly taller than Emerson, but not much.

Dr. Jones shuffled and said, "We don't know how it could go."

"How it would go?" Belen said. *Just say it.*

"It could go either way."

"You mean if he will live or die." *I am not so delicate,* she thought. *Do you think I've have lived this long, this far by being delicate?*

"Yes." The doctor sighed and said, "I have to ask you a difficult question. If he should pass . . . or, I mean, his heart should stop. Do you want us to revive him?"

"No," said Emerson.

"Yes," said Belen. She looked at her son, disgusted. "He will live," she said quickly. "He's all . . ." She had almost said, *He's all*

I have. He wouldn't leave me, leave this earth because he knows, my Jory knows he's all I have. With Emerson standing right there, she quickly changed her statement and said, "He's always been strong. He'll pull through."

"Mrs. Lalaban," Dr. Jones began. "Just prepare for the worst."

Bastard, Belen thought. *Rude, rude, RUDE. He may be young but he had no right to say that. "Prepare for the worst." Why don't you say, "Let's hope for the best." Say something hopeful to make the family feel better.*

Belen was not stupid. In her nursing career, she had encountered situations like this when families faced similar tragedies. She knew the family needed hope. Even if it's false. Give us false hope for a little while. *Bastard.*

"He was hurt pretty badly. I hope you understand what I'm saying . . ."

"I know what you are saying! I'm a nurse."

Belen wanted to slap him but felt pity for Dr. Jones. There was an Ivy League ring on his finger, but not a gold band. He thought that separating your professional life from your personal life was as simple as taking off your white coat and going to play racquetball. No, she would not slap him, but she would push him. Yes, she would do that. She pointed at him, pounded her index finger into his chest and said, "I know what you are saying." Each word was emphasized with her finger jabbing into the good doctor's sternum.

Dr. Jones stepped away, nodded, and rubbed his chest.

Belen returned to the hospital room to be with her husband.

EMERSON

*E*MERSON WATCHED HIS mother enter his father's room and Dr. Jones step away to speak to some nurses. He stood in the hallway and looked at the hospital's walls: white, sterile, antiseptic. He stared at the walls, identifying with the blankness there.

Rrrrrrrrrrrring.

Emerson saw a television monitor positioned at the corner of the ceiling. Beneath it was a pay phone. Rrrrrrrrrrrrring. He rushed to it.

—Hello, hello, hello, Emerson said.

—It took you long enough.

—I couldn't exactly answer a phone that no one else could hear now, could I? It would have looked stupid. Emerson looked around, cradling the phone between his ear and shoulder. He whispered into the receiver, Did you see what happened to Dad? Oh, God.

—I know.

—What the fuck's going on?

—It might get worse, Emmy.

—How can it get worse that this?

—It just might, little bro'.

—What am I supposed to do?

—Just hang tight. Keep it together.

—What's going on?

—Look up.

—I don't feel like the optimist now.

—No, I mean look up. Look up and I'll call you later.

Emerson hung up the phone. He stepped away and watched the television monitor above him. *Breaking News* was imprinted across the screen.

"This just in," a news anchor said, "there was a shooting at the Edelman Center, a Jewish day care facility."

Emerson watched children milling about, being walked from the school to waiting cars. The children looked small, no taller than his waist. He remembered being that little when he and his older brother Jun were taken to celebrations where their father Jory Lalaban was a desired guest. Memories come at the most bizarre times, Emerson knew. You're in your car, cursing the traffic, then a song comes on the radio, a song so associated with Before that you stop for a moment. And breathe. Maybe that's why there's traffic because a song is playing on the radio making people breathe. Memories come out of order. They pierce like arrows, unaware of when or where the next one might hit.

"A child and an adult at the day care center have been rushed to the hospital," the anchor said. The monitor switched to a father standing by the gate of the Edelman Center. The camera is focused on his worried face.

"Where's Edward?" the man said. "I'm looking for my son Edward. Edward! Where's my son?"

"Sun, I call you," Jory used to say. "Sun, Moon, I call you. Watch over this house so the people may grow wealthy."

"I can't find Edward?"

Emerson watched the helpless father. Emerson believed his father was never helpless, possessing the skill to cast spells. Emerson and his brother served as assistants. At parties, long ago, Emerson, nudged by his mother, delivered a glass to his father, followed by Jun carrying a bottle of wine. Emerson wanted to carry the wine because it was more prestigious. However, at a *Kanyao* a few months earlier, Emerson dropped the bottle, breaking it, and his mother wouldn't let him carry wine again.

The camera switched back to the news anchor. The anchor said, "Relatives of the children are encouraged to call this 800 number."

"Relatives of this family join us," Jory said. "Come. Come to this house in Gardena, California. We honor you, we trade you food and wine for blessings upon this family, the Aquiapao family." After a ceremony, people approached his father and thanked him, adored him. Thank you, Mr. Lalaban, for coming all this way. Mr. Lalaban, I can feel the house is already warmer. Jory, I'm sure our marriage will be successful with your blessing. Can you come to my sister's house next month? She will be giving birth soon.

These people were familiar with the Lalaban's past, but the Curse seemed to have lifted. Look! Belen can have children again! Also, the next *mambunong* was hundreds of miles away in Las Vegas.

While the adults thanked Mr. Lalaban, kids approached Emerson and Jun to ask for favors.

"Are you a witch like your dad?" a girl asked Jun.

"Witches are girls, wizards are boys," Jun said.

"My dolly is sick. Can you make her better?"

"Sure." Jun waved a hand over the doll's head. "I command all the evil spirits to go away. One, two, three! You're better."

The little girl smiled and ran off.

"Can you make my baseball magic?" a boy asked.

Emerson took the ball, closed his eyes, and like his brother, waved his hand over it and said, "I give this ball special powers to fly." For special measure, he wriggled his nose like that pretty blonde woman on the reruns of *Bewitched*.

At the end of each *Kanyao,* which usually went into early evening, Emerson and Jun sat in the back of the Nova listening to their parents gossip about the family they had just left.

"Did you see how tired Jane was?" Belen said.

"Yes, I did. She was only married last year." Jory responded. "She is going to leave her husband, you'll see."

"Jory! That's a terrible thing to say."

"It's true. Getting married was not something she wanted to do. She listened to her parents too much. She was twenty-seven years old, and they wanted her to get married. I knew she didn't want to go through with it. It was on her face."

"It was not on her face. I was there, too. She seemed happy."

"I saw it on her face. She had dead dreams by her eyes."

"That's ridiculous. She was happy."

"I saw dead dreams on her face!"

"Maybe she just woke up."

"All the same, it was a bad omen to see dead dreams on a newlywed."

Emerson wiped the corners of his eyes with his thumb and forefinger. He saw the smallest remains of yellow crust on the tip of his fingers. No one had to tell him dead dreams were seeping out of his head. He wanted to call Michael for the one-hundredth time. He wanted to hear his voice. He decided against it. Michael was flying now. Emerson knew that Michael was still furious. Emerson, yet again, did a real good job at screwing up a good thing.

He grabbed the pay phone underneath the television and hoped that Michael found it in his heart to return at least one message. He threw some coins into the phone and checked his voice mail. There were two messages. *Please be there,* Emerson thought. *Please.*

"Emerson, it's Eric," the first message began. Eric Mori, his boss at the Asian-American Equality Center. "Emerson, I'm sorry to hear about your father. Take all the time you need. Is that clear? All the time."

The second message. "Emerson? It's Daisy. I'm here for you," she said. Emerson smiled. She continued, "I'll take over your workload, okay? Do you want visitors? Also, a lot of us are putting together a card. Which hospital should we send it to?"

No Michael. He hung up and dialed Michael's cell phone. It rang four times when voice mail picked up. It was in Chinese with an English translation soon to follow. At this time, comfort no friend, no relative could give.

"Michael, here," the voice mail said, "I car you when I'm on the ground." Beep.

"Michael. It's me. Something terrible happened. My dad's in the hospital. He was shot. Call me, all right? I need to talk to you." He hung up and sighed. He hoped this emergency would cause sympathy, arouse some degree of forgiveness in Michael.

Emerson stepped back to catch the end of the news broadcast. "It appears that the shooting of a nearby postal carrier is connected to the crime at the Edelman Center. At this time, authorities are currently looking for the shooter who injured a counselor and a child. The counselor and child are listed in stable condition. No word yet about the postman. Next up: are you ready for Halloween? Roving consumer reporter Adele Bayless shows you where you can get the best costumes at the lowest prices. Join us for your evening news at eleven."

JORY

WHATEVER IT WAS that Dr. Jones injected him with made Jory weightless, the kind of lightness associated with dreaming. In that hazy, heavy cloud of unconsciousness, Jory thought he could see the Moon, a burned God. During his life, he had developed a relationship with that celestial being, judging His moods, His emotions. When the Moon was full, Jory cried. *Don't be ashamed,* Jory said to Him in the backyard of his home. Don't be ashamed.

Jory awoke on a beach and was confused. He looked up and saw the Sun; to the side, a faint distant orb hovered. He looked around and saw endless shore. He stood up and discovered his body was free of injury. He stretched his arms, then bent over to stretch the back of his legs. Jory put his fists on his hips and sighed. He decided to run. He ran along the shore. He was aware of the sun on his face. It was warm. He was running along the Pacific Ocean, he realized. That was the only ocean he was familiar with. He flew over it when he and his wife chose to leave the Philippines, remembering it would be this Ocean that would put an end to all that misery. That's what the Maker of Prayer told Jory, then what Jory told himself over and over and over again: curses cannot cross water.

He and his wife hooked themselves onto a tail of an American dream shaped in the form of an airplane, taking them to California. He boarded the plane, with his entire life savings with him—$250—and he noticed that the air felt different.

"It's the change in cabin pressure," his wife told him. They laughed.

"No, it's not. It's different. It's cooler."

"It's the air conditioner."

He looked at his wife, and she knew to shut up. She rubbed his arm and nodded. "It is different," she said. "It WILL be different." She folded her lips inward, stifling a cry. Jory put his arm around his wife and comforted her. He was twenty-eight years old. His wife just turning twenty-six. He felt them leaving the misery behind.

Now almost sixty, he ran along the ocean. He started his life on one side of the Pacific. He would end his life on the other side. He didn't know it would end like this. He ran hoping to see familiar sights like the Santa Monica Pier. He didn't. He stopped to rest, looking to his right, then to his left. The beach was endless.

Jory looked up. The Sun was golden, splendid. He bowed his head, as if to receive a blessing. The Sun covered the halo of his scalp with a gentle warmth. He smiled, put his palms together, bowed slightly and whispered, "Thank you."

He walked along the shore, taking off his shoes and socks to enjoy the feel of sand underneath his feet. He saw that his toes were different. His feet didn't look like his feet. At least not the feet he woke up with. His feet looked younger, the skin was tighter. The yellowed toenails were clear. The crooked toes were straight.

He looked at his hands, and they, too, looked different. The brown spots that peppered his hands were gone. The dryness that usually cracked his skin was gone. His bumpy, brown palms were soft and pink. He touched his face and could tell that had changed also. The skin that sagged around his jaw was firm. The sunken cheeks had become full again. He extended the hair from his head, looking upward to inspect the color. When he combed his hair earlier in the day, most of his strands were gray. Now, there were only a few strands of grayness, but mostly it was black. He unbuttoned his shirt and saw the falling skin on his chest had risen again. The paleness from his torso was gone, back to a golden brown.

Jory couldn't resist his next inspection. He unbuttoned his trousers, pulling the band of his underwear away from his skin. He looked at his penis and saw that it had also changed. It was no longer a shriveled, shrunken old thing. It was full, protruding from his body, hanging quite comfortably and rather handsomely at that.

With no mirror in sight, he wasn't sure how young he'd become. He tried to remember the stages of his body, the metamorphosis of child to man. He knew that he wasn't terribly young, not a child or anything like that. He wasn't skinny the way he was when he was eighteen, the time he met the woman he loved: Belen. The woman who gave flavor to the Moon. As he entered his twenties, his body began to get wider, sturdier. He judged his body to be older than twenty or twenty-five. His body appeared to be of a man in his thirties, maybe just entering his thirties.

He heard a sound coming from somewhere he could not place. It was the sound of electricity, something buzzing. He looked around but could find nothing. He looked up and saw the Sky. It was a beautiful baby blue, from one side of the earth to the other. He saw a spark of light in the air, a small wisp of lightning. There were no clouds, and Jory did think it odd that lightning should appear in such a clear sky. He saw the baby blueness above him crack, splitting and moving. The Sky appeared to be re-creating itself.

There were sounds, too: voices coming from the Sky like turning the knob of a radio, trying to tune into just the right frequency. "I—I can't—can't—can't believe." Jory recognized the voice immediately. It was his. "I—can't believe you—took those—with you. I—I can't believe you took those records with you."

"I—I couldn't leave," another voice responded. It was a woman's voice. He knew that voice. It was Belen's. "I couldn't leave—leave—leave these—these—these behind. I couldn't leave these behind."

Then there was music, Filipino music. The lyrics were inaudible, but within a few notes, he knew the words of the song. The sound became crisper, the sparks above happened more frequently. Light was leaving, slowly becoming evening. In a matter of moments, daylight faded. The incoming night made the sparks in the Sky more rich, brightly yellow against the darkening heavens.

"I can't believe you took those records with you." He heard again.

"I couldn't leave these behind," he heard his wife say. The sparks in the Sky became more dramatic. Jory shielded his eyes, afraid that the sparks might somehow blind him. The sparks tore the Sky apart, adding more color to the blueness. Small explosions happened here and there, one right after another, leaving colors behind, creating swatches of reds, greens, and yellows. The sparks flew and Jory watched as the sky, marked with hues, created a picture of some kind, a photograph. He looked up, and when the last spark hit, he saw it was himself and Belen. They were younger, newly American. They were in their living room. It was evening. They had decided to buy a stereo, and Belen couldn't wait to use it. That is what it was. The Sky was filled with this image of a time when Jory was younger. He gasped.

The picture moved.

"I can't believe you took those records with you," the man in the Sky said.

"I couldn't leave these behind," she responded. She was by a suitcase, examining old records.

Jory knew what would happen next. Belen would choose a record, the one with Filipino love songs, and she would play them. They would dance. The boys would come from their bedroom, awakened by the music. Jun-Jun would rub his eyes, while Emerson, although fully two years old, could not stand by himself. Emerson is assisted by his older brother who is keeping him steady on two legs. That's exactly how the scene unfolded in the Sky above him.

He knew that Belen would pick Jun up and dance with him. Jory would try and teach Emerson to walk. All the while Filipino music filled the house. Jory watched this in the Sky, a scene from his life. His mouth agape. He cried because it was a simple scene, nothing that would ever be noted in history, but it was moving to him. Even more so was seeing Jun-Jun alive again. That beautiful, beautiful boy.

The picture in the Sky froze. Jory was stupefied, wondering what would happen next. He watched the Sky fall. Rather, the image he watched fell. It folded and crumpled like a parachute cut loose from its strings. It floated down and Jory was sure the image would come crashing down on him.

Jory fell back onto the sand watching the image of himself, of his family flutter downward. It looked like it would cover the whole surface of the beach and ocean. He watched the faces of his family become larger and larger, the image coming closer and closer. Then, from the center of the picture, he saw the point where the picture pulled back toward the Sky, the family image following the trajectory. The edges of the picture were still sweeping toward earth, waiting to be taken with the upswing. Jory saw the edges falling downward, finally whipping upward. The picture came painfully close to Jory, feeling the breeze it created when it came to the beach. *Like a tissue pulled from a box,* Jory thought. It was like that. He saw the picture go far into the distance. He saw it fly into the blackness of the universe.

Damn, thought Jory. Never, NEVER had he seen anything like this. Watching a scene from his past in the Sky, seeing it fall, only to be plucked back into the heavens. Father Aga, the Catholic priest who mentored him, would be shocked.

He continued to watch the Sky, wondering where the picture went. The vision of seeing Jun-Jun still alive remained with him. He was shaken and thrown at seeing his oldest son walk and talk. He still missed that boy. Jory teared up just thinking about his son.

Wind blew from behind him, a whistling wind, a warm wind that forced his hair to fall onto the sides of his face. He turned, and the wind pushed against his cheeks, forehead, calling him. He heard the wind speaking, whispers coming from the air.

"Moon, Sun, Ancestors," Jory heard a voice say. "I ask you to bring my dad back to me."

He walked toward the sound.

BELEN

*B*ELEN SLEPT IN the hospital lounge, waking to find Emerson gone. She assumed he went home and silently cursed her son for leaving at such a critical time. *That boy,* she thought. *Always going.* She patted her hair down and blew into her palm. Her breath smelled awful. She pulled out a mint from her purse, popped it into her mouth. She rolled her head around and sighed. She stood up on unsteady legs and made her way to the nurse's station.

She would greet the incoming nurses, tell them she was a nurse, too. Spouses of nurses got better treatment. Mentioning that she was a nurse was useful at times. She learned to reveal this tidbit of information if a police officer pulled her over. She would say, "I'm sorry, officer. I'm a nurse, and I didn't want to be late for my shift." The officer would let her go, knowing there may be a time when a nurse's services might be needed.

Belen stood at the far end of the hall, watching the women in white. They were chatting, laughing. They were younger, women in their thirties, early forties maybe. How strong you look, she thought. You deal with the sick or dying, and you still manage to wake up in the morning to go to the same job with more sick and dying. You lead normal lives with husbands and children.

In Belen's early years in America, that is who she was. Back then, there was so much hope. Amidst all the ailing people in all the beds, there was still so much to look forward to. She secured a job at a big, prominent hospital, making good money with full benefits. (It was her salary, not Jory's, that helped secure the loan for the house.) Then Jun died, and everything went upside down. She couldn't take the pressures of working in such a high-paced hospital and moved to an easier job at the seniors' home, a place where people died at the end of their lives, when people are supposed to. "Hello, I'm Belen Lalaban," she said to the women at the nurse's station. "I'm a nurse, too, at A Place of Rest. My husband is here in room 417."

"It's all over the news," one nurse said. "That poor day care center. It's just terrible. They're still looking for the shooter."

The shooter? Belen thought. She had forgotten someone else was involved in this. Someone who had shot Jory.

"They think the shooter was a racist or something," the nurse said. "Those poor little Jewish kids."

Those poor Jews, Belen thought. They've gone through so much. With Hitler and everything. People using the Bible to hate them—it's terrible. But her husband? He didn't do anything. The Bible doesn't say anything about Filipinos. She thought for a moment, then decided, yes, that's right: nothing about us, not a single reference.

She went to Jory's room, opening the door. She saw Emerson sitting in a chair next to his father, his head on the bed, asleep. Belen entered quietly and watched them. Emerson's head was turned toward her. She studied her son's face. There wasn't a trace of a single tear. She shook her head. If Emerson ever cried, surely it would have been over something like this.

She shuddered at the thought of how her son would react if it were she in the hospital. He probably would throw a party. She mentally slapped herself for thinking such unkind thoughts. She didn't mean to let her son become so cold, so distant toward her. Yes, there was THAT fight, the one that almost obliterated any relationship they had. She knew things started way before that.

Emerson always preferred Jory over her, she knew. When Emerson was a teenager, he got it into his head that he wished to learn Ibaloi, the language of their province. Emerson asked his father to teach him.

"*Shanom*," Jory said. "It means *water. Shanom.*"

"*Shanom*," Emerson repeated.

"*Pamilja.* That means, Family."

"*Pamilja.*"

"*Si fay ngaran mo?*" Jory said. "That means *What is your name?*" Emerson repeated again.

In the hospital, watching her son sleep by his father, she felt wounded. *Emerson could have asked me to teach him Ibaloi,* she thought. After all, it was me who taught the language to Jory in the first place. He could have asked me, but he didn't.

She dug into her purse and pulled out a small black leather bag. She opened the small bag and retrieved a rosary. She was about to begin her prayers, but decided that Jory needed these beads more. She approached the bed, careful not to wake Emerson.

Belen wrapped the rosary around a metal bar, part of the bed frame. *Now,* she thought, *Our Lady, please help my husband.*

Belen noticed there was an uneaten meal of chicken and wine not too far away. *Let's forget about everything, Emerson,* she thought.

Let's forget about that fight. It's been—how many years? What do you want me to do? That is what I believe. Things had never been the same since that fight. Now is not the time to be distant.

If things were different, Belen thought. *If only things were different.* How many times did she think this? She thought it when she left her mother's home, beaten and scared. She thought this when she left the Philippines, beaten down, but hopeful. She thought this when Jun flew up and away.

She didn't want to be here: not in this room, not in this hospital, not in this country. She would have been content to have lived on her island with servants in a large hacienda perhaps, socializing with politicians and lunching with grand wives. She would have enjoyed shopping on Session Road, the main boulevard of Baguio City, enjoyed lunch at the Terrace Hotel, picnicking atop mountains so high you had to look down to see clouds.

If things were different, Emerson would not be cursed. He would be married, make a good husband to a wonderful girl, a smart Filipina anxious to have children. Emerson could certainly achieve that. Emerson is a good-looking man, she believed. He is better looking as a man than when he was boy. He was so plain, but, then again, any child paled next to the beautiful Jun.

As a girl, Belen herself was not particularly stunning—pretty, yes, but not remarkable. Her hair deeply black with just enough oil to make it shimmer. Her eyes a little too far apart and her nose small, a button nose, someone might call it. Her lips weren't particularly full, but they were red. What made her attractive, what made her a prize was that Belen believed she was more appealing than she really was.

Since girlhood, her mother fussed and preened over her. Ermaline Dubabang had servants style Belen's hair, adorning her head with satin bows or fresh flowers. Belen walked down Session Road and women, girls gasped. Belen mistook their reactions as a comment on her looks, her face and figure. She believed that her clothes, bows, shoes, and flowers complemented her and not the other way around.

She watched her son's back as he slept. She marveled at how he had his father's build, with the same kind of broad shoulders. Who would have known that Jory would produce a son of similar stature, but would lack the kind of charm that made the original sparkle. Jory had a way about him that she had never known with another man. She had known men who were attractive. Offers of marriage came in when she was only twelve. The boys didn't make the bids to wed. The fathers did. She sat at the dinner table when a family friend offered a cow at the nuptials of Belen and his boy. Belen blushed, knowing that a pig was a decent offering for any girl in the province. She knew the boys, some of them were certainly pleasant to look at.

"She won't be marrying for a while," said Ermaline. "She will finish school first. Besides, when I was married, three cows were offered. I want to make sure she goes for more than me." Year after year, proposals of marriage came in for Belen. By the time she was sixteen, her mother had refused well over a dozen. Some of those offers were quite substantial, including entitlement to land and deeds to businesses.

"Are you sure you know what you're doing, Mama?" Belen asked.

Ermaline gave a perfunctory nod and said, "They're not good enough."

From her earliest memory, Belen knew that her mother was her most important advocate. Belen held great respect and adoration for her mother. She hoped to be a fraction of her mother's being.

When Jory came to Our Lady of Mercy, Belen knew something was wrong. Jory was introduced, and she, along with a dozen other girls (perhaps even a boy or two), swooned. Jory's black hair fell onto his stern angular face.

"This is Jory Lalaban," Father Aga said.

Jory Lalaban, she thought to herself, repeating his name over and over again in her mind, *Jory, Jory Lalaban.* Then he smiled. Smiled! His mouth parted, and a thin gap separated his front teeth. For the first time in her life, Belen felt conscious of her appearance. She adjusted her modesty veil, buttoned her front collar, afraid of showing this man, this Jory too much. She felt slightly off kilter at seeing the handsome boy introduced as a teacher. Feeling slightly off kilter was not something Belen was used to.

Jory's simple hello to the students at Our Lady left Belen dumbstruck. At night she could barely sleep, keeping her hands between her legs, feeling things she had never felt before. She wanted to rest, feel refreshed when she returned to school the next day. Finally! Something to wake up for. She arrived at morning prayers a half hour before commencement to have Jory walk out and see her. She did this for weeks.

There were other girls who had crushes on Jory, too. They giggled when he walked by or chatted nervously with the young seminarian. Belen did none of that. She did not laugh because what she felt for this man was serious business. She did not speak to him because she had no voice with him. If she sat with him all day without saying a word she would have been happy.

Belen looked at the rosary that she wrapped on the railing of Jory's bed. Jory would not have liked it there. She put it there more for herself, reminding her of the presence of the Virgin. Belen had a long history with the rosary. Oh, how the rosary had gotten her into trouble. Once a nun slapped her for clicking her fingernails on the beads of her rosary during morning prayers. A nun slapped her for wearing the rosary around her neck. "The rosary is NOT a piece of jewelry!" the nun proclaimed.

Belen hated those nuns. She was also slapped for keeping the top button of her blouse unbuttoned. She was slapped for running her fingers through her long wavy hair during Mass. "Vanity!" one nun said, "Belen Dubabang! You are guilty of shameless vanity! There is a reason you wear a modesty veil!" She was slapped for wearing lipstick. It came to the point that Belen simply turned her face and waited to be backhanded.

In this hospital room, she wondered what the nuns would think. She stared at her husband and son. She took several deep breaths, then she saw Jory stir.

EMERSON

*E*MERSON SAW HIS mother had fallen asleep in the hospital lounge. He craved a joint, but a cigarette would have to do. He smoked cigarettes sparingly during times of duress. He thought this evening counted. He walked out of the hospital and noticed the crowd of postal workers were gone.

Emerson got into his Galaxie, reached inside the glove compartment, retrieving a pack of American Spirits. He lit a cigarette, lowered his head, and exhaled a cloud of smoke. He thought of his mother sleeping in the lounge. How could she sleep at a time like this? It's probably for the best. If she were awake, he'd talk to her, something that was always difficult to do.

There were times growing up when he dreaded going home, knowing his mother would be there. He sensed that she felt the same way about him. If it weren't for the male prostitutes on Santa Monica Boulevard, he would have gone bonkers.

He extinguished his cigarette in the ashtray, put his key in the ignition, and drove out of the parking lot. *Just a few minutes,* he thought. *I'll go, then come right back.* He wanted to hear his engine rev, feel his car in motion. He got on the on ramp, speeding up his Galaxie. Twenty-five miles per hours, thirty, forty, fifty— there was power in this. He pressed on the accelerator and rolled down his window. Cold wind filled the car. Emerson was not like the other gay men he knew, feminine guys who liked stylish clothes and furniture and had long drawn out conversations about art, boyfriends, and love.

He preferred masculinity because it moves. Masculinity doesn't dwell or remember. Masculinity strengthens when a heart is broken. Masculinity doesn't weep over such things. It doesn't shed a tear when death rolls by.

He needed only one hand to remember how many times he'd shed tears, and, even then, he didn't need all his fingers. The last time was when he "came out" to his mother. He hoped revealing his secret would bring his family closer to together. That's what one of the prostitutes had said—coming out actually made things better.

On the freeway, with lamplights whizzing by, he saw the signs of businesses along the ways. Pep Boys, Wal-Mart, Kentucky Fried Chicken. He had bought a bucket of extra crispy, biscuits, mashed potatoes, and gravy when he came out. Emerson, just turning twenty-two, sat at the kitchen table with his parents and said he had something to tell them.

"I wanted you to know," he said, plopping gravy onto a thigh. "I was wondering whether I should tell you, but you're my parents. And I guess you should just know. That's all."

"That's okay. We still love you," Jory said.

Emerson smiled and looked down at his plate. That filament he'd always felt for his father strengthened.

He turned on the radio of his car, cruising at a comfortable sixty miles an hour. The black road ahead made him calm. The radio blasted a song by the band Journey, he couldn't remember the title but it was from the *Escape* album.

"That's right. We still love you," Belen said. That was one of the few times that he recalled her telling him that. Emerson looked at her, and realized that, perhaps, he could love his mother, really love her. He was willing to forget about when he was kid and his mother believed the wrong child had died. He saw how she adored Jun, worshipped him in death. His photo was still on the mantle. Emerson's photo tucked away in photo albums, never prominently displayed. If you walked into their home on Carondelet, you wouldn't know a second child grew up there.

Belen continued, "That's right. We still love you. The Curse comes, but you can fight it. You can try."

Emerson tapped the steering wheel, in keeping with the rhythm of the song. He'd always liked the raspy voice of Steve Perry, Journey's lead singer.

"This is part of the Curse," Belen said. "Making you this way. The Curse doesn't want you to get married and have children. The Curse is trying to get you—"

"Belen," Jory said. "This is not right for you to say—"

"But you can change things, Emerson. You can. You can fight it."

Steve Perry sang, and Emerson joined in. "Don't stop belieeeeeevin." He continued beating the steering wheel. His opened hands balled into fists.

"You think I'm cursed, Mom?"

"Oh, Belen," Jory said. "This is not that. This is Nature. This is. It happens that way sometimes. At the orphanage, there were these two boys named Mariano and Jo—"

"Listen," Belen said, "the curse made you this way. You can change."

Emerson changed lanes, accelerating to seventy miles an hour. His old car still had a lot of life in her.

"Dad, did you hear what she just said. Did you hear? Mom thinks I'm cursed." Emerson thought of his dead brother, the major victim of the Curse. His mother equated his being gay with the most tragic event that had ever happened in his life, one that led his father to temporarily lose his sanity. Emerson believed something was not quite right in the world once he saw the lifeless body of his brother crumpled on the ground. For Emerson the Curse became as real to him when he stood by Jun's coffin. However, Emerson did *not* believe it was the cause of his gayness. "This was a mistake. Coming out to you was a big, fucking—"

"Calm down," Jory said. "And you don't have to use those words in this house."

"I am not fucking cursed," Emerson said, his voice cracking. He turned away and shut his eyes, hoping that tears would not squeeze through.

"This is part of it," Belen said. "You being this way. It is part of the Curse."

Emerson saw his mother stand and point her finger at him. "You don't know what's going on. You don't know that. You don't know what it's like to run from something you can't see! You don't know when it's coming. You don't know what it's like to run. My mother told me—"

"I know what your mother said. You're just looking for another excuse to hate me," Emerson said.

"Quiet!" Jory said. "The both of you be quiet! I don't believe this is part of the Curse."

"Thank you, Dad."

"But there is a Curse."

After twelve minutes of silence, Emerson left the kitchen. He could not be alone with his mother after that. Jory had to be present.

Emerson tried to make another lane change, but a Thunderbird wouldn't let him in. "Let me through, Goddamnit!" Emerson yelled out his car window. He exited the freeway. The sound of speeding cars were gone. The blur of lights became steady glows. Emerson drove up to a large sign that said: SPIRITS FOR SALE. Below it was a smaller sign that read, SPIRITS FOR SALE, THE BEST IN BEER AND WINE. He parked his car on the curb, went into the store, asking the man behind the counter if they sold saki. The man instructed Emerson to a row of glass doors that kept booze cold.

You're supposed to keep saki warm, moron, Emerson thought. He bought a bottle and saw a nearby diner half a block away. He held the saki in one hand as he walked to the restaurant. He ordered a fried chicken plate to go. He walked to his car and drove back to the hospital. His mother was still asleep in the lounge. He entered his father's room and arranged the chicken and saki by the night stand. He went to the window, looking out at the vastness of the sky. He knew his father worshipped the heavens. Emerson wasn't quite so convinced. But he knew his father believed. That was all the faith he needed. Emerson brought his hands together, bowed his head, and whispered, "Moon, Sun, Ancestors, I ask you to bring my dad back to me."

He pulled up a chair and rested his head by his father's arm. He fell asleep, waking only to hear his mother scream, "Jory! He's awake."

JORY

*H*E WALKED TOWARD the origin of where the wind blew. There was something tugging him. It came from a darkness in the distance. He moved closer, the warm wind grew stronger, and something in it made him calm. It was this calmness that drew him deeper into the darkness. He stopped momentarily and turned to the beach. The dark Sky still crackled; strings of electricity appeared in the air.

With each step he felt himself get weaker, and the youthful body he encountered on the beach faded. Jory saw his skin lose its firmness. Small buttons of pain surged on his back, and he stopped walking. The pain grew so intense that he fell to one knee, then to all fours. He closed his eyes and collapsed.

He felt himself rolling. The warm wind spinning him. *What?* Jory thought. *I feel like I'm inside a dryer.* The spinning stopped, but his head kept turning. He felt himself slip under something heavy. Someone had buried him in hard cement. Some. Buried.

Ment. His thoughts separated and fell like bricks down the chasm of his mind. Someone had put a funnel to his ear and poured cement into his head.

He opened his eyes and saw a thin line of whiteness spread across his vision. It was so bright, he closed his eyes again, resting for a moment. He tried again, preparing himself for the blinding light. He saw a hazy whiteness with blurry dark lines. He tried to focus, and the dark lines became more pronounced, the whiteness became flatter. He was in a room. He felt someone put a hand over his mouth, and he almost gagged. He looked down and could see a clear plastic cup hugging his jaw. He moved his right hand to pull the cup off his mouth, but he could not move.

He heard someone scream his name. A figure came into his sight lines. *Belen!* he thought. *Get. Somebody. To. Pull. This. Concrete. Off. Me.* One sentence spoken in his mind took his breath away; he rested for several seconds before attempting another thought.

Another person entered his sight lines. Emerson. He watched them both stare down at him. He thought, *What. Happened?* He heard other sounds enter his head. A beep, then another beep. Then another beep. Then constant beeping. It resounded in his head like nuclear explosions. *Stop. The. Noise,* he thought.

What. Happened? He remembered the dream, but nothing before that. He was on his route, delivering mail, then he was dreaming about being on a beach, now he was here.

There. Was. A. Snake. Somehow a snake was involved, Jory thought. *I. Fought. A. Snake.* It must have been a mighty battle, he knew. *That. Stupid. Snake.*

He looked around the room and saw the remnants of a meal. Fried chicken and a bottle of liquor. Whatever happened must have been bad, he knew. For someone to invoke the *Tawal*, a spell to call you back, there must have been fear that his soul had wandered off.

Emerson. Emerson. Called. He. Celebrated. Me. This thought comforted him. *Emerson is a good boy. Just. Like. Me,* he thought. He laughed again, coughed again. In his younger years, Father Aga said Jory was a good boy, a considerate youth, for taking the time to visit families. Father Aga could not make such visits himself. Father Aga was too busy tending to the daily operations of Our Lady. (Church upkeep had become a struggle. The war had been over for ten years now, but the mentality of war was far from over. The Masses were always packed, but parishioners tended not to give much to the offertory.)

"Dad?" Jory heard Emerson say. "You're back."

Yes, Jory thought. *Maybe. I'm. Back. Because. You. Called. Me.*

Father Aga had tried to discourage the practice of local superstitions like calling ghosts, spending money to buy meat for rituals.

Idiot, Jory thought. *Father Aga. Idiot.* He could tell from the soft brightness of his room that it was morning. The Sun was building momentum, gaining heat. Father Aga preferred the Sun over the Moon. The locals used the cycles of the Moon to plant rice or arrange weddings or funerals. The use of the lunar calendar went against the Christian calendar of solar cycles. Father Aga told the farmers that harvesting around the cycles of the Moon was inadequate and certainly paganistic. The farmers, who recognized the Moon as a God, simply said that they had been working with the lunar calendar for centuries with great success. Why should they stop now?

Father Aga ruefully reinforced the moving away from local spiritual and cultural habits with all who taught at his school. If the current generation of Igorots could not be saved, Father Aga told Jory, the following generations would be. Father Aga was born at a time when the Philippines was a territory of the United States. He was born an American, and heading the people toward Western life and American ways was his own personal goal. He was furious when the Philippines had refused statehood, leaving the country to fend for itself. If he had his way, the Philippines would still be colonized by America.

Father Aga had boasted that in his years, he had actually met William Cameron Forbes, nicknamed "Father of Baguio," appointed by President Taft as Governor General of the Philippines. Father Aga had great respect for W. Cameron Forbes, the grandson of the fine poet Ralph Waldo Emerson. It was Forbes who made sure that the rest of the world had access to the mountain provinces, building roads to the hard-to-reach area.

It was the monotheistic approach that the West had adopted many years ago, and those in the East should follow suit, Father Aga told Jory once over dinner. He knew other countries in the Orient, like China or Japan, practiced polytheism and the ridiculous notion of worshipping one's ancestors. He was grateful that Christian missionaries were making their way into those countries, leading them into enlightenment.

"Honey?" Jory heard Belen's voice, a voice he'd heard for decades. *Belen,* he thought, *speak to me.*

"Jory, honey. I was so scared, so scared."

I. Scared. Too.

"Jory," Father Aga said, "you are part of a younger generation that would continue necessary conversion."

"So scared," Belen said. "I didn't know what to do."

The sound of his wife's voice had changed over the years, but there was still a kind of breathiness and rhythm that she'd maintained.

"I'm glad you came back," Belen said.

Glad, Jory thought. One of Belen's favorite words. She'd used it many, many times. Belen was always glad. She was glad when they met for the very first time, attending a Halloween feast at the Dubabang home. Father Aga instructed him to be extra

nice to the Dubabang clan for they were the biggest contribu-
tors to the church. Ermaline Dubabang's contribution helped
pay for the new missals, which were bound in leather.

A car was arranged to pick Jory up, and he knew immediately
this was not going to be an ordinary visit. He'd gone to several
parties already, usually taking a *jeepney,* or small bus, or simply
walking. No one had ever sent a car.

He was dropped off at the front of the largest house he'd ever
seen. Crowds of people milled about. Tables of food in the front
yard, more than he'd ever seen at previous feasts. Seeing one
roasted pig on a table was what he was used to, and even then that
was an expensive meal.

A pleasant-looking girl—someone he'd seen in town
perhaps—greeted him, but he couldn't quite place her. If she were
beautiful, he might have remembered her, but she was not. She
was pretty, and even that description was generous. She did, however, have a style about her that made her a little more striking.
Her posture straight and her head high.

"Hello," she said. "I'm Belen Dubabang. I'm glad you could
come." She was casually dressed, but Jory could tell from the
severe neatness of her appearance that her casual facade was carefully honed. She extended her hand, and he noticed it was cold.
The poor girl was nervous, Jory assumed, stuck with greeting and
entertaining the clergy. He saw girls like this growing up at his
orphanage, girls who came to church. They were proper, well-
coiffured girls who were meant to be exhibited, not touched.
Belen's cold hands made her human.

The girl guided him to a table and fixed him something to eat.
He noticed the small gold crucifix hanging from her neck when she
bent over to pile food onto his plate. He saw the image of Christ sus-
pended in air, swaying when she moved from one dish to another.

In preparing the plate, Jory saw that her back was straight, even when bending. She handled the serving spoons with a steady hand. Her lips were pursed and her brows raised, giving him the impression that she was capable of serving but didn't particularly care to do it.

She handed him the food with both hands and he noticed that she closed her eyes when he accepted, bowing her head, treating the plate like a generous gift. It was in this state of diffidence that Jory recognized her.

"You're the one who attends morning prayers so early," he said.

"Yes," she said, smiling, turning a tinge of red.

She guided him to the front steps of the house, and Jory was aware of the people who parted for her, including several people with their backs to her. They felt her presence approaching and, as he followed behind her, he felt it to. Perhaps she was confident, perhaps she was proud, but somehow this pretty, but not beautiful, girl became remarkable.

They sat on the steps of the house. Jory felt inadequate sitting next to her. If it weren't for his seminarian clothes, he would not be eating with her now. She would not be pouring such attention on him. His dark clothes gave the appearance that he was associated with God. That association elevated his social status, one closer to hers.

"I'm sure your family is proud to have you as a priest," Belen said.

Jory stopped chewing. He cleared his throat and said, "I don't have any family. I was raised in an orphanage." That admission made him put his plate aside.

"You don't have anyone?"

"No."

She took him into the house where more people were gathered, talking to articles of clothing neatly arranged on the floor.

"What are they doing?" Jory asked.

"They're talking to my dead grandparents," she said. "My grandparents are being told of the latest gossip in town. Or people confide in them, telling them secrets. Maybe they're asking guidance."

"They're praying to them."

"Yes. Do you think it's stupid?"

"No, not at all."

She brought him into a room with dozens of photos and paintings.

"More of my relatives," she said, indicating the images on the wall.

He noted that each wall had dozens of photos on them.

"Yes. Most of them are dead though. These are my grandparents," she said. She waved her hand like she was revealing a prize. "In the mid-1800s, my grandfathers went below to the lowland provinces to become educated. Schools were rare here.

"When war broke out, my grandmother wanted to save these photos and paintings. She protected them as best she could and buried them."

"You have so many pictures."

One corner dominated the room. There was a marble table with well over a dozen pictures of one man. Bouquets of flowers were on the floor and five full plates of food surrounded a large painting with a gold frame. The painting was of a stern-looking man with short, cropped hair.

"That's my father," Belen said. "His name is Valentino. Tino, they called him."

"He looks . . . powerful."

"He died in the war," she said.

"Was he killed by the Japanese?"

She lowered her eyes, and Jory felt he had asked an inappropriate question.

"Would you like to meet him?" she said.

"Who?"

"My father." She smiled and looked up

"Yes, of course."

She led him toward the rear of the house and opened the back door.

"Here he is," she said.

Less than twenty feet away, five sarcophaguses lay. They were intricately designed with roses, bearing dates of birth and death. Jory was truly impressed that this family could afford to bury their relatives in such a manner. As a member of the clergy, he believed there was some rebellion in this action. This family chose not to bury their ancestors in hallowed ground.

"These are my grandparents," Belen said. "And this is my father." She walked closer to the stone coffins and ran her fingers along the one with the name Valentino Dubabang. Flowers and plates of food lay on his sarcophagus. "That's why we're having a party; we're honoring them, particularly my father's soul, on Halloween. I'm told that it was my father's spirit who led my family and others in our village to safety."

She lifted a cookie from one of the plates of food on the grave. She bit into it. She offered the remaining half of the cookie to Jory and said, "My father's spirit has graced the cookie. We don't usually offer the food to people outside of the family, but I don't think he would mind if you had some."

She stepped closer and brought the crumbling cookie to his face. He bit into it and felt the tips of her nails, painted pink, against his lips. He laughed as the cookie crumbled around his mouth. Her touch was kind and turned into a delicate caress as she wiped the food away from his chin. He thought he detected affection there and was ashamed of thinking she held feelings for him. It was obvious that she was better than he. She was meant for someone better. And knowing this, he began to feel something, something that could be called Desire. He felt what young men feel when they meet a girl who they know is too good for them, somehow having her elevated him to her level or lowered her to his. It's usually the latter.

"Over there are others," she said.

He saw small granite squares on the ground. She guided him to that place where her ancestors rested. He followed her, not because he was interested in learning more about her family. He followed her in the way men watch a movie they don't care to see or pay for a dinner they can't afford. He hoped at the end of it, he would be rewarded: she would undo herself, undo her hair, pulling it from a rubber band, undo her clothes, slipping the buttons from the eyelets on a blouse, and let him enter.

As he stood on the graves of Belen's dead relatives, he whispered a question under his breath. He asked them for their permission to have her.

BELEN

"*J*ORY!" SHE YELLED, leaning over her husband, touching his face. "I was so scared. So scared. Jory, honey. I'm glad you came back."

Belen caressed Jory's face, paying close attention to the area by his temples. Her husband had a headache, she knew, and she wanted to massage it away.

See, I told you he would be okay.

Thank you, Blessed Mother. A million thanks, Belen thought and made a mental note to put a few more dollars in the collection box next time she attended Mass. She moved the hair away from his forehead, running her fingers along his scalp. Years of lovemaking with this man taught her that Jory always found comfort in this action. She noticed how his breathing steadied and how his panicked eyes settled.

You're safe, she thought. *Safe with me.* She wiped the crust, or Dead Dreams, from his eyes. He blinked. In this hospital, as devastated as her husband was, she felt no greater joy than sitting with him, not saying a word, feeling to some small degree like she was a girl again. Being alone with Jory was something she always looked forward to when she was young.

She jumped when her mother said, "Father Aga asked you to tutor the new priest."

"Me?"

"Yes, Jory Lalaban asked for you to teach him Ibaloi. He said you were bright."

Belen watched her mother beam with pride. Belen lowered her head, grateful that she had made her mother happy.

"Did you hear that?" Mrs. Dubabang said, turning to the women working in the kitchen, "Father Aga asked my daughter to tutor the new priest."

"He's not a priest, yet, Mama. He's learning."

To be alone with Jory, truly alone, not at a party, not with relatives nearby. Alone with Jory. It was agreed that they'd meet at the Dubabang home. The servants were instructed to stay out of the house, so there could be as much quiet for instruction as possible. Mrs. Dubabang stayed in her room to nap.

The first lesson in the Dubabang living room was not a productive one. In the hour that they had together, Belen taught Jory three phrases: My Name Is Jory; What's Your Name?; and What Time Is It?. It took about fifteen minutes to learn how to say those sentences. She spent the rest of the hour nervously talking about other things with bouts of awkward pauses.

"Which movie star is prettier? Juvy Cachola or Priscilla Valdez?" Belen asked, touching her hair.

"Juvy Cachola by far," Jory responded, then coughed. "Don't you think the actor Eddie Gutierrez looks like Elvis?"

She laughed for no apparent reason and answered, "Oh, yes. I think so."

Silence.

Belen sat with her body turned away, arms folded over her breasts. Ever since she had seen Jory in church, she experienced a kind of tingling in different parts of her body. By turning away and folding her arms, she hoped that Jory could not see how her nipples had become firm. She was self-conscious of the possibility that her passion for this man could be seen right through her bra and blouse.

The quietude was interrupted with the footsteps of Ermaline Dubabang, waking from her nap, and descending the stairs. Hearing her mother, Belen stood and walked to the opposite end of the room.

"I hope you gained something today," Mrs. Dubabang said.

"Yes, ma'am. Yes, I did," Jory said.

"Would you like some juice?"

"No."

"Very well then. You'll be coming by again at what time?"

"Day after tomorrow."

Jory left the room, and Belen felt like a rope was tied around her waist, tugging at her. She followed her pupil out of the room, watching him leave the house, seeing him turn around to wave good-bye not once, but five times.

"He seems like a nice boy," Mrs. Dubabang said. "He'll make a good priest."

In the hospital room, Belen smiled, touching her husband's face. *Yes, you would have made a good priest, a very good priest,* she thought. There were times when she wondered what would have happened if she simply taught him the language and left it at that.

"Have you heard the songs of Gloria Abanez?" Belen asked Jory, believing that he would learn the language better if it were put to music.

"A little."

"Here, she sings some songs in Ibaloi."

Belen played the record. She sat, eyes closed, swaying to the music, then said, "Gloria Abanez is saying, 'Don't leave me, my dear. I love you. I love you.'"

"Maybe . . . you could show me different parts of Baguio?" Jory asked.

Belen opened her eyes, nodded, and said, "But maybe we should not tell anyone that we are meeting at other times."

"I think you are right."

She told no one of her secret meetings, timing her walks so that no one might see her. She took long detours to meet Jory. Their usual spot was by the mouth of Crystal Cave located on the side of a mountain, imbedded in trees. The entrance had slimy walls, but in the late afternoon sun, the walls shimmered. The cave had caverns that led into darkness. It was shrouded with mystery, as it was known that people had entered the caverns and lost their way, never finding their way out.

She met him outside and discussed little things like what was going on at school and what the latest movies were. She praised the glorious voice of Gloria Abanez who sang peasant songs, sometimes in various dialects. Though critics had chastised Gloria Abanez for singing songs in languages that many people from different parts of the Philippines could not understand, Gloria Abanez held firm saying that some songs needed to be sung in the context of the language they were written. This would maintain the purity of the lyrics.

When Belen held his hand, conversation ceased: words became unnecessary. She sat with her fingers entwined with Jory's, looking away from him. If her eyes met his, she knew that what she was doing was somehow incorrect. She knew that their paths should continue without each other. Their lives should be parallel lines, not an intersection.

Sometimes Jory squeezed her hand a little more, his grip a little more firm. She had to turn toward him. Even then, she could not look at him. When her lips touched his, it was a slow and gentle meeting. With his kiss, she was locked away somewhere, a place with no sound and no calendar. There were times when her lips touched his, it was daylight. When her lips parted from his, the moon was in the sky. Shaded in evening, then and only then, could she look at him. Her eyes could meet his when the moon illuminated his face. Her modesty and shame fit well in darkness.

One afternoon while she was holding his hand, ready to kiss, she heard a group of children playing nearby. She became scared and pulled Jory closer to the entrance of Crystal Cave, away from view. He held her closer. The children passed. Belen motioned him back to their original tree, but Jory did not move. She let him kiss her neck, pulling her into the cave. She hesitated at first. She looked into his face and saw a yearning that she had never seen before. She acquiesced. She entered the dark mouth of Crystal Cave, a place known for people losing their way.

Belen looked down at her husband's exhausted face. His eyes were half-way closed. She leaned in and placed her lips to his forehead, providing him with a small, gentle kiss. She sat down thinking of what she gave up to have a lifetime of kissing Jory.

Secretly meeting him was a joyous experience, but it also caused her some degree of guilt. She was not a dedicated Catholic, but she was still Catholic. She grew up revering men dressed like Jory, but when she held him close, felt his stubble against her neck, she crumbled. When he placed his arms around her back, any guilt absolved itself. Feeling him close to her, he was not a man of God. He was a man who belonged to her. She belonged to Jory.

Unfortunately, hiding her relationship from her family was incredibly difficult, causing her a great deal of stess. She stayed out later, telling her mother that she was spending time at the library or in deep prayer in the church. She had never lied to her mother before, but what made it worse was that it wasn't only her mother she was hiding from. She hid from her whole province.

She did this for months, and the servants whispered. They stopped looking at her and quieted down when she entered a room that they were cleaning. Once a maid had brought in her laundry while she was in her room and said, "Miss Belen, I'm sorry that it took longer to wash your clothes. I noticed that they were more wrinkled and more dirty than usual."

"I'll have to be more careful."

"Yes, Miss Belen, you should."

Her friends inquired about her whereabouts, and her brothers worried. They asked her where she was spending her time, and she said she wanted to be alone to think. This made people suspicious because Belen was not the type of girl who went away to think about anything. If she said that she wanted time to paint her nails, *that* would have been more believable.

She refused to go to morning prayers and never looked at Jory in the hall. She passed him silently, with the understanding that they would meet later in the day. She gave the appearance that she wanted nothing to do with the seminarian. Unfortunately, it was this behavior that made her friends and brothers know that she was spending time with him somehow.

Belen felt the curious stares cast upon her from the servants, her friends. This caused her to eat irregularly, wake in the middle of the night, perspire almost everywhere she went. Perspiring was something that Belen had never done before. Her muscles seemed to tick, and her fingers became clammy. Her body seemed to betray her, and it made her nervous. The only time she was calm was when she was with Jory; otherwise, she was a nervous wreck. She became extremely worrisome when her period stopped coming.

What Belen did not know was that the servants knew the daily running of that house. They were on a routine schedule on when to dust and when to scrub. They knew that Ermaline Dubabang preferred her rice cakes sweeter than usually prepared and liked her hair brushes in a row. They knew that the Dubabang boys, Oliver and Cesar, liked their trousers creased and their shoes polished weekly.

They also knew the cycles of the women in the house. They knew when to leave swatches of cloth in the bathrooms and to have warm tea readily available. They made sure that laundry was scheduled for this time. The maids certainly noticed when laundry was lighter than usual.

For the first month, the servants kept quiet about their discovery but watched Belen carefully. They observed her moodiness and nervousness but had no explanation. Now, they did. The second month rolled around, and they noticed the laundry remained light, there could only be one possible answer.

A maid in the Dubabang home told her sister who was a seamstress on Session Road, who told her fiancé, who was a waiter three doors down, who told his best friend, who mopped floors in the bank, who told an accountant who was working late, who told his wife, who was a teacher at the university, who told a trusted student who helped her grade papers, who told her cousin who attended Our Lady Catholic School that the daughter of Ermaline Dubabang was pregnant. The cousin, in turn, who knew Belen, said she had a crush on a young seminarian named Jory Lalaban and relayed all of the suspicious gossip that Belen and Jory were seeing each other.

"She's carrying the child of a priest?!?!?!" one maid gasped.

"Yes, that Jory Lalaban. Belen gives him lessons," another maid said.

"I wonder what she had been teaching him."

"Yes, it all makes sense now."

It did *not* make sense to Mrs. Dubabang when she discovered that her daughter was pregnant. She was furious. Not only because her daughter's suitor was an almost priest, which was bad luck in itself, not only because Jory was poor and had no decent offering to make to their ancestors, not only because this Jory had no relatives or past to speak of—where family lineage was extremely important to Mrs. Dubabang—or that Belen had not received her period in months. What infuriated her was that she had to hear this from other people.

The rumor mill operated as efficiently as Mrs. Dubabang's lumber mill, and she confronted her daughter. Belen admitted that the rumors were true. Ermaline fumed. Her eyes widened and her fists throbbed

"Idiot girl!" Mrs. Dubabang said, removing her wooden slipper, rushing her daughter and beating her with it. Belen's screams were heard throughout the house. Servants or other relatives responded by running to the living room, witnessing Ermaline beat her daughter. One by one, they left the living room to let the reckoning take place.

Mrs. Dubabang grew tired, lifting her left forearm to her forehead, her right hand, holding the slipper, to her side. To her dismay, Belen crawled away. Mrs. Dubabang would have forgiven her had she stayed there, huddled and scared. It would have been a sign of humility and submission, as if to say, *I'm sorry and I'll make everything right again.* Instead she was leaving.

Belen crawled through the living room, she heard her mother say, "They will curse you, Belen."

Belen did not have to wonder who "they" were. She looked up from the floor to see the imposing image of her mother. Behind her were paintings and photographs of grandfathers and grandmothers, uncles and aunts, cousins, nieces, and nephews. She knew that her family, every person she shared blood with, were displeased.

Except her father. In the corner of the room, she saw the pictures of her dad, and she took comfort. She knew it was her mother's hand that killed him.

"They will curse you, Belen," Mrs. Dubabang said. "God will curse you."

How did I know? Belen wondered in the hospital, looking at her husband. *How did I know that the Curse would get this far?* She heard a knock at the door. Emerson sat against the wall, and she almost forgot that he was there. The door opened and her neighbor Mrs. Kim stuck her head through. It must have been at least 9:30 A.M.

"Look, Jory, the Kims came."

Belen had been living next to Mrs. Kim for over two decades, and they had become quite close over years. It was Mrs. Kim who dragged her to the sidewalk, providing comfort, when Jun's body went into the air.

EMERSON

"*Y*our father might need blood later," Dr. Jones said. "Especially after the operations. We'd like to be prepared. You, being his son, would naturally have the right blood type."

Emerson got an appointment to have his blood drawn. He sat in a crowded waiting room with a window connecting the waiting room to the lab. The Bloodtaker, a phlebotomist with dark hair and muscles, appeared at the window, called Emerson's name, and gave him a small card to fill out. He returned to his seat among the middle-aged women, poised with a pen. Have you used injection drugs? No. Are you diabetic? No. Then the question: have you had sex with a man since 1980?

Emerson looked at the piece of paper and drew a deep breath. He knew he was HIV negative. He had consistently tested for HIV every year for over ten years. He first tested several months after he had been penetrated. Emerson would hang out with the prostitutes on Santa Monica Boulevard and met a man who said he was twenty-eight years old. Emerson didn't like to remember too much about this person, except that his name was Doug.

Have you had sex with a man since 1980? He hunched over his card so none of the women sitting next to him could see his answer. He checked the box that indicated Yes. He approached the window and gave the card to the dark-haired man. Bloodtaker read the card, then said, "I'm sorry. You don't qualify."

Emerson looked behind him at the waiting room, hoping no one was nearby. He forced a smile and said, "Look, my dad really needs me to give blood."

"I'm sorry."

"My dad was the postman who was shot. Can't you make an exception this one time?" He looked at the man across from him. No reaction. "He's hurt, really badly. He needs blood, and I'm his only son." Still, no reaction. Emerson clamped his jaw, whispering through his teeth. "You want me to get tested? I'll do it right now. I'll show you I'm negative."

"I'm sorry." Bloodtaker got up to leave.

Emerson grabbed his arm. "My blood is good."

"Sir, let go. When your father needs it, we'll try and find blood that matches."

"You take my blood and get it tested. You'll see. There's nothing wrong with it."

"Let go of my arm."

"I want to talk to somebody about this. Your supervisor."

"I am the supervisor." Bloodtaker leaned forward. "There are certain guidelines that we have to follow. I really am sorry."

Emerson, inches away from Bloodtaker's face, whispered, "If someone like you can give blood, so should I."

"Actually, sister, I can't give blood either." Bloodtaker looked at him directly in the eyes. "Now, let go of my arm, sweetheart, or you'll leave a bruise."

Emerson released his grip. "I apologize. I just want to help my dad."

"I understand you're upset," he said. "If I could change things I would. At this time, we can't. Believe me. I would change things, if I could."

Emerson looked up and saw the bright fluorescent lights. "I made a mistake. I checked the wrong box."

"Sir, don't do this."

"Do what? I'm straight. I have a girlfriend."

Bloodtaker lowered his lids.

"Her name is Donna. We've been high school sweethearts. We were supposed to get married, but she wants to finish grad school first. Which really made me mad. You see, I want to be a husband. A father with kids."

"You don't have to do this."

"So, I said to her, 'Donna, look, my biological clock is ticking. I'm not getting any younger. I wanna get married.' You know what she said? She said she wants to pursue her doctorate degree next."

"Sir."

"'Doctorate?' I said. 'You know how long it takes to get one of those?'"

"I'm leaving."

"Wait. You know, what I think the real reason is. The real reason she doesn't want to marry me is 'cause she doesn't think I'm worth marrying. I see some of the guys she goes to school with, smart guys, guys who went to Yale, guys with a future, guys who *want* a future. And I don't measure up. I'm not one of those guys. I didn't go to college or anything. I didn't want to go to college. I'm not ambitious like that. I just don't have it in me. Donna's mad at me because I've had only one promotion in twelve years. She wants me to want more. It sucks knowing there are guys out there who are better than me, because they want more, want something else."

"They're not better," Bloodtaker said.

"I'll show you I'm straight." Emerson turned around to the waiting room and said, "Any young woman wanna go on a date? I'll bring you flowers. A box of candy, too."

Emerson felt a tug on his forearm. This time it was Bloodtaker gripping him. He said, "Honey, don't humiliate yourself."

"I'll humiliate myself for my dad. Now, will you take my blood or not?"

Bloodtaker slowly shook his head.

"Fine. Any single woman wanna go on a date?"

"Don't make a scene."

"How about a married woman? Your husband doesn't have to know." Emerson approached a middle-aged woman in a yellow dress. "Hey, beautiful. You have the prettiest eyes. I think I could really get into you."

"I'm calling security."

"I've got *Playboy* magazines in a drawer at work," he said. "I pull them out when I'm bored. I look at pictures of naked women. I'm not supposed to have girlie mags at work. I could get fired, but a picture of a naked girl just brightens up a whole day. I think girls are hot. I do. I'm straight. I am."

"Did you do it?" his mother asked later in the day. "Did you give blood for your father?"

"No," Emerson said, "they won't take blood from men like me."

His mother looked confused, then comprehension filled her face. She nodded.

Emerson hated that nod. To him, it said, "See, you are cursed."

JORY

*T*HE MORNING SUN hurt his eyes. The Sun has that kind of affect on people, on beings sometimes. The pain medication made his insides numb, leaving his outer layer, the skin, more sensitive. He felt Belen's hands caress his face. *Oh, Belen, the woman who let me taste the Moon.* Those hands. Still warm. They have become a little rougher through the years, but still warm, so warm. The first time he had touched them, under a plate, they were cold, cold out of nervousness. That was the only time. They were warm when he held them those many years ago. They were warm when she gripped his back when they made love.

He watched her beautify her hands, place a ring or two on fingers, paint her nails various shades of red, but nothing made her hands more beautiful than the warmth that radiated from them. He took a deep breath, enjoying the touch on his face. Her touch was worth it, all of it, including the wrath of Father Aga.

"Aaaaaah," Jory said. He tried to say, *Aga. Remember Father Aga?*

"Do you like the way that feels, honey-bunny?" Belen said, continuing to caress Jory's face.

"Aaaaaah," Jory said again. He didn't know why he could not formulate words. They were in his mind, but somehow it was not properly connecting in his brain.

"Just rest, Jory. You're very medicated."

Father Aga found out that Jory had gotten a girl pregnant and was infuriated. Not that Jory had had sex—he was still a young man after all and that was forgivable—but it was who he had sex with. He impregnated Belen Dubabang. If he had had sex with some peasant girl, something could be done. The girl would be whisked away, taken to a parish on another island. They would make up a story of how the girl had lost her husband in some tragic accident, maybe pay the girl's family a few pesos to stay quiet. Jory had to screw the most prominent girl in the region, and ruin the most stable financial relationship the church had. And for that, he would make sure that Jory Lalaban would pay.

Father Aga summoned Jory into his office, and before Jory could close the door, Father Aga backhanded the young man.

"What were you thinking?!?!?!" Father Aga yelled, grabbing hold of Jory's head with two hands. Father Aga thought of the tiles in the rectory that wouldn't get replaced, the pews that wouldn't get varnished.

"I love her, Father," Jory said.   .

"Love her? What do you know about love? Inserting yourself into a girl doesn't mean you love her." Father Aga thought of the cement base carrying a statue of the Virgin, below her feet read the inscription *Our Lady of Mercy*. It was the first thing you saw when you drove up to the church. Through the years, the cement base had withered away, the letters of the inscription had faded, reading *O Lad of Mer.* Father Aga had hoped the Dubabang family would replace the base. Now it seemed unlikely. Some quick maneuvering was required to save the relationship. Father Aga had an idea. "You will go to her and you will marry her. You will beg for forgiveness, and you will do as Ermaline says. If she wants you to cut off your right arm to save the family honor, you will do that. These Igorots are a weird bunch, and the Dubabangs are at the top of the heap. You've disgraced them, don't you know that!"

"Yes, Father."

"You listen to me. I will marry the both of you myself. I will treat it as a wonderful thing that two children of God have found each other. You will stand in front of the entire congregation and beg for forgiveness. Is that clear? Beg. Beg like you've never begged before.

"You will continue religious training. You can't become a priest, of course, but you can become a deacon. I think the Dubabang's would appreciate a deacon in the family. We will restore their family honor, and you will help strengthen the ties between us."

At the end of his harangue, Father Aga was almost grateful that such a scandal took place. He wanted to congratulate himself on his brilliant plan of uniting the Dubabangs with the church. He took a deep breath and said, "Do you understand?"

"No."

"No? What part of this don't you comprehend? We are rectifying this shameful situation. The Dubabang's name will be restored. You get to marry the girl that you say you love *and* continue your religious training."

"Father, I don't wish to be a priest."

"You won't be a priest, you'll be a deacon."

"I don't wish to continue my training. I don't wish to be a part of the church."

"What?"

"Emerson left the church."

"What are you talking about?"

"Ralph Waldo Emerson left the church. When his wife died, he was affected by her death."

"What's wrong with you?"

"Ralph Waldo Emerson studied to be a man of the cloth. He had lots of potential. He left the church because the world didn't make sense to him. If things don't make sense, answers might be somewhere else. I think I want to go somewhere else."

"Go lie down. You are not making sense. I am trying to fix things."

"I don't think things need to be fixed, Father Aga. Just changed."

⸺

CHANGE THEY DID. Jory prepared to leave the church. He was not prepared for how welcomed he would be by the Old Ones in the province. He did not know that Makers of Prayer would be elated that there would be one less Filipino man teaching the preposterous theories of this new Christian religion that had invaded the area.

The old people of the province noticed that more and more of their young were paying less and less attention to their customary spiritual laws and giving more credence to the strange God known as Jesus Christ. There was a time when a *mambunong* or a Maker of Prayer was an important person at any function. The *mambunong* presided over births and deaths, marriages and anniversaries. The *mambunong* offered prayers to the stars and to the Gods of Earthquake or Thunder and called the souls of the dead to visit. They were often poor, old men and women who were taken as wise.

As the *mambunong* made more functions, said the blessing of a home, the *mambunong* noticed other Makers of Prayer were there, too. The new Makers of Prayer or priests and nuns were followers of Christ, wearing clothes of midnight. The *mambunong* wore clothes of radiant color, stripes of reds and yellows, blues and greens. The *mambunong* worried that the mountains of the Philippines would become like the rest of the country, deeply entrenched in worshipping the sickliest God ever seen.

The *mambunong* may have been old men and women who lived in rural parts of the mountains, but they had certainly wandered into the makings of a church. They would go inside and see Jesus on the crucifix and were horrified. This is what people are worshipping?

Gods should be strong, not sickly, emaciated beings. They had heard that Jesus was killed. What kind of God would allow himself to be killed? If Jesus was the son of another god, what kind of god would allow his own son to be treated that way?

The *mambunong* did agree that humans have souls. They did not agree that *only* humans have souls. They believed that *everything* had souls. Animals had souls, trees had souls, the fabric worn on your body had souls.

Most of the Makers of Prayer were old enough to see the change coming, see the withering of their religion, one they had been practicing for centuries. Most of the Makers of Prayer started their training in the late 1800s and heard stories of how they fought dear and hard for their beliefs, they fought the Europeans who attempted to climb up the mountains, and they even fought other Filipinos, inhabitants of the lowlands, who joined the legions of Spanish Christians who wished to convert them in the name of Christ.

The Americans beat Spain in the Spanish-American war in 1898, and the *mambunong* thought they would be free from Spanish Catholicism. They didn't know that the Americans would keep the Philippines and other countries like Puerto Rico, Cuba, and Guam.

The Americans were not so eager to give up their trophies. Headed by the Republican Party, it was decided the Philippines would not be granted independence but remain a possession of the U.S. This added more headaches to the old ones in the mountains. Not only did they have to contend with Catholicism, they had to put up with other Christians intent on spreading the word of Christ. The Makers of Prayer were overwhelmed with one Church dedicated to Christ; now they had others: Anglicans, Episcopalians, Baptists.

When a road was built in 1912 successfully connecting the lowlands to the mountains, the swell of Christianity became unbearable. They brought fancy cars and never before seen sweets and ridiculous fabric to clothe the *entire* body. Imagine wearing fabric to cover the pores of your skin? The Makers of Prayer were told it was to make up for the sins of one named Adam and one named Eve who, upon being deceived by a snake, discovered shame and that shame made them embarrassed about their nakedness.

It was a remarkable story, but to the *mambunong* it didn't make sense. If a snake was that deceitful, they should have killed it. They had heard the Christian God had banished Adam and Eve from His very beautiful garden. As He should for creating two people foolish enough to be deceived by a snake! At the very least, Adam and Eve should have threatened to eat it.

Some of the *mambunong*, particularly the old women, wore the vertebrae of snakes in their hair to protect them from lightning. Snakes were kindred spirits of lightning, and lightning in the sky would never strike its own on earth.

The Christians taught tales of Adam and Eve to the children of the mountains. The Christians were very deceptive, luring the children into their Christian schools, the only places of learning in the area, encouraging them to forget old ways. If families refused, the Christians kidnapped the children, taking them to lowland schools. It became so bad that the *mambunong* began kidnapping the children of the nearby villages to teach them how to perform the *Abasang,* a ritual performed when a child is born, the *Pachit,* a ritual to commemorate peace and prosperity, the *Saad,* a ritual to cure sickness caused by the lingering souls of the dead.

There were fewer and fewer *mambunong* being groomed. The Christians brought television and radio. A huge building was built in Baguio City showing movies about faraway places like Paris or New York or London. The children of the mountain province wanted to go there. And the parents were more than willing to support them.

The old ones were disheartened when one of their own returned to the mountain, wearing shirts and pants and shoes. And underneath those clothes, there were more garments. The younger generations were being taught Adam and Eve, stupid individuals who didn't know how to handle a snake. For this mistake, children of their province began to know shame. How disgraceful it was to teach children to feel such things.

Imagine the *mambunong'*s surprise and delight when one of *them,* a Christian priest named Jory Lalaban, chose to leave Christ and learn about worshipping the Moon.

⌒

JORY SAW THE Moon through the hospital window, grateful that Fall had arrived and Winter was approaching. He believed the Moon was in better spirits during these months when the evenings were longer, allowing the Moon to dominate the Sky for more hours. Soon the Solstice will arrive, and what a wonderful night that will be.

Moon, Jory thought, *help me. They're going to operate on me, Moon. They're going to take another bullet out of my back.* He wanted to say this. He always spoke his prayers out loud. If not loud, disguised in the breath of a whisper. As long as the words left his tongue, and lifted themselves into the Sky.

He could not speak and feared his prayers were trapped in his head, floating about, unable to transcend his skull and rise to the Sky. He was able to nod or turn his head to the side to indicate No, but when he opened his mouth, only a croak came out.

Jory looked out his window and saw his God—at least his very favorite one. Gods were everywhere, but from the very beginning, the Moon held special significance for him. Jory always knew the Moon was sympathetic, showing the scars inflicted by the Sun, and for the first time in his life Jory understood. With bullets in his back, he understood. He thought he knew difficulties when he'd tried to support his wife and unborn child in the Philippines. He was free from the church but not free from husband responsibilities. Finding work to support his new bride was not easy. While Belen went on to university, partly on scholarship and earning money as a teaching aide, Jory found himself being turned away from many of the businesses in town. The businessmen were loyal to Ermaline Dubabang and didn't want to hurt relationships with her, a woman who influenced commerce in the area.

The only job he could find was in a newly opened restaurant in Baguio City, started by a Manila businessman who was not familiar with the Dubabang clout. The Manila businessman had his own money and could care less about a provincial woman who may be wealthy, but certainly not as wealthy as money made from the largest city in the country.

Jory and Belen had found lodging in a small, rural, one-room house made of corrugated metal. They paid very little rent on the house, because it was all but abandoned. There was no electricity or running water. They bathed in a stream a tenth of a mile away and kept food in a metal box packed with ice. There was one window in the house, and on moonlit nights, a soft glow fell into the otherwise dark room.

Belen said she did not mind losing the material possessions she once had. Jory knew she was lying. This made him cherish her even more. Belen could live without fancy furniture, but she could not live without food. Her meager salary certainly could not feed them both and a child on the way.

He was able to get some meals from the restaurant but not enough to keep a family alive. Jory, like so many people before, turned to God when troubles came his way. He decided to go on a spiritual quest. He went to the old men and women he had been so fascinated by when he had reached the mountain for the first time. He knew who they were and where they lived. There were several Makers of Prayer who lived in the province. They were old and poor but respected.

He approached one of them in the marketplace to formally begin his spiritual training. He wanted to learn about the God of Thunder and his wife Agamayo; the Ampasit, spirits that live in wood; the Timungau, spirits that live in water. He became particularly interested in the Pasang, spirits that lived in the air. The Pasang became very, very important to Jory and Belen. It was, after all, the Spirits That Live in The Air that determined whether or not a woman would give birth.

Jory took to his new studies with a passion that he hadn't had while studying to be a priest. He noticed there were great similarities in his training to become a Catholic priest and his training to become a Maker of Prayer. Like his priesthood training, there was ritual and there were prayers attached to that ritual. In praying the rosary, there were prayers set to the counting of beads: the Hail Mary, the Our Father, the Apostles' Creed were among them. There were also saints that could be petitioned for special intervention with God. If you lost something, for example, you could ask St. Anthony, Patron Saint of Lost Things, to help you find whatever it was you lost.

As was the case in becoming a Maker of Prayer. If someone was ill, a ritual would take place, and there were certain prayers that accompanied that ritual. The ritual consisted of placing a cup of rice wine on the ill person's forehead. The cup would have a leaf on it. A special prayer to the Moon, the Stars, the Sun, all of the Sky would take place.

In both instances, whether it was in a church or in a field, blood was involved. The Blood and Body of Christ was offered to the congregation to taste, while the blood of a chicken was offered in *this* situation. There was sacrifice of some kind in both matters, Jory discovered.

Jory knew that Christianity's roots were in paganism, carrying some of the most basic rites of original worshippers: the sacrifice of blood and the offering of prayers. Whatever the spiritual practice may be, Jory observed an innate need for human beings to ask for forgiveness, request salvation, and receive wisdom.

There were several Makers of Prayer in the province; each had a different way of doing things. Each had their own remedies for making coughs disappear. You must offer the God Kabunyan a chicken, one might say. A chicken isn't necessary, another might say, but you must make sure the rice wine offered was of the highest quality. He likened this behavior to the way Catholic priests had a way of doing things. Father Ryan introduced American ideologies in his sermons, taking into account the work of Ralph Waldo Emerson, while Father Aga maintained a more conservative point of view, taking direction only from what the Vatican pronounced as true.

Regardless of the point of view, whether it was priest or whether it was Maker of Prayer, the absolute rule was a sincere devotion to God and Godly things, which included a sincerity in prayers.

When Jory set out to pray to the Moon for the very first time, he was nervous. He had tried praying in church with not much success. He was afraid that if he prayed to the Moon, he would have the same kind apathy that he had for Christ.

While Belen slept in the shack, Jory went outside to pray. He got on his knees and clasped his hands the way he had done before. He lowered his head and thought of the Moon. His mind was blank. He didn't know how long he kneeled, but his knees hurt. In church, he had padded knee rests to comfort him, but now he only had the grit of the ground. He sat back and wondered if he would ever get the purpose of praying.

There was pitch blackness around him, and he could barely see the shape of the little house he shared with his wife. He saw the outlines of trees and mountains around him, but not the fullness of their beings. In the darkness, he saw the top of things, the small glow of the metal roof, the glint of light that the leaves of trees reflected back to the Moon, the ominous shape of black mountains against a dark, dark blue Sky.

There was nothing but quiet and the faint sense that the trees, the mountains, the metal house that he lived in were lifeless things that no one would have noticed if it weren't for the dim light of the Moon.

He remembered a tale that one of the Makers of Prayer had told him, a tale that Jory latched onto, somehow relating to its meaning. There was a time when the Moon was as bright as the Sun. They shared the same power of light. The Sun had decided to find a spouse, but was not successful. The Moon laughed at Him for failing. The Sun became angry and threw ashes on the laughing Moon. The Moon was unable to show Himself fully again, his brightness dimmed. There are some nights that the Moon will show you where the Sun had scarred Him. The dark parts in a quarter moon or half moon are where the Sun had burned Him. When the Moon is full, He is ashamed, only revealing the handsomest part of Himself. For years, Jory loved this story. He could comprehend not wanting to show the pained part of one's self. Now, in this hospital, on this bed, Jory truly understood.

He looked through the hospital window, looked up at the glowing orb in the Sky. This night He was full.

May I see, Jory thought. *May I see . . . where the Sun hurt You? No need to be ashamed. I know that You were once bright, as bright as anything. But sometimes . . . sometimes things happen to us. Someone hurts us, maybe. Yes, hurts us. Maybe someone will hit you or cheat you. Or shoot you. You are a great God, so great that even damaged by the Sun You still maintain magical powers. You could make eyes water the earth, make eyes fill up with moisture too great for lids to dam up. Moonlight is only that part You are willing to show people, not the hurt part, not the burned side.*

Jory thought of all the nights that he went outside and looked up, like the night he stole his son's body and honored it properly. He always reveled in the brightness of the Moon, ignoring where the Sun had thrown ashes on Him. Those nights, the Moon unveiled Himself. He saw the darkness that resided there, but didn't pay attention. Like a battered wife who shows her bruises slowly, Jory turned away. Not anymore.

He looked at the Moon and shared in the sorrow of someone hurting you. In this bond Jory felt comfort, too. Out there, in the universe, a celestial being was damaged and was in dire need of consoling.

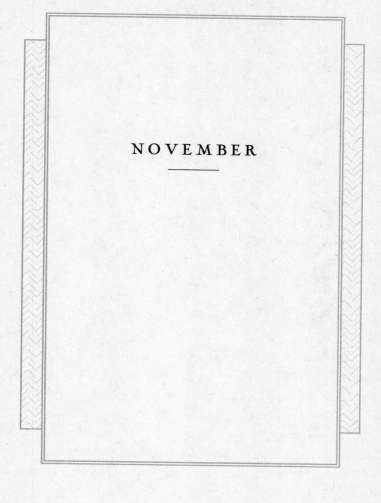

NOVEMBER

MICHAEL

*I*T TOOK ONE evening to change the direction of Michael Zhang's life. One day he is a happy-go-lucky flight attendant, satisfied with his life, happy to have escaped working in a Taipei fish factory, which was the history of his family for three generations. He couldn't ponder gutting, then drying fish that would be packaged and sent to stores all over Asia.

The thought of coming home smelling like deepwater fish every day, something his father reeked of for thirty years, so repulsed him that he vowed to fulfill his dream of seeing the world someday. He was reading the pages of a fashion magazine and saw a picture for Taiwan Air advertising cheap fares to places like New York, Sydney, and Toronto. Michael knew this was his fate. He called the corporate office only to discover that part of flying internationally was having the skill to speak another language, preferably English.

The next day he found a school that taught English. Two years later he spoke it competently, albeit with a thick accent, but enough to qualify him for flight attendant school. He had flown for two years, and in that time had seen all the countries he'd wanted to see: India, Jamaica, England, Germany, France, Spain, Tahiti, Japan, Canada, Nigeria, Brazil, Mexico, and, of course, the United States. He established a regular route of Bankok to Taipei to Los Angeles and back again.

He enjoyed his life. He didn't know that tremendous heartache was soon to come. He leafed through the *LA Times*'s Calendar section and saw an ad for a play, a musical of some kind. He called to make a reservation for one. He didn't invite his fellow flight attendants because he didn't think they wanted to better themselves like he did. After two years of flying, having seen Buckingham Palace in London, the temples of Kyoto, and Carnaval in Rio de Janeiro, in the back of his mind, he saw himself as a fish factory worker in disguise.

He'd never been to a play before but he knew Pearls, a nickname he called fancy people, went to plays. If anyone asked him what he did last Saturday night, he wanted to say, "I went to the theater." He practiced saying, *I went to the theater,* hoping to sound nonchalant, hoping to sound like going to the theater was as common for him as going to the bathroom. Pearls always said things like that, always talked about doing extravagant things like it was daily routine.

He arrived at the theater, East West Players, and didn't know it was an Asian-American theater. He was stunned at how many Orientals were there. He sensed, however, these Orientals were not from Asia. He got that immediately. He listened to their conversation and knew from their English that they had been in America for a very long time, maybe even born and raised in the States. If he had known this, he wouldn't have attended. He didn't particularly like Orientals from America; they always thought that they were better than people from the Orient. Then again being better, acting better was such an American trait, he believed.

He should have left, right then and there. If it weren't for that girl dressed like a boy! She stopped him. The girl, who appeared to be Chinese, said something in English that sounded like "Thank you fuh cumin. Wa presha you spa." He understood basic English. The girl said, "Thank you," but he didn't pick up anything after that.

"You're welcome," said Michael, hoping that was the right response. He couldn't judge. He just knew to say You're Welcome whenever he heard Thank You. He remembered that from his English class as he prepared to be a flight attendant. You're Welcome.

The Chinese girl pinned something to his chest, smiled, then spoke in Chinese. Michael, who spoke Mandarin and Cantonese, was thrown off. In Cantonese, the girl said, "Thank you for coming. We appreciate your support."

The girl's Cantonese was atrocious, heavily American accented, as if the language was recently learned. Michael had some idea of how his English must sound to others—painful. Regardless, Michael was grateful for providing the right response to her statement.

"You're welcome," Michael said, reverting to his native tongue. "I wouldn't miss it for the world." He liked English phrases like I Wouldn't Miss It For The World. They were so dramatic, so nonsensical. Other phrases he liked: I've Gone To Hell And Back and You Think Your Shit Don't Stink.

"So, you're Chinese?" Michael said to the girl.

"Chinese-*American*," the girl said. He should have left right there. He should have walked away from this girl and gone straight home. Michael took a deep breath, always amazed at how

American Orientals distinguished themselves as different from those Orientals from Asia.

I was too polite, Michael would think months later. *I was too polite and should have left that theater.* He would think this after he left Emerson's apartment for the last time, sweat falling from his forehead, his voice hoarse from screaming at Emerson.

"I was born here in LA. I really wanted to work with the Asian community," the girl continued. "So when a job opened up at the Asian-American Equality Center, I jumped at the chance. We're happy that East West Players donated this evening to help us raise funds. Since I speak Cantonese, I work with the Chinese community."

Michael felt sorry for the Chinese people she helped, if they had to hear her earsplitting Cantonese. Michael should have run from this girl, who was definitely American: she spoke nonstop about herself. If he had left, he would have escaped. He didn't know it then but he was only moments away from meeting his future X-boyfriend. That is what he would be known as for the rest of Michael's natural life: X. They may have been boyfriends for months, but the title of X would remain for years. The world was made up of current boyfriends and X's. Michael had a feeling the world had more X's out there than boyfriends, the globe harnessed by a metal fence of heartbreaking cast-asides.

He almost got away, too. Almost. There were times at work when he shook his head thinking of how he almost escaped. A man approached this Chinese-American girl to give her more pins. Michael was stunned. This man was a dead ringer for his favorite singer, pop star Andy Lau. He was a little darker, but still, his eyes, his face, his hair were that of the romantic Chinese crooner.

There, his direction was changed, eventually leaving him twirling and jagged like barbed wire. Michael had spent many nights listening to Andy Lau, had attended five of his concerts.

He sat fourth row center, screaming and cheering when Andy Lau finished a song. He almost lost his voice when he attended one of his concerts, screeching, "Andy, I love you!"

"Hi, Emisuh!" the Chinese-American girl said to the Lau look-alike in English.

"Hah uh you, Daahsy?" he said to her. "Eting see gowe."

Michael cursed himself for not knowing more English. Later, post-break-up, he would curse himself for knowing too much. It's understanding too much English, or the need to, that got him into this bitter emotional shit hole in the first place.

"I think wi ma luh money . . ." the man said. "We shu do mar stud li dis. I tank I well elp ti op ar ay shuns. Mah de it give rahz."

Daahsy laughed at this. Michael began to hate Daahsy, hate her for being so familiar with Emisuh. Michael noticed Emisuh glancing at him, glancing at him often.

His heart melted when Emisuh offered his hand, saying, "Thank you foh cumin."

"You're welcome," he said.

"Ohmygod." Daahsy's face exploded, her hands went into the air. "Wer ah mah mans herz." Daahsy laughed some more and spoke to Michael in Cantonese. "Where are my manners. This is Emerson. We work together."

Emerson, Michael thought. *Emerson. Beautiful name.* Later the mention of that name would cause migraines, but in the beginning, it was beautiful. Emerson. The sound of it echoed like wind chimes on a hot summer day.

"Ah you he wit the Chinese coslit?" Emerson said.

"Are you here with the Chinese consulate?" Daahsy interpreted. Michael laughed, flattered that he was mistaken for an ambassador of some kind. Then, as quickly, he looked around to see if the real Chinese ambassadors were there.

"No, I just love the theater," Michael said. Daahsy told

Emerson what he said. Emerson nodded. Then there was a brief silence that made him uncomfortable. He had been in this situation before, been with people who didn't speak the same language. There was an awkwardness, wondering what would come next. He had dated other English speakers, some of those dates went on for weeks, before becoming part of that chain link fence of X's that circle the earth. They all inevitably ended because they had nothing else to say. Rather, they had a lot to say, but couldn't say it at all. This is what happens when you date people who don't speak the same language, Michael thought. After Emerson, Michael swore he would only date men who spoke Cantonese. All it takes is one, one person to banish the men of the world, reducing your pickings to those who speak the way you speak. You can't be honest, truly honest if you don't even share the same word for Honesty.

"Mah name is Michael," Michael said in English, directing it at Emerson, hoping to keep the conversation going, hoping this Andy Lau dead ringer would talk to him.

"I'm Daisy," Daahsy said. "Thank you for coming, Michael."

"You Chinese, Emerson?" Michael asked.

"No, I'm Filipino. Filipino-*American.* May I show you to your seat?" Emerson said, looking down at the ticket in his hand. He knew exactly what he said, because, as a flight attendant, he had said this so many times to English-speaking passengers.

"Yes, please," he responded. They left Daisy to stab more people with pins. Through the lobby, he held his arm. He had a nice grip. He also noticed how people looked at him, looked at them. He knew they looked good together. Emerson was several inches taller than he. He liked slightly taller men.

Emerson led him down the aisle of the theater, looking at his ticket. Down the aisle, Michael thought. He had known Emerson for all of thirty seconds, but already had thoughts of marriage and adopted babies.

Emerson pointed to a seat in the middle and said, "I'll cum fah you at intamisha."

"Huh?"

"I'll. Come. For. You. At. Intermission."

Michael watched him leave. He watched him turn around several times. He smiled, watching Emerson watching him back.

Shit, Michael said to his fellow flights attendants, to anyone who would care to listen, *I didn't know what I was in for.*

BELEN

*B*ELEN SHOULD HAVE been overjoyed when she read the gunman was in custody. She had taken her vacation time to spend it caring for Jory. For close to two weeks, there was no word about who and where the gunman was. She couldn't wait for the bastard to be caught. Reading about the gunman only filled her with dread. She read that William Baylor from Little Rock, Arkansas, turned himself in at a police station in Sacramento and claimed responsibility for the shootings.

It was reported that William Baylor, a former member of a youth Nazi organization, had been in custody previously for beating his wife. When William Baylor was escorted from the police station he yelled obscenities at the press, calling on other white Christians to take on the struggle and fight the holy war against that evil known as the (expletive) Jews and the new evil entering the United States, meaning the (expletive) immigrants who are draining the country's resources, and the (expletive) government for letting down the American people.

What made Belen shiver, what made her crumple the newspaper in her hand and throw it onto the floor of the hospital was that William Baylor also screamed that he was acting in the name of the Lord, calling himself an "Agent of Christ."

She called Emerson and said, "You won't believe what I just read. William Baylor is an Agent of Christ."

"Huh?"

"In the newspaper. The man who shot your father. He was acting on behalf of God."

"Mom, you don't really believe—you don't really think that this is part of the Curse."

"I do, Emerson. It has to be. What else then?"

"Mom, just relax. I'll be there soon. People from the District Attorney's office will be coming. We have to talk, okay?"

Belen hung up. She couldn't believe Emerson's attitude. This confirmed for Belen, once and for all, that God was damned mad, had never forgiven her, and had sent someone to claim Jory. She knew the power of God's wrath, a searing reminder that He controlled all. The arrival at this conclusion is forever scarred in her mind. It happened during the first month of her marriage. Jory slept behind her, his arms entwined around her body. The warmth of his being gave her the feeling of being nestled in a golden ball of sunlight. His head rested by the nape of her neck, and Belen felt his nose pushing tepid breaths of air onto her skin. *This should be God,* she believed. This safety, this warmth.

She slept in one of Jory's old shirts, a plaid, worn-out, button-down with holes in the elbows. When she left her home, she took with her some things that she thought a sixteen-year-old girl might need. She took most of her favorite clothes, her photo albums, records, and a stuffed bear. She did not think of taking her nightgowns, silky, satiny things that her mother bought for her, close-fitting, floor-length dresses with bows and baby animals sewn in. Belen wore them to bed, often pulling the hem above her knees, so her legs could stretch wide and far apart. In Jory's old shirts, with fabric that reached just below her hips, she could bend or splay her legs any way, any time she'd wanted.

Her hair fell across her face when she slept; she felt the black strands move across her cheeks. When she was living at home, her mother insisted that she keep her hair bound up in rubber bands. Her mother said that the oil in her hair would surely give her face pimples if it wasn't properly tied. She also said that her hair would get severely tangled and matted in slumber. Belen was also ordered to keep her hair tied up to prevent loose strands from falling onto the sheets or the floor, ruining the crisp neatness of the bedroom.

Lying next to Jory, with her legs resting any which way, her hair falling however it might, Belen felt complete. She was glad that she didn't have to sneak around town to meet her love. That whole experience left her tense and wound up. She didn't have to hide anymore. And her body felt a relief it hadn't felt in months. Once she left her parents' home, she and Jory went over to City Hall and in less than an hour, she was Mrs. Jory Lalaban.

She knew her mother was mad at her but felt sure that she'd come around eventually. Ermaline would take to her and Jory once the baby was born. Then she could leave the little shack that she and Jory found and move back into the big house, and Jory could sleep in her big bed. Her mother would be delighted in being called grandmother. Everything would be fine in several months, a year at the most. In the pitch blackness of night, she nuzzled closer to Jory and fell asleep.

One night she felt her insides move. She felt fluid passing through her. It was a familiar feeling, she had been experiencing it since she was twelve. She opened her eyes, knowing that this was a mistake. Her period stopped coming months ago. It stopped coming because she was with child, with Jory's child. She sat up and put her hands between her legs and felt the blood there.

Jory woke and said, "What's the matter?" He got up and lit a candle. He saw his wife sitting on the bed, the mattress stained red. "Oh, no."

"It's nothing," Belen said. "It's just my period." She was shocked at how casually she said it. "Hand me that towel . . . and go outside."

She wiped herself and dried the bed as best she could. She turned the mattress over and decided to take care of it in the morning. She took off the shirt she was sleeping in, found some scissors and began cutting it up. The scissors didn't seem to work fast enough. Belen shred the shirt with her hands, ripping it apart, making little strips of fabric that she could use for the next several days. The sounds of ripping the shirt appealed to her. There was a part of the fabric, near the shoulder, that was particularly hard to shred. She gripped the fabric and tried to tear it asunder. She closed her eyes, wrapped her fingers tightly around the garment, and pulled. When it wouldn't give, she tried again, screaming this time. Her voice filled the little shack, left the window and traveled some distance away.

Jory came into the room and saw her naked, his old shirt ripped apart on the floor. He lifted her up, pulled her into bed with him and held her as she cried.

This was cruel, she thought. *So, so cruel.* To make her unpregnant was beyond what she'd expected from the heavens. For the next five years, Belen prayed, went to church on Sundays, went to morning Mass when she didn't have class, paid homage to saints— female saints mostly, hoping women would be more sympathetic to her plight—so that someday she would become pregnant again.

It was on her knees with her hands clasped together that she felt comforted. Yes, she went to church to beg members of the Kingdom of Heaven to give her a child. She'd come to appreciate the aloneness she received in deep, silent prayer. In her younger years, as a naïve girl, she paid little attention to praying or church. She had no problems then. She needed no assistance from God. As a childless woman she chided herself for not getting that relationship earlier.

What she discovered when she prayed, earnestly prayed, not merely going through the motions of reciting memorized words, was that there was peace there. In the quietude of the church, her misery didn't go away, but was complemented. She went to church and knew that Jesus suffered, the Blessed Virgin suffered, the saints suffered. Suffering was the one true constant in life.

She took comfort in the rosary, repeating: "Hail Mary, full of grace, the Lord is with thee, blessed art thou among women . . ." *yes, Mary, you are blessed,* Belen thought, *the most cherished woman in all of Christendom. You must know what it means to want a child. I honor you. You are kind, more understanding.*

Whispering below her breath: "Blessed is the fruit of your womb, Jesus . . . As much as I respect your Son, He is a man and cannot grasp what it means to want a child growing inside of you. I cannot pray to a man about such things, Holy Mother. I can ask you, Blessed Lady, to ask Him. You understand. Bless my womb."

By then, Belen had not spoken with her own mother for several years and truly missed that relationship. She valued the bond of an older woman, a person who yearned for her to be the very best, someone who championed her. Belen missed Ermaline Dubabang's voice, insisting that she have it all, that she deserved the finest things in the world. Belen felt the void in her life known as her mother; one of her motivations in going to church was to find a substitute.

Running her fingers along the beads of her Rosary, quietly saying: "Holy Mary, Mother of God, pray for us sinners now and at the hour of our death . . ." *Yes, we are sinners,* Belen believed. *I've sinned,* she thought. *And I am sorry. Pray for me, pray for me, pray for me. Holy Mary, go to your Son, and speak into His ear, and tell Him that I am worthy of mercy. Can you do this for me? You are His mother. He will listen to you. He won't listen to someone like me. Ask Him to grant me mercy.*

I'll see what I can do, dear, Mary replied.

It would take several more years for an ounce of mercy to arrive.

⁓

BELEN OPENED HER eyes to see the walls of the hospital room. The tips of her fingers were indented from the rosary beads that she'd been gripping. She saw her husband asleep. His condition had improved slightly, but he was still listed in critical condition. He wasn't out of danger yet. He could barely move, could hardly speak, but his eyes were alert. His eyes let her know that he was still here.

It was ten o'clock in the morning, and October was gone. Winter will be in Los Angeles. Winter Solstice, Jory's favorite day of the year, would be here soon. Would it rain? Probably not. In over thirty years in Los Angeles, she remembered more mild winters than extreme. It would probably maintain a steady 75 degrees throughout November, December, and January. Winter is the only season that holds the years together; it comes late in the year and stays through the beginning of the next. It is the moment that binds yesterday and tomorrow. It is change. She forgot this sometimes as LA kept its warm, constant weather. It's not like other parts of America, where cold and snow blankets everything, making everyone know a shift has occurred. Winter in a warm climate is deceiving. Change happens but no one notices.

She looked out the window at the sprawling valley and remembered when she thought this place, this Los Angeles, was Holy Land. In her first week in America, she bought a map of California and noticed she was surrounded by Catholic deities. To her west was the beach named after St. Monica, valleys named after St. Gabriel, St. Fernando; further south was the city of St. Diego; further north were the cities of Saints Barbara and Francisco. Within a year of her landing, she was pregnant and happy, so happy. She believed it was the protection of these saints that had granted her wish. And the huge Pacific Ocean that distanced her from Before.

She heard a knock and turned. Emerson's head peeked through the door.

"Mom, some men from the district attorney's office are here. They need to talk to us?"

"What do they want?"

"I talked with them earlier. They want to talk about specifics."

"Jory," Belen said to her sleeping husband. "I'll be right back." She stepped into the hall, following Emerson to the lounge. There were two men and one woman waiting.

"I'm Thomas Fielding. I'll be handling the case." Thomas Fielding was tall, well over six feet. His dark hair was slicked back. He reminded Belen of a movie star from the forties. "My colleagues Art Rodriguez and Diane Mailer."

Belen nodded at them and took a seat next to Emerson.

"As you know," Thomas began, "William Baylor turned himself in. The Attorney General's office assigned us to the case."

"Attorney General?" Belen said.

"We're making it into a federal case."

"The U.S. government is getting involved in a shooting in Los Angeles?"

Thomas straightened his back. "Yes, your husband was a postman, correct?"

Emerson nodded, but Belen didn't get the connection.

"Dad was a postman, Mom. That makes him an employee of the U.S. government, making it grounds for a federal case."

"We have agents looking into William Baylor's past, interviewing people he came into contact with. We're deciding what to charge him with."

"Will he go to prison?" Belen asked.

"He's going to prison anyway, but for how long is the question."

"Isn't he going away for the rest of his life?" Belen asked.

"That would be ideal, wouldn't it?" Thomas said.

"Life imprisonment is too kind," Emerson said. "He should be put on death row."

"The death penalty won't be pursued."

"Why not?"

"Because . . ."

"Because what?"

"Because technically William Baylor hasn't killed anyone."

"Well, my dad is nearly dead. Have you seen him?"

"We're gathering information for the case now. There are a few things that we already know we're going to charge him with. There are several counts of the use of a firearm in the commission of a felony, a count of being a felon-in-possession, possession of an unregistered firearm. Am I clear?"

"Can't you just put him away?" Belen said.

"We want that, believe me, we do. It just takes some time. Mrs. Lalaban, Emerson, if we want William Baylor to go away, he has to be charged. With every charge, there's a penalty. Each charge may carry a weight of ten years, maybe more, maybe less. If Baylor's attorneys are persuasive, he may get less. So, the strategy is, if Baylor is charged with as many crimes as possible, the longer he will stay in jail."

"That's good," Belen said.

"What else will you charge him with?" Emerson asked.

"We'll also go after a hate crime charge," Thomas said. "Baylor has called this a holy war against minorities. With the attack on the Jewish day care center and your father being Asian, it's a crime motivated by race and religion. If found guilty of a hate crime, that alone could add several more years to his prison term."

This was all new to Belen, and her head swarmed with unclear thoughts. *A holy war against minorities? He thinks we're evil?*

"We're also going to charge him with an act of terrorism," Thomas said.

"Terrorism?" Emerson said.

"Yes, we think that his intent was not just to hurt minorities, but to send a kind of message."

"I'm not sure what you are saying," Belen said.

"Mrs. Lalaban, William Baylor did what he did to symbolize something."

"Symbolize what?"

"He wanted other Jews, Asian people, other minorities, who knows . . . to be scared. We have agents investigating his past. And we'll have our chance to question him."

She saw Mr. Fielding stand. Emerson and the other two colleagues stood also. She chose to remain sitting. She watched Emerson shake their hands as they left. *Winter is coming,* she thought. *Change will happen, but will anyone notice?*

EMERSON

*E*MERSON WALKED THOM Fielding and the other attorneys to the parking lot. He shook Thom's hand and said, "Thank you for the work you're about to do."

"I'm sorry for what happened, and I wish we could have met under better circumstances."

"Me, too."

"There's going to be a press conference this afternoon at the Edelman Center. There'll be lots of people there. It'll be later on today. Will you be present?"

Lots of people, huh? Emerson thought. He said, "Um, no. I'd rather handle this my own way."

"I understand. Here's my card. Call me if you need anything."

Emerson watched them drive off. He turned to look at the hospital. He thought of saying good-bye to his mother, but decided against it. He would be back in the early evening. He'll talk to her then. He got into his car and drove home.

As soon as he entered his apartment, he went straight to the kitchen, pulling open a drawer, reaching to the very back. He pulled out a crumpled ball of aluminum foil, unfolded it and picked up a pathetic looking joint. He lit it up and took a drag, knowing that was all he needed to set him at ease.

He'd always been a lightweight when it came to smoking pot. One of the prostitutes on Santa Monica Boulevard pointed that out to him. He stubbed out the joint, folding the aluminum foil over it and placing it back into his secret hiding place.

He sat on a couch in his living room. It was a crappy couch, one he paid next to nothing for at Goodwill. All of his furniture was crappy, bought from the garage sales and thrift stores in the area, but it was comfortable, crappy furniture that he'd collected over time. In the back of his mind, he knew the furniture held stories, other people's lives imbedded in the velvet upholstery of the couch or rubbed into the grain of a table. Everything has souls, his father told him. Maybe that is all a soul is made of: stories, deeply imbedded inside.

Emerson had the same apartment for thirteen years. He left his parents to live in a one-bedroom apartment in the hills of Silverlake. Back then in the 1980s, Silverlake was an affordable place to live, certainly something an eighteen-year-old kid making less than twenty thousand dollars a year could afford.

His first boss recruited kids off the streets and gave them decent jobs as peer workers, people from the street helping other people on the street. His one-bedroom was going for $375 a month then.

When Emerson first moved in, he invited his parents to take a look at his new place; his father insisted that he bless the home. His mother insisted that she properly sanitize it. Jory brought candles and food. She brought rubber gloves, three cans of Lysol, Ajax, and a bucket.

In the living room, his father performed the *Okat*. A long time ago, his father told him, the *Okat* was performed when someone died to send his soul on his merry way. A sacrifice was given, a pig perhaps, and prayers were offered to the Sun, Moon, and the souls of the dead. He said aloud the *Sabosad*, a story of how the Sun and Moon had fought, then became harmonious, and how Thunder and Lighting had quarreled, then became friends.

"This," Jory said, "will get rid of the spirits who are lingering and make the house peaceful."

"Now do we kill a pig?" Emerson said, a poor attempt at sarcasm. His father smacked him in the back of the head. Emerson took it as his cue to break open the Saran Wrap covering the *lechon,* roasted pork, that his father had bought from a Filipino restaurant.

He knew that his father was special. As a child, the ceremonies, like the one conducted in his apartment, were grand affairs with lots of people and lots of food. People danced, clanging and hitting gongs, well, most people didn't have gongs so they made do with regular pots and pans. A whole roasted pig, with skin a honey brown, was unveiled as the centerpiece of the meal.

Emerson arranged the food on the kitchen counter of his apartment. His father went into the bedroom to light candles. He heard the spray of Lysol in the bathroom. He went into the living room and saw the slightly open door of his bedroom and the slightly open door of his bathroom.

"The food's ready," Emerson said. His father and mother opened the doors of their respective rooms almost at the same time. His father was blowing out a candle and his mother was removing rubber gloves.

The smell of candle wax with the dissipating smell of aerosol came at him, causing him, to cough violently.

"I better do the *Sigop*," his father said. Emerson knew it was a ceremony to cure coughs. His father had conducted it whenever Emerson had a cold.

"See," his mother said, "I knew this place has germs." She put on her rubber gloves again.

After his last cough, Emerson said, "Let's eat first. No more praying and no more cleaning." His parents looked at each other and prepared to eat. Emerson had no furniture to sit on and only a desk in his living room. He had bought the paint-chipped desk for three dollars at a garage sale down the street. He didn't particularly need a desk, except to have something to lay things on other than the floor.

He had no plates either, but his mother came prepared with paper ones. They each left the kitchen to sit on the living room floor. Emerson noticed that his mother left the kitchen with two plates of food. She placed one plate on the desk, next to his cordless phone, and got her bag.

"I brought some things to make your apartment more like home," Belen said. She pulled out some small picture frames from her purse. "What's a home without family pictures? Here, this one is of your dad and me dancing."

Emerson examined the photo. His mother wore a strapless gown, and his father wore a traditional *barong*, a white sheer long-sleeved shirt, and black slacks. He had to admit that they looked like a handsome couple. He placed the photo on the desk, next to the cordless phone.

Belen showed Emerson the other picture, a small 4×6 framed photo of Jun-Jun. She placed it onto the desk next to the extra plate of food.

"Look, Jun-Jun," his mother said, smiling rather excitedly. "This is your brother's new pad."

"Let's eat, Mom."

"Okay, okay. First show your brother your new place."

"Mom, I'm hungry."

"Oh, c'mon. Show your brother."

Emerson paused for a moment. His mother was looking at him, and he sensed his father was looking at him from behind.

Emerson approached the desk, looked down at the picture of his dead brother. He grabbed the frame and said, "Hey, Jun, welcome to my new apartment."

He detected the tone of flippancy in his voice and was sure that his parents could detect it, too. He looked at the picture and as always was dumbfounded at what an attractive child his brother was. His black bangs were evenly cut, hovering over big brown eyes. He had a look caught between joy and sadness. Looking at the image of his fallen brother, Emerson started over again.

"Jun, this is my apartment," he said, genuinely.

He saw his mother smile and his father slowly approach him. He turned the picture around, so the face of his brother looked out. Emerson tilted the picture downward.

"This is my first piece of furniture!" he said, referring to the desk. His mother laughed.

"Yeah, his first piece," his father said. "He bought it with his own money. At his first job."

Emerson turned the photo to another part of the apartment. "Here's the living room. See the gray carpet. The landlord just painted the place. It's almost the same beige color of our room.

"This is the kitchen. It's kinda small, huh? Look, I get a view of a parking lot from here." Emerson walked over to the window of the kitchen and pressed the photo against the glass, so his brother could see that he wasn't lying.

"Soon, Emerson is going to get his own car, aren't you?" his mother said.

"Yeah, there's this guy selling his old car, Jun. I saw a FOR SALE sign on it. He's selling it for three hundred dollars. I have half of it already. I can get the other half with my next paycheck."

Emerson walked out of the kitchen, through the living room, and into the bathroom. He held the picture next to his face, hoping his brother could see what he saw.

"Look, Jun," his father said, "the tile is your favorite color. Light blue."

"That smell you smell is mom's Lysol," Emerson added.

"Show him the bedroom. Show him the bedroom," his mother said.

"And here's where I'll sleep." Emerson held the photo with one hand, using his other hand to show the area where his bed would go. "What do you think?" Emerson turned the photo toward himself. And for a second, he expected the picture to answer him. Emerson went back into the living room, with his parents following behind, and said, "This is it. My new place."

He looked at his parents. They both seemed to have a satisfied look on their faces.

Rrrrrrrrrrrrring. Emerson looked at his cordless phone on the desk. Rrrrrrrrrrrrring. He grabbed the phone and said to his parents, "Uh, I'm expecting a call from my landlord."

He went into his bedroom.

—Lo?

—You have the coolest place, Emmy. Thanks for showing it to me.

—No prob. You really like it?

—Yeah, you did good. Can't wait for you to buy the car. Maybe you can come up to the Bay Area and see me?

—You think?

"Time to eat," he heard his mother say in the living room.

—Gotta go, Emerson said.

—Okay. Congrats on the apartment again.

He walked back into the living room. Emerson placed the phone on the desk.

They ate relatively quietly. His mother suggested different kinds of furniture for the house. Emerson was acutely aware that he sat on the floor with his brother's picture facing him.

"You know, when me and your mom got married, our first place was a shack. It was made of metal." His father talked and laughed with pork in his mouth.

"Yes," his mother said. "Oh, it would get so cold."

"Luckily, we had each other to keep warm." Jory winked at his wife. Her lips spread into a thin smile. "That picture we gave you was of me and your mom when we first got married. We danced. I had one good *barong*."

"I had one good dress," Belen said. "The dress—"

"Seconds, anyone?" Emerson offered. His mother and father shook their heads.

"If Jun had grown, I wonder what he'd be doing now?" his mother said.

At once, Emerson felt the air in the room become heavy.

"Well, there is no use thinking like that. No use," his father said.

"He probably would be living up north," Emerson said.

His mother said, "You think so?"

"'Cause I think he would be going to college right now, finishing his last year at a school like Stanford maybe. He was smart, you know. He prolly liked it up there and would have lived in San Francisco or something. Get a cool job later."

"Maybe," his mother said.

"Maybe," his father also said.

Once they finished eating, his mother put on her rubber gloves and went to work in the kitchen. His father went outside to clear away any trash or dead leaves in the small yard attached to his apartment. He knew his father would be praying to the gods of the trees or the sky as he cleared away stuff. He hoped he wasn't speaking aloud, so the neighbors wouldn't hear him.

Emerson went into his bedroom to unpack the two boxes he brought from home. Two boxes filled with clothes, some books, a skateboard, and a few other things that he wanted to have with him in his new home. He took the box of clothes into the living room to unpack. He didn't want his parents to see what he brought.

When they had cleaned all they could, his parents left, reminding Emerson to eat the food by Jun's photo to add to the good luck of the apartment. Jun's photo remained in the same place for many years, along side the photo of his parents.

He knew Jun's killer was still out there somewhere, forgotten about now. That was wrong, simply wrong. He looked at his watch. The news would be coming on soon. He turned on the television, channel surfing. He stopped on a channel with a news anchor talking; behind her was a small picture of William Baylor.

"Now, with the latest on the shooting at the Jewish day care center is Jane Marquez live at the Edelman Center."

"It is a somber day," Jane Marquez said. "Leaders of the Jewish community and other activists gathered today to respond to William Baylor's call for a holy war against Jews and other minorities. Security has been tightened since Baylor's capture. The Edelman center has actually been getting phone calls *in support* of William Baylor. They've also been getting letters threatening violence if William Baylor is not released. We have tape of the press conference of civic leaders denouncing the crime."

"The families of the children are devastated," a rabbi said. "In this day and age, it amazes me that such crimes still occur. To speak to us is a mother of one of the children."

A middle-aged woman approached a mike. "My name is . . . "

she began. Emerson remembered how his mother reacted when Jun died. There was the same look of loss. "My name is Sylvia Jacobs. My son Peter might lose his arm because . . . because a bullet severed a tendon . . ." She broke down and had to be led away.

The camera pulled back, and an array of people stood there, some of them he recognized: community leaders that made a name for themselves fighting for the poor, the elderly, the minorities. It was an impressive sight. He saw a man in a dark suit, with movie star good looks, standing to the side. It was Thomas Fielding, the prosecuting attorney.

Emerson turned off the television, and looked at his apartment filled with junk. The pot he'd smoked had already settled in and he was dozing off.

Rrrrrrrrrrrrrrrrring.

Emerson leaned over and picked up the cordless.

—Hey, Emmy.

—'lo.

—How you holding up?

—All right, I guess.

—Why weren't you at the news conference?

—You know why. I don't feel comfortable around all those people, those cameras.

—It's scary, but I think you should have been there.

—They did just fine without me.

—You know no one cared when I died.

—That's not true. We all cared. It tore us up.

—The search for my killer just stopped. After a while, my file was left in some drawer, because another crime occurred.

—Well, that won't happen here, because William Baylor's in custody. Baylor will get what he deserves. He's going to prison. There's no doubt about that.

—My death disappeared over the years because I became a

file, just a file. Just a kid in the city who died. I became name-less, faceless.

—This case has a face. Sylvia Jacobs, the mother—

—And she was great! She was called and she answered. You're being called, Emmy. As your older brother, I am ordering you to respond.

—But—

—No ifs, ands, or buts.

Silence. The conversation ended. Emerson pulled out his wallet and dug out Thom Fielding's card. He called and Thom picked up.

"Fielding here," Thom said.

"Thom, this is Emerson. I saw you on TV and I think it's great that this kind of news spreads."

"Yes, it'll help gain public sympathy."

"Next time, please let me know when something like this takes place. I'd like to be a part of it. You know, show support."

"Sure, there will be another conference in a few days. The mayor is expected to attend."

JORY

"*W*AAAAAH," JORY SAID. He meant to say *water,* but his vocal cords hadn't been quite right since he'd been shot. He mainly croaked. "Waaaaaah." He spoke only when it was absolutely necessary. With every word he attempted, his chest felt like it was going to cave in.

"What would you like?" Belen said.

"Waaaaaaaah."

"What, honey-bunny?"

He moved his eyes to his left, indicating the cup on his nightstand.

"Water?" Belen said.

Jory nodded. His wife lifted the cup to his lips, and he sipped. The cool drink relieved his parched throat. *Belen,* he thought, *remember when you let me drink the Moon?* She lifted the cup again. He sipped some more. He was dry. His whole body seemed to be dry all the time. His wife kept applying Vaseline to his lips and lotion to his limbs, shifting him around so he wouldn't get bedsores.

"Are you ready for your shave?" Belen said.

"Yuh."

She pulled a Bic disposable razor from a plastic bag, and he felt her pressing the blade against his cheek. He heard the scraping sound and felt the pressure, but didn't feel the actual razor. *Get a real razor,* he thought, *and slash it across my neck.* He couldn't speak well, but it no longer hurt to think. He was able to construct full thoughts without it being an effort.

The weeks he had been in bed he had grown depressed, something the doctor said was to be expected. His mobility was mainly from the waist up, though his arms felt like boulders, unable to lift them. The doctor said it was still too hard to tell how much nerve damage was done. The bullets had hit key areas in his back.

"There," Belen said. "You look handsome again." She threw away the plastic razor. "The shooter was caught."

"Huh?" Jory widened his eyes at hearing the news. He tried to lift his head, raising it about half an inch, before resting it back on the pillow, exhausted. He had been given painkillers, leaving him in a state of floating numbness.

"Yes, he turned himself in," Belen said. "William Baylor. I hope he gets a hundred years for what he did."

Jory inhaled, gritting his teeth. *Just five min—no, make that ten minutes with that* baboy—*that pig.* Of course, Jory wanted to make sure that when he had those ten minutes with William Baylor the criminal was properly tied up. In his present state, Jory couldn't exact the kind of revenge he wanted.

Bite him, Jory thought. *Keep him tied down, lead me to him, and I'll bite him. Chew him. Sink my teeth into that animal.* Ten minutes of biting greatly appealed to Jory. He reveled thinking about it.

"Why are you smiling?" Belen asked.

"Biiiiiiii."

"Buy what?"

"Biiiiiiii. Skiiiiin."

"Lotion? You want me to buy more lotion for your skin?"

Jory shook his head. He saw Belen sit next to him and take his hand. She massaged it. It felt good, really good to know that he could feel her touch, though he couldn't squeeze back.

"Can you feel that?" she said, pressing his hand against her cheek. "I can feel you, Jory. Can you feel me?"

He nodded and smiled. Jory turned his head and saw a wall. Half of it was covered with cards, bright cards with Get Well Soon sentiments.

"They're from your coworkers and our neighbors. Some people from my work sent cards, too. And people from Emerson's job sent that big one over there. They all signed it. Wasn't that a nice thing?"

There were chrysanthemums, yellow and full, on the floor. The site of the flowers eased him. He turned his head to Belen.

"Gaaaard."

"Guard?"

"Gaaarden?"

"Oh, don't worry about that, honey-bunny. The Kims are keeping a good eye on your garden. Mrs. Kim is good with plants. You know that, though she is not as good as you. She said she will take care of it. Don't worry about that."

Jory nodded. He closed his eyes, remembering the green grass of his yard. The birds of paradise, star lilies, carnations, roses, moonvines he'd planted years ago. And the tremendous sunflowers—all six of them—that towered over the garden.

"Hooo," Jory said.

"Hmmmm?"

"Hoooome."

"Home?"

"Taaaake."

"Take what home? The flowers?"

Jory shook his head.

"Take the cards home? You don't want them here?"

Jory inhaled.

"Take home what?"

With all his might, he squeezed out one perfect word. "Me."

⌒

IT AMAZED JORY how full circle his life had run. Once he was the healer. Now, he needed to be healed. Of course today, healers weren't what they once were. Dr. Jones comes in, looks him over, and moves on to the next patient. Sure he tries to appear caring, appear concerned. Appearance is all it is.

Where are the Wandings of today? Wanding, the man who taught Jory how to cure. Wanding knew all of his patients, and they knew him. Oh, what it was back then. Jory will never forget that morning in the spring of 1963, when Jory met Wanding and went to the home of an old woman suffering from headaches. Wanding was called to cure it. The curing of headaches required the *Nansaang*, a simple ceremony. All that was required was the offering of *Tapuy*, rice wine, a chicken, and some prayers. It was so simple, in fact, that Wanding was sure Jory could perform it.

They showed up at the house of the old woman. Jory requested that the ceremony be conducted later in the afternoon when Belen was done with nursing school. He wanted his wife to be at the very first ceremony where he would not be a student, but the actual Maker of Prayer. Belen agreed.

The old woman was brought into the backyard, while members of her family sat beside her. Well over three dozen people came to witness the healing of the old woman, the mother of six, and grandmother of fifteen.

Jory could tell that the family was dreadfully poor. The wooden house was quickly eroding and, from the way the trees had been cleared, most of the family probably slept outside, under the branches.

Wanding approached the old woman and said, "Ah, my old friend, I hear you have spirits in your head that won't go away."

"Yes, Wanding," the old woman replied. "They are causing my head to ache. Please get rid of them."

"Of, course, my good woman. I shall not conduct the *Naansang*. My student will do it."

"He looks too young."

"He will have more strength to fight the spirits with."

The old woman nodded.

Jory conducted the ceremony exactly as he had been told. He poured the rice wine in a cup and placed it on the woman's head. He placed a leaf over the cup and was given a live chicken to hold. The chicken squawked at being handled but Jory held the chicken by its feet, waiting for the bird to calm. The chicken fluttered its wings a bit, then stopped.

"God of the Sky," Jory began, "Sun, Moon, Stars, I will trade with you. I give you this rice wine, this chicken to trade with you. You, the Gods, who make this woman's head ache, I trade with you. I offer you wine and food to honor you. Souls of our dead, come pray with us. Pray with us, and you will cure this woman."

Jory saw the relatives of the old woman looking at him. For a moment he was self-conscious. He looked down at the woman with the cup on her head, her sad eyes looking up at him. *They want relief,* Jory thought. *This old woman and her family want her pain to go away,* and he understood, for the very first time, his purpose, the purpose of anyone doing what he or priest or nun or shaman is expected to do: simply relieve them, make things a little bearable.

"Sun, I trade you. Moon, I trade you. Big Dipper, I trade you. This food to honor you, remove the aches of this woman."

The prayer was over. Jory held the chicken in his hand and looked at a smiling Wanding. He stood there, trying to remember what came next. He held the chicken, waiting for someone to take it away and prepare it for dinner.

Wanding approached Jory and stood behind him.

"Kill it," Wanding said.

Jory turned around. The mouth of Wanding an inch from his ear.

"Kill the chicken," Wanding repeated.

"What?" Jory said. He was well aware of the fact that he needed to sacrifice the fowl. Animals were sacrificed at other celebrations. For the most part, Jory had only seen it after the fact; the hogs, the chickens were already dead, then brought in. He had never seen an animal actually killed. Knowing he had to kill the animal was different from actually doing it. Killing a chicken was common knowledge for anyone who grew up with livestock, but Jory grew up in an orphanage where food came from the marketplace.

Wanding gave Jory a knife and whispered, "Cut the chicken's head off."

"I don't know how," Jory whispered back.

The crowd rustled and even the old woman blinked in wonder.

"Lay the chicken by the old woman," Wanding commanded. "Hold the chicken's head down and slice the neck."

Jory hesitated, feeling Wanding's breath on him. Jory held the chicken's feet with one hand and with the other firmly pressed the chicken's body to the ground. The chicken fluttered and squawked. Jory couldn't keep the chicken from moving.

Wanding grabbed the chicken's head in his hand and said, "I'll hold it. You cut its throat." Wanding looked up and smiled at the assembled crowd. "He is young. I'm teaching him. He will make a good Maker of Prayer someday."

Jory looked to Belen, hoping to find solace there. He was confused when she looked back at him as if to say, *Go ahead and kill the bird.*

Wanding held the head and body of the chicken firmly in place, leaving a wide margin at the neck for him to slice. He placed the blade by the neck and stopped.

"Cut hard," Wanding said, "I sharpened the knife this morning, press the metal with all your strength."

Beads of sweat accumulated on Jory's forehead. He tried to steady his hand. He put the knife to the chicken's neck, took a deep breath, closed his eyes, and plunged the blade into the fowl.

He opened his eyes and saw the separated head from the body. Jory exhaled, feeling triumphant. His first sacrifice. He looked up to see the smiling faces of the crowd and the pleased look on his wife's face. Soon the chicken's feathers will be removed and the bird cooked. Jory lowered his head in relief.

Wanding was still holding the bird down, the head neatly severed. When Wanding let go, Jory was not prepared to see the headless body of the chicken take flight. It flew against his chest, bouncing to the ground. Jory screamed, and to his dismay the decapitated bird waddled around on the floor for several seconds before collapsing.

The sight of the moving bird caused Jory's stomach to churn. He felt his legs weaken and his head become heavy. He leaned sideways, falling against Wanding. Jory was reminded of the time he fell against Father Ryan when he caught the lovely smell of the pretty girls in church. Wanding caught him and laid him down.

The crowd rushed the fallen Maker of Prayer and the old woman lifted her head, causing the cup of rice wine to spill from her forehead onto her face. She screamed.

"It's all right," Wanding said. "The spirits are leaving the old woman and are trying to take over Jory. But Jory will fight them off, won't you? It's all right, stay back." Wanding put a protective hand over Jory's shoulder and whispered, "How are you? It's your first sacrifice. I felt the same way when I killed my first animal."

"Jory," Belen said, "What's wrong?"

"I'm okay. Take care of her," he said, looking at the old woman wiping rice wine from her face.

"I'll get her a glass of water," Belen said.

Jory sat while Belen disappeared. He felt foolish for fainting, but knew that he would be all right. He was satisfied. He knew what to expect now.

He watched Belen return with a glass. Belen held the cup while the old woman drank out of it.

After several moments, Jory was on his feet. He watched the bird taken away and prepared for eating.

Belen left the cup of water for a relative to continue quenching the old woman's thirst.

"Have her drink all of it," Belen said. Jory noted her tone. She was beginning to sound like a nurse.

"I'm proud of you," she said, taking her husband's arm.

When the woman had finished drinking the water, she sat up, massaging her head. "Wanding, your apprentice may be young, but I think he cured me of my headaches."

MICHAEL

$\mathcal{M}$ICHAEL DRAGGED HIS carry-on through the terminal in Taipei. "Forget about him," a fellow steward told him—as if Michael didn't know this, as if knowing that yearning for a guy who deceived him was worth remembering. He felt foolish for even thinking of starting a family with Emerson. Forget about him. As soon as he left Emerson's apartment, just before chewing out the Filipino *American,* all he tried to do was forget about him. He'd been trying to forget about him for weeks, ignoring Emerson's phone messages—all forty-two of them, deleting them as soon as his number appeared on his cellphone, refusing to let the jerk say Hi. He even went out to bars, finding a few men to sleep with, hoping other men would quickly erase the one man who caused him incredible heartache.

He exited the terminal in Taipei, passing television monitors with news from around the world. One caught his attention because the screen flashed news from the States, Los Angeles to be exact, a city he refused to fly into. The monitor had the face of a woman crying about something, a shooting that happened.

Another reason not to go back to that city, the state of California. You get your heart broken *and* you can get shot. *A few more weeks,* Michael thought, turning his attention away from the monitor and down the white tiles of the terminal. *A few more weeks, a few more men, and Emerson Lalaban is out of my system. In a few months, the pain becomes an annoying ache, and by next year, I won't even remember why I was upset.*

He hoped that eventually, Emerson would be filed away as "someone I used to know" and memories he had of the man would disappear. He smiled, waiting for the day he wouldn't remember a thing about *that* time in Los Angeles. He won't recall their first date—on a Sunday. He won't remember having Emerson pick him up at the Shangri-La Apartments, where he and his fellow flight attendants shared a place. He won't remember how he wanted his fellow flight attendants to check out his new prospect.

"He looks like Andy Lau," Michael exclaimed to his roommates. He knew Andy Lau's name alone would illicit a favorable response.

"Is he Chinese?" one roommate asked.

"I don't know. He's Oriental-*American,*" he said. His roommates rolled their eyes before bursting into laughter.

"Does he speak Chinese?"

"Who cares. If he looks like Andy Lau, he could speak Greek for all I care," said another roommate. "If he looks like Andy Lau, maybe you won't be speaking at all."

Michael won't remember how he blushed at the insinuation or how they waited in the Shangri-La lobby, hoping to get a glimpse of the Oriental American. Michael wore a red silk shirt and tan linen trousers. His hair was combed back, stiff with gel.

Emerson arrived in brown shorts and a black shirt. Michael was almost offended that he'd dressed so casually for a first date. One of his roommates gasped, "He *does* look like Andy Lau."

Michael introduced them and was embarrassed when his roommates laughed, acting like starstruck teenagers.

Emerson took him to his car parked by the curb, and Michael was disappointed. He may look like a wealthy pop star, but the comparison ended there. He looked at the badly dented car, an old, old car. Michael saw Emerson in shorts, wearing a beat-up shirt, next to a beat-up car, and he knew: Emerson was a loser. At twenty-nine, he had dated enough men to spot a loser.

Michael should have listened to the voice inside of himself that politely screamed, *Don't get into that car!* Michael would relive that moment in his mind dozens of times, filed in his memory banks as a "near escape."

Emerson got into his side of the car and pushed the passenger seat door open. The door flung out, with a horrible creak.

"Get in," Emerson said.

I feel sick, Michael should have said. He should've walked away and never called this loser again. Weeks after breaking up with Emerson, Michael slapped his own forehead wondering what got into him for not taking that option. Emerson peeked through the passenger side, his face beaming with a smile. His teeth were perfect.

That smile, Michael thought, *fuck that double, triple piece of shit for having a great smile.*

"Something wrong?" Emerson said.

"Maybe my car, take?" That should have been the tip-off, the tip-off Michael should have been aware of. He *never* drove anywhere on a date. He was always picked up or driven. That was the first concession he'd ever made, and he should have known he was slipping.

"Your car?"

"I drive Satin?"

"Satin? Saturn? You drive a Saturn?"

"Yes."

"Next time. Hop in."

Michael slid in. His trousers got caught in a tear in the upholstery.

In the car, Emerson asked, "Wha wu yoh fren laf fung?"

"Huh?"

Emerson repeated himself, speaking more slowly, more carefully. "Why. Were. Your. Friends. Laughing."

"Oh, They. Taught. You. Looked. Like. Someone."

"Who?"

"Andy."

"Who. Is. That?"

"Singer."

Michael wondered where they were going. Ed Debevic's? Gladstone's? Kate Mantilini? They were restaurants that Michael wanted to go to but never had. He couldn't read the menus. Now, with his English-speaking companion, he could certainly order what he wanted, well, at least one of the "specials."

Michael could not ignore the smell of his car. It reeked of old vinyl. The air freshener, shaped liked a pine tree, hanging on his mirror didn't seem to help. They drove into a restaurant parking lot. A diner of some kind. He could make out the name of the restaurant, Astro.

"This is my favorite place to eat," he said.

They parked next to a police car then entered the diner.

He looked around at the gaudy place with frog green stools and brown wood paneling, confirming that, yup, this guy Emerson was a loser.

A hostess took them to a booth—a booth next to blue-haired men with piercings on their faces. Michael's stomach churned. He didn't think he could eat anything next to these men. The hostess presented them with menus then took their order.

"I. Hope. You. Enjoyed. The. Play. Last. Night," Emerson said.

Last night. He looked so handsome, wearing a dark suit. His hair pomaded to the side. He looked like *somebody*. Now, with his hair falling on his forehead, shirt wrinkled, he looked like anybody. *But* there was still that strong resemblance to Andy Lau. Michael had most of Andy Lau's music. He had made love to his music.

"Yes. I . . . enjoy . . . very much." In fact, he had a miserable time. He didn't understand a word of what they were saying. It was a musical about the Tiananmen Square uprising in Beijing. It seemed like a good play. The audience looked like they were having a good time. He did think it was odd, seeing an American play, written for Americans, about China, with Oriental performers singing in English in what was supposed to be the Chinese language.

Something that he did grasp about the play was there was a love story angle. The best stories have a love story angle. Michael was a romantic at heart and always enjoyed seeing people fall in love, starting a family, adopting a child, a girl from China maybe.

"It. Was. A. Charity. Event. For. Us," he said.

"Charity?"

"Yes, when people give money. For. Good. Cause."

He's working for a place that needs money?!?!?!? What kind of person would work for a place like that? And what kind of person would let other people know he worked for a place like that? Charity. A word that he would never forget. Never date a man who needs Charity.

The food arrived. They ate mostly in silence. Emerson said a few things. Michael nodded. Michael said a few things. Emerson nodded. Then his date said something, a phrase he recognized.

"You're beautiful," he said.

He knew this phrase. Men said this to him. He liked it when men said this to him. He made sure his hair was properly conditioned, his skin properly moisturized, his nails properly manicured, his chest exactly seven inches larger than his waist—he read in a magazine that is the proper proportions of an ideal torso. He exercised, dieted, made sure to keep those scheduled appointments at the salon, so he could fit into that category of men termed Beautiful. No one would ever mistake him as a boy from a farm.

"You really are beautiful. I'm. Flattered. You. Are. Out. With. Me. I'm really happy you said you would go out with me."

If this were Taiwan, Michael thought, someone who looked like Emerson would have his pick of guys. Michael knew he was good-looking, even very good-looking, but there were far more attractive men than he in Taiwan. If this were Taiwan, Emerson would be with someone taller, someone more educated, someone more wealthy. He would be with a Pearl. *Not someone like me,* Michael thought.

In Taiwan, Emerson would not be working for a company who needed money. His looks alone would have conditioned him to be better than what he was. Michael also knew that Oriental Americans never saw themselves this way. Oriental men in America had no concept of who they were, and certainly how attractive they may be.

For all of the Oriental Americans he came across, for all their high-faluting qualities, they had no concept of themselves. Michael viewed them with sadness, really. What it must be like to grow up in a country where no one looked like you, to watch television where the heroes were not you, where all the beauty looked nothing like you.

"You. Handsome," Michael said. He watched Emerson's face go blank. "You. Handsome. You. Look. Like. Star." Emerson's face remained blank.

He didn't know, Michael thought. He didn't know how good-looking he was. Even though Emerson looked like Andy Lau, one of the most famous, most handsome men in Asia, he did not grasp his appeal.

"You. Do. You look like star."

He watched Emerson's brown skin reach a tinge of red. Emerson laughed, brushing the hair out of his face, shaking his head, and laughed some more. Emerson threw back his head, still laughing, and Michael saw a glint of silver in the back of his mouth.

"Why you laugh?"

"No one has ever said that to me before. No one ever said I looked like a star."

Michael laughed, too, because he'd never said that to anyone else, either. For a moment, he stopped, struck with irony. Here in Los Angeles, no one thought of Emerson as a star, or even an actor. He was ordinary here.

BELEN

*I*T WAS CLOSE to midnight. She sat in her house; the lights in her kitchen, living room, and bedroom were on. She took comfort in the brightness of her home, particularly during that time of the month when she set aside one hour to pay bills. She saw the pile of mail on the floor, letters fallen from the slot in the door. She leafed through them, separating the junk from the important things.

She looked at the gas bill with the signature blue flame on the white envelope, opened it, and saw that she owed sixty-three dollars. She immediately pulled out her checkbook to pay it. She liked being square with her finances, always had. She was the one who spearheaded the buying of their home, filling out the paperwork for a loan. She made sure that they had the money for the down payment and had the income to pay the mortgage. A few more years of payments, and the house would be theirs.

She wrote out the check for the gas bill. She did the same for water and power. Another check to the phone company. She had almost no credit card debt, using her Visa sparingly, usually at the end of the month just before payday. She opened the credit card envelope and saw that she spent seventeen dollars on cosmetics. She bought new lipstick, eyeliner, hair conditioner, and a new shade of nail polish. She wrote out a check for that, too.

With all of her bills done, she took a deep breath. Her mind began to wonder about other bills, namely the cost of Jory's stay in the hospital. As a nurse, she was certainly privy to the rising medical costs of hospitalization. She pulled out a yellow notepad and pencil. She guessed the cost of a one-day stay in the intensive care unit, where her husband lay, to be roughly six thousand dollars a day. She pulled out a calculator to estimate a two-week stay, including the various doctors who examined him, the nurses who took care of him, the medication prescribed to him. The number she came up with was $110,000.

She gasped. One hundred and ten thousand dollars! Her savings didn't even come close to that amount. She stared at the zeros in front of her. One hundred and ten thousand dollars. The numbers echoed in her brain.

Belen, dear, she heard in the back of her mind. *Take a deep breath. You have insurance, remember? Go to sleep, dear. You will able to handle this in the morning.*

Are you sure? Belen thought.

Yes. Just go to bed.

She thought about the insurance that would take care of the hospital bills. Thank the Lord for insurance! Insurance sounded like such a wonderful thing to have: life insurance, insurance for the house, the car, and health insurance. She'd always had insurance in whatever medical establishment she worked, far better than Jory's. In fact, it was always Belen's insurance they went with, not Jory's meager insurance package at the post office. She would call in the morning. *Yes, call in the morning,* she thought.

She sighed, relieved. Then another thought came her way. The hospital insurance wouldn't take care of the mortgage, food, water and power, or Pacific Bell. Heck, even insurance needed payments to be maintained. She'd always incorporated Jory's salary in figuring out the month's budget and sat wondering what to do. She made a mental note to contact the post office to inquire if her husband would be getting any kind of disability payments for his situation. She was sure things would work out, at least she hoped.

She saw all the brightness in her home. She ran from room to room, turning the lights off. *It's a waste of money,* she thought, *to use all this electricity.* She sat in the darkness of her living room, bewildered. *One hundred and ten thousand dollars,* she thought. The numbers wouldn't leave her mind, despite the Virgin's words.

She struggled earlier in her marriage and Belen never liked that feeling. It was okay to be a little financially dopey in your youth, but she was not young anymore. Being on top of financial matters became a priority as she aged. She thought of her mother and how Ermaline was literally possessed with a keen sense of business. Her mother never seemed to doubt how money should be spent or raised. She was a fine businesswoman, building a successful lumber company. Belen knew how that became so; her father's spirit guided the Dubabang fortune. His spirit owed that much to Ermaline, considering that Ermaline had the task of murdering him, a story that had become legend.

Belen thought about her father Valentino Dubabang, a man everyone in their village admired. During the war, he became ill and weak, unable to walk. Belen was only a baby when they fled their town to hide. Valentino could not keep up, even with the aid of other men carrying him. Ermaline, carried the babe, Belen, while the two sons, Cesar and Oliver, trudged through the night by her side.

It was reported that the Japanese were getting closer. The villagers feared what the Japanese would do to them if they were caught. Reports of rape and murder were kind. It was the stories of excruciating torture, lasting days and weeks, which clung to the night air like cobwebs.

Valentino could not go on, explaining it was his presence holding the villagers back. He asked to be left behind so the others could continue. He had one last request: let him die before the Japanese found and tortured him to death. Weak and feverish, he could not do it himself. He asked one of the other men to kill him immediately.

"I'll be better to you dead," Valentino said. "I will guide you after, show you where to go."

Everyone understood this, and the thought of a kind spirit leading them to safety was certainly appealing.

"Kill me," he said. Several men took up the only gun they had, but put it down. One was even brave enough to put the barrel to Valentino's head before backing away.

"Someone kill me before the Japanese do."

"I'll do it," Ermaline said, stepping into the circle of men surrounding her husband, arranging to have her children taken several yards away. Ermaline could not say that she loved the man she married. Her nuptials, like the women before her, was arranged. Valentino, however, was a good man, a good husband, a person who did not cheat and who did not beat her. He offered several cows for her, a wealthy statement of how he considered her worth as a woman. He was always kind to her, always provided for her. And if the situation were reversed, she'd want no other person to end her suffering. She may not have loved Valentino, but she respected him. A woman worth several cows was expected to be dutiful. A man like Valentino deserved a death befitting his life, not one at the hands of the enemy.

Ermaline held the gun to her husband's sweating head. She took a deep breath and tried pulling the trigger, but it wouldn't give.

"Use both hands," Valentino said.

With her two fingers against the trigger, she put the barrel by his temples and closed her eyes.

"Open your eyes, Ermie," Valentino said. "Or you might miss."

Ermaline was raised to believe that a dutiful wife does what her husband instructs. She widened her eyes, looked down at her husband and exhaled. The gun went off, Ermaline collapsed, and the men rushed to her side. She came to several minutes later and asked if Valentino was dead. She hoped this was so, because she could not bring herself to pull the trigger again.

"He's gone," someone said. "Which way should we go, Ermaline—I mean Mrs. Dubabang." After that moment, her first name was never used again. She was twenty-two years old, and her status had been elevated to that of the most respected.

Dazed and grief-stricken, she led them this way and that. No one questioned her judgment for surely the spirit of her husband was guiding her. She never uttered a word and walked in a trance. She lifted her arm and pointed. Other women held the hands of her children as she walked. Men rushed before her, cutting down branches, clearing the ground of debris, guessing her next step. They let her guide them for weeks. When she couldn't walk, men made a carriage of their arms and carried her. They had been alive longer than they'd expected: Mrs. Dubabang was possessed by someone from beyond.

As soon as the war was over, Ermaline chose to live close to an area where her family and Valentino's family were laid to rest. She erected a huge house from the small lumber mill her husband owned, every nail and every stick of wood with her husband's memory in mind. She sent men to find her husband's body to properly bury him in the back of the house to keep his spirit near.

The war had ravaged homes and buildings, and the need to reconstruct took over the province with a fury. The Dubabang Lumber Mill became very rich, and everyone who remembered knew it was the soul of Valentino Dubabang that made it so.

⌐

IN THE MORNING, Belen was tired. She rolled around in bed, reaching for a husband who was not there. At 6:00 A.M., she was up and pacing, scratching her head. Her morning coffee made her more anxious.

As soon as the hands on her wall clock made that perfect 45-degree angle—the small hand on the 9, the big hand on the 12—she was on the phone. She called St. Joan's billing department. Her $110,000 estimate was not far off the mark. She was told that Jory's stay thus far would cost $115,732.52.

"My God," Belen said.

"Oh, Mrs. Lalaban," said a perky voice on the phone. "This should be the least of your worries. We'll figure out the bill when your husband leaves the hospital. I'm sure your insurance will kick in and everything will be fine."

"I just want to be prepared. Thank you for your help," Belen said and hung up. Her next call was to Jory's supervisor, who told her that Jory had saved up a few months' worth of sick leave and vacation days that could be used while he was recuperating. He informed her that many of his fellow postal workers had donated their own sick leave and vacation days, which would help for a few more months. She felt better about switching to working part-time so she could be with her husband more. She and Emerson arranged a schedule. She would be with him until she had to be at work by five in the afternoon. Emerson changed his schedule to work from 8:00 A.M. to 4:00 P.M., going to the hospital to relieve his mother by five.

She called her insurance company who told her that Jory was insured for up to $100,000 for an emergency hopitilization. Jory's two-week stay had already exhausted that amount. She was told that insurance would cover 80 percent of the bill, but reminded her that she was responsible for the remaining 20 percent. So far, she would have to pay approximately $3,500 for Jory's two-week stay. This was certainly good news, but the calculator in her mind kept working. If it costs 115,000 for a two-week stay and insurance would cover 80 percent of that, she would be responsible to pay $23,000. Jory was far from recuperating and in a month's time, hospital costs would be close to $50,000. This was far beyond anything Jory and Belen had saved in their lifetime.

By the end of the year, she thought, I would have to pay close to $200,000!

Belen blamed herself, believing she should have known better. Somehow she should have known that something like this would happen. The Curse returned. She berated herself for not being wiser. "Mother was right," she whispered. "I am stupid. Stupid!"

She walked around her home in a daze, thinking that every decision she'd ever made was foul. She faulted herself for not making more money in her lifetime. Early in her career, she had a good income working in the emergency room at a respectable hospital, with her sights on becoming head nurse someday. If she had stayed at that job, she would have received 100 percent hospital coverage for herself and for Jory.

"I could have had one hundred percent coverage!" Belen screamed in her living room. She picked up pillows on the couch and threw them across the room. "Why did Jun have to die? Why?" It was the death of her firstborn that made any ambition she possessed simply disappear. Dealing with the stress and blood of an ER was something she could not handle anymore. She switched to a job that was a little more bearable. She transferred to A Place of Rest, an old folks' home, where everything seemed calmer. If anyone died, it was because they had lived a long life and it was appropriate. It also changed her insurance package. At the time, it seemed like a fine decision. Being insured for up to $100,000 seemed like a lot of money. Paying only 20 percent of anything after that seemed like a good deal.

Jory's situation might require him to stay in the hospital for several months. *What will happen then?* she wondered. Six months' worth of hospitalization would cost over half a million dollars. She would be broke for sure. She inhaled and tried to calm herself. In her mind, she devised a plan.

I'll wear heavy sweaters to bed, she thought. Winter was approaching and nights were already getting cold. She chuckled to herself. She might owe half a million dollars and her best strategy was to wear sweaters to save a few dollars. *Well,* she thought, *it was something.*

She decided to stop using heat, stop taking hot showers, stop watering the lawn, eat sparingly, use the phone only when she absolutely had to, cancel the cable TV and the newspaper delivery, use electricity only when necessary—even if it meant walking in darkness most times—stop buying clothes, use cosmetics only on select occasions. She shuddered at the thought of losing the house.

She never thought at this stage in her life that she would be leading an existence that mirrored her earlier life, one she would rather not repeat. Many years ago when Jory came to her and told her that there might be one way to break the Curse, she readily agreed. Even if it meant going to her mother to beg. She wanted the Curse to end, yes, so she could have a baby, yes, so she and Jory could finally have that family they'd always dreamed of. She had another reason, one she never told Jory: she wanted the Curse to end because she was tired of being poor.

She was raised with money, and, frankly, she missed it. Something a rich girl who loses her riches hopes for is to be rich again. Jory had said that he wanted to be wealthy one day. Belen was convinced that he did not know what he was talking about. Poor people only have a vague idea of wealth. They think it means buying whatever you want. Wrong. You don't buy whatever you want, but you have the confidence in knowing that you can. It was that confidence she missed. She didn't buy *every* dress that she found attractive. She knew that if she went home and the dress stayed on her mind, she could send a servant to retrieve it.

It wasn't until she left her family's money that she yearned for every blouse that appeared in a shop window, every shade of lipstick on a counter, and every expensive meal on a menu. It depressed her knowing that she couldn't have it.

When she stood in the backyard of the house she grew up in, anxious to see her mother, she could feel that old confidence come back. She looked at the graves of her ancestors, and even though they might be mad, she prayed to them, silently asking for their help. She prayed to them for weeks that her mother would meet with her. When her mother said yes, she assumed it was due to their assistance. She asked dead members of her family to help undo the animosity that her mother held for her, so she could be rich again, rich in every way.

Even though they could not afford it, Belen and Jory, who had become a fine *mambunong,* conducted a small *Kanyao* to ingratiate themselves to the souls of her ancestors and to the God Kabunyan. It was a pathetic offering of rice and *Tapuy*, rice wine, but she hoped that the souls they were asking assistance from noticed that the *Tapuy* was expensive.

Without telling her husband, Belen also went to church to pray to Jesus and recited the prayers of the rosary, hailing Mary. She figured in dealing with Ermaline Dubabang, she should ask the assistance from as many deities as possible. Her mother Ermaline was strong, she knew. Ermaline was a woman with will, the kind of might that any man would fear and that had earned her the reverence of all the women. As she stood ready to ascend the first step to her girlhood home, she hoped this power would work in her favor. She bowed her head to the graves before she entered.

The screen door opened and a pretty, young girl stood there. She was dressed in clothes that Belen recognized as her own.

"Hello," the girl said.

Belen could not speak, still taken by the Filipina at the door wearing fabric that she handpicked herself. She gave a slight nod.

"My name is Esther. I'm new."

"I'm Belen—"

"I know who you are. I've heard—I mean . . . I know who you are. Please come in."

Belen swore that she wouldn't cry. Her mother probably chose that dress specifically for Esther to wear that day to let Belen know that the only daughter of the Dubabang clan was no longer a part of the family. She felt her confidence fading.

She entered the kitchen and was overwhelmed by her past, the lingering odor of fried sausages, a favorite of her mother's. The floor emanated a slight stench of bleach and the air was tainted with Lavender Sunset, a perfume her mother bought to cover the smell of the bleach.

Led to a nearby table, Belen sat and watched Esther leave the room. She clutched her purse in her hand like so many of the women who had sat at that table. Her mother discussed—no, told—what these women, new maids, were expected to do. (These women were newly married and poor. To ensure a successful, happy marriage these women and their husbands conducted their own *Kanyao,* asking the Dubabang family for meat to offer the Gods and their ancestors. In exchange for the meat, services would be rendered. The women became maids, and the men became employees at her mother's lumber mill.)

Belen wore her best dress, colored an azure blue, her mother's favorite color, and heels that were no taller than an inch and a half. Her mother believed that only prostitutes wore heels two inches or higher.

Her hair was twisted in a bun and she wore little make-up. She tied a gossamer scarf around her neck, hoping to add a touch of modesty to her appearance. She checked her nails, grateful that she removed the Ring Around the Rosey Red nail polish earlier that morning.

She reached into her purse for an aspirin. Thank the Lord for aspirin. She popped it into her mouth and waited. After several minutes, Belen couldn't take the silence. She stood up and paced. She knew her mother was doing this on purpose, making her wait to reinforce the fact that she was gliding on her mother's time. Everyone else's schedule was dependent on Ermaline Dubabang.

An hour later, Belen worried that her mother had chosen not to see her. She spent days wondering what outfit to wear, choosing what words she would say at their first meeting. It would be just like her mother to make her go through that kind of preparation and simply not show up.

Belen picked up her purse, ready to leave. She decided to take one look at the house before she left. She quietly walked into the dining room and touched the blonde wood dining table that seated twelve, ran her palm against the padded, velvet seats of the chairs. She peeked into the living room with the big, bulky, furniture, gazing at the pink, satin curtains her mother chose because of the built-in sheen of the fabric.

Lastly, she stepped into the room where her mother had beaten her, the room with paintings and photographs of her ancestors. She took in every image, inhaling and exhaling, hoping every inhalation brought in good luck and joy.

She approached the corner that held the images of her father: big pictures, little pictures, medium-sized ones; paintings and photographs representing Valentino's transition from boy to man. Belen picked up the smallest impression of Valentino, a black and white photo framed in gold, no bigger than two inches. She put it in her purse and quickly turned around when she heard footsteps.

Ermaline Dubabang entered, wearing a pleated skirt and a plain white blouse. To anyone else, her mother would have been taken as a handsome woman, choosing to wear simple, tasteful clothes. Belen was hurt. She knew that her mother could have dressed a little more stylishly, added a little more flare. She had done so many times for distant relatives stopping by or to greet a business associate. By not dressing up for a daughter she had not seen in several years, Belen knew that her mother regarded her as plainly as the women who cleaned the house.

"What are you doing in this room?" Ermaline said.

"I was in the kitchen, but you didn't come. I thought I would take a look. Just a look, especially pictures of Dad."

"Your father was a good man. I hated putting that gun to his head."

"I know."

"Sometimes we have to do things, horrible things because it's right." Her voice was flat, dry. "You wanted to see me?" Mrs. Dubabang sat on an armchair, leaning back.

Belen lowered her lids. "Thank you for agreeing to meet me. When I sent you that note, I didn't know what to expect. Then when you responded, I . . . I . . . was so happy."

Mrs. Dubabang remained silent.

Belen sat on a chair across from her mother and said, "How is Cesar? Oliver?"

"Your brothers are fine. Cesar is going to get married."

"Cesar? Married? That's wonderful." Belen smiled.

"Wonderful? He's marrying the girl *he* wanted to marry, not the girl I wanted him to marry. A decent family wouldn't allow their daughters to marry into ours. They're afraid your bad luck will get to them."

"Mother."

Mrs. Dubabang put her hand to her head and stood up. "Cesar is marrying the daughter of a fish seller. Can you imagine! Well, at least we know where the girl is from. We know her name." Mrs. Dubabang massaged her forehead.

"Are you all right?" Belen said. "Mother—"

"Don't call me that."

Belen sat still, then she plunged into her bag for a tissue. No luck. She undid the gossamer scarf around her neck and put it to her face. "What . . . what do you want me to call you then?"

Belen looked up from her scarf and could see that her mother had her head in her hands.

"Belen, you should be at a party. Right now, you should be at a party. You gathered people for morning *merienda,* because you want a break from your studies. You are getting your master's degree in something, perhaps literature. It doesn't matter because you're not going to use it, but it will be good for you to have. You're supposed to be in Manila, at the University of Santa Tomas. Friends come to your house, a small one that I bought you."

"I didn't . . ."

"There will be two young men who go to your *merienda*. One is a young politician, another is a student studying business."

"Mama, stop."

"They both court you, but you choose the politician because

he is more handsome. He is more charming. He is also from here. He sends his parents to meet with me. They are educators of some kind. We discuss Bands of Marriage, what we shall give and what they will give. They offer a generous seven cows and three pigs for the *Kanyao*. I am pleased because that is more than what was offered for me. The meat will be needed to feed the hundreds of people who will attend your weeklong wedding celebration."

"Please, stop it."

Mrs. Dubabang laughed and shook her head. "Father Aga will be so mad. He is so mad that we spend so much money on your wedding. I don't care because we want everything right for you. You are my only daughter. I want your marriage properly blessed.

"You stay in Manila because there is a better chance for your husband to pursue a career in politics. You have babies. You become familiar with other politician's wives. You develop a strong friendship with these women. When you turn thirty, you find yourself the wife of a senator. You decide to find a charity to work with, something dealing with children. It is satisfying work. You shop for the newest clothes and have your hair done to fit the latest style. Your husband tells you he might want to become president someday."

"Jory is a good man."

"Your husband tells you that he must start winning support now. He works with his political connections, promising jobs to those who help him. You must do your part, too, he says. You begin traveling the Philippines. You befriend wealthy ladies in cities like Cebu and Davao."

"Mother—"

"Don't call me that."

"Mo—I need to ask you something. A favor."

"When you turn thirty-eight, your husband runs for president. He is smart and savvy, and you are beautiful and sophisticated. He loses the election by a small margin. Still, you put up a good fight. He will run again. Next time he will win. You are forty-six and—"

"I need to ask you."

"I know what you are going to ask me! I know why you came here. Your life is ruined, and you want to fix it."

"My life is not ruined."

"You're twenty-three, and your life is already over. I hear about you. I hear you became a nurse. Typical. I suppose I should be proud of you for putting yourself through school. I'm not. How many women train to be nurses? You were not supposed to be like so many women."

"Jory and I want children."

Mrs. Dubabang's laughter echoed through the house. "But God won't let you. You stole something from Him, Belen. He took your babies away from you. You were pregnant, then you were not."

"I learned in nursing school that a lot of things make that happen. I learned that when a girl gets nervous or pressured, she can lose her . . . then it comes back again when she is better."

"Call it what you will, Belen, you thought you were going to have a baby, and you didn't. And you can't. God was mad at you and our ancestors were mad at you for not properly honoring them. They're still mad at you. How does it feel?"

Belen was quiet, feeling ashamed. As much as she hated to admit it, she knew her mother was right. Regardless, she pressed on. "I can have children. The doctor told me I was okay and Jory is okay."

"Then why do you want to leave? Word gets around fast. You should know that. You want to go so the Curse won't follow you.

You want to break the spell. You could have been First Lady of the Philippines, instead you're damned."

"The Curse won't follow us over water. Jory and I have applied to go to America, but it would take years for papers to be processed, maybe even a dozen. I know you can talk to somebody, maybe cut those years in half, maybe make it less."

"You want to go? You want me to talk to someone to arrange your flight? I'll do that. I'm not doing this to be kind. I'm doing this so a girl who betrayed me will never have to call me mother again. I'll help you.

"I killed your father because it was the best thing to do. It was war. He was in pain. I hoped after his death, you, me, Cesar, Oliver would do everything we could to honor him. Not do a single thing to blemish the name he gave us. Valentino Dubabang's spirit would be remembered for having saved our lives.

"With our name alone you could have had anyone, been anything. You could have been First Lady, Belen. Our Jackie Kennedy. Jackie Kennedy!" Ermaline took a deep, deep breath and said, "Now, you're nothing. Our name, the Dubabang name, reduced to gossip. I'll help you. Just get out. Out of my house, out of the country. Just go."

Belen's insides crumbled. She felt hollow. All she could think of to say was, "Thank you."

Ermaline remained quiet, and Belen took that as a cue for her to leave. She headed for the front door, well aware of her mother behind. She turned the knob and stepped out of the house. She became aware of the fact that she would never see this house again. She turned to take one last look. Her mother was at the entrance, and what Belen saw scared her. Her mother looked dead, expressionless and distant. She watched Ermaline slowly close the door, and what would happen next, Belen would relive and ponder for years to come. Ermaline stood, with the door almost shut, her face barely peeking out of the entrance.

"Belen."

"Yes?"

"May you live . . . a *very* full life," Ermaline said, then shut the door.

Many years later, Belen would realize how damning those words were.

EMERSON

"I'M GLAD YOU'RE here," Emerson said to his coworkers on the day of the press conference. He planned to sit in the crowd as activists spoke from an erected stage in the Edelman Center yard. He knew he would be nervous with all those people around. He knew he would sweat. He knew he would get queasy.

"No problem," said Daisy, pressing tissue against his forehead. "You're here for your father."

"You're doing this for your dad, don't forget that," said his boss Eric Mori.

"Emerson!" someone yelled.

Emerson jumped at the sound of his name. He turned and saw Thom Fielding heading his way, along with a man and a woman.

"Emerson," Thom said, "this is Rabbi Shultz and Sylvia Jacobs."

Emerson introduced Daisy and Eric.

"I'm glad we can stand together," the rabbi said.

"Is your father okay?" Sylvia asked.

"Better. Not great."

"Shall we take our seats?" Thom said.

Emerson watched Thom, Sylvia, and Rabbi Shultz walk to the stage. He followed Daisy and Eric to the watching crowd.

"Emerson," Thom said. "Where are you going?"

"I'm going to sit in the audience."

"We arranged to have you sit up here with the other family members."

Emerson froze.

"C'mon," Thom said walking toward him. Thom held onto his elbow and led him onto the stage.

"I'd rather sit with my friends," Emerson said.

"Nonsense. You being here is important. Remember to keep your remarks short."

"Short?"

"Yes, Emerson. We hoped that you'd say something about what you've been going through. I assumed that's why you wanted to come."

"I don't have anything prepared."

"You'll be fine," Thom said.

He sat on a white chair, next to Sylvia Jacobs. He sat while the mayor made a speech about the crime.

"This is truly a shame," the mayor said. "That something like this should happen in our city is devastating. Our city, our state, our country will not tolerate this kind of hate."

Applause came from the audience. The applause shook Emerson. His palms became clammy, and he rubbed them against his slacks.

The mayor continued. "I have served this city, this country. First, in Vietnam, then as part of law enforcement. I have fought for freedom for others and fought to maintain order in Los Angeles. It is a crime that this kind of tragedy should happen."

More applause. More sweat from Emerson.

"We have some brave people to speak to you. Family members that were affected by this crime. First is Ms. Jacobs."

Emerson watched as she talked about how her life would never be the same. Emerson wanted touch her. She, it seemed, knew what he was feeling. Emerson didn't how to relay his feelings over the incident. He was afraid to get in front of all those cameras, all of those people to tell the world that having your dad shot by a racist was shitty, downright fucked up.

The mayor introduced other speakers who spoke of changed lives and doomed livelihoods. With each new speaker, Emerson felt faint. He was bound to speak soon, and he was aware of the others looking at him. People in the audience, people on stage wondering what the son of a victim might say.

He saw Sylvia Jacobs look at him. She nodded her head, smiled tentatively, as if to say, *It'll be all right. You can relay the story of your life, the pain of this incident. It'll be good for you, therapeutic in a way.* He saw the prosecutor Thomas Fielding standing at the corner of the stage, wearing a black pinstripe suit, staring at Emerson. He saw his coworkers in the audience, Daisy Chan and Eric Mori with stern faces.

All of the speakers who were supposed to speak had spoken and Emerson dreaded the fact that he was saved for last. The son of the shot-up postman.

"And now," said the mayor.

Emerson began to breathe hard. *What the fuck am I gonna say,* he thought. *What?* He uncrossed his legs preparing to stand and approach the podium.

"Thank you all for coming," the mayor said. "Thanks to all the families for coming out. This concludes our conference."

The mayor was ending the program. People on stage looked around in confusion. There was one more speaker, and the politician was saying farewell. Sylvia Jacobs straightened her back, wondering what was going on. Rabbi Shultz raised his hand, trying to get the mayor's attention. It was no use, the mayor's back was to him.

"Have a good day," the mayor said.

Emerson sighed, believing that there was a God. He wouldn't have to speak. He was forgotten. He could go. He came. Everyone saw him come. Now, he could go home. He touched his forehead, wiping away perspiration.

Rrrrrrrrrrring.

Emerson looked up.

Rrrrrrrrrrrring, he heard to his left. Rrrrrrrrrrrrrring, he heard to his right. Rrrrrrrrrrrring, he heard from somewhere in the audience. *What the . . .* Emerson didn't finish his thought when he heard a Rrrrrrrrrrrring from behind him. Beeeeeeeeeep, he also heard. A pager was going off. Beeeeeeeep. Beeeeeeeep, he heard again. Rrrrrrrrrrrring. Rrrrrrrring. He looked at the audience. No one else was hearing that irritating ringing sound. Everyone watched the mayor say his final words. Rrrrrrrrrrrring. Rrrrrrrrrring. Beeeeeeeeeep. Beeeeeeeep. Rrrrrrrrrrring. Beeeeeeeep. Beeeeeeeep. The sounds were going off together, coming from every direction. He knew it was his brother trying to contact him, demand that he speak. Rrrrrrrrrrrring. Rrrrrrrrrrrrrrrrrring. Beeeeeeeeeeeeeep. Rrrrrrrrrrrrrrrrrrrring. Rrrrrrrrrrrrrrrring. Beeeeeeeeeeeeeep. Rrrrrrrrrrrrrrrrrrrring. Rrrrrrrrrrrrrrrrrring. Rrrrrrrrrrrrrring. Beeeeeeeeeeeeeep. Rrrrrrrrrrrrrrring. Rrrrrrrrrrrrrrrring. Beeeeeeeeeeeeeep. Rrrrrrrring. Beeeeeeeeeeeeeep. Rrrrrrrrrrrrring. Rrrrrrrrrrrrrrring.

Emerson couldn't take it anymore and yelled, "Stop!"

The mayor turned around and looked at Emerson. Sylvia Jacobs put a hand on his back. The audience was staring straight at him. He saw Thomas Fielding approach the mayor and whisper in his

ear. The mayor nodded and said, "But! Before we call this conference to an end, we have one more person who has something to
say. His name is . . . he's the young man whose father was shot."

Emerson slowly stood up. His legs were weak. He suddenly
remembered a poll done by a newspaper that wrote most people
fear public speaking more than death. Emerson understood this
completely. He would rather jump from a plane than face a
crowd of people. He slowly approached the podium. There were
several microphones secured to a stand. The mikes had logos on
them. ABC, CBS, NBC, FOX, CNN, and others he didn't recognize. He saw the kind face of Daisy Chan looking up at him, nodding, urging him to go on like a mother watching her child give a
piano recital. He rolled his tongue around the insides of his mouth,
trying to relieve the dryness there. He was no longer sweating, all
the moisture from his body was gone. There was a glass of water on
the podium. He sipped from it and bowed his head. He heard feet
shuffling around him and could see, in the corner of his eyes, camera men looping cords around their arms, preparing to leave, believing they got whatever footage they needed for the evening news.

He raised his head, opened his mouth to speak, hoping a sound
would come out. Nothing. Words weren't coming. He didn't
know if words would ever come. He looked out at the crowd, and
his nerves kicked in. He was terrified, more terrified than he'd
been in his life. He didn't like being up here. He didn't like having to be in front of these people. He didn't like having a father
in the hospital. He didn't like it at all. He gripped the podium
and said the only thing that came to mind, "Damn it." It was a
whisper, but through the speakers it echoed through the Edelman
schoolyard.

The cameramen stopped looping cords, picked up their cameras, and aimed them at Emerson. People shifted in their seats. The
shuffling of feet stopped, and a dead silence blanketed the area.

"Damn it," he said again. "I don't like being here. I don't." He lowered his head, exhaled, inhaled, raised his head. "I . . . I . . . I don't like having my father . . . who can barely move, b-b-barely speak—lying in a room at . . . St. Joan's hospital." He held his breath, refusing to let tears build up. He would not cry. He didn't like to cry. He never cried in front of people. He would not be vulnerable in front of strangers. He would not. He went the other route. He hit the podium and said, firmly, without a quiver in his voice, "My dad should be at work, doing his job. How *dare* William Baylor do this. How *dare* he ruin my dad's life. Who is William Baylor to think that he could do this to other people's lives?" He heard a cell phone go off in the back. It wasn't a Rrrrrrrrrrring. The phone played the tune Happy Birthday. "I wish I could call this a nightmare, but you can wake from that. This is a life sentence. William Baylor is scum, nothing but scum."

Emerson stepped away from the podium. He was aware of the silence he left behind. He took his seat next to Sylvia. She grabbed his hand and held it. Emerson held hers just as tightly. He looked at the ground. Then he heard people move, feet came into view. He heard the tentative sounds of clapping. It grew to a hearty applause. Emerson looked up and saw people crowding around him. Rabbi Shultz lifted him up by the elbow. He saw that everyone was standing.

Daisy had a tissue in her hand, waving at him, crying. Eric Mori had his fingers in his mouth whistling. Reporters with notepads or small recorders rushed him.

"Do you have anything more to say?" a reporter asked.

"How is your father doing? What's his status?" another reporter asked.

"St. Joan's?" a journalist yelled. "In the Valley?"

Rabbi Shultz led Emerson away, whispering into his ear, "You did good, my boy. You're going to get those Nazi bastards mad, I'm sure. I don't know if you are aware of what you just did."

"What do you mean?" Emerson asked.

"You'll see. You'll see."

JORY

*J*ORY LOOKED AT the wall that had Get Well cards taped to it. In the days since Emerson's broadcast, the number of cards had tripled. Emerson's words—"William Baylor is scum, nothing but scum"—were replayed over and over again on national news. The cards overlapped, and Belen had to tape more cards to a different wall.

"This one is from St. Louis," she said. "And look at this." She held up a large manila envelope. She opened it up and pulled out a large piece of flipchart paper. "This one is made by a second grade glass from Dallas, Texas. Look at that, Jory. The kids drew a picture of a field with all sorts of animals running around. Isn't that sweet?"

"Sweet," Jory confirmed. It was becoming easier for Jory to form words without it exhausting him.

"This card is from Norfolk, Virginia."

"Norfolk? That's far." It became so easy, in fact, that Jory became adept at spewing out several words at a time without getting severe headaches.

The most remarkable thing about his recovery was that he was able to move his hands and arms, showing that the nerve damage wasn't as bad as Dr. Jones had thought. He still had problems with his legs, though. A physical therapist was brought in to help Jory use his limbs again. The physical therapist gave him an exercise which required him to open and close his fists, an activity that caused beads of sweat to form on his forehead. He found that his left hand was far stronger than his right. Still, it was a wonderful thing to hold Belen's hand and give a tentative squeeze back.

He was also able lift his head and look around, although lifting his torso was still hard to do. There were still two bullets lodged in his body that Dr. Jones didn't know what to do with. One bullet might have to go, causing fear of infection, but the other might be left in permanently. Those two bullets felt like bricks inside of him.

He saw the door open and Emerson step in. He looked different, looked stronger somehow. His face seemed brighter. *Maybe he should appear on television more often,* Jory thought. He carried a paper bag.

"Hey, Dad," he said. "Look what I've got." He opened the bag and emptied letters onto the hospital bed, different colored paper falling at his feet. "They're letters from everywhere. I've been getting them at home. People have been calling me at work and at home, too, asking how you are."

"How did they find you?" Belen asked.

"They looked me up on the internet, I guess. Found me in the phonebook."

"What do they say?" Jory asked.

"They want to know if you're okay. If you're getting better. Maybe I should think about changing my number or getting it unlisted. I went home and there were seventeen messages asking about you. One guy said he was calling from Toronto, a woman called from Maui. So many calls."

"We've been getting calls here at the hospital," Belen said. "It got so bad the nurses are screening them."

"All these people want you to get better, Dad."

"He is getting better," Belen said. "Look, the color is back in his face. Maybe we can take him home soon, huh? Maybe you can be back by Thanksgiving."

"Yeah, I would like that," Jory said. His hope of returning home overwhelmed. It was the motivation to eat, to sleep, to wake. Returning to that house on Carondelet was his goal when the physical therapist said, "Lift your arm this high." Even though the act of lifting his arm caused great pains at first, he did it anyway.

"You need to strengthen your arms so you can operate a wheelchair," said the therapist.

The thought of being in a wheelchair would have disgusted Jory before, but in this case, it sounded better than a hospital bed. Mobility was important to a man who was used to walking for blocks at a time.

"He also seems less depressed, huh, honey-bunny," Belen said.

Jory raised his hand. Belen knew to take it. She wore no make-up, he noticed. Her hair tied in a pony-tail and she still looked beautiful. He wanted to touch her, remind her of when they were young, new to this place called America. He looked at Emerson reading the letters at his feet. This man, his son, grew inside the woman whose hand he held. The concept astounded him. There was actually a time when these two people were one, absorbed into each other.

He recalled moving his palm on her pregnant stomach, a belly that was forming Emerson. He created circular patterns with his hand around her naval. Round and round, imitating the broken rocks swirling around Saturn. Being that close to his wife, the woman that he had given up God for, he felt like he had become one of the mythic Greek figures in the Sky. He was Sagittarius, the Archer, and he chose to leave behind his bow and arrow to rest with Virgo, providing polite kisses on her stomach. He put his ear to it, listening intently for the slightest bit of sound.

That was 1969, and he had never felt more happy. In that year, he had also never felt more angry. The Moon had been desecrated by astronauts. He spit on the ground, looked up at the night Sky and said, "Goddamnit!" He balled up his hands and raised them high. He shook his fists at the heavens, then brought them to his head. He grabbed his hair and groaned.

"Come back in the house," his wife said on the back-door steps, their firstborn on her hip, their second waiting to be born. "Come inside. What can you do? It's progress."

"How could you let them do it?" Jory screamed into the darkness. He spit some more.

"Jory, the neighbors will think we're crazy. This is a good thing that happened. I know you don't think so, but this is history. Come inside and watch. This is the first man on the moon, Jory. The first man on the moon!"

Jory turned around to look at her. With that look, Belen withdrew into the house, quietly shutting the door.

It'll never be the same, he knew. How could he worship the Moon knowing that man had stepped all over Him.

He spit one more time, bowed his head, then entered the house. For the next several days, Jory was despondent. He had been working as a postman for three years, and his coworkers knew him to be a cheerful man. People who received mail from him greeted him kindly, knowing they would get a jovial How Are You Today? from the mail carrier.

Jory dragged along in his days, listening to stories of the

stepped-on Moon. When those famous words rang through the airwaves, making the headlines of newspapers and filling the television news, Jory, for the first time in his life, called in sick. They were words that Jory despised: one small step for a man, one giant leap for mankind.

"The Moon, Belen. The Moon! They're stepping on the Moon. Can you believe that? They're stepping on *Him!*"

"What can you do? This is America. They do things like that. They go to places and step on things. It is one-small-step-for-a-man to do this."

"How dare they speak for all of us. They are—what is it? Arrogant. This is one small step all right. It's one small step backward!"

Belen waved her hands in the air and went to make baby food for Jun-Jun.

"Backward, I say." Jory knew what they were doing, doing what they were doing for centuries. They were making everything tangible. When God was too great to conceive, notions that men could somehow be connected to greatness had to be conceived as well. Men had to be half-Gods at some point, whether it was Hercules or Jesus. It was that too-strong-of-a-connection to holiness that Jory feared. There were simply things that man could never be. Gods were one of those things. When men too closely associate themselves to God, all hell could break loose.

There should be a distance, Jory thought, *between greatness and the ordinary.* Man should stay closer to home. If they want to believe, if they want to experience grandeur, walk outside, see the sky, see the trees.

Ralph Waldo Emerson knew the wonder of nature, of water, of dirt, of leaves. Jory knew that Mr. Emerson was blasted for too strong of an emphasis on nature as a source of strength, and on the diminishment of church and God in humanity.

Wherever he went, the Moon landing was everywhere. It filled the racks of every news stand, supermarket, and liquor store he went into. He caught a glimpse of one magazine and leafed through it. It was *National Geographic,* with a pictorial of a landscape so striking that he had to read further. It was about a place called Joshua Tree, part of the desert just outside of Los Angeles. He saw pictures of those bizarre rock formations and decided to go. It looked like what the Moon would look like, Jory believed.

He was unsatisfied with the pictures that NASA provided to the world, black and white grainy things, making Him look flat and unattractive. He tasted the Moon, a flavor his wife provided for him, and there was no way in heck that the Moon could look so uninspiring.

He planned a trip to visit Joshua Tree as soon as his second child was born. He wanted to go sooner, but Belen's pregnancy prevented them. Belen couldn't sit still for long. Even when she slept, Jory noticed how she tossed and turned—their second babe restless inside her. She found herself running to the toilet every few hours. Belen refused to sit in a car for two hours each way, away from a bathroom.

A few months after Emerson was born, Jory packed a picnic lunch, Belen got the babies dressed, and they were on their way to the Moon. They got into their Nova, hit the freeway, drove away from the city to that sandy place where men had died in olden days.

They paid a toll, got a brochure informing them about Joshua Tree. They parked the Nova and Jory, holding his oldest son and a wicker basket of Filipino food, set forth. His wife held the coddling infant Emerson and followed.

Jory stepped onto land and could move no further. He saw the oddly shaped rocks, the smooth, rust-colored boulders, and thought, *Damn.* He'd never seen anything so beautiful. He had seen the rice terraces of the Philippines, and he had experienced the caves of Luzon. He had been down to the splendid beaches of his old country, but nothing could beat this!

"Watch out," Belen said, "the brochure said there are snakes."

"Snakes won't hurt us," he said. He honestly believed that. He was told that snakes are kindred spirits to lightning. Some Filipino men ate snakes to improve their virility, and when he and Belen desperately tried to conceive, he'd take a trip to Chinatown to buy some snakes in a bottle. He was sure it was making a meal of those snakes that led to the birth of his two healthy sons.

Jory found a clearing to sit in and they ate among the rocks. He barely spoke when they ate. He couldn't find the words. He sat and digested his meal, looked at his wife feeding their young ones, among the walls of what could be the Moon, and he knew he was experiencing something divine.

Something divine, Jory thought, as he read the different letters that Emerson brought him. He was amazed at all of these people caring about him. He was sincerely touched. Something divine.

MICHAEL

*M*ICHAEL WALKED THROUGH the aisle of the 747 making sure everyone was ready for take-off. He reached the end of the plane and buckled himself in. *Off to America,* he thought, *damn it.* He'd been avoiding this trip for two months, refusing to head in the direction of Emerson. He flew Taipei to Bangkok and Bangkok to Taipei, never completing the last leg of the flight of Taipei to Los Angeles. He informed his boss, another gay man, about Emerson, stating that the state of California made his heart sink. He would rather not fly there. His boss, an amenable man, said he would allow Michael to mourn the loss of his relationship, but he would eventually have to start flying to America again. In November that time eventually came.

"I can't fly to Los Angeles."

"Michael, be reasonable," his boss said. "The other flight attendants deserve some time off."

"I told you California makes me ill. I loved Emerson. I told him so. I waited for him to say that he loved me, but he didn't. Well, he did, but in a chickenshit way. How hard is it to say I love you? I can't go back to Los Angeles."

"I know. That's why you're flying into Las Vegas, Nevada."

"But—"

"No, buts, Michael. You're going."

So off to Vegas. It would take several hours to get to the land of bright lights and casinos. He was in the air when he felt himself getting misty. Flying to America forced Michael to recall all sorts of things about Emerson, including their second date, when Emerson took him to a merry-go-round in Griffith Park. Brass poles came through the backs of horses. Michael sat on the saddle of a white horse with a blonde mane. Emerson stood next to him. The merry-go-round started, and Michael almost lost his balance. Emerson stood there keeping him steady.

They left the merry-go-round and walked through Griffith Park. Michael noticed the golf course and the well-dressed people playing. There were golf courses, playgrounds for Pearls, in Taiwan, too.

"Do. You. Play. Golf?" he asked.

"Naw. I'm. Not. A. Golfing. Kind. Of. Guy."

Michael knew this was probably true and swore he would not have a third date with this man who did not, would not, or had no aspiration to play golf. Michael cried when his relationship ended with Emerson, and he would recall the last definitive moment of strength: when his goals were intact and his ambition came first. He had one goal in becoming a flight attendant, one goal in learning English, one goal in bettering himself—going to places like the theater, one goal that he would truly miss the world for. That goal was that someday, he would be a Pearl himself. Something he knew was that Pearls only hook up with other Pearls.

When snot ran onto the silk slipcases of his pillow, he remembered clear as crystal the decision he made, one he should have stuck to. It was made with such conviction, the kind of conviction a person of worth would make. Michael decided: this second date with his Andy Lau look-alike would be his last. It being the last, he was going to have fun. He had often wondered what it would be like to make love with Andy Lau, always wondered what it might be like to have the singer on top of him. He decided Emerson might be the closest thing to it.

"What your place look like?"

"It's a regular place. Nothing special."

"Show me."

When they arrived at his apartment, Michael agreed: it was nothing special. He stood in the middle of the living room, eyes to the floor.

"Music?" Michael asked.

"Uh, yeah, sure." He turned on the radio. A commercial was ending, saying, "You're listening to the quiet storm." Jazz entered the air. The muffled sound of kissing filled the room.

Michael found himself on a bed. With his eyes closed, he thought to himself, *Andy, hold me, Andy.* He clung onto him like he'd never held anyone before. *Andy, love me.* He could tell the way Emerson kissed him, touched him, the sex was going to be good.

I *love you, Andy. Love me back.*

Now, Michael had had flings before. After each one, he became better at handling them. He learned to depart quietly or in the morning, stating, "I have to fly."

He awoke close to midnight with Emerson by his side. He stealthily slipped from the covers, and found his clothes bunched on the floor. A lamp in the corner emanated a soft glow. He saw Emerson shift on the bed, and he almost said, "I have a prane to catch." Emerson didn't wake.

Michael put on his clothes, satisfied, feeling like he'd finally known what it was like to make love with his favorite singer. Andy Lau was remarkable. He orgasmed twice. If he had left right then and there, Michael knew, his life would have gone on as planned. Emerson Lalaban would have been remembered as Emerson who? Or even better as Em? Evan, Everett—his name was E-something.

If it weren't for that shoe! That goddamned other half of the Kenneth Cole pair that he couldn't find. Even with the help of the lamp, he couldn't find his left shoe. He looked under the bed, and there it was. He could see the black leather shoe clearly. He got on his back, reaching for it. He grabbed it and felt it hit something. Once he got his missing Kenneth Cole, he looked at what it had hit. It was a toy, a skateboard. It struck Michael as odd that a man Emerson's age would be playing with a skateboard.

Michael froze when he heard Emerson rustle. He peered over the bed to see if Emerson woke, and something he saw made him pause. He looked at the sleeping face of Emerson, of this man, on this bed, under the soft glow of the light. He ceased looking like his favorite pop star. He looked like someone else. He looked ordinary, ordinary in a way that's attractive. As if he could offer a life, not an exciting one perhaps, but a good, stable one. Examining Emerson's face, he decided to disrobe. He slipped back into bed, sliding his arm around Emerson's neck bringing him close to his chest.

With Emerson's head by his face, he smelled his hair. It smelled like American Crew pomade. Michael caressed the sleeping man's back and held him. He was struck with that look on Emerson's face as he almost stole away, that look that Michael could never forget, no matter how hard he tried, that look that changed the direction of his life.

He landed in Las Vegas and went straight to his hotel. He turned on the television and channel surfed. He stopped on CNN.

He felt ill. He saw Emerson on the screen being interviewed about the recent tragedy.

"My father getting shot was—is devastating. We're hoping that he'll recover," Emerson said.

"We all wish you and your father the very best," the host said.

Emerson looked different, hurt. Michael's thoughts reeled back to that time when he should have left Emerson's apartment, but stayed due to that hurt look on his face.

He dialed Emerson's number—a number he still remembered—recalling that one-night stand that turned into a relationship. In the closeness of midnight, as Michael almost made a clean getaway, he looked at Emerson's face, which jittered and sank. In his slumber, Emerson looked like he was going to cry.

BELEN

*S*HE LEFT THE administration offices of St. Joan's with half of her and Jory's life savings gone. She paid for the last two weeks and the next two weeks. She asked the financial aid counselor what her options might be when she ran out of money. He told her payment arrangements would have to be set up—say at one thousand dollars a month—or Jory could be moved to a less expensive hospital, County hospital perhaps.

Belen hated the idea of Jory in County Hospital. She didn't like the idea of her husband possibly sharing a room with several people, which was the case at County. She also knew that Jory would be sharing that room with some of the city's most indigent communities. She hated the thought of Jory lying next to some homeless person who hadn't bathed in weeks or a drug addict who'd overdosed on some disgusting drug like heroin.

She agreed to make payment arrangements when the time came. The calculator in her head continued. Starting in two weeks, she would owe them one thousand dollars a month for the next fifty months, eventually one thousand dollars a month for the next twenty-two months. On and on it went. She shuddered at thinking that if Jory's health didn't progress, she would owe one thousand dollars for the next one hundred months. She would be paying a thousand dollars a month for the next ten years! She didn't know how she could add a thousand dollars *and* meet other expenses like the mortagage.

Blessed Lady, she thought, *what will I do?*

You could sell the house.

How she loathed that suggestion.

Maybe you can get another mortgage?

She became sick at the idea of having payments until she was in her eighties. She didn't want to work when she was eighty-five years old. She wanted to rest.

How about selling things? You know, those earthly possessions you humans always hold dear.

She thought of every stick of furniture in her house, every piece of jewelry, all of her clothing and wondered if anything was worth selling. No. Everything she had was junk. Well, it became junk over the years. When she bought her sofa at Sears basement, it was such a buy, with upholstery that would last for twenty years. Twenty years seemed like such a long time when she bought it. Now that she was at the other end of those twenty years, she wondered how time managed to file itself away.

My dear, I've given you several good suggestions, and you refuse to take them. What's a Mother to do?

She walked through the parking lot, making her way to the Intensive Care Unit where Jory lay. She decided not to tell Jory about the cost of his hospitalization. She wanted him to be worry-free so he could recuperate faster. She had to tell Emerson. They may have had their differences in the past, but he seemed like a changed person since he started making public appearances, a change she welcomed. He was more upbeat, more like his father. Emerson would help somehow. *If not for me,* she thought, *for his father.*

For a brief moment, she was grateful that her son was gay. If he wasn't, he might be married with children. His financial commitment would be to his own family, not to his parents.

Gay people, well, the ones she'd see on TV, were always so carefree and stylish. And they always seem to have money to burn. *Maybe God meant for him to be gay,* she wondered.

That's preposterous. We frown on such things. And no amount of justification would make it right.

I know, Lady, Belen thought. *I just want to make sense of things. How things work. Why things work. That's all. Please don't get upset.*

She inhaled the November air. It was fresh, and it reminded her of the beach. Oh, how she loved the beach. Jory loved the desert, and she enjoyed going to Joshua Tree. It became a yearly event to visit the Moon, as Jory called it. After the sixth trip, Belen went more out of obligation than a sheer need to see the place. By the ninth trip, Jun had died and Belen stopped going. It just didn't feel right. Jory who had accepted that life would never be the same after the death of their oldest son, continued to go.

Belen looked at her watch. Visiting hours would begin in fifteen minutes. She decided to wait at the entrance of the hospital and stand for a bit, just a bit and enjoy the fine weather. She loved Los Angeles for that, the continuous presence of the sun. She loved being able to go to the beach in the middle of winter. She made her way to the beach whenever she could. On weekends, she'd persuade her family to eat crabs at Redondo Pier, shop at the open-air vendors in Venice Beach, and give the kids a few quarters to play in the arcades in Santa Monica.

She'd walk along the wooden slats of the Santa Monica pier and see the sea below her feet. She watched the seagulls fly above her and put out a few bucks for fried oysters from one of the cheap restaurants there.

There were many days when she went to the beach without her family knowing about it. She'd always managed to find work in West LA, closer to the beach. Sometimes during lunch, she'd venture out to the water and simply look out at that expansive ocean. She knew way out there the Philippines floated.

When she was younger, she wondered about her family and hoped that her brother Cesar had received the baby photos of Jun-Jun and Emerson. *Please tell Oliver hello for me,* she'd write, *I miss my brothers.* She'd dot the "i" in *miss* with a heart, something she'd learned to do in America.

Whenever she sent off a letter, she'd remember her childhood and how she loved being the sister to two strapping boys. They were rough with each other but always treated Belen with care. It ached her that they were put in the middle of this feud with her mother. She loved her brothers and wanted the best for them.

She got letters from her brothers every once in a while, telling her about Mom, their lives, and their families. *My wife gave birth to our third daughter*, Cesar wrote. *Oliver married a nice girl from La Trinidad, but no kids yet. It was a good thing because it looks like they're going to get a divorce anyway.*

Peppered in the letters was news of Ermaline. *Mom loves being a grandmother, but she wants a grandson. Which Oliver and I have failed to provide. She* has *grandsons,* Belen thought, thinking of her own children. She began to fume. *The lumber business is not going well. Another lumber mill was built here and it's giving mom a competition she'd never had before.*

Without having to say it, she knew that she was being blamed for their misfortune. Whether they have no grandsons or the lumber mill was experiencing difficulty, her mother blamed her for bringing bad luck into the family. *How much more do you want me to take?* Belen wondered. Something she learned was that most times you have to take responsibilities for your own fate. She thought, *You can't keep blaming for every little thing!*

Something Belen did, that she would never forgive herself for, was write her mother. Jun-Jun had died and she wrote Ermaline telling her what she was going through. She wrote:

> *Dearest Mama,*
>
> *I know we have had our differences in the past. But I have to tell you something terrible happened. Jory Lalaban, Junior, my oldest, died last year. It is a terrible thing. My heart feels like it was ripped apart. I was not going to tell you because I know you don't care about me. I just thought you might want to know that my son, your grandchild, is gone.*
>
> *Sincerely, Belen*

She told Jory what she had done.

"Why did you do that for?" he asked.

"I just wanted her to know, that's all. She should know if her grandchild dies."

She didn't tell him her real reason. She wrote that letter hoping that, in light of recent tragedies, her mother would find it in her heart to end this squabble. This was enough! It had gone on for way too long. She wanted her mother to write back and tell her that a death of a child is truly a horrific event. She wanted a letter, written in her mother's hand, saying, *Let's put this whole thing behind us. I forgive you. Please be my daughter again.*

She waited for months for a response. She went to the beach after work to look out at the ocean, thinking about what her mother must be feeling. She imagined Ermaline Dubabang opening the letter and reading it, feeling regret and sorrow for being so cruel.

She hadn't seen or heard from her mother in almost ten years, not since that day she entered the back door of her home, like a servant woman interviewing for a job, to ask for help in getting to America.

She wanted to see her mother again. When Jun died, Jory said a child's soul cries for his parents. Jory was wrong, children don't cry out for their parents when they die, they also cry out when they're alive and grow to become adults. She had always missed her mother, wondering what she was up to or if she was well. Her mother was mean, yes, but Belen believed that she gave her good cause for it. Belen believed that she deserved to be punished, but it had gone on way too long. She'd proven herself, taken every emotional dagger that her mother had thrown at her. It was time to stop. She hoped her mother felt the same way.

Her desire to see her mother intensified when Jun died. There was something missing in her soul. She came to believe that by bringing someone else back into her life, her pain would be alleviated. Her mother would be that person.

By simply writing *Dearest Mama,* she felt better. She felt cleansed at making things right with her mother. She imagined getting a letter back, red ink on delicate salmon-colored parchment. Belen knew that her mother kept such paper in a desk drawer near her bedroom window. She remembered her mother writing letters to a dear cousin living in Tokyo with that paper. She wrote letters of invitation to a party to friends in Manila with that paper.

Belen would leave work, go to the beach, look out at the ocean, wondering if her mother had written the letter and sent it. She'd stand on the sand and breathe deeply, knowing her mother would answer eventually. She was sure that she would leave the beach, drive home, and a salmon-colored letter in a salmon-colored envelope would be there, the flap of the envelope held closed by a red seal.

She would arrive home, tear open the letter and read that her mother was grateful to hear from her, that the tragedy of losing a child should not be dealt with alone. In that letter, her mother would offer to fly to Los Angeles and provide the kind of solace a mother should provide to her daughter at a time of crisis. Then Belen would call home—oh, calling home, what a wonderful thing to be able to do—and hear a maid's voice answer.

"May I ask who is calling?" the servant would ask.

"Yes, this is Belen. I'd like to speak to—"

"Oh, Belen, we've heard all about you. I'll get your mother."

Then they would speak, speak about the lost years. They would both cry and agree that those years were ridiculous years. Thank God, they're over with.

When Belen got that letter, it wasn't salmon-colored or written in delicate parchment. It was a postcard. She wondered if Jory, who delivered mail to their home, had seen it. It was buried among bills and junk mail, and she assumed that Jory simply didn't bother leafing through it.

The postcard was of a church she'd never seen before. The church looked serene and romantic with stained glass windows of flowers. On the back of the card, there was black ink that read:

I'm sorry for your loss.

Ermaline Sagat Dubabang.

Belen noticed that her mother used her full name, the way she signed a check. Belen kept that postcard in her purse for days. She didn't tell Jory. She believed that Jory would not understand these things. He didn't know of the invisible tug that parents sometimes had on their children.

After carrying that postcard for a week, she went to the beach, pulled it out of her purse and looked at it for a very long time. She gritted her teeth and let go a furious, frustrated scream. She ripped the postcard in half, then into quarters, then smaller, then smaller again. She held the bits of postcard, images of the church destroyed in her hands. She walked to the shore and stood there waiting for the tide to come in. When the water reached the toes of her white shoes, she threw the bits of postcard inot the water, letting the tide carry it away. She watched the paper toss and turn in the small waves, eventually floating away from her, and back, back to where it came from.

She would return to the beach. It was still her favorite place. The water meant something else to her now. It meant distance. She stood on the shore of her new home, America. Far off, far away, somewhere out there was a woman. Just a woman. A woman in a house with servants. She has two sons with three granddaughters. She has a lumber mill that is doing poorly. She would hear that the woman, named Ermaline Sagat Dubabang, would pass in her sleep. And Belen could feel nothing for a woman she did not know.

Belen looked down at her watch; visiting hours began five minutes ago. She turned, walked through the sliding doors, and stood at the closed mouth of the elevator, waiting to be lifted to the man she loved.

EMERSON

"*T*HANK YOU FOR calling," Emerson said into the phone. "My father is doing better. He can speak. I really must go, really." He hung up. That was his third call that day from some well-wisher who had seen him on television. The phone rang again and Emerson sighed. *Not another one,* he thought.

"My father thanks you for calling," Emerson began.

"Hi, it me," Michael said.

Emerson took a deep breath. He closed his eyes and gripped the phone. "Hello, Michael. Hi, *Chino.*"

"I sorry about you dad."

"I'm sorry, too. About everything. Thanks for calling. It's been crazy, but your voice has already made things a million times better." For the very first time in a long, long time, Emerson felt like crying. They'd be tears of relief. If Michael was calling there may be hope. Emerson had been feeling hopeless about a lot of things. Finally, this call gave him something to feel good about.

"I see you on TV."

"Where are you?"

"Las Vegas. You dad, okay?"

"He's better. More alert. Hey look, about what happened . . . I am so sorry. I don't blame you for being mad. I should have told you how I felt. I shouldn't have disguised it that way."

"You hurt me. I wait for months for you to tell me I Love You."

"I'm sorry."

"You should be."

"I'll make this right. I promise."

"You deserve smack in face."

"I really, really am sorry."

"You sorry you deceive me or you sorry I discover?"

"Can we meet? Can we talk or something? With everything that's going on, I just need to see you, hold you."

"I sorry about you dad. If things different, I go to you now. I hurt. I be here for you. We talk if you want, but I cannot be in same city as you now. I be you friend far away."

"I don't want you far away."

"You take care of you dad. You tell him things you should have tell me."

"What?"

"You say to you dad what you say to me?"

"No."

"Because he understand what you say. You no fool dad. Like you fool me."

"I didn't fool you."

"Yes, you fool me. Your dad is a man. Me is a man. Some time man like to talk. Sometime, man like to listen, too. It's nice to hear kind words. You say to dad what you say to me?"

"No."

"That's shame. Before my dad die, I make peace. Good son

makes peace with his dad. You only son left, it make it more important."

"Look, my dad knows how much I care for him."

"Like you care for me? You don't say what you say correct. All this time, I think you don't care for me. I tell you I love you, and you not say it back."

"I want to see you. I need to see you. I'll say anything you want me to say. Just promise to see me."

"Take care of you dad first. I don't want to see you right now. I too mad. Be with you dad first."

"Can I call you? Or can we talk later, *Chino?*" A beep interrupted his call. "Someone is trying to reach me. It might be my mom."

"I call you later."

"Okay."

Michael hung up.

"Wait. When later?"

Emerson clicked over and said, "Yes?"

"Is this Emerson Lalaban?" a male voice asked.

"Yes, this is."

"The same guy on the news? Whose dad was shot?"

Emerson smiled. It was another stranger calling to tell him things would be all right or that he is being prayed for.

"Yeah, I saw you on TV talking, calling William Baylor scum. I have something to say about that."

"What?"

"I think you're scum. It's people like William Baylor who's keeping this country from going to hell in a handbasket. I hope your father dies and you go back to your own country, rice paddy boy."

"Who is this!?!??!"

"None of your fucking business! I know where you live, asshole. I'm gonna come and cut you to pieces. It's people like you who are draggin' the country down. You hear me?"

"I hear you, you ignorant fuck. You come near me, and I'll rip your face off."

"Tough talk from Mr. Chinky. Look, you stop calling William Baylor scum or else."

"I know you're this way because of inbreeding, but don't you EVER call me again."

"If you don't stop calling Baylor scum, I'll post your fucking telephone number on the Web, and you'll get calls from more people like me, shithead."

Click.

Emerson stood in his living room, wondering what just happened. He got on the phone with Thomas Fielding and said, "Hey Thom, I just got a phone call this afternoon, some nut who said some pretty shitty things."

"We can try to get something like that traced. Did he threaten you?" Thom said.

"Yeah."

"Cases like these bring out all sorts of creeps, which is something that Baylor hoped for."

"Well, the last thing I want is for Baylor to get anything he wants. Is there something we can do? Something I can do?"

"Well, you're already doing it, talking publicly about what's happened. It did a lot of good. It'll pressure people, maybe a judge, to make sure that Baylor gets what he deserves. In the meantime, I think you should get your phone blocked, so you don't get calls like that again."

He hung up and walked out to get some air. He picked up his mail. More letters for his father. They appeared to be sympathy cards. There was one letter that looked peculiar. There was no return address and the envelope looked crumpled. He opened it, and it was a letter written in scrawled, jagged print. It read DEAD RICE PADDY BOY.

Below those words was an illustration of a bloody body with a dagger through its heart. A swastika was drawn into the handle of the dagger.

He thought about his mother. Had she been getting threatening letters or phone calls? He got into his car, preparing to relieve his mother of her shift. He arrived at the hospital. She sat with his father, massaging his arm.

"Mom?"

She looked up. She had a worried look on her face.

"Mom, can we talk outside? There's something I need to tell you."

"Yes, let's talk," she said. "I need to let you know about something, too."

JORY

An OPERATION TO remove one of the two bullets left in Jory's back was successful. The remaining bullet, Dr. Jones had said, would have to wait, maybe stay there permanently. He didn't want to interfere with it just yet. Another operation would be scheduled later.

Jory slept. He dreamed. He found himself on the beach again. His body regained its youthful appearance and strength. He jumped in the air and reveled at how his body was able to move again. He walked along the shore, skipping even. He knew he was dreaming. Soon, he would wake and return to his damaged body. For now, he was slumbering and was determined to enjoy the pleasure that the deepness of sleep brings.

The Sky above him moved, shifted. An image came into view. Jory sat back, smiling, watching the colors shoot across the Sky. His face grew grim when he saw the scene unfold above him. He turned away, but something forced him to look.

Above him, he saw Jun-Jun on his skateboard, maneuvering the dips of the sidewalk. Emerson walked on the lawn following a moth with rust-colored wings. The door to the Lalaban home was wide open. Belen sat on her small stoop to watch her children play. Jory was inside fiddling with the TV antenna, trying to make the green lines of the screen disappear.

The neighbors gardened, talking to each other over their chain-link fences. Mr. Kim was on his porch trying to decipher the directions of the new sprinkler he had just bought from Sears.

A car was heard speeding up and everyone looked. It accelerated down the street, and the vroooooooming of the engine made everyone nervous. There were children playing out there, the neighbors knew. Parents counted heads of their brood, making sure everyone was accounted for.

The car sped down and everyone heard thunder in the hot summer afternoon. A crash. Mr. Kim saw a small body rise into the air, flip-flop and fall. He saw the car speed by him.

Mr. Kim heard screams. He dropped his sprinkler. Jory shot out of the house. Belen's hands were in the air. Mr. Kim ran into his house and called an ambulance. He thought of calling the police, but he felt the need to call the ambulance first. His wife woke from napping on the couch.

"The Filipino boy was hit by a car," Mr. Kim said.

Mrs. Kim rushed outside. The neighbors gathered. Mrs. Kim approached the crowd and saw Mrs. Lalaban screaming. She ran to the hysterical woman, putting her arms around Belen. Mrs. Kim held on tightly as Belen tried to bust free. Mrs. Kim pulled Belen to the ground, trying to calm her.

Mrs. Kim searched her mind, thinking of the English words that she knew. She knew how to say My Name Is Mrs. Kim. She knew how to say How Are You Today? She knew how to say, Good Morning. She said Good Morning to people even when it was night. She did not know how to say Everything Will Be All Right. She held her crying neighbor and became immediately grateful that she did not know English because no words—English or Korean—could possibly say what needed to be said, especially seeing the blood on the road.

She saw the body of a child crumpled on the street. *Thank God it was not one of my own kids,* she thought. She had her kids spend the day with her cousins at Magic Mountain. From the angle of the body, Mrs. Kim couldn't quite tell which boy was hit. Was it the lovely boy or the other one?

When Emerson emerged from between two parked cars, Mrs. Kim got her answer. Mrs. Kim saw Emerson approach his older brother lying on the street. She saw the young boy bend down and touch his brother's shoulder.

He does not know he's dead, she thought. With one arm around Mrs. Lalaban, she offered her other hand to the child. *Come here,* she wanted to say. She racked her brain for the English words for the simple phrase Come Here. *Good morning,* she whispered.

Mrs. Kim saw Mr. Lalaban rush toward his sons. He picked Emerson up and fell to his knees, keeping his son's head away from the blood and the dead boy. Jory's hand hovered over Jun's head, eventually stroking the fallen boy. Jory looked up, and Mrs. Kim saw how the sun created shadows on his face, dark hideous spots by his nose and under his brows. She saw Jory open his mouth to scream or yell, and Mrs. Kim braced herself for an ear-splitting noise. Instead his mouth remained open, but no sound emerged.

An ambulance came, then the police.

"Did anyone see what happened?" an officer asked. Mr. Kim yelled, "Car. Blue car."

"What kind of car?"

"A Comet," Mr. Kim said. "A Mercury Comet."

Medics approached the Lalaban family. One medic said, "You have to get back, okay? You have to move back, so we can get to him."

Jory, slowly moving backward, fell on his butt. Emerson held on tightly to his torso. He watched the police and medics look down at the body, wondering how to proceed. How do you lift a bleeding boy with a broken body from the ground onto the stretcher? A small pool of blood surrounded Jun-Jun, a thick, wet puddle.

The medics picked up the crumpled body and put him into the ambulance. One of the medics offered his hand to the Lalabans, offering a ride to the hospital. Jory took one tentative step forward when he heard his wife scream.

"This cannot be. No. It is not," Belen said. Mrs. Kim slowly walked Belen to the ambulance. She stepped into the metal van, followed by Jory and Emerson.

"Which hospital you go?" Mrs. Kim asked. "We follow."

"Queen of Angels," the medic said.

Belen muttered all the way to the hospital. She kept saying, "This cannot be. This cannot be."

"This cannot be," Jory said, pounding his fist into the sand of the beach. He stood up and screamed at the Sky. "This cannot . . ."

"Shhhhhhh," Jory heard. He looked around the beach.

"This cannot be," Jory whispered, falling down onto his knees, letting himself collapse onto the sand.

"Shhhhhhh, honey-bunny," Jory heard in the darkness of his mind.

Jory saw the Sky fall, the tragic image overwhelming him. Suddenly, the image was dragged back into the Sky. Jory closed his eyes, repeating, "This cannot be!"

"Shhhhhhhh."

Jory opened his eyes. He saw Belen sitting by his side. Emerson was at the end of the bed.

"You're having a nightmare, Dad," Emerson said. His face breaking into a slight smile. "Just a nightmare."

Jory was groggy. The familiar feeling of painkillers drenched his body.

"You're doing great, Dad. They took out another bullet. One more to go."

He looked up at the ceiling, feeling nothing.

"Good news, Jory," Belen said. "Dr. Jones said if you get a little stronger, you can come home. So rest, okay. Rest and get better."

Jory nodded his head and thought, *Home.*

DECEMBER

JORY

"*T*AKE ME HOME," Jory said, sitting upright. It had been a week since the operation, and it pained Jory to sit that way. However, he wanted to show the doctor that he was well, at least getting better. He had been in the hospital for two months, doing the exercises the physical therapist instructed, though one side of him seemed stronger than the other. He built his strength so he could go back to the house on Carondelet Avenue.

Emerson said, "Dr. Jones, what do you think?"

"He is making remarkable progress."

"He can be discharged then?" Belen said.

"Well, I don't know," Dr. Jones said.

Jory watched as the three adults talked about him.

"I think my father can handle it."

"Yes, me, too," said Belen.

"We can discharge him, but he might have to be back for another operation. Looks like that remaining bullet is pushing against some nerves. That's why you're feeling weaker on your left side."

"That's fine," Belen said.

"Maybe we should keep him here until the last bullet is removed."

"What?" Belen said. "More days in the hospital? We can't afford—afford him being miserable here. He would feel much better at home. It would put him in a better frame of mind to be operated on. You know this, Dr. Jones. A patient must feel better, emotionally as well as physically, when he gets operated on. My husband doesn't like it here. He can recuperate at home."

I'm a chair, Jory thought. *A chair. Everyone is talking without consulting me. That's the way Jun was treated,* Jory thought. *Like an object.* When Jun-Jun was pronounced dead, the doctor wanted to know what was to be done with *it.* The doctor said, "Which cemetery would you like *it* to be moved to?"

Jory said, "I'd like to take *him* home."

"I'd like to take Jory home," Belen said. "Let him recuperate there."

"Yes," Jory said, "I would to take *him* home. I'd like to take my son home and bury him in our back yard."

The doctor smiled and said, "Oh, you want to get your son cremated, then take him home? Sprinkle his ashes in the garden, perhaps?"

"No, I want to take his body home and bury him whole in the back yard."

Jory explained to the doctor that his child needed to be buried there. He needed to be close to his parents or else Jun-Jun's spirit would get lonely; so lonely, in fact, that Jun-Jun would call others to join him. Perhaps even take away his other son Emerson from the earth. Jory knew this to be true. When Andres died in the orphanage, three more children followed. He wanted Jun buried at home, in the back yard. The way Belen's relatives were buried.

"I know this sounds strange to you, doctor, but they do this in the Philippines."

"Well, this isn't the Philippines and you can't take *it* home," the doctor said. "You certainly can't bury it in the back yard. You just can't."

"I want to take *him* home. Yes, I will bury *him* in my back yard."

Jun's body was in the hospital morgue for two days while the doctor did everything that he could to change Jory's mind. The doctor assumed that Jory, being Filipino, like so many other Filipinos he'd encountered, was Catholic. The doctor brought in a priest, a man he'd become familiar with from giving last rites to past patients. The doctor was dumbfounded when Jory did not listen to the priest, but yawned several times as the priest spoke. However, the doctor was determined to have his way and urged a nurse, a Filipina, to talk him out of it.

"We're in America now," the nurse said. "Do things the American way. Mr. Lalaban, you'll have trouble. What if you move? If you move, you'll have to take the body with you. I wouldn't want to move into a house that had a dead body in the back yard."

Jory did not care for this nurse, not one bit. He could tell she was from Manila. Big-city people have no concept of life in the province. He saw her name plate. Her name was Maravic Applegate. She obviously had married someone who was not Filipino and bought into her husband's American ways.

Jory went to the hospital two days in a row, waiting for the body to be handed over. In that time, Jory had constructed a coffin, a skill he learned from burying the orphan boys in the Philippines, and dug an open hole in the back yard. He was adamant about his decision, sitting in the hospital lounge, arms and legs crossed, arguing with the hospital to surrender the body. He planned to have his son's body wrapped in blankets from home, placed in the backseat of the Nova, and to bury him among the chrysanthemums.

The doctor was relentless, stating, "Well, there are city ordinances or something that won't let you do that. You can't just bury a dead body in your back yard. It is illegal."

"Illegal or not. I want to bury him there."

The doctor brought in the hospital's legal council to convince Jory that what he wanted to do was somehow against the law. The attorney stated that there were health and safety codes in place to prevent a dead body from being buried somewhere that wasn't a cemetery.

"You could go to jail," the doctor said. "Do you want that?"

A week later, Jory sat at Matson Mortuary, a funeral home in his neighborhood. Jun was dressed in his best suit, prepared for burial the next day. The viewing was widely attended by Jun's classmates and people in the neighborhood, including the Kims, who went out of their way to be helpful. People passed the coffin, taking one long look at the child. There were bruises on Jun's face, but makeup was heavily applied to make Jun's face appear unmarred.

"We should go now," whispered Mrs. Kim to Jory. "This place close soon. You go, too. Your wife need rest and it children sleep time."

"I don't want to go yet," Jory said.

"Jory, I'm tired, so tired," Belen said.

"Go with the Kims and I'll see you back home."

Jory did not look up as he heard the footsteps of the Kims and his wife and son taper away. He looked around the room. Everyone was gone. Jory opened the casket and lifted Jun out. His son felt like a stiff, wooden doll.

"Don't be afraid," Jory whispered into his son's ear. "I'll take you home where you belong." He held Jun's body tightly, sucking back tears. *You belong near us,* he thought. He proceeded to the Nova.

When he reached his home, the house was dark. His family was sleeping, Jory knew. He drove the car as far up the driveway as possible. He went into the garage and retrieved the small coffin. He placed the coffin by the hole near the garden. The faces of sunflowers looked down at him.

He went to the Nova and took Jun from the back seat. He laid the boy delicately into the coffin, clearing Jun's forehead of stray hairs. He looked up to the dark Sky and said, "Moon, Stars, and Sky, guide my son. Lift him, lift him high. Take him to the place of his ancestors. Jun, you must go. Go and never come back. Join your ancestors and, in time, we will come."

Jory bowed his head, looking at the corpse of his child. He thought of Ralph Waldo Emerson. His wife Ellen Tucker died. A year after her death, he opened her coffin, an act that would change his life, leading him to become the writer he became. Staring into the decay of what was once a creature who breathed and laughed and ate and stirred so much joy, Jory understood why Ralph Waldo Emerson had so much reverence for nature. Nature breathes, taking what was left of the dearly dead and exhaling them back into the world.

Jory put the lid on the coffin, and lowered his child into the shallow grave. He pushed dirt into the hole, hearing the clumps of soil hit the coffin. Jory kneeled before the grave and continued to pray, "Sun, Moon, Stars, Trees, Mountains, take him. Lift him to the place of his ancestors. Take him home."

"Doctor," Jory heard Emerson say. "What would we have to do to take him home?"

"Well, you'll need a wheelchair and a hospital bed."

EMERSON

*E*MERSON BROUGHT HALF-A-DOZEN letters to a press conference where two police officers agreed to meet and show support for the families of the shooting. The press conference would be held inside a classroom. They couldn't hold it in the yard, afraid that it might rain. He showed the letters to the police officers. They seemed to be written by the same person, and all the letters threatened death to Emerson.

"That's to be expected," Officer. No. 1 said. "Now that you're being more visible, talking publicly about what happened to your family, you're going to have to expect this."

"I've told my mom not to open suspicious letters."

"How is your father doing?" Officer No. 2 asked.

Emerson looked at the two men. *Leave him alone,* Emerson wanted to say, but he said, "Much better. It looks like we're going to take him home."

"Can we talk to him at some point?"

"He . . . he . . ." Emerson said. He looked at the two officers in front of him, and his stomach became queasy. He looked beyond the police officers and saw people preparing for the press conference. Someone attached a mike to a stand near the podium.

"Question him about the incident."

"Um," Emerson said, walking away toward the makeshift stage where he would sit.

The officers followed him and one of them asked, "We've been holding off 'cause he's in bad shape. Can we talk to your father?"

"I don't know about that." *Leave him alone.*

Officer. No. 1 said, "If we could talk to your father, get some perspective on what happened the day he was shot, it could really help."

Emerson heard knocking. He turned and saw a man tapping the mike to see if it worked. The knocking continued, and Emerson thought of the time just after Jun died. Knocking from the front door woke him. He was only six years old. He got out of bed and opened the front door. Two policemen were there. "Good morning," one of them said.

"Hi," Emerson said to the two policemen at the door.

"Good morning." The older policemen spoke in his kindest voice. "Are your parents home?"

"If we could talk to him," Officer No. 2 said. "It would really help."

Emerson remembered that the policemen at the door looked serious. He went to his parent's bedroom. His father wasn't there, but his mother was asleep, slightly snoring. Emerson watched his mother and knew, even in rest, she was miserable. He tapped her shoulder, but she wouldn't budge.

"Mom?"

She continued to sleep, her mouth slightly open. He shook her. She stirred and said, "Jun?"

"No, it's me."

She opened her eyes, and Emerson will never forget the disappointment in her face when she saw it was him standing there.

"What? Is it time for the burial?"

"No, some police are outside?"

"Police?"

Emerson brought his mother a robe and followed her to the front door. She patted her hair down as she spoke.

"Yes?" she said.

"Um, ma'am. We got a call from Michael Matson at Matson Mortuary. He said that, uh, a body is missing."

"I don't understand."

"Apparently someone took the body of your son."

Emerson saw his mother fall forward. One of the policemen caught her and said, "Are you all right?"

"Yes," she said. She put her hand to her mouth and looked around the room. She turned around and slowly walked toward the back door. The policemen joined her. Emerson followed. They were in the back doorway when Emerson saw his father looking up to the sky, whispering something.

Emerson stood in the doorway as the two officers drew their guns and pointed it at his father.

"Sir," one of the officers said. "Put your hands in the air and please step away."

"Jory," his mother said. "Do what the men say. Please, honey-bunny."

Emerson watched his father raise his hands and walk away from the mound of dirt in the back yard. He watched the policemen handcuff him.

Emerson ran to his father, yelling at the policemen. "Leave him alone," Emerson said, kicking the older police officer. He pushed and shoved as the policemen led his father to the squad car.

"Leave him alone," Emerson said.

"Sure, if that's how you want it," Officer No. 2 said. "At some point, when he gets better, we'd like to interview him. Just talk to him. Your father's testimony would help a great deal."

"I said, leave him alone . . . for now. Maybe in a few weeks."

⌒

THE USUAL CAST was at the press conference: Sylvia Jacobs, Rabbi Shultz, families from the Edelman Center, and Thom Fielding walked in just in time for the start of the conference. There was only a handful of press who arrived, mostly Jewish and Asian press. None of the major papers and no television crews were there.

"Where is everybody?" Emerson asked Rabbi Shultz.

"They've moved on," he said. "I've seen this a million times. They're more interested in the son of a president whose plane recently crashed."

"Is the mayor coming?"

"Probably not. He's been so busy. Besides, he's let us know he has our complete support."

"Really?"

"Yes, he made a personal donation to the Edelman Center. And he's visited Sylvia several times."

"Yes," she confirmed. "He came personally to visit my son. Even sent flowers. He'd visited Diane, the counselor who had been shot. Of course, he made it a point to have all the Jewish papers there, reminding them to support him in the next election."

"Politicians," Rabbi Shultz said, shaking his head. "Anything for a photo op."

"Well, he's never visited my family," Emerson said, sitting back in his seat, crossing his legs and arms.

"His press secretary came to represent the mayor's office," the

Rabbi said, pointing to a balding man sipping coffee. "Maybe you can ask him why."

Rabbi Shultz started the press conference by demanding that Baylor get the maximum sentence for his crime. He said, "Any judge who will not sentence him to the maximum should not be a judge in this city."

As he spoke, Emerson looked out at the pathetic crowd, half of what it was when Emerson first spoke. Even Daisy Chan couldn't make it. She said she had a full workload that day. He noticed that there were less people showing up at all the events. This saddened him.

He looked around the classroom. Drawings done by children were on the wall. A long strip of paper lined one wall, showing how to write capital and lowercase letters. There was a similar strip in his classroom when he was a boy. A few days after Jun's death, he was asked to stand in the front of his class, underneath the strip of paper with examples of the alphabet. His teacher said, "Emerson, we all know what happened and all of your classmates thinks it's terrible, don't we, class?"

Emerson saw two dozen heads nod.

The teacher wrote three phrases on the blackboard. The teacher went over the phrases and asked the children to repeat after her.

"I'm sorry for your loss," the teacher said.

"I'm sorry for your loss," the children repeated.

"You have my deepest sympathies," she said.

"You have my deepest sympathies."

"Now this might be a hard one, class," the teacher said. "If there is anything I can do, don't hesitate to ask."

"If there is anything I can do . . ."

"Together, class. Don't hesitate to ask."

"Don't hesitate to ask."

"Very good, everyone. Now, Emerson, go back to your seat and know that everyone is very sad about what happened. Let's open our books, and who can tell me what a vowel is?"

Emerson sat down and a child leaned over to him and whispered in his ear, "I am sorry for your loss."

That sympathy went on for years, something that Emerson couldn't seem to escape. As he grew, he left Rosemont Elementary School, went onto Virgil Junior High, then Belmont High School. Throughout his childhood and adolescence, kids were overly kind to Emerson, never forgetting that hot summer when a boy never returned to class. Especially when rumors hit that the family had gone off the deep end, the Lalaban house was haunted, and the neighborhood was stained with the boy's ghost. No one ever found the Comet.

Nondescript children who grew to become teenage academics offered to help him with his homework. Emerson always said, "Thanks, but no thanks." Pony-tailed girls who grew to become pony-tailed cheerleaders said a preening and obligatory "Hi, Emerson" in the halls. Emerson nodded. And even little boys who grew up to join neighborhood gangs told incoming gang bangers to leave that Emerson guy alone. Don't beat him up, don't steal from him. He's been through enough already.

Every one knew about the blue Mercury Comet that was never found. And everyone in that neighborhood had a feeling as to why. The Mexicans knew, the Salvadorans knew, the Chinese knew, the Koreans knew, the smattering of white people knew, other Filipinos knew, and the black people who lived there shook their heads because they knew before anyone else did.

Even though there may have been good intentions in finding the speeding Comet, someone else got shot or robbed or arrested for drug dealing. The death of this child would be racked up as yet another tragedy that occurred and was labeled Unsolved.

Emerson looked at Rabbi Shultz speaking about injustice. He

looked out into the audience and saw the press secretary with a cup of coffee in his hand, looking at his watch.

Rabbi Shultz introduced Sylvia Jacobs as the second speaker. Everyone watched Sylvia talk about the progress her son is making. She thanked the mayor's office for their continued support.

Emerson couldn't believe how poorly attended this press conference was. There were mainly Jewish papers and Asian papers sitting the audience. He'd gotten on a first-name basis with most of the reporters from the Asian papers. They'd been very good about reporting the story. Soon, they might go away as well. Just like Jun's death, this tragedy will simply be overtaken by another tragedy. This Emerson refused to have. His father deserved more. His dad certainly deserved more than having the mayor's office send an underling

"Thank you, Sylvia," Rabbi Shultz said.

"Families will never be the same after this incident," said the Rabbi. "And now, to give an update on his father, is Emerson Lalaban."

Emerson stood and approached the microphone.

"Thank you for coming," Emerson said. "It is truly unfortunate that I had to meet Rabbi Shultz and Sylvia this way. They are good people, and I wish we could have met under better circumstances." Emerson saw the press secretary still sipping coffee and checking his watch. Emerson continued, "It's too bad the mayor couldn't be here."

He saw the press secretary look up.

"Then again, my family hasn't had much opportunity to spend time with the mayor or really sit down to talk about how troubling it was that an Asian man was shot down like this."

He saw the press secretary spill his coffee on his suit.

"I hope our fine mayor considers all his constituents important."

He saw the press secretary hastily pat his suit with a napkin. A hand went into the air. It belonged to one of the Asian reporters.

"Are you saying the mayor is not providing the kind of support that he should?" the Reporter asked.

"Not at all," Emerson said. "I know the mayor is busy. Running a city takes a lot of time. Like going to the opening of that new opera last week in downtown."

The press secretary looked around the room, fussing with his suit.

Another hand went into air.

"I'm Nancy Sekizawa with *Asia America Today*. What has the mayor done to show his support for you and your family?"

Emerson smiled. "You mean besides forgetting that I was part of the press conference we held last month? Give me a minute, I'm sure I'll think of something."

He saw the reporters furiously writing on their pads. He saw the press secretary watching this, too.

"Perhaps," Emerson began, "you can ask his representative. I believe his press secretary is here. Would you like to comment?"

The heads turned around.

"Well," the press secretary said, "the mayor is personally invested in this . . . and . . . he's . . . he's scheduling a visit with the Lalabans shortly."

MICHAEL

*M*ICHAEL STOOD IN the shower, vigorously scrubbing his body with Purity soap, a product he'd buy in Asia, one that promised to "whiten and tighten" by incorporating the ancient ingredient of crushed pearls.

Water splashed onto his face, and he wondered what Emerson was doing right now. Michael was tossing a mental coin as to whether he should give Emerson a second chance or not. Heads, give the bum another opportunity. Tails, dump the bastard. He was leaning toward heads—but not by much. He wondered about that emotional place that led to the point of their breaking up, thinking that, maybe, the course of their relationship would have blossomed if Emerson handled things differently.

Michael had been dating Emerson for four months when he uttered, "I love, I think. You." Michael never said it again, hoping that Emerson would respond in a similar way eventually. When he didn't, Michael acted like it was no big deal, acted like he'd said what he said by accident. In actuality, Michael was crushed. Saying I Love You was the beginning of other phrases like Where Do You Want To Spend Our Next Vacation or What Shall We Name Our Newly Adopted Baby?

He waited, yearned for Emerson to say those three words. Michael had never felt this way about anyone, and it confused him. It remained thick in his mind, and he wondered if there was a way to make himself more lovable. He lost five pounds he didn't need to lose, conditioned his hair more thoroughly, conducted more facial scrubs, and scraped his mouth with wax that had magic emollients that kept the lips soft and supple. Michael put gel into his hair, moisturized his skin, and dabbed antipuffiness cream under his eyes with the potential of hearing I Love You by the end of a date. When it didn't happen, he looked into the mirror and wondered what imperfection did he overlook? What gruesome flaw stood in the way of Emerson fully embracing him?

There was nothing more physically that Michael could do and so he arrived at the conclusion that there must be some character flaw he needed to address. Especially when he entered a room and saw Emerson speaking to someone on the phone, quickly hanging up when Emerson saw him standing there.

"Who that?" Michael asked.

"Nobody. Nobody," Emerson would say.

"You seeing somebody else?"

"No, just you."

"Then who you keeping talking to? This John or June person."

Emerson took Michael's hand and said, "A friend. From up North. We've known each other for a long time. I'm not seeing anyone else. I don't *want* to see anyone else. Just you."

Just you. Michael took those words as poisonous confirmation that despite his grooming and honing of physical beauty, despite his efforts to better himself like going to the theater, despite learning to say You're Welcome to someone's Thank You, all his aspirations to Pearlhood were for naught. He was and forever would be: just. Just a guy, just a steward, just a piece of rock yearning to be a jewel.

Michael's only recourse was to behave more jewel-like, behave in a way he assumed Pearls always behaved: happy and carefree. He decided to be in a perpetually good mood, accommodating his needs to meet Emerson's, agreeing to see a movie he didn't particularly care to see and paying for dinners he couldn't afford. He took NoDoz to pep himself up after a long flight and forced a smile when he was in a sour mood. He laughed at times that didn't warrant a chuckle and made love when he wasn't sexual.

In their screwing, Emerson spoke, saying things Michael mostly did not understand. He understood a few things that were said during passion, the basics like I Want You or God, GOD! But for the most part, he didn't understand what Emerson said. He thought nothing of it. It was simply a man whispering (sometimes yelling) words lost in sex.

Michael was sure I Love You was coming when Emerson held him as they slept or kissed him when he left. Emerson appeared loving. It was then that Michael became curious.

"What you say to me?" Michael asked.

"Huh?"

"What you say to me when we sex?"

"Nothing."

"Yes, you do. You say something."

"I don't remember what I said. Probably something about how beautiful you are and how much I dig being in bed with you." Emerson pulled Michael into him. "C'mon. It's nothing, *Chino.*"

The next few times they had sex, Michael waited for Emerson to speak. He didn't. Michael had to fly and would be gone for a few days. He often worked business class, serving executives cocktails.

Some flight attendants hated business class because the men and women were so snooty sometimes. Despite specific instructions to turn off all mechanical devices before flight, they remained on their cell phones till the very last minute or refused to turn off their computers.

Michael didn't mind that. He liked working business class because he secretly hoped that he would meet a Pearl among them who would sweep him away, keep him in some luxurious apartment in Hong Kong. To no avail. He knew that there were gay men in business class. He could tell the way one of them looked at him a little too long or a casual conversation about the weather lingered longer than it should.

He flirted with these men, but they were often very cautious, probably afraid of any indiscretion that would jeopardize their standing as business people. Instead, Michael saw them lurking in the gay parts of Taipei or Phuket or Tokyo. They weren't in suits but in casual clothes, drunk, hitting on men, trying to score before they returned to their offices in their homeland, maybe even to their wives.

Business people were the same around the world. He had been flying for four years and had heard every language spoken in that neat part of the plane separated by curtains. He heard Cantonese, Mandarin, Japanese, French, German, Spanish, English, Thai, Vietnamese. They spoke about money or transactions or appointments, Michael assumed. Every once in a while a person would call his family saying he would be home soon.

Once Michael returned to Los Angeles, Emerson was at it again; in the heat of orgasm, Emerson spoke words, phrases Michael did not understand. Michael was so frustrated that an hour after their first sexual encounter, he coaxed Emerson into another round of pleasure. Michael wanted the sex to last longer, listened intently to what Emerson was saying. He heard the syllables, phrases, memorizing them in his mind, and when Emerson was through, his body heaving then shivering, signaling that he had reached the height of ecstasy, Emerson held Michael in his arms and proceeded to go to sleep.

Michael slowly pulled himself away, got up, found a piece of paper, and wrote out what Emerson had said. He looked at the words and could not recognize its meaning. Pee pee ya ti ha. He would ask his friends who were better at English to tell him the meaning later.

Michael had called every English speaker he knew, reciting the phrases to each person. Each person, including a woman who studied American literature, said they could not decipher what he said.

"Are you sure you're saying it correctly?" a friend asked.

"I'm positive. He say it just like this," Michael said, rattling the phrases off.

"Maybe he's saying, *People pee then they yawn?*"

"Why he say that?" Michael said, almost disgusted.

"You must be saying it wrong, because that doesn't sound right to me either. Are you sure it's even English?"

Michael had a date with Emerson later that night. He wondered if maybe Emerson was simply moaning during sex or excreting animalistic sounds that sex often evokes in people. They were the frivolous ramblings of a man in the throes of excitement. Why, Michael had one lover who used to scream, "Take me over the mountain! Take me over the mountain!" when he orgasmed. He once dated a man who yelled, "I am Godzilla, stomping out Japan." And then there were those who made gorilla-like grunting sounds or cooed like birds. There were those who made inaudible noises or sighed like it was their last breath. What did it matter what Emerson said? He was just releasing in sounds what his body was feeling.

With this resolve, Michael continued to have sex with Emerson not thinking of what was being said. Emerson's arm or leg draped over him. Feeling Emerson's breath on his neck. Emerson's body aligned with his. Resting his head on Emerson's chest, just below the nipple. Partaking in weird conversations that would have sounded ridiculous or encroaching months before, but now sounded sublime.

"You have dead dreams on your face," Emerson said, wiping the crust away from Michael's face in the morning.

"Dead dreams?" Michael said, closing his eyes, waiting for Emerson to finish clearing his face.

"That's what my dad called them. He said when you sleep, you dream. Sometimes you wake up before the dream finishes in your head. It has no where else to go, so it dies and squeezes out of your eyes."

"You have dead dreams on your face, too."

"Yeah, I know."

⌒

MICHAEL TOWELED HIMSELF off. The phone rang.

"Herro," Michael said.

"Hi, *Chino.*"

"Emerson, you okay? You papa?"

"Better. Much better. My dad is coming home next week."

"Cool."

"The mayor is coming for a visit, too. I fixed it so he can come when my dad is at home."

Silence.

"How are you, *Chino?*"

"Why you keep using different language when you talk to me?"

"I didn't mean anything by it. It was just something I learned when I was a kid, s'all."

"Sorry. Don't mean to jump on your throat."

"Don't be sorry. I deserve it. May I see you? Please? When will you be in LA again?"

"I fly into Vegas only."

"I'd like to see you."

"Why?"

"Because . . . you make me happy. I feel good when I'm with you."

Michael lowered his head. He looked out the window of his hotel. He could see a big cowboy, an attraction to a casino, lit up in lights with his arm moving back and forth. He hadn't seen Emerson in almost three months and, as much as he loathed feeling it, he missed that sack of shit.

"All right," Michael said, "I see you for a while. You come to Vegas."

"What?"

A sense of power came over Michael, one that delights any spurned lover. He would be in control. "You cross desert for me?"

"Yeah, I would. I would do anything to see you. Not for long though. I gotta be in LA cause my dad and everything. Just for a day maybe?"

"I pick you up at airport."

"Uh, I'm a little tight on money right now. I'll drive. I'll leave early in the morning and be there by noon. Then I'll go back to LA at night."

"Okay. When?"

"Saturday. Where?"

"I meet you in gay part of Vegas. On Paradise Road."

"Anywhere in particular?"

"Um, the biggest landmark is Hard Rock Hotel."

"Hard Rock on Paradise. Gotcha. I'll see you at noon. And I'm really looking forward to it. I miss you. I miss you more than you know, Michael. I've never felt this way about another guy."

BELEN

"CAN YOU PLEEEEEASE feed Mr. Addison?" the girl asked.

"No," Belen said to the youngest nurse on staff. "You lost the coin toss."

"Please, Belen, he makes me nervous. That cane of his has a mind of its own. I just hate it. I can't feed him. I just can't"

. Belen looked at this nurse, all of twenty-five years old, too inexperienced to handle the Addisons of this world.

"Belen, I was told he has to eat. Be on a regular diet. That's what his daughters ordered."

"He can starve then."

"Belen, please. I'll let you have one of my vacation days. I know you need 'em."

Belen looked at this naïve young thing, offering a well-earned day of rest because she didn't know how to handle a fool. She took it as an opportunity to spend another day with Jory. Her husband was doing quite well, but Belen was cautious. The Curse has a way of throwing surprises.

She picked up the tray of food and headed toward Mr. Addison's room. He sat on his bed, one hand under his blanket. His cane a safe distance away. A good sign.

"Why, hi there," Mr. Addison said.

"Hello, Mr. Addison. Are you going to behave yourself?"

"Always do."

She approached his bed, laying the tray on his lap.

"Can you put the napkin on me," Mr. Addison said with a smile that indicated folly.

"Mr. Addison," Belen said. "I'm not in the mood to play games." *No more games,* she thought. *I don't want to be a chess piece anymore. I don't want to be sacrificed for someone else's gain.*

Jory was coming home, and she hoped all would go well. One bullet was left in his body. One operaton left. She hoped this would be the last one. She knew that every time someone was operated on, anything could go wrong. People have died during the simplest procedures.

"C'mon, put on my napkin. Don't want to ruin my pajamas," he said. "I'd do it myself but my arthritis is acting up again."

Belen undid the cloth napkin, letting the metal utensils clatter onto the tray. She placed the napkin around his neck and felt his hand on her breast.

"My arthritis is feeling a lot better," he said, grinning.

My life is in chaos, she thought, *and you have the nerve to touch me. My husband's life is ruined, my life will never be the same. I'll have to pay for another operation I can't afford, wondering if my husband has the strength to survive another operation, and you, Mr. Addison, think you can do whatever you please.*

Belen picked up the butter knife, wielding it at the old man, and said, "Mr. Addison, you touch me again and I'll cut off your last good testicle!"

Taken aback, Mr. Addison looked at her and said, "Yes, ma'am."

She left the room with Mr. Addison mumbling, "You can't talk to me like that. I pay good money here. I'll tell my daughters about you. You'll see."

⌐

IT WAS ELEVEN in the evening when she got home. She looked around the house and thought, *Oh, there is so much to do, so much.* She had four days to get the house ready for Jory's return home. And the mayor! Belen whispered some small profanity under her breath about Emerson inviting the mayor over, too! So little time.

She started with her bedroom, pulling off her sheets, bundling them up, then throwing them into the washing machine. She pulled out the vacuum and went over the carpet with it. She sprayed Windex onto all the windows and realized one of the curtains was torn. She took it off the rod and reminded herself to properly sew it. She dusted the bureau, the end tables, and the lamps.

Next is Jun and Emerson's room, she thought. *Why do I keep doing that? Next is Emerson's room.* She looked at Emerson's bed. She turned to the wall that Jun's bed used to be pushed up against. *That's where the hospital bed will go,* Belen thought. *Where Jun used to sleep. After all these years, that space will be occupied.*

Her oldest son's bed was long gone, delivered to Goodwill. That was something Jory wanted to do as soon as he was out on bail: donate all of Jun's things, including his clothes. Belen refused.

"I don't want to get rid of these," Belen said, referring to a neatly folded pile of shirts.

"Honey," Jory said, "we should give them away. It's best."

"Let's keep Jun's clothes. It's a waste. Emerson will wear them soon enough. He'll grow into them." That was a stupid idea, Belen knew. Jun's clothes would never look right on Emerson, but she continued, "Yes. We can save money that way. We'll keep them and when Emerson outgrows them, we can get rid of them."

She saw Jory pack the clothes into a box and asked, "What are you doing?"

"I'll put them in the garage. We can get them later," he said.

"Don't pack them," she said, shaking her head. "Just keep them in the drawers. Why put them away? Bugs will get into them or something. They'll be destroyed. We'll just have to get them all over again. The way Emerson's growing, he'll fit into the clothes in just a few months. We'll just keep them in the drawers and save them. Just keep them in the drawers."

Jory left the clothes alone, and Belen put away the Hang Ten shirts with tiny footprints on the chest, the Ocean Pacific corduroy pants, the Toughskins jeans. She put the brightly colored shirts on hangers, placing them in the closet. She delicately folded the jeans in a way to insure a crease. She patted them when she placed them in a wooden bureau.

Still, so much to do, Belen thought. She decided to do the bathroom and kitchen last, something she would get to in the next couple of days. She turned to leave the room, but went to the bureau. She pulled open a drawer and saw the empty space there. Emerson did wear the clothes, and they were eventually given away, except for a few items that were tucked away in a closet.

"Ay!" she said. She forgot to light Jun's candle! She ran to the mantle in the living room, picked up the matches next to the candle and said, "I'm sorry, Jun-Jun. I just got so caught up with things, you know. Your dad is coming home. The mayor is coming, too." She lit the candle and stared at the photo for a long time.

The telephone rang.

"Hello?" she said, still looking at the photo.

"Hey, Mom."

"Emerson, what's the matter? Is everything all right?"

"Yeah, sorry for calling so late. I wanted to let you know I need to go away on Saturday, something I need to do. I'll be there tomorrow, Friday, but I need Saturday to do stuff. Dad's a lot better now, and I know you usually spend the whole week-end with him anyway. Would you mind if I don't go that day?"

"No, I don't mind." *How sweet,* Belen thought. Emerson never checked in with her before. "What do you need to do?"

"I have to visit a friend. I haven't seen him in a while."

"Okay, but you'll be back Sunday?"

"Yup."

She hung up the phone. She stared at Jun's image, closed her eyes and prayed that Jun was okay wherever he was. This was something she did immediately after Jun's death. She'd sit quietly, hoping that her oldest son's spirit was peaceful somewhere.

"Mom, what are you doing?" Emerson asked when he was a boy.

"I'm praying."

"What does it do?"

"It keeps my head together," she said.

"What's it like?"

"Well," she said. "I think things, wonder about things. Maybe I have a question. I pray, and sometimes I get the answer."

"Does somebody give you the answer?"

"You can say that."

"How do you know it's the right answer?"

"I don't. I hope it's the right answer."

"How does it work?"

Belen thought about it for a second. "Well, it's like the telephone. You talk into it and you can't see the other person, but you know someone's there. Then when you talk, someone talks back. A little voice talks to you. Prayer is like that."

She wished she had a better response, something more wise. Maybe Emerson would have had a better sense of godlier things if she did. At the time, that was the best she could do. *So much to do,* she thought. *So much.*

JORY

"*H*OW ARE YOU today, Dad?" Emerson asked.

"Good," Jory said. "I can't wait to leave this place."

"Mom and I were scared."

"I was a little scared, too."

"Dad, some men are here to ask some questions. You've been doing well lately. I said it was okay if they came by."

"Sure. Sure."

Emerson opened the door. Two officers entered, along with a man in a suit.

"Thank you for meeting with us," Officer No. 1 said.

"Your account will help," Officer No. 2 said.

"No problem," Jory said, looking at the two men in black. Emerson stood by the foot of his bed with Thom Fielding.

Officer No. 2 said, "I've seen buddies gunned down, and I wish they recovered as well as you."

"My dad," Emerson said, "still has another bullet they have to pull out, but he's doing good."

"You'll make an excellent witness," Thom Fielding said.

"You're the one who's going to get the sonofabitch," Jory said. The men in the room laughed a bit.

"Yes," said Thom. "I'll get the sonofabitch. He's in custody now. He's pleaded guilty, and we're just waiting for trial. We're going to prosecute him with all we've got. He won't be out for a long time."

"Good!" Jory said.

"Dad, I'll show these guys out. I think the nurse has been holding off on your bath until we were through. I'll be back when she's done."

He watched Emerson exit his room taking the men with him. Jory hadn't dealt with policemen since he was arrested. It was just as long since he'd spoken with a lawyer fighting on his behalf. The last time was when he had to go to court for taking Jun's body.

"The family has been through a lot, Your Honor," his court-appointed attorney said to the judge. "My client has agreed to move the body to a cemetery."

The judge took pity on him and only fined him five hundred dollars. The judge said, "Mr. Lalaban, do you understand that what you did was wrong?"

Jory replied, "I understand what I did was illegal."

"Now, Your Honor, Mr. Lalaban and his family have the task of finding a burial plot for their son."

Jory shook the attorney's hand, thanking her for all her work. He did what the attorney said he would do. He went to Forrest Lawn Cemetery and was told of some lovely areas with flowers that would make a beautiful place to bury his son. He visited the different burial spots and was shown one area where his son might lie.

It was near a bed of pink carnations. He walked around the area, looking down at the metal plates surrounding the plot where Jun might be laid. Anna Melissa Morgan, 1932–1976; R. Sloan Perry, 1918–1960; Joseph Heng, 1925–1967; Elliot Sean Davis, 1919–1973; Elena Lopez, 1910–1972. Jory said the area wasn't quite right. He was shown other parts of the cemetery, grassy pieces of land with trees and birds singing. Jory looked to the ground reading the names and dates. He shook his head and decided that those areas were not the right places either.

He was shown one plot and next to it was a grave that read: Tommy Delaney, 1960–1969. There were fresh flowers laid on the grass and a little football placed by the metal plate. *The boy was loved,* Jory thought. He knew this was the site where Jun must lay.

"Hello, Tommy," Jory said, kneeling down. "I don't know why you died, but I hope it wasn't too painful." He pulled dried blades of grass from the ground. "My son didn't suffer at all. At least that's what the doctor said. He was hit by a car, but his body went into shock. His body didn't feel anything after a while. I'm grateful about that.

"Tommy Delaney is a good name. I'm sure your parents miss you and you miss them. It is lonely being the youngest one here. I hope the adults here don't treat you bad.

"I'm going to lay my son next to you. He is a good boy. He is smart and friendly, always did good in school and can teach you many things. He is good at games and never cheats. He would make a good friend to you, Tommy Delaney. I know you are a good boy, too, because no one your age can have done anything so bad. I don't want to put my child next to those adults. Their spirits might not be kind to kids.

"My son will make good company. Yes, he will. I hope you will get along because boys your age need friends. You know, someone to talk to. So, if you can make him a good friend, I will appreciate it. I will treat you like one of my ancestors, too. Yes, so you won't be forgotten.

"I will talk to Jun and tell him to be good to you, too. He will listen to me. Listen to his dad. He will make a good friend to you, Tommy."

Several days later, Jun was laid next to Tommy. From the cemetery, Jory drove his wife and son, parked the car in the driveway, and watched what was left of his family enter the house. Jory stood outside and looked at the street, studying the path of the road. The white concrete had a pattern of dark stains. He wished they were oil droppings from passing cars. They were not.

He went inside. His wife was in the bedroom sleeping, and Emerson sat frozen in front of the television, watching a cartoon of a rabbit fighting with a pig. Jory sat on the sofa and willed the day to end. He picked up the newspaper, searching its contents. He stumbled upon the obituaries, and read notices of famous people, accomplished people passing on. So-n-so, age 75, was the head engineer at Boeing, died from heart attack, survived by a wife and three daughters. So-n-so, age 82, was the first woman to receive a PhD from the male world of academia at a prestigious private college, died from cancer, survived by one son and two grandchildren. So-n-so, age 71, was a musician influencing the jazz scene in Los Angeles, died of brain tumor, survived by his wife.

Jory thought of his son's obituary. Jory Junior "Jun-Jun" Lalaban, age 8, perfect attendance in school, four gold stars in art, survived by two parents and one brother. *Dead children should have their own section in the newspaper,* Jory thought, mentioning accomplishments that could have happened. Jory Junior "Jun-Jun" Lalaban could have been an artist, could have been a father.

He looked through the window, watching the shades of light change, from a luminescent white to a yellow to a violet to a brown, eventually a deep blue, finally blackness. All the while

Emerson sat in front of the TV, getting up once for an apple, then sitting down again.

"*Anak,* child, it is time to sleep." Jory said. Emerson turned around, nodded, got up to turn off the TV, then headed into his room. Jory waited, checking his watch. It was a little past nine. *It is too early,* he thought.

He surveyed his living room. It was empty. He knew it would always feel this way. Even if this room were filled with people, it would still be empty. He took a deep, deep breath, and he sensed that Jun-Jun was almost gone. His scent was present, but his presence was not. The boy had only been buried for several hours, but he could feel his son leaving. *His soul was too young,* Jory thought, *too young to stay attached here.*

He noticed early on that Jun-Jun took to bright colors like yellows, light blues, reds and purples, colors you'd see on a parrot's wings. His oldest son was all Sky. He was meant to float upward.

In his living room, Jory was alone, fully alone. He didn't have to console his wife or watch his son—his only son. He didn't have to be strong, didn't have to be a man. He sat on his sofa, sinking into the cushions. Jory laid back and let his muscles relax. His head leaned to the side, almost touching his shoulder. His hair falling from his crown, curtaining his forehead. His lids fell halfway down his eyes, and his breathing slowed to a hush. With the masculine accoutrements aside, Jory felt like a stuffed doll, bent every which way. Like the dead orphans he saw as a boy. Men with no manliness are lumpy, raggedy, stitched-together dolls.

He heard his watch ticking. He twisted his wrist so the face of his Timex faced him. It was close to midnight. It was time. He inhaled, summoning himself back. His torso and extremities rose to life again. It was time to be a man again.

He lifted himself up to his feet, quietly walking into the kitchen. He went to the sink, bent down, and opened the two small doors there. He pulled out a bucket, which contained a scrub brush. He turned on the faucet, letting the water fill halfway up the bucket, the scrub brush floating to the top. He heard the dull echo of the water filling the plastic cylinder. He turned off the faucet, left the bucket in the sink, bent down, and looked for cleaning fluid, maybe Ajax powder. There was none.

He looked on the counter top and settled for Joy dishwashing liquid. He took the bucket of water and the dishwashing liquid out the back door, through the driveway, and stood on the street. He got on his knees, pulled out the scrub brush, letting some of the water fall on the brown spots, dried blood stains. He scrubbed. He squeezed some Joy onto the road, letting the clear liquid ooze onto the ground. He scrubbed some more. Bubbles formed. At first they were white, then they turned red. The bubbles foamed over the brush and over Jory's hand, his fingers sticky with blood and Joy. When he was out of water and soap, Jory stood up, got the hose, and sprayed the ground. When the stains were gone, he knew he was done bathing the earth.

⁓

"ARE YOU READY for your bath?" said a nurse, bringing in a bucket and wash cloths. "How is our little celebrity today?"

Jory chuckled. The nurse helped him turn to his side. Jory could swear that he could feel the remaining bullet turning inside him. He heard the nurse behind him placing the cloth inside the bucket, then wringing it out.

"I hear the mayor is going to drop by when you go home," she said, undoing the back of his hospital gown.

"Yeah, that's right." Jory felt her wiping his back, inspecting the sutures.

"And you had all those visitors today, too."

"One of those men was a lawyer. He's going to get that bastard who tried to kill me." He felt the nurse lift his arm to scrub his armpit.

"A lawyer? You're not paying him, are you?"

"No. He's a government lawyer." He felt her move the cloth to his lower back. He sensed she was heading toward the buttock and legs, but he couldn't feel that part of his body. He couldn't look as she lifted his leg to wipe his thighs.

"That's good you don't have to pay," the nurse said. "Okay, now let's move you, so I can wipe your front side. I can't imagine having to pay a lawyer on top of the hospital bills."

"Well, we have insurance." He rested on his back again, letting the nurse sponge his chest and stomach.

"Yes, but still, Mr. Lalaban. I mean your insurance is paying most of it, but not all. We have to write down every bit of care you get, and it still comes out to a pretty penny, even with insurance."

"What do you mean?"

The nurse walked around the bed, wiping his other side. "Well, Mr. Lalaban, most people have to make a copayment, so your family must be paying something."

"Knock, knock," he heard Emerson say. He was facing away from the door, and Jory hoped that Emerson had not walked into the room while he was half naked.

"May I come in?" Emerson said.

"We're almost done," the nurse responded. "Wait outside."

Jory felt the nurse adjust his hospital gown, covering him up.

"We're done!" the nurse yelled.

Emerson walked in, approached the bed, and said, "You did good, Dad. Talking to those officers will help put Baylor away for a long, long time."

The nurse adjusted his pillow and walked out. Jory looked at the wall with all the Get Well cards. Some of them were drooping; the tape attaching them to the wall was losing its stickiness. The flowers in the room were drying out; dead leaves had fallen to the floor.

"Emerson," Jory said. "I was wondering, you know. How you and your mother are doing."

"We're fine."

"I mean, you know, how you're doing with me being in the hospital?"

"We're doing fine, happy you're better."

"How about moneywise?"

"Don't worry about it, dad."

"I want to know."

"Me and mom worked things out. Just get well."

"Is it a lot?"

He saw Emerson's eyes shift.

"Nothing we can't handle," Emerson said. "Really. We figured it out."

He noticed how his son tried to sound cheerful.

"Tell me."

"Not much, Dad. Really."

Jory looked at his lying son and said, "All right. If you say so."

"Yeah, don't worry about it. Just get better."

Jory took a deep breath and coughed. Even though, he didn't feel like it, he yawned. He said, "Emerson, I'm getting tired. Let me sleep a while."

"You want me to go?"

"Yeah, just for a while."

As soon as the door closed, Jory turned to the phone by his bed. He slowly reached for it, feeling aches run down his side. He used both hands to lift the phone. It felt like he was lifting a boulder. He placed the phone onto his bed and called information, getting the customer service number of his bank. Belen may have been in charge of the money, but he knew basic information about their account. He called and a woman answered.

"Hello," the operator said, "This is Elsa, how may I provide you with excellent service today?"

"I want to check on my account."

"Sure. Account and social security number, please?"

Jory rattled off the numbers.

"This was an account shared with Bel—"

"Yes."

"I show that account was closed."

"Closed?"

"Yes, it closed due to insufficient funds."

"But we had over twenty-thousand dollars."

"Yes, there were withdrawals, with money placed into your joint checking out."

"How much money is in there?"

"I show a balance of seventeen dollars and twenty-four cents."

"That's all?"

"There were sums of several thousand dollars paid to St. Joan's Hospital."

"Thank you."

"Certainly. You have a nice day."

EMERSON

*E*MERSON GOT UP at five o'clock on a Saturday morning, preparing to leave at seven, making sure he'd have plenty of time to arrive at the Hard Rock by noon. He got directions on the internet, reading that it would take approximately four hours to arrive in Las Vegas.

He looked outside. It was dark, quiet. His apartment was still. When his brother never returned, the bedroom they shared took on this kind of silence. He never realized how Jun's breathing had been such a strong part of the walls or how the shifting of blankets caused life in space.

There were times when he and Jun waited for the very last click of the very last light switch, signaling their parent's retirement to bed. Jun crawled out of his sheets, grabbed the flashlight in his drawer, illuminated his face, and pretended to be a ghost. Emerson looked at the bright light creating shadows on his brother's face and giggled. There was nothing scary about Jun, nothing scary at all. He giggled louder.

"Shhhhh," Jun said, sitting on Emerson's bed, waving the flashlight around. A white ball roamed the walls of the room. "That's the Moon that Dad prays to, Emmy. It's flying around. See?"

Emerson watched the bobbing ball of light skim the floor, illuminating a skateboard and a plastic ball. It skidded up to the corner of the ceiling where an abandoned cobweb floated. It passed the pictures of actors that Jun held dear. When Jun died, his father took down the pictures of the Fonz from *Happy Days*, photos that Jun tore out of *Tiger Beat* magazine. He took down a poster of Bruce Lee that Jun-Jun begged to have when they walked down Hollywood Boulevard. The poster was of the martial arts star in a fighting pose with blood on his chest where someone had scratched him. The torn down pictures left white spots on the wall.

His father took away the toys that he thought Jun-Jun played with, like the glow-in-the-dark Hot Wheels race cars or the little green men who were supposed to be soldiers. Emerson played with them, too. His father didn't know that. He did not protest when his father took away his toys. Instead, Emerson came to accept that when someone dies, things that belong to you disappear, too.

Something else disappeared: safety. Whenever Emerson was scared, waking from a bad dream, he crawled from his bed to Jun's, slipping under the sheets with his older brother. When Emerson learned the alphabet, memorizing all the way up to Z, he'd always forget what came after P.

"Q," Jun whispered.

"Oh, yeah. Q, R, S, T, U, V, W, X, Y, Z."

Any confidence that Emerson felt went away when a Comet whizzed through Carondelet.

One night, Emerson stared at the posterless wall of his bedroom and wished his brother would return, wished to all the Gods and Goddesses that he was knew of, from Santa Claus to the Tooth Fairy, that Jory Junior would return somehow.

He looked out the window and saw the moon illuminating the back yard, giving a hint at the small bump of earth that refused to flatten. He tried to sleep, but heard laughing. He got out of bed and peered out the window. He saw two teenage boys and a girl standing in the back yard. The teenagers were drinking and whispering.

Emerson knew those people shouldn't be there. His father taught him that the places where the dead had lain should be sacred. He went to the back door and could hear them talking. They looked quite a bit older, maybe high school students.

"Go ahead. You said you would," one boy muttered.

"Okay, do you have the camera?" the other boy replied.

"Yeah, I got it."

"This is wrong," the girl said. "We shouldn't even be here."

"It's all right. Just one picture." The boy with the camera aimed it at his friend lying next to what was Jun's grave. The guy on the ground lay there with his arms across his chest. A small flash went off and the boys laughed.

"Be quiet. You'll wake someone," the girl said.

"Look. It's just one picture. The guys at school didn't think we'd do it. Now, we have proof."

Emerson opened the back door, watching the teenagers stand in the yard. He walked, with bare feet, toward them. Emerson became aware of the cold night air. His white T-shirt and white pajamas with images of Donald Duck did nothing to protect him form the chill. He thought of going inside and getting a sweater, but he wanted to tell the teenagers that what they were doing was wrong. This land was holy.

The teenagers fidgeted with the camera, their backs to Emerson. "This is going to be great," one boy said.

"Maybe we should take another one. Just to be sure," the boy with the camera said.

You shouldn't be here, Emerson thought. *You're like the driver of the Comet. You don't care that my brother went into the air and landed dead. My brother used to sleep here and you don't care.*

"Go away," Emerson said. The teenagers turned around. Emerson walked closer to them, watching the teenagers step back. "I was sleeping but I heard you."

"Shit!" one of the teenagers said. "It's the dead boy!"

"Don't come any closer," the youth with the camera said. One hand was in front of him, trembling.

"We're . . . sorry . . . sorry that we woke you . . . from your rest," the girl said, sounding like she was going to cry.

Emerson saw the footprints left on his brother's former resting place and felt a hot surge rise from his feet to his throat. He said, "You should be punished for stepping on this land. Punished for what you did!"

The girl screamed, and the teenagers ran past Emerson into the dark night. *Punished,* Emerson thought. He patted the ground, trying to erase the footsteps of the trespassers.

"I'll guard your spot, Jun," Emerson said. He raised his hands in the air the way he'd seen his father pray. His arms got tired, and he lowered them, not understanding how such an act seemed to make his father happy. He closed his eyes the way he'd seen his mother pray. He thought of Jun in his mind, but he was unsatisfied with the still image of his brother in his head. He tried to listen for that little voice his mother said comes when you pray.

He went back inside, dusted himself off, and went to bed. He stared at the bare space of his room. He missed his brother, missed him more than anything. He cried the way he'd cried every night since Jun's death.

L, M, N, O, P . . . , he thought, hoping to hear the voice of his brother who always knew when to help him out.

P, he thought on the verge of sleep, then he heard: Rrrrrrrrrrrrring.

He got up and thought of answering it, but he was told not to pick up the phone. Only adults were allowed to do that. He went into his parent's bedroom. They slumbered. He went to his father's side of the bed, nudged him and said someone was calling on the phone.

Rrrrrrrrrrrrrring.

"I don't hear anything," his father said.

"The phone is ringing," Emerson said.

"You're dreaming. Go back to bed," he said.

Rrrrrrrrrrrrrring.

Emerson went into the living room.

Rrrrrrrrrrrrrrriing.

He looked at the phone.

Rrrrrrrrrrrrrrring.

—Hello? Emerson said.

—Hi, Emmy.

—Jun!

—Shhhhhhhh.

—I have to tell Mom and Dad.

—No, don't.

—Why not? They wanna hear from you.

—No. I just wanna say thanks for telling those guys in the back yard to leave. They were stupid.

—Yeah. Lemme wake Mom. She'd wanna talk to you.

—Noooooo.

Emerson never figured his brother to whine.

—I just wanna talk to you, Jun said.

—Me?

—Don't you wanna talk to me?

—'Course.

—Then you can't tell Mom and Dad. Just 'tween us. They couldn't hear anyway. They're sad I died. Don't tell 'em I called. They'll just get more sad.

—If you say so.

—'Sides, I wanna talk to you. Only you.

—Can I call you if I want?

—Nah. You have nowhere to call.

—Where are you?

—Here and there. Sort of around.

—When'll you call again?

—Don't worry 'bout that. I'll know when to call. Just don't tell Mom and Dad, or I won't call again.

—I won't do that.

—'kay. Emmy?

—Yeah?

—It's Q.

～

EMERSON GOT INTO his car. It was exactly 7:00. He hit the freeway. There were almost no other cars on the road. He accelerated, enjoying the speed, enjoying the movement. He remembered discovering the thrill of wheels when he walked home from school one day. Two weeks after Jun was buried, Emerson passed the Plymouth Skylark, a car that had been abandoned on his street, and noticed a wooden object sticking out from the front fender. Emerson approached it and recognized the tip of Jun-Jun's skateboard. He guessed that when Jun was hit, the skateboard merely rolled away, parking itself under the jalopy. He pulled it out and saw that the skateboard was undamaged.

He picked it up and took it home. He slid it under his bed and kept it there. He didn't want his parents to see it because he knew that they wouldn't want it in the house. His father had taken out all of the things that belonged to Jun-Jun, and Emerson wanted to keep one thing that belonged to his brother.

Sometimes on rainy days, he'd shut his door and pull out the skateboard, pushing it from one end of his room to another. Sometimes Emerson pulled out the skateboard just to look at it. There were dark footprints from where Jun used to stand on it. The varnish was almost gone. The red plastic wheels were nicked and turning brown.

Once, Emerson took the skateboard outside and tried using it. He fell twice, but by the third time, he was able to stay on. He only went in one direction. He eventually figured out how to turn. You lean left to turn left, lean right to turn right.

In a few months, he handled that skateboard as easily as breathing. He grew an inch and three quarters and took to wearing his brother's clothes. He traveled past the Manila Grill restaurant, past Kim's liquor store, past Visaya Bakery. Some people who saw him turn a corner had to look twice, thinking that Jun-Jun himself had risen from the grave to claim his rightful place in the neighborhood.

⁓

HE FELT GOOD in his car, going somewhere, anywhere. He was making good time. He saw the sign to Needles, California. He'd be in Las Vegas shortly. A few drops of rain appeared on his windshield. He looked out his window and heard a loud crack. Thunder. Then he saw lighting. More rain appeared on his windshield. He turned on the wipers.

There's something about wheels, Emerson knew. Whether the wheels are attached to an engine or a piece of wood, wheels mean distance. They mean getting away. He'd known this for years, beginning with that skateboard that was his ticket to freedom. He secretly used his skateboard to take to the neighborhood, wearing out wheels, then using his allowance money to have them replaced. The wooden board managed to keep its sturdiness, though.

Emerson saw the rain moisten the desert between Los Angeles and Las Vegas. The desert was a place his father was drawn to. His mother was drawn to the sea. Emerson was drawn to the city streets that bent, curved, and dead-ended. At sixteen, with a newly minted driver's license, those yards of neighborhood streets that he skateboarded on stretched into miles, and each mile delivered him further from his house and closer to Somewhere Else.

His mother came home from work in the late afternoons and slept the rest of the night. Emerson took the keys as soon as she laid them on the mantel. His father knew that his son was taking the car, but didn't seem to mind. He seemed to understand the importance of distance. Emerson took his mother's Nova as far south as Sierra Madre, as far east as Alhambra, as far north as Lancaster, and as far west as he could go, which meant the ocean. Each direction was at least forty-five minutes from his home. He covered all directions before he began to worry when his parents would begin to notice. A few extra miles in each direction would mean getting home at a time that would be noticeable. *That* would have meant no driving in any direction; his parents would take the car away. He also made sure to replace the gas he'd spent.

He drove around Los Angeles, checking out the neighborhoods and their inhabitants. One place that he'd always enjoyed was Hollywood. It wasn't far from his home, and there were different types of people who wandered the night. Young actors and actresses, who looked like they just leaped out of a music video, walked to a trendy club. Tourists with backpacks strolled along Sunset Boulevard. Older people, who remembered when Hollywood was a small little town, warily stepped around Hollywood Boulevard preparing to see a show at the Pantages or have a meal at Musso and Frank's.

And then there was Santa Monica Boulevard, a street that Emerson loved. He'd read about a crackdown of male hustlers on this street, and he was compelled to check it out. It was those hustlers that drew Emerson to the place. He wasn't attracted to them because those men were lewdly sexy. Lewdly sexy men, gay and straight, were everywhere in Los Angeles. He wasn't attracted to those men because they slept with men. If that were the case, he would have driven further into West Hollywood, the gay part of town.

What Emerson found attractive about them is that these guys, some about the same age as Emerson, stood on a street, hoping to be picked up like a gift under a tree. They appeared lost, displaced. It was that displacement that Emerson found familiar. It was that that made Emerson park the Nova and join them.

He'd park his mom's car on Western, walk up a block to Santa Monica Boulevard, then walk the few miles west to La Brea, then back to Western. Those blocks were made up of immigrant-owned stores and run by working-class folk. That stretch of Santa Monica Boulevard wasn't listed as a place to visit in tourist handbooks. It was notorious.

Emerson would walk with his head down, but his eyes were alert and wandering, looking out of the side of his face to see male prostitutes hanging out on a corner. He passed dozens of them, some of them teenagers, others well into their thirties.

The first time he walked Santa Monica Boulevard, he walked briskly like he was late for a class. The third time, he slowed a bit to actually see the businesses around him, like the dry cleaners or furniture store. He saw the chow mein in the window of a Chinese take-out joint and the purple dog collars in a pet store. By the fifth time, he'd stop walking and simply stand there, looking up to see the dark blue sky. He watched the prostitutes straggle by; every once in a while one of them got into a car and drove off.

He noticed that Santa Monica Boulevard changed when he walked. It was primarily black and Latino guys when he started, near the freeway off ramp, at Western, then he saw more white guys as he ventured further west.

Some of the guys were really handsome, well dressed with scrubbed faces, and some of them were down right creepy looking, obviously homeless with greasy, matted hair. They stood there by a bus stop or corner, leaning against a wall or perched on a curb. They looked into cars, trying to make eye contact with potential clients.

Cars drove by real slow, checked out the merchandise, picked up somebody or quickly drove off if nothing on the shelf appealed to them. Sometimes he saw a car pull up, a window roll down, and a prostitute peer into the car. Once, Emerson heard them discuss prices.

"Forty bucks," one prostitute said.

"Only got twenty."

"Sorry, forty bucks for what you want me to do."

The car drove off, and Emerson was proud of the prostitute for sticking to his price. He continued walking. Every so often, a car cruised by him real slow, a window rolled down, and somebody asked him, "Need a ride?" Emerson kept walking. "Excuse me, you know where Malibu is?" Emerson walked. "Cutie, how much?" He kept his head down and moved one foot in front of the other.

Emerson's sojourns to Santa Monica Boulevard happened two, maybe three times a month. He sat in class, listening to the teacher discuss American history, and the thought occurred to him: what was the Boulevard up to? He wondered about the boys on the sidewalk and if they were okay. He hoped that they were eating and that they found a place to sleep. Winter was coming and he prayed that the weather would be mild.

He went home, did his school work, and waited for his mother to arrive. He ate with his family, bowing his head, waiting for his father to summon ghosts.

"Come," said his father, "eat with us. Belen made this food for you to trade. My son offers you his food to trade. Come."

Then the clink of spoons and glasses began.

"Are you doing anything exciting in school?" his mother asked.

Emerson took a deep breath and said, "No, nothing exciting at school. Just the regular stuff."

"Do you have a girlfriend yet? Some parents don't want their children to date. I think if you want to have a girlfriend, you can have one," his father said, smiling.

Emerson looked down at his food. "No, nobody." He sectioned his rice into four parts. He spooned *kare-kare* stew onto his plate. A main ingredient of the stew was peanut butter that gave the dish an orange coloring. He let the stew fall between the sectioned rice, reminding him of a Martian river. "I wanna use the car tonight."

"Why?" his mother asked.

"There're some friends I want to meet."

"The same friends from before."

"Yeah."

"Why don't you bring them home? We want to meet your friends."

"Yeah, sure. Sometime."

"Why don't you feed your brother," his mother said.

Emerson dug into the *kare-kare* and scooped some of the orange stew onto the plate next to him. This is why he never brought friends home. He didn't want to explain that empty space at the table where Jun's spirit sat.

"Can I go now?" Emerson asked. Sometimes he felt that empty space at the table extended to his relationship with his parents.

"Go ahead and take the car," his dad said.

Emerson grabbed the car keys and headed out. He parked on Western and walked among the boys on the Boulevard, nodding to them. By then, he'd become a familiar face, and everyone assumed that he was a hustler too. Or if not that, a druggie of some kind, a homeless runaway trying to get away from the father who molests him and the mother who drinks her way half crazy.

"Name's Albert," one guy said.

"My name is . . ." Before he could finish, Albert yelled at a guy across the street.

"Hey, Funny Bones, what up?"

A skinny boy crossed the street and hi-fived Albert.

"How things goin'?" Funny Bones said.

"Slow. Hope things pick up."

Funny Bones turned to Emerson and said, "How things goin' with you, *Chino?*"

Emerson didn't speak Spanish, but knew *Chino* was Spanish for *Chinese.* He didn't correct him. Frankly, Emerson was honored that these guys were even talking to him. Emerson was playacting at being a prostitute. They were the real deal. They weren't fakes like Emerson. Emerson offered, "You guys want something to eat?"

"You payin'?" Albert said.

"Yeah."

"T'anks, *Chino.*"

"Yeah, *Chino,* thanks," Funny Bones said.

Emerson led them to a nearby burger stand. They were almost there when a black and white car pulled up next to them. An officer peered out his window and said, "You boys up to no good?"

"Give us a break, officer," Albert said. "We're just going to get a sandwich."

"Make sure that's all you get. I want a nice quiet evening tonight, all right?"

"Yeah, yeah."

The policemen drove away.

"Fucking cops," Funny Bones said. "They ruining business."

Emerson ordered three burgers and pulled out a twenty to pay for them.

"Where'd you get the money for this? It's been kinda slow for me." Funny Bones asked.

"Me, too," Albert said.

Emerson fumbled with the change. He didn't want to tell them that his parents give him allowance money. "Um. . . ."

"I been out here all day," Albert said. "No one's propositioned me for nothin'."

"Well," Emerson said. "I . . . I have this regular customer. I meet him at his job and do stuff for him. He pays me."

"Sweet," Funny Bones. "Wish I had a regular. All the guys I come across are one-timers. Wham, bam, here some money, thank you, man."

Emerson stood by Funny Bones and Albert as they finished the last bites of the burgers. He thought the guys would leave him, eat the food he provided and say, "See ya." Instead the guys hung out, leaned against the wall or shifted from side to side. The night was still young and they knew that business wouldn't pick up for a while.

"Wanna smoke?" Albert said, patting his pocket. "It's the good stuff."

"Yeah. C'mon, *Chino,*" Funny Bones said.

Emerson was led to a nearby alley. Albert pulled out a small piece of aluminum foil, unwrapped it, produced a joint, and lit it.

He inhaled and blew smoke that Emerson had never smelled. Funny Bones took a hit then offered the joint to Emerson.

"Go ahead, *Chino,*" Funny Bones said.

"Never done it before," Emerson said.

"You never smoked weed before?"

Emerson shook his head.

"Then just take one toke."

Emerson held the little cigarette, brought it to his lips and inhaled. He violently coughed.

"Take it easy, *Chino,*" Albert said.

Emerson's eyes watered, and he swooned. Funny Bones held him up.

"Damn, lightweight, ain't you."

"I guess," Emerson said, enjoying the feeling of leaning against Funny Bones.

"Here, just sit for a while."

Emerson crossed his legs on the floor, feeling weightless, feeling unencumbered. *If anybody were to walk by,* Emerson thought. They would have seen this Albert and this Funny Bones and this Emerson and believed them to be friends, just guys hanging out on a weeknight, prolonging the day before morning comes, signaling the start of school. Emerson liked that, liked thinking that he had friends. As it was, he was sixteen and wandered the halls of Belmont High School by himself.

This Filipino boy wanted to make friends. It's just that he didn't feel any connection with people he went to school with. His classmates were pretty jovial and sociable. Most of them he'd known since elementary school, most of them knew he had a brother that died and a father who stole his corpse. And most of them had heard about the spirit of his dead brother haunting the neighborhood, stories that Emerson wasn't surprised by. His brother was a remarkable creature. Of course Jun's essence was still present.

He understood why he never made friends at school. They knew about his brother and, no matter what happened, the death of Jun-Jun would always be between them. His brother's death floated under the desks of every class he'd ever attended and sat on every window blind he looked through.

On the Boulevard, watching Albert cruise the cars passing by, watching Funny Bones breathe into his palm to make sure his breath didn't stink, Emerson wanted to know these guys. He wanted to know the boys on Santa Monica Boulevard, guys who didn't know him from dried gum on the sidewalk, guys who walked in darkness and stood on corners hoping someone would drive by and want them. He sensed that these guys had a Jun story, a tragedy that drove them to this street.

"Why do they call you Funny Bones?" Emerson asked.

"Well, *Chino,* my real name is Martin, but I could do this." Funny Bones stretched out his arms and bent them at the elbows, giving the impression that his arms were broken. "I'm double-jointed."

"That freaks the shit outta me every time you do it," Albert said.

"That's kinda cool," Emerson said.

"Hey, let's get a Coke," Funny Bones said. The three of them walked down the street like they'd know each other their whole lives.

⁓

THERE CAME A time when taking the car and disappearing for hours caused worry with his parents. He never forgot that time his father cooked rice and a special meat dish in a pungent sauce. The meat dish was diced into small cubes and Emerson scooped a ladle full onto his plate.

"Is Mom going to join us?" Emerson asked.

"No, she is with Mrs. Kim. They're going to talk."

"All right."

"Your mom wants me to talk to you, because you go out at night and stay out late."

"Yeah, I'm just hanging out with friends." Emerson looked down at his food, spooning the diced meat into his mouth.

"Believe it or not. Your mom and me would go out when we were your age. We would go out and Hang Out. So, if you Hang Out, you should be careful."

"I'm not doing anything wrong."

"Sometimes, when you Hang Out, things can happen. Then you're a father."

"I'm not doing *that*, dad."

"I know what it's like."

"I'm just visiting friends," Emerson said, helping himself to seconds of the diced meat.

"Well, you visit who you want. Hanging Out is fun. Just be careful. I know you stay out late. It takes a lot of energy to have fun, stay alert. What you're eating will help you," Jory said, smiling.

"What do you mean?"

"You will feel more strength. More better when you Hang Out."

"Huh?"

"Snake will make you Hang Out good."

"What did you say?" Emerson said looking at his plate. The diced meat mixed into his rice. His mouth full of the stuff.

"Snake. It will make you, what do you call that? Strong. Mighty. It wakes you up."

"You're feeding me snake?"

"I began eating it before we came to the States. I buy it in Chinatown. Eating snake helps me stay young. And—"

Emerson spit his food into a napkin.

"Don't worry, Emerson. It won't kill you."

Emerson held his breath, trying to convince himself not to vomit.

⸺

EMERSON FELT THE blow. He pulled his car to the side, stepped out, feeling the rain gradually dampen him. He saw the tire. It was flat. *Shit,* he thought. The rain fell harder. He retrieved the spare and the jack. He looked at his watch, knowing that changing this tire would affect his time to Las Vegas.

He got down on one knee. The ground was wet, and his shoes and pants were getting soiled. The rain pelted his head, and Emerson felt a whisper of rage rise within him. *Why now,* he thought. *Of all the times to get a flat, why now?* Why on the day he was going to meet Michael, the best guy he'd encountered.

The jack lifted his Galaxie into the air. The best guy. He twisted off the bolts, pulling off the flat and threw it onto the side of the road. In addition to being wet, he was sweating, trying to fix the tire, hoping to gain back the time he'd lost. He had to be at the Hard Rock by noon. If he was late, Michael would take it the wrong way, think that he was inconsiderate, unable to make a crummy appointment.

He couldn't afford to make another mistake with Michael. On a spectrum of men he'd known, Michael was at the far end, being the best guy he'd ever had relations with. The worst would be Doug, a man he met standing on the Boulevard. Emerson's presence on Santa Monica Boulevard became as ordinary as sand. After school, he'd frequent the shops in the neighborhood, hang out at the liquor store parking lot. He lied to people and said he had a rich sugar daddy who was helping him out. That's where he got his money, and he didn't need to hustle anymore. He still liked the street, though, and people were flattered that a "kept boy" still wanted to hang with them. A director at a social service organization took notice of Emerson and offered him a job as a peer counselor to help the prostitutes. Emerson had just graduated from high school with no prospects of work, so he jumped at the opportunity of making money.

Emerson's job was to talk to other young people on the streets and inform them of their options. He met Doug while on duty. Doug was leaving a bar and smiled at him. Doug walked over to Emerson and said, with a smile that lit up the dark night, "Are you working?"

"Yeah, I'm working. But not as a prostitute, I mean. I'm a social worker." Emerson knew that there was a big difference between a peer counselor and a social worker. The latter required several years of schooling and thousands of dollars toward a degree. His job as a peer counselor required knowledge of the population he served and a sincere need to help them. He was always proud of saying that he was a peer counselor, but looking at the man with wavy brown hair and shoulders that stretched from one side of the street to the other, Emerson had the need to better himself a little.

"A social worker, huh?" Doug said. "That's a nice thing to be. You do look kinda young to be social worker though. How old are you?"

"Nineteen."

"Do you have a boyfriend?"

"No."

"No? Someone as cute as you not having a boyfriend? You must have high standards."

"No," Emerson said, "I mean yes. Well, I never had a boyfriend." Emerson looked toward the ground, missing Doug's smile turn into a grin.

"Never had a boyfriend, huh? I guess that means I have a head start. Can I call ya?"

"Yeah, sure," Emerson said and stood there, truly flattered that a guy who looked like this, who wore his shirt tucked into his trousers and had no crud under his nails, would want to go out with him.

"Uh," Doug began, "this is the part where you write down your number."

Emerson's brown skin turned rose, because he'd never given a number to a guy before—well, at least not his real one.

Emerson said, "If you could be kinda careful when you call, that would be great. My parents don't know . . . about me."

"You're really new."

"I guess."

Doug called the next day, insisting on a date. They went to a fancy restaurant—fancy for Emerson. It was a Mexican restaurant across the street from the Paramount studios. He sat in their booth the way he'd always sat at a booth at Astro Diner or Denny's or International House of Pancakes: his back against a wall, his legs resting on whatever chair space the booth had available. He was embarrassed when the hostess asked him to please sit with his feet on the floor.

The dimly lit restaurant had pictures of movie stars on the walls. Emerson had been to restaurants where pictures of actors hung on walls before, but these pictures were of real famous people, and they were autographed!

Doug paid for the meal and Emerson—who was used to eating one-dollar burgers—was impressed, particularly when the bill cost more than fifteen bucks. On their second date, Doug took Emerson to a jazz restaurant on Western and Wilshire. Doug paid for that, too. On each date, Doug was a perfect gentleman, and Emerson felt comfortable with him.

"What do you want to do with your life?" Doug asked over an appetizer, a sampling of cheese.

Emerson looked over the brie, feta, and blue cheese and wondered what to make of it. The cheese he was used to eating came on a meat patty, between buns. "Um, I guess I just wanna be happy."

"Well, what does happiness look like?" Doug cut into the blue cheese, smearing it on a cracker.

Emerson copied his date, hoping that he didn't look stupid putting cheese on a cracker that wasn't salted. He popped it into his mouth, the way he had done with peanut butter on saltines. Emerson wasn't prepared for the pungent flavor of the cheese and gave a slight cough.

"You know," Emerson said, "have a job and be happy."

"Do you want a great job? Or will any job do?"

"I like my job now. Helping people."

"You're young. And you sound it. I want you to be happy, Emerson. I wish you to be more happy than anyone."

Emerson looked at Doug and somehow felt satisfied. The aftertaste of the cheese had settled in the back of his throat. No one had ever wished him happiness before, and he didn't know how to respond. All Emerson could think of to say was Thanks.

After a week of dating and half a dozen meals bought, Emerson began to talk with Doug, talk with him like he'd never talked with anyone before. "My dad is a magical person."

"Yeah?"

"He casts spells and things."

"Interesting."

"I was his assistant. When I was little."

"I bet you were cute."

"I don't know about that. Do you believe in God, Doug?"

"I suppose. He brought you to me."

"I don't believe in God, I don't think. My mom believes in Jesus and Mary and those guys. My dad believes in the moon and stars and shit. They have to believe because they say we're cursed."

"Do you believe in anything?"

"I don't know. I guess I do. I think God is a lot of things. I think God's out there maybe."

"Maybe."

They kissed passionately when their dates ended. Emerson didn't want to go any further than that, something Doug respected for the most part. There were a few times when Doug tried to unbutton Emerson's button-fly jeans, but Emerson led his hand away.

On their seventh date, Emerson thought their relationship had grown to a point, and he let Doug undo his pants. Doug said he wanted Emerson's first sexual experience to be memorable, so he led Emerson to a full-length mirror.

"I want to do it standing," Doug said and disrobed himself and Emerson.

"Hey, Doug?"

"Yeah?'

"Before we go any further, I wanna say—I just want to let you know that I love you. I do." Emerson felt a joy in uttering those words. He felt a vulnerability that was pleasing. He said it again, "I love you."

"Stand over here. In front of the mirror."

"I love you, Doug. Do you love me?"

I Love You Doug would follow Emerson for years, making him think twice, thrice, and four times before saying I Love You again. (And even when he said it, he said it in a way that only a small population of the earth could understand.)

"Look up. Look into the mirror," Doug said.

Emerson saw his skinny reflection and lowered his head at the sight of his naked body in the full-length mirror. His nudity was unbearable to him. He looked like someone you'd see in *National Geographic,* some starving child with a too-prominent ribcage.

Doug said, "You're so delicious."

"Do you love me, Doug?"

Emerson felt Doug caressing the inside of his buttock, wiping something slippery there.

"This is the best lube," Doug said. "It doesn't dry out."

"I love you. Do you love me?"

"Keep looking at yourself. Look at yourself in the mirror."

"I love you."

Emerson watched himself, and saw Doug's face nestled in the blackness of his hair. "Keep looking into the mirror, just watch yourself. Watch me enter you."

He jumped forward, away from Doug. "Do you love—"

"Yeah, sure, I love you. Relax, baby," Doug said, pulling Emerson back to him. "It'll hurt for a bit, but for only a little while. Just keep watching yourself in the mirror. You don't want to miss this."

Emerson cringed.

"Look at yourself in the mirror. Look." Doug was firm with his direction. Emerson watched his reflection and felt Doug behind him, entering. Emerson felt a searing pain that catapulted up his hips.

"Doug, I don't want to do this. Please."

"Just relax."

"I wanna go," Emerson said, trying to pry himself away.

Doug slapped him and said, "Look, princess, I've been patient enough with you."

Emerson was stunned. "Why'd you do that—"

Before he could finish, Doug grabbed him by the hair, forcing him to his knees, eventually flat down to his stomach. Emerson thrashed about, fighting back. Doug picked Emerson up a few feet from the floor then slammed him down to the ground, knocking the wind out of the Filipino boy. Doug said, "Now, now, don't fight me."

Doug's hand kept Emerson's face to the floor. Doug climbed onto Emerson's back, spreading his legs, then forcing himself into the teenager.

Emerson gasped and cried, "It hurts. Please stop."

Doug was relentless, wrapping himself around Emerson. Emerson felt imprisoned in the cave of Doug's body. He felt the weight and force of Doug's body behind him, ripping into him, destroying him.

Doug pulled Emerson's head back by his hair. Emerson saw his reflection in the mirror.

"Are you watching?" Doug said. "Are you watching yourself? Answer me, bitch. Do you see your reflection in the mirror?"

Emerson felt a shooting pain—excruciating—rise within him, then fall away, only to rise again.

"Do you see yourself? Do you see me inside you? Do you see yourself?"

He saw his face: contorted. His teeth gritting. His hair awry. A mask of anger and fear on his face.

Doug whispered into Emerson's ear: "This is what you look like when your Innocence is being taken away."

After Doug orgasmed, he pushed Emerson away and crawled into his bed. Emerson lay on the ground, feeling like he'd just been cut up then discarded. He wept while Doug snored. He found his way to the bathroom. He closed the door before switching on the light. Emerson cried and felt stupid, felt like he'd been taken. His virginity was ripped from him, taken by a man who said I Love You in a way that it should not have been said: frivolous. What was worse, Emerson gave him something else. He talked to Doug about his dad and God and stuff. He felt like he'd given him a personal bit of himself that no one was supposed to reach. Only in that bathroom did Emerson realize that this man, this Doug, could have given a rat's ass for what Emerson felt about his dad or his God or his stuff.

The johns on Santa Monica, who paid for sex, were far better men that Doug. Those men were up front, honest about what they wanted and what they were willing to pay. Doug was deceitful, saying words he didn't mean and listening to conversation that he'd forget about once his ambitions were met.

Emerson walked back to the bedroom. He looked down at Doug and narrowed his focus. He whispered, "Doug, what you did was wrong. *Takalajo.* I call on all those who came before me, my ancestors, to find a punishment that suits you. I cast this spell on you."

He went into the night, vowing never to see Doug again. Later, when Emerson left his job, moving to other ones doing similar things, when other lovers came, Emerson was wary. If there was one Doug, there could be two. Emerson dated other men, usually those born elsewhere and with a rudimentary understanding of English. He couldn't get too close to a man if he didn't understand what he was communicating. Some of these men from countries like Korea, France, Brazil claimed to love him. Emerson loved them back—in his own special way, a way all of his English-as-a-second-language boyfriends didn't comprehend and were to frustrated to figure out. Except for one: Michael.

MICHAEL

*M*ICHAEL WAITED FOR Emerson in the lobby of the Hard Rock. That morning he went to the gym, lifted weights, bench-pressed, did three hundred sit-ups so when he met his X, he would look and feel his best. He sat on a chaise by the entrance, leaning back with his legs crossed. He saw a model posing this way in a Ralph Lauren ad and wanted Emerson to feel like he was stepping into the romantic pages of a magazine.

He imagined Emerson entering the lobby, seeing Michael lounging on the chaise; then an elated Emerson would run toward him. Michael would sit up, while Emerson rushed forward, getting down on one knee and begging for forgiveness.

"My love," Emerson would say, "give me one more chance to prove myself. I vow to never disappointment you."

Michael would look around, blush in embarrassment, while a crowd gathered, applauding them for getting back together.

As the minutes went by, Michael relaxed his pose. It was 12:15. Emerson was fifteen minutes late. Michael felt beads of sweat form on his forehead. He wiped it away, afraid perspiration would somehow ruin the affects of the facial he had the night before.

He sat there with the slot machines in the back ringing, people walking by with cups of coins in their hands, ready to gamble.

"Damn it, I lost!" Michael heard someone say. He turned and saw a blonde woman hitting a slot machine. She was angry, but not as angry as Michael was waiting for Emerson. Michael was not violent and he never understood why other men had the need to brawl. He believed that one of the best things about being gay was that he lacked the crude hormones that seemed to overwhelm straight men. Bars throughout the world can share the story of some man causing a ruckus after one too many beers. Wars were started because straight men had the innate ability to destroy. He thought that was purely a heterosexual trait of the male species. But in business class, for the first time in his life, Michael understood the instinct to kill.

Three months ago, Michael boarded the plane in Bangkok. The announcement was made to turn off all cell phones. He noticed a businessman still speaking into his cellular. Michael approached him to ask him to end his call. As he got closer, he heard the man speaking a language that was vaguely familiar. The rhythm and sounds of his words resounded in his ears. He looked at the man. He was Asian but Michael didn't know from which country. He could guess. From his darker skin, he was probably from a Southeast Asian country, perhaps from Thailand or Cambodia.

He stood there listening to the man, waiting in the aisle. The passenger looked up, nodded to let Michael know that he would be getting off the phone soon. The dark-skinned man smiled, laughed a little, and said something else. And what he said caught Michael off guard. It was familiar, more than familiar. It was what Emerson had said to him when they had sex, what Emerson said was nothing.

The man turned off his cell phone and put it into his pocket.

"That is pretty language," Michael said.

The man looked up, somewhat surprised. "Oh, it's Filipino."

"I heard language from Philippines. It not Tagalog?"

"No, it's different. From a different province."

"Oh, what you saying?"

"I was talking to my wife."

"What was that part you say? You say, people pee and then they yawn."

The passenger laughed, then corrected Michael. "*Pipiyanta ha.*"

"I sorry. What that mean?"

"I was telling my wife, I love you."

I love you, Michael thought, smiling. *Pipiyanta ha. Emerson was saying I Love You when we were screwing.* Michael became giddy. He rushed to the rear cabin of the plane and told his fellow flight attendants that his Andy Lau look-alike boyfriend was saying I Love You.

"Isn't that sweet?" Michael said. "He was saying I Love You."

"That is sweet," said one attendant. "But why didn't he just tell you so you could understand? And if he did love you, why did he deny not knowing the meaning of his words when you asked him?"

"I don't know. Maybe he was nervous. Maybe . . ." Then Michael's exuberance began to wane. *Whey didn't he just tell me "I love you," especially when he knew I wanted to hear it. I lost weight,* Michael thought, *I changed my attitude. I did all I can to be more lovable, only to have him say "I love you" so I can't understand? My English is not that good and I still managed to find the words to say how I feel. Emerson can't do the same?*

Michael landed in Bangkok and was going to stay the night. He would make the return flight in the morning. He wandered the city, pondering why Emerson didn't say I Love You in English, so he could understand.

Bangkok was really a remarkable city, old and new at the same time. It was beautiful. He saw many tourists, especially men from Australia or Germany or America. He entered a bar and sat down and ordered a beer. Next to him was an older Australian man with a Thai girl half his age. *Gross,* Michael thought.

"You're beautiful," the Australian said.

The girl laughed.

"Maybe I'll take you back to Melbourne with me. Would you like that? You can be my little angel."

The girl laughed some more, nodding. Michael noticed the wedding ring on the Australian's finger.

"God, I love your smile. I could make love to you all night. Make you my little play thing. Do what I want with you."

Michael thought the girl would slap him for being so forward. Then he realized that she doesn't know what he's saying. She doesn't understand English. The Australian knows she doesn't understand English. He says whatever he wants . . .

It was this bit of enlightenment that made Michael's ears grow hot, caused his lips to tighten, and his teeth to clench. It caused his heart to beat so fast that, if a doctor were to listen, he would have heard a series of thumps so close to together it could have been mistaken for one long drone.

In the morning, when he retuned to Los Angeles, Michael snapped at passengers who wanted a pillow, handled blistering food trays with his bare hands, and scolded parents for allowing their children to run freely in the aisles. He became militant about wearing seatbelts when the seatbelt light was on and staying seated when the slightest bit of turbulence hit the plane. He ordered passengers not to wait in line for the lavatory no matter how badly they needed to pee. In one instance, he gave a styrofoam cup to a man and told him to use it to relieve himself.

He sat quietly while the plane landed at LAX. He waited for the passengers to deplane, not bothering to clean up along with the other attendants. He exited the airport as quickly as he could. His fingers tingled, preparing to clench Emerson's throat.

Michael sat in his red Saturn watching Emerson drive up. Emerson smiled, parked, then approached Michael's car.

"Aren't you gonna come in?" Emerson said.

Michael slowly turned his head. The glare on his face made Emerson step away from the car.

"Something wrong?" Emerson said.

Michael followed Emerson into his apartment. Emerson opened the door and once inside, Michael yelled, "*I know what you say to me!!!*"

Emerson jumped back and uttered, "What?"

"I know what you say. When we sex, I know what you say. *Pipiyanta ha*. I know meaning. Why you not say in English? You know I want to hear."

"I . . . I . . . wasn't ready."

"You full of shit. You full of fucking shit. I say I Love You and you say nothing back to me. I wait for you to say I Love You back. I wait and wait. I think something wrong with me. I think I not good enough. I act happy for you."

"You don't understand," Emerson said.

"I understand. I know, you get off on saying I Love You. It make you happy. But it come with responsibility. You get to say I Love You with all the happy, but with no responsibility. You full of shit. You think I'm some girl in bar you can say nice things to then leave for Australia the next day?"

"What?"

"Never mind," Michael said, storming out of Emerson's apartment.

⌒

MICHAEL LOOKED AT his watch. It was 12:45. He decided to leave. All that waiting for nothing. Emerson is a waste of time. A big waste of time. He heard screaming behind him. He turned and saw a man and woman jumping up and down. There was a large slot machine that rang with lights flashing. The tinny sound of coins dropping filled the air. Other people gathered around the man and woman, including children. Children. He still wanted to adopt. It may not be with Emerson, but someday it would happen.

"Fuckin' A," someone in the crowd said. "You won! You won!" More people came around, watching the couple hug and kiss each other. They wanted to be around the luck, Michael knew. Maybe some of it would rub off on them.

"Sorry I'm late," Michael heard from behind him. Emerson. Michael shook his head, getting ready to blast Emerson for his tardiness. He turned, then stepped back. Emerson looked awful. He was drenched. His hair wet and flat. His clothes soiled. His face oily and worried.

"What happened to you?" Michael said.

"I got a flat, and it rained. The directions I got off the internet were wrong, and nobody could tell me exactly how to get to the Hard Rock. It's on Paradise Road, I'd say. No one knew where Paradise was."

Michael watched the pathetic man in front of him speak, scratching his head, shifting from side to side. He looked exhausted and drained. Michael placed his palm against Emerson's cheek. Emerson looked up, shocked from the touch.

"I just," Emerson said. "I just wanted one day for everything to be right. Just one fucking day. One day without worrying about my father, wondering how we're going to make ends meet. A day where I wouldn't get a fucking hate letter. I get hate mail, you know that? From some Nazi. I just wanted one day when everything went right. You'd figure I could at least get that."

No, Michael thought, *you don't get things just because you hope for them.* Michael put his arms around Emerson, feeling this Andy Lau look-alike crumble into him.

"I just . . . I just, just," Emerson said.

"It all right," Michael said. "Shhhhhh."

Emerson quieted. Michael felt Emerson's arms go around his waist. Emerson's head resting on his shoulder. He felt Emerson holding him tightly, a firm grip filled with need, such incredible need. It felt good to be needed.

"I'm sorry," Emerson said. "So, so sorry."

"Let's walk," Michael said. Michael guided Emerson out of the Hard Rock, walking him down Paradise.

"Hungry?" Michael asked.

"Starving."

Michael indicated a Mexican restaurant across the street. He opened the door, letting Emerson in first. At their table, Michael asked, "How is you papa?"

Emerson lowered his head and said, "Can we not talk about that just yet? I just don't want to talk about what's going on in Los Angeles for a while."

"Sure," Michael said. He saw that Emerson was troubled, confused, things he'd never before associated with Emerson. *He came to me,* Michael thought, *because he's looking for relief, a little bit of cheer.* Emerson had been through so much in the last several months that Michael decided that it was his duty to raise his spirits. Michael saw it as a challenge and planned to meet it.

A waiter appeared at their table. The waiter had a name tag on his chest.

"How you say that?" Michael asked, pointing to the plastic plate on the waiter's chest.

"Jose," the waiter said.

"Jose," Michael said. "I like that name. My name is Jose from now on."

Michael saw Emerson look up, a little smile on his face. *It's working,* Michael thought.

Michael continued, "Jose, I'm Jose, too. I decide right now."

"Okay, Jose," the waiter said. "Why do you want to change your name?"

"I look for new American name. Michael is my name, but I change."

"Why? Michael is a nice name."

"Everyone name Michael."

"A lot of people are named Jose, too."

"I want good name. And I speak small Spanish. *Como?*"

"Chimichanga is a good name," said the waiter. "It's the name of one of our specials."

"Okay, my name is Chimichanga."

Emerson laughed and said, "We'll have two of those."

The waiter left and Michael leaned in, examining Emerson's face, relieved that he was feeling slightly better. Michael looked out the window of the restaurant and saw a little boutique with a sign above the door.

"What that say over there?"

"*Joyeaux Noël.* It's French."

"What that mean?"

"Well, *Joyeaux* means Joyous, I guess. Or happy."

"Happy?"

"*Noël* means Christmas. *Noël.*"

"You mom and dad observe Christmas?"

"Not really. I got presents on Winter Solstice, a few days before Christmas. Dad said that's the origin of Christmas anyway."

"Nowhere."

"Noël. No-Well."

"No-where."

"Skip it."

"You good at different language."

Emerson looked away. "I'm sorry about that. I said I Love You to this guy once and it was a disaster."

"Disaster?"

"Mess. A great big mess."

"It's a mess now."

Michael saw Emerson pick up a salt shaker, move it from one end of the table to another. Emerson looked up and said, "I love you. I really love you. I wanted to say that to you for a long time, but couldn't. I know I hurt you. I know I hurt us because I couldn't say those words."

"Are you happy you said it?"

"Yeah, I am. I'm sorry. Can we get back together? I want you back in my life. Michael?"

"Jose. My name is Jose now. *Sí.*"

"See what?"

"*Sí* mean Yes in Spanish. I know other language, too. *Sí,* we can get back together."

Emerson smiled and said, "I missed you, Michael. I missed your smile and your eyes and your touch. I missed having you in my life."

"I miss you, too. Don't blow it this time."

"I won't." Emerson sighed. He looked around the restaurant and said, "I've never been to Las Vegas. I've never been outside of Los Angeles."

There's a whole world out there, Emerson, Michael thought. *It's big.*

"That's sad, huh? Never leaving home."

"No. I go all over to find home."

"Hey, Michael or Jose, you wanna come home with me? Come back to Los Angeles."

"I have to fly away in a few days."

Michael saw Emerson's face darken with disappointment. "Maybe, I change and fly out of LAX."

"Please."

Michael made a mental note to call his boss, informing him that he needed another place to fly.

BELEN

$\mathscr{A}$T WORK, BELEN heard laughter coming from Mr. Addison's room. She detected the sounds of his daughters Ava and Lana. It was time for their monthly visit, she assumed, bringing with them their home-baked zucchini bread. *Thank the Lady,* Belen thought, the daughters could feed the bastard. She went to her station and was preparing to fill out some paperwork when she heard her name.

"Belen!"

It was one of Mr. Addison's daughters.

"Belen, can you get your ass in here? We wanna talk to you," one of the daughters yelled.

Belen hesitated, then heard, *Belen, dear, no use putting off the inevitable. You have to face the fact that you wanted to cut that poor old man.*

Belen sighed, put down her pen, and went into the room. She stepped in and saw Mr. Addison in bed and Ava sitting beside him. Ava had a stern look on her face. She heard the door close behind her. She turned around and saw Lana, larger than the door-frame, standing there.

"There she is," Mr. Addison said. "That's the cow who almost killed me."

"Shhhh, Pop!" Ava said. Lana walked around the room, joining her sister.

"I want her fired," said the old man.

"Belen," Lana said. "I know you've been taking care of our dad for a long time. Still. We don't pay all that money to have pop's life threatened."

Belen could hear it, her boss chastising her for taking a knife to a patient. She would be reprimanded, even fired for that.

"Before we talk to the head nurse, we want you to know that we're fair women," Ava said.

Belen worried that she would have no job and wouldn't be able to pay for Jory's recovery.

"Fair women," Lana said.

I was stupid, Belen knew. *I shouldn't have been so angry with Mr. Addison. I'm a nurse for God's sake.*

Lana continued, "So, why'd you do it? Wanna kill Pop?"

Because I was tired, she wanted to say. You are not the only people with relatives in bad shape. She was tired of being professionally kind when her own world went bad. She was being crapped on. The world was crapping on her and she, as much as she could help it, didn't want to be crapped on anymore.

"Yeah," Ava said, "we want to hear your part of the story."

And she still didn't want to be crapped on. Belen crossed her arms and said, "Yes, I threatened to hurt Mr. Addison. And I still do."

Lana put her hands on her hips. Ava's jaw fell.

"Your father," Belen said, "grabbed my breast. I picked up a knife and threatened to cut off his testicle."

Dead silence filled the room. Then laughter. Ava and Lana laughed!

"Well, shit, Belen," Ava said. "I didn't think you had it in ya."

Lana said, "Pop, you didn't tell us the part about grabbing her titty."

"You didn't ask," said Mr. Addison.

"Castration is too good for you, Pop." Ava turned to Belen and said, "You're my kind of woman. You want some zucchini bread?"

⌒

SHE SURVEYED THE house the morning Jory would return. At 7:00 A.M., she walked from room to room. Spotless. The morning sun came through her windows and her home had never looked more lovely. The metal chrome of the wheelchair she ordered for Jory sparkled by the door.

Her husband would be pleased. She was pleased, too. She was told her husband's prognosis looked good, the remaining bullet would be extracted in a week or so. Just one more operation. One more hump. Dr. Jones told her that Jory still had a lot of rehabilitation he would need to undergo. A process that would take months, possibly years. She'd never be able to pay for his rehabilitation, other trips to the hospital, and mortgage payments, even with Emerson's help. The cost of the wheelchair and hospital bed alone was a small fortune.

"Mom, I'll move back home," Emerson said. "I won't have to pay rent, and we can somehow make things work."

She told him no. She loved him for offering. If there was one small consolation to this sordid mess it was that she and Emerson were on much better terms. When he offered to move in, he felt like a good son. When she knew that she couldn't have him do that and told him not to move back, she felt like a good mother. She had gotten a good life, one with Jory. Emerson had a right to his own. She was certain Emerson's own life did not mean moving back with his parents and taking care of his father.

Blessed Lady, she thought, *am I making the right decision?*

I support you, dear, in whatever choice you make. You have free will. I feel just terrible that you were put in this situation, but you can handle it. I know you can.

"Another option," Emerson said, "is to get another loan on the house. I can cosign."

That was an option she refused to take. The Curse was something she and Jory were stuck with. She would not have her remaining child taking on remnants of the Curse, which meant being saddled in debt that he'd still be paying long after she and Jory were gone. Besides, he was dealing with his own part of the Curse: Emerson will never know the joy of marriage and having children of his own.

She would not tell Jory of planning to sell the house. At least not now. She would wait until he was stronger, after his last operation. She sat down with a cup of coffee, wondering where she and Jory could go. She wasn't sure which part of town to live in or how high rents were. She decided to call Emerson and ask him to help her find a place. Even though her son would be home later that day, she wanted the whole afternoon to be nothing but cheer with no talk of selling the house or of where to live. Belen got on the phone, dialing her son's number.

"Herro," someone said.

Belen hung up. She dialed again, more slowly. It rang.

"Herro?"

"Hello?"

"Hi."

"Is Emerson there?

"No. He sleeping."

"What?"

"Bed. Dreaming."

"Oh, please tell him his mother called. I need—"

"Hi, Emerson's mom. I sorry about you husband."

"Thank you."

"You pretty lady."

The voice on the phone sounded cheerful, an element she hadn't had in her life in quite some time. "Pardon?"

"You pretty. I saw you picture that Emerson have. You pretty lady. You wear beautiful dress in black-and-white picture."

"Oh, it wasn't so beautiful."

"Yes. It gorgeous. What color was dress?"

"I think it was blue. Sapphire blue."

"Very strong color."

"Yes, I thought so back then, too."

"Not every girl carry sapphire blue. I bet you carry good."

"Well, I did get a lot of compliments on the dress."

"Taffeta?"

"Yes, it was taffeta. It came with a matching cape, but I didn't wear it in the photo."

"No, it hide shoulders too much. You have good shoulders."

"Oh, thank you. Don't tell anyone. I chose that strapless dress to show off my shoulders a little."

"I tell no one. You Pearl. I can tell."

"Pearl?"

"Pearl is classy person no matter what. You put pearl in jewelry box, you put pearl in trash can. But it still pearl wherever you put it."

"What's your name again?"

"My name Michael. But I think I change, maybe Jose."

"Why?"

"I think I find better name."

"Oh, no, I think Michael is a good name."

"You think so?"

"Yes, it sounds more handsome."

"Okay, I keep Michael just for you, pretty lady."

"Oh, I'm not so pretty anymore."

"Woman who wear sapphire blue, always pretty."

"You're making me laugh. Will you tell Emerson to call me when he gets up."

"Sure."

"Michael, how do you know Emerson?"

"I, um, his friend."

"I don't remember Emerson talking about you."

"I hard to talk about. I visit from Taiwan."

"Oh, I hope to meet you. I don't know a lot of Emerson's friends. Are you close?"

"You could say that. But Emerson can be so difficult."

"Don't tell him this, but I think he gets it from me."

"Like mother like daughter."

"What?"

"Sorry. My English not so good. I forget how saying goes."

"Will you be dropping by today when my husband returns?"

"Sadly, I have plane to catch. I be back next week."

"Oh, have a safe trip. Don't forget to tell Emerson to call me."

"I not disappoint you, pretty lady."

JORY

"***D***AD," EMERSON SAID. "You'll be home soon."

"Yes," Jory said, grateful that his son was there to help him leave.

"Mom's at home. She's got everything ready."

"Mr. Lalaban," the medic said, rolling him down the hall. "We'll take you back on the stretcher. Once we get you home, there should be a wheelchair waiting for you."

"Okay," he said, watching the nurses wave at him.

"Good luck," one nurse said.

I'll need it, he thought, especially when his wife and son would have to break the news of having no money. *They were waiting for me to get better, I'm sure,* he thought. *I'm feeling better now.*

"Say hi to the mayor for me," another said.

I'll do that, too.

The medic pushed him through two sliding doors, and the fresh morning air kissed his face. He inhaled, deeply. The air, laced with dew and sunshine, was a far better thing to take in than the antiseptic odor of a hospital. He coughed, causing a slight ache in his body. He knew it was the bullet inside of him. He couldn't wait for it to be removed. December 22 was the day set for the operation. A good day, he knew. Winter Solstice. Some call it the shortest day of the year. *Oh, no,* Jory thought. *That is the longest night in the calendar, when the Moon has more time to shine.* He was lifted into the ambulance.

"I'll see you at home," Emerson said.

"Yes. Home."

He saw the two doors at the back of the ambulance close; the engine started, and Jory, facing the rear of the automobile, saw the hospital through the window going farther and farther away. He smiled.

"Hang tight, sir," said the medic. "We'll be there lickety split."

"Lickety split," Jory repeated. On the freeway, he watched cars behind the ambulance turn on their blinkers to shift lanes. Several cars did this. One car attracted his attention. It was old, but shiny. It lingered there for a while before putting on its left turn signal. The car sped up, almost parallel to the ambulance. Jory looked through the side window and saw the word *Comet* on the side, just above the tire. The window he looked through was tinted, so he couldn't make out the color of the car. He saw a child stick his head out the window, smiling, enjoying the wind in his face. The car continued to accelerate, leaving the ambulance behind.

"Almost there," the medic said.

Jory saw exit signs for cars going the opposite way on the freeway. Silverlake, Vermont. The ambulance slowed, then made a curve. It must be his exit, Benton Way. He looked out the window at the familiar neighborhood, and his heart pounded. He saw the Mobil gas station and the twenty-four-hour donut shop. He saw the sign for Temple Street, and his palms began to perspire.

He felt the car turn. He didn't have to see a sign to know it was his street, Carondelet.

The ambulance came to a stop. The doors opened, and the first faces he saw were Mr. and Mrs. Kim.

"Welcome back," said Mrs. Kim, while Mr. Kim shook his hand, the weak one caused by a bullet pushing against nerves.

He heard clanging noises as the medic and Mr. Kim secured the metal legs of the stretcher on the ground. They turned the stretcher in the direction of the house, and, for the first time in months, he saw the front entrance to his home. His wife and son stood on the front steps.

He looked up and down, side to side, taking in the full view of this house. Beautiful. The medic moved the stretcher toward the entrance of his home. Emerson stepped down to help lift the stretcher up the stairs and through the doors.

He smelled coffee brewing. Jory tightened his lips, stifling a cry.

⌐

A FEW DAYS later, Jory found himself in front of a table with a cake on it. Around him were his wife, son, and neighbors. People from the post office came in uniform and threw confetti at him. Everyone sang, "For he's a jolly good fellow, for he's a jolly good fellow, for he's jolly good fellooooooooow, that nobody can deny!"

"Welcome back, Jory," said Mr. Kim.

"Yes, good to have you home—where you belong!" said Mrs. Kim.

There was music playing and kids from the neighborhood running here and there. Jory clapped his hands when the cake was being cut. German chocolate, his favorite. His home had a life to it he hadn't seen in a long time. It was a festive season, and people wore holiday colors of white and red.

There were strangers there who quickly became friends: people from Emerson's office; nurses from Belen's work; and people from the Edelman Center, Rabbi Shultz and Sylvia Jacobs. She brought her little boy who was hit by a bullet. The boy's arm was in a weird contraption to help it heal where the bullet hit him.

"Let's take a picture," said Belen.

And there they were, a boy and a man who had bullets in them from the same gun, side by side. In the picture, they were smiling. Not a hint of tragedy. The little boy gave the older man a hug, and Jory whispered a little blessing on the boy, granting him a long and joyful life.

There was a loud knock at the door, and Emerson answered. A man in a dark suit entered, followed by two people. One of them had a camera. The man in the suit looked familiar. Emerson shook his hand and led him toward Jory.

"Dad, the mayor is here. He dropped by to wish you well."

"Why is the mayor here?" Jory asked.

"Because he's worried about you and wants to make sure you're well."

The mayor! Jory thought. *He came to check up on this old Filipino man.* Jory was honored. The mayor extended his hand while cameras flashed. Belen handed the mayor a plate of food. The mayor loosened his tie and sat down to eat.

With this buzz of voices and music around him, he felt joy. Jory savored the moment and asked for a slice of the German chocolate cake.

EMERSON

*E*MERSON ARRIVED AT his parents' house at seven in the morning, just before starting his job at eight. He positioned the wheelchair by the bed, took hold of his father's paralyzed legs, gently pulling them over the side of the mattress. Emerson thought it would be easier if he lifted his father's whole body from the bed to the chair—a process that would have taken all of ten seconds—but his dad would have no part in it.

"Do you think I'm helpless? You think I'm a baby?" Jory said.

Emerson hunched down, letting his father put his arm around him, best-friend–style, and tried lifting him into the wheelchair. His father grabbed hold of the bed's metal railing with his other arm to steady himself. It took several tries to get his father into the wheelchair, usually taking three counts of three to get him going.

"One," Emerson said, "two, three!"

He and his father rose about an inch before Jory let his arm buckle and he'd have to be set down on the bed again. Emerson fastened his arm firmly around his father's waist.

"One, two, three!"

This time they almost made it to a full standing position. Well, standing for Emerson, with Jory leaning against his son. His father's balance was off, and they slumped back onto the bed.

"Dad," Emerson said, "just move with me, okay? One, two, three—"

Before his father could respond, Emerson lifted his father, swung him over, and landed him into the wheelchair. Emerson was breathing hard. His father was breathing hard, his hand on his chest.

"I can feel it," Jory said.

"Feel what?"

"Bullet is right here."

Emerson put his hand on his father's emaciated chest and rubbed it.

"Not there. On my back."

Emerson stood behind the wheelchair and massaged his father's back. He could feel the raw skin that had been cut open and sewn back up again. He said, "The bullet will be out next week."

Just before he wheeled his father into the kitchen to eat the breakfast his mother was preparing, he looked up at wall, where his father's bed had been pushed up, and saw the different Get Well cards taped to it. He took comfort in seeing that the wall was full of life again.

MICHAEL

*I*N THE AIR, between Bangkok and
Taipei, he noticed that there were fewer Westerners traveling. He
knew that Christmas was nearing, and most Westerners didn't
like to work around that time. His family observed Christmas,
but was not rabid about it the way Westerners were. Growing up,
his family had a small tree about a foot high tucked away in the
corner, and his mom made an American dish like hamburgers to
eat on Christmas day. As far as he was concerned his favorite part
about Christmas was when it ended; he made it a point to be in
the States on the twenty-sixth to take advantage of the incredible
sales offered at Neiman Marcus and Saks.

Lunar New Year was the really big celebration that his family
observed, and Michael had the romantic, funny idea of bringing
Emerson home to meet his family. His mother would love
Emerson's flawless English, and his younger siblings would gawk
at the fact that his American friend looked like Andy Lau.

He thought a trip to Asia would be good for Emerson, because to be an Asian man in Asia is much different from being an Asian man in the West. He is more secure. He is treated better. His opinion is more valued. That is what happens when you're a part of the majority. Plus, there are more hair care products designed for him.

It would be good for Emerson to travel more, take reprieves from Los Angeles. He couldn't believe that Emerson's first trip outside of LA was Las Vegas, with facades of New York, France, Italy, and Egypt. Michael could get a travel pass and take Emerson to the real Manhattan, the real Eiffel Tower, the real gondolas, the real pyramids and more, so much more. The temples of Kyoto, the bright lights of Hong Kong, the tallest building in the world in Kuala Lumpur, the beaches of South America. Michael saw himself walking with Emerson on the sands of Tahiti, holding hands. No matter where he was in the world, Michael, with Emerson at his side, would feel at home.

Someday they would make a trip to China. A girl. They would adopt a girl there. And, maybe a boy. A boy from the Philippines.

BELEN

*B*ELEN COULDN'T WAIT to get home to sleep. Her day at A Place of Rest left her tired and ragged. If she had to shove another bedpan underneath someone's ass, she'd scream. She was doing enough of that on her off time with Jory. At work, she had to take it a step further. She examined the shit to see if it was a healthy color.

She pulled up and saw Emerson's car parked in front. A light was on in the living room. Her spirits lifted at seeing life in that house again. Emerson was probably putting his father to bed. She was grateful Emerson took on the task of lifting his father into and out of that wheelchair. She knew how to do it herself, but the weight of her husband's body was handled much more easily by a younger man.

She opened the door, thinking of the bed that awaited her. She came onto Jory and Emerson sitting across from one another, a game of checkers going on between them, the checker board placed on the handles of Jory's wheelchair where his elbows rested. There was something about that scene that revived her.

"I thought Dad might wanna play or something," Emerson said.

It was a lovely sight, one she hadn't seen in a long time. The scene wasn't complete though. Music needed to fill the air. She let her bag drop to the floor, yanked out some LPs, put one of them on the stereo, and turned up the volume just a bit. Filipino songs filled the air. She saw Jory's head bounce from side to side and Emerson's foot tap.

She hummed to the songs, everyone once in a while contributing a few nonsensical words to the tune, la—dee—lie, la—dee—lie. She swayed to the music, lifting the hem of her dress a little to simulate a lavish ball gown.

"You look like you're going to fight a bull," Jory said. Emerson chuckled. Belen, for the first time in what seemed like years, laughed. She let go of the hem of her dress, put her hands on her hips, stomped her foot, and said, "So what's wrong with that?" And returned to dancing, arms in the air, legs going from side to side.

"King me," Emerson said.

"Where?" Jory said.

She twirled and twirled. The tiredness left her body. She could have gone on all night. She stopped dancing to the rhythm of the music, she moved out of sync, listening to the ordinary sounds checkers make, hopping along cardboard.

⁓

LATE AT NIGHT, long after Emerson had gone, Jory invited Belen to his bed.

"Lay down with me," her husband said.

She slid next to him, her head against his chest. What a warm and familiar feeling! It was nice to feel this familiar with Jory again.

"After all this," he said, "let's go on a vacation."

Belen was quiet.

"We can use some of our savings to go somewhere, maybe Hawaii. Wouldn't that be nice?"

"Yes," Belen said. She closed her eyes, listening to the beating of Jory's heart.

"Will we have enough money?"

She remained silent.

"Belen?"

"Yes. We'll go away. We are the richest people in the world." Belen lifted her head, pleased to see her husband's face so close to hers. She moved closer and kissed him, kissed him for a long, long time. She felt him pull away.

"You know," Jory began.

"Yes, honey-bunny?"

She saw Jory look up at the ceiling.

"The worst part of this, this whole thing . . . " he said.

"What?"

"I can't love you the way I want," he said, touching his legs. "I can't feel anything down there."

"I can still give you the moon," she said, smiling.

Jory laughed.

Belen liked that sound. She undressed.

JORY

"ARE YOU GOING to do this every day, Emerson?" Jory asked, slipping his arm around his son's neck.

"One, two, three."

"Emerson?"

"Dad, you're not even trying. We have to get going. You have one more night at the hospital, then they get that last bullet outta ya in morning One, two, three—"

Jory landed on the plastic seat of his wheelchair. He asked again, "Are you going to come every day to help me?"

"I hope not," Emerson said.

Jory heard the weariness in his voice.

"I mean, I hope you'll learn to do it yourself," Emerson said. "That's why we're paying for physical therapy."

"Is everyone ready?" Jory heard Belen say. She stood at the doorway of the room, adjusting her coat.

"I don't like that physical therapy," Jory said. "I can exercise my arms myself. Maybe save some money."

"Don't be ridiculous, Dad. People at the hospital are pros. They'll know what to do to get you into tip-top shape."

"What are you talking about?" Belen said.

"I think Dad is getting the hospital jitters."

"Honey-bunny, it's the last operation. Then you don't have to go back."

He felt Emerson push his wheelchair to the door. Jory put the lock valve in place, freezing the movement of the wheels.

"C'mon, Dad, stop farting around."

Emerson reached down to release the wheels. Jory swatted it away and said, "I keep waiting for you to tell me."

"Tell you what, honey-bunny?"

"That we're broke."

He saw Emerson step away, walk to his mother. They stood looking at him. *They're ganging up on me,* he thought.

"Everything will be fine," Belen said. "We'll figure it out."

"Yeah," Emerson said. "I've got some money. It'll be all right."

Jory was unconvinced. His face must have reflected his thoughts, because Belen clasped her hands together, raising them to her chest, the way he first saw her praying. It was a sign of pleading.

"Jory," she said, walking toward him. She got on one knee and said, "We didn't tell you because we didn't want you to worry. You have to get better, stronger. You don't have to worry about this money stuff. It's only money anyway. We can deal with it."

Jory looked down to the ground.

"Yeah, Dad," Emerson said, his voice unusually chipper. "It's no big deal. I said I'm helping out. You know, I'm expecting a raise later this year. That'll help. You don't have to worry about this. You don't."

Jory shut his eyes and said, "Okay. Maybe if things get really bad, we can sell the house."

"We've thought about that, right, Mom?"

"Yes, Jory, we already thought of that. We probably won't have to do it for a little while."

"When?" Jory said.

"Maybe later next year," Belen said. "We can find an apartment. Emerson said he'd help us look."

"Yes, Dad. A real nice apartment in a better neighborhood. Maybe in the Westside where mom works."

"So, things will work out," Jory said, looking up, forcing a smile.

"Of course!" Belen said. "Now, enough of this. Let's get ready to go."

"You'll feel better tomorrow when the bullet is out of your system," said Emerson.

Jory's son walked behind him, unlocked the wheels, and pushed the chair to the rear of the house. He gently maneuvered Jory down the steps of the back door. Jory waited for Belen to pull the car up.

Jory looked at the back yard. The sunflowers were still high, the branches of some of the bushes were bare. The grass was drying. The place where Jun was buried still wasn't flat, the earth slightly raised to remind him that a child lived and died here, a family landed on this very spot to start again. And again.

He'd hoped someone would say, "That's ridiculous. What were you thinking?" when he mentioned the hideous idea of selling the house. He'd hoped Belen would say, "Jory, are you crazy, crazy, crazy? This is our *home.*" He'd hoped Emerson wouldn't say anything. Just laugh. Just laugh at the notion that they would get rid of the house where he shared a room with Jun.

I walked miles, Jory thought, *so we could live here.* Delivered mail for years, decades. Miles. He ran his hands down legs he could no longer feel. And Belen working at that old folks home, a place they could never afford themselves. Belen, a woman who helped him drink the Moon, was young when she started there and now she was reaching the age of the people whose heads she placed pillows under.

"Dad, are you ready?"

Jory nodded.

"Okay, one, two—"

"Just carry me, Emerson. It's easier."

TOGETHER NOW

*T*HE NIGHT BEFORE the operation, Belen slept.

Michael shopped.

Emerson smoked a joint, then went to bed.

Jory dreamed. He returned to the beach, building sand castles, watching waves roll in, roll out. The Sky began to break. He looked up and saw movement, intense shifting of two people. The picture became more clear. It was a scene in his bedroom. Jory was inspired to make love to his wife on the first night in the new home on Carondelet.

Jory celebrated, buying sandwiches and four bottles of San Miguel Beer. He sat with Belen on the small mattress, by the window. Jory disrobed. Belen followed. The curtains were drawn, and he couldn't see her. After rolling on the bed for several minutes, Jory had to confess that he was aroused but could not rise.

"I think it was too much beer," he said. Jory got up and stumbled around in the darkness. He went to the window and parted the curtains just a bit so he could take in the view of their new street. Quiet. There were no cars to be heard, even the boulevards on each side of Carondelet were silent. He turned, got down on his hands and knees, feeling the ground for the last bottle of San Miguel. He found it a few feet away from the bed. He popped off the lid and took one long swig. He got up to offer a sip to his wife. What he saw caused him to sigh, caused him to put the San Miguel down, and sigh again.

A thin line of moonlight fell from the window and landed across Belen's torso. Her head tilted to the side, her lovely profile imbedded in the blackness and fullness of her hair. The line of moonlight ran down the wall, traveled the floor, up the bed, crossing Belen's body, beginning at her left ear, journeying between her breasts, running down her stomach, her belly button, ending at her pubis.

Jory shivered. There was nothing more beautiful than his God and his love meeting, creating a divine image on this bed, in their home. He got down on his knees, inching forward, humbly and quietly, head bowed like an obedient servant. He studied the beam of light on her body. The path of Moon appeared to be a glowing stream rising to that white ball up there. He kissed Belen's feet, kissed her calves, kissed her knees, slowly positioning his head between her thighs.

He heard her giggle. "Shhhhhhhhhhhhhhh," he said. The moonlight changed the landscape of her body. Her breasts became small mountains, between them, a valley. Her belly moved, shifted like the rolling waves of an ocean. He felt like he had gotten closer to the universe, tasting a river that made its way from the Moon.

On the beach, Jory watched the Sky. Like before, the moving picture fell, almost touching earth. Jory reached for it, but it lifted away, back into the Sky. He wept.

⌢

BELEN WOKE, SHOWERED, and prepared for her day. Jory would be operated on at 7:00 A.M., just a few hours away. She wanted to be there before the anesthesia was administered. She exhaled, walked over to the mantel, and caressed the picture of Jun. She pulled out the small picture of her father and caressed that, too.

"Take care of Jory today," she whispered to the photos.

Take care of Jory today, she prayed.

I will, she heard.

She set off for the hospital and when she arrived, she found Jory awake, sad. She rushed to him.

"What the matter?" she said.

"Thank you, Belen."

"You're welcome," she said, though she wasn't quite sure what he was talking about.

"You gave me the Moon."

⌢

EMERSON STEPPED INTO the hospital room and discovered his father depressed, miserable. His mother brushed the hair from his father's head, cooing, "What's the matter, honey-bunny? Don't be sad."

Rrrrrrrrrrrrrrrrring.

He saw the phone by his father's bed. He ignored it. He approached his dad, took his hand, and said, "Hey, is everything all right?"

"Jory is just a little nervous, aren't you, Jory?" Belen said.

Rrrrrrrrrrrrrrring.

Emerson looked at the phone, looked away. Dr. Jones came into the room. He said, "All set." An orderly came in and took his father away. Dr. Jones and his mother followed. Emerson was alone in the room.

Rrrrrrrrrrrrrrring.

—Yeah? Emerson said.

—Tell Dad you love him.

—What?

—Tell him, go and tell him.

—He knows I do.

—I know he does. It's more for you. So, you know he knows.

—I'll talk to him after the operation.

—Tell him *now!*

—. . .

—Go!

Emerson hung up, walked into the hallway. His father, mother, Dr. Jones, and the orderly waited for the elevator. Emerson's pace was brisk. Once he heard the ding of the elevator, he ran. He jumped into the elevator and looked down at his dad. His eyes were bloodshot. His breathing slow.

"Dad?" Emerson said. He looked up, saw Dr. Jones and the orderly pressed against the wall of the elevator. He felt self-conscious suddenly. He wanted to say I Love You, but the presence of the two men hindered him.

"Dad," Emerson said. *"Pipiyanta ha."*

"Pipiyanta ha," Jory said.

~

IN TAIPEI, MICHAEL narrowed down his choices to three shirts. The mall would be closing soon, and he couldn't quite settle on a gift for Emerson. He looked at the black oxford shirt. It was handsome, and Michael knew that Emerson took to dark colors. Still, it didn't seem right. There was something about the front pocket on the breast of the shirt that bothered him. He never recalled Emerson wearing shirts with pockets. He looked at the emerald green polo shirt with vertical stripes and solid collar. He felt the shirt and didn't approve of the cotton polyester mix or the thinness of the material. He raised the third shirt, a dark brown short-sleeved button-down. It was well made and handsome, but the color would simply blend right into Emerson's skin. He returned the items and strolled through the men's section. He stumbled onto the athletic department and saw something that appealed to him. It was a simple V-neck T-shirt, thick and 100-percent cotton. There was really nothing extraordinary about it except for the color. It was baby blue. It made Michael smile. He bought it and believed he had made a wise purchase.

~

JORY WALKED ALONG the beach, waiting for the operation to be over. He would wake and return to Belen and Emerson. He walked and walked, knowing that when he woke, his useless legs would return. And he would have to deal with the fact that the house he'd called home for thirty years would be gone.

It would've been better if I'd died on the first day, he thought.

~of

BELEN STOOD WHEN Dr. Jones entered the lounge.

"Everything went perfect," Dr. Jones said.

Belen turned to Emerson and smiled. Her son smiled back.

"He's recovering. You can visit him in a few hours."

~

RRRRRRRRRING.

Emerson left his mother, approaching a pay phone in the corner. He looked around, then picked it up.

—Dad's fine.

—I heard.

—He'll be up in a few hours.

—We'll talk then.

⌒

MICHAEL PERUSED THE international papers at the duty-free shop. He bought an issue of *USA Today*. It was two days old, but it was something he could read on the plane. He also bought a card that he would give to Emerson along with the shirt. Inside the card, he wrote: "I love you."

⌒

BELEN SAT QUIETLY in the room, watching Jory sleep. She checked her watch. Jory should have been awake by now.

⌒

EMERSON WAVED HIS hands around in a corner of the parking structure, trying to rid the area of marijuana smoke. He waved his arms about, believing the smell was dissipating. A mother and child strolled by. The child wondered why this man was flapping his arms, trying to fly.

⌒

BELEN APPROACHED THE nurses' station.

"My husband hasn't woken yet. Something's wrong."

The nurse looked up from her paperwork and said, "Let's go take a look."

⌒

"X-RAYS?" EMERSON asked with surprise.

"Chest and a brain scan. Just to make sure," Dr. Jones said. "It's probably nothing."

⌒

ON THE PLANE, Michael looked out the window. He saw the separation of day and night. He was entering a part of the flight where light and dark shifted.

He leafed through the paper. There was a diagram showing the importance of the Winter Solstice, marking the beginning of Winter. This Winter Solstice is particularly appealing because it will have a particularly full moon. A full moon on a Winter Solstice hadn't happened in 133 years. It would be a large moon, fourteen percent larger than usual.

⌒

THE SKY MOVED. Jory sat back, watching.

"You'll wake them and you know Emerson doesn't sleep good," he heard a voice say. Jory laughed. He knew that voice was his. He knew what he would say next, "Belen, if Emerson gets up. I will not put him to bed. You do it."

"Of course, I'll put Emerson to bed," Belen said.

Jory laughed some more. What a wonderful evening that was.

⌒

BELEN LOOKED AT the X-rays Dr. Jones presented her.

"As you know, problems can arise. A blood clot formed right here," Dr. Jones said, circling the area with his finger.

"A pulmonary embolism," Belen said. "You'll prescribe blood thinner, then?" she said. It was a strategy to loosen the clot.

"Yes, but, as a nurse, I'm sure you know . . ."

Belen looked at him. Her gaze firm. *I know,* she thought.

⌒

"HI, THOM," EMERSON said into the phone. "I got your message. So, you found the guy whose been sending the hate mail?

He's been writing Baylor, too? Yeah, my dad was operated on this morning. He's recuperating. Thanks. They're gonna do some X-rays—"

"Emerson," he heard from behind him. He turned and saw his mother. There was something in her face that made him say into the phone, "Thom, gotta call you later."

～

MICHAEL HEARD HIS cell phone ring. He answered it.

"Michael, I know I shouldn't call you when you're flying but I didn't know who to call. I just don't know," Emerson said.

"Slow down. What happened?"

"My dad isn't waking up. They might have to put him on a machine or something."

"I get there soon."

"Promise?"

"I promise."

～

EMERSON RUSHED TO the hospital cafeteria, buying a small box of chicken and a can of Mountain Dew. He went back up to his father's room. He laid the food out on a table near his dad's bed. He looked out the window; evening came quickly. The moon was perfectly round. *He's up there somewhere,* Emerson believed; somewhere up there his father's soul was wandering. He remembered the *Tawal* was a ritual meant for dying people to return to health. It worked the first time.

"Soul of Jory Lalaban . . . " Emerson said, trying to remember how his dad used to say this prayer. He tried again, "Soul of Jory Lalaban, you have gone away. Come. I am calling you." He bowed his head and improvised his own prayer, "Dad, you're up there somewhere. You cast a spell on me that I cannot break. Your wizardry is immense. I bow to you. Now, I shoot a spell into the sky and command you to return to me."

～

JORY LOOKED AT the Moon, full and bright. The Moon was showing him only the most beautiful part of Himself.

"It is Your night," Jory said, looking up. "Winter Solstice. For one night of the year, most of the hours of a day are Yours. The Sun is the farthest away and cannot overpower You, Moon. Tonight, You own the Sky."

"Dad?"

Jory looked around. *Emerson?*

"Dad, I'm calling you."

"Not now, Emerson. I'm talking to the Moon."

"I'm calling you."

"Emerson, it's Winter Solstice. It only comes once a year."

"I command you to return to me."

"Command? Don't order your father around. Now, go play. I'm busy."

～

THE NEXT MORNING, Dr. Jones said, "If things persist, I think you might want to consider other options, maybe turn off the machines?" Belen wouldn't hear of it.

"I'll respect whatever decision you want to make, but are you sure you know what you're saying?"

"Of course, I'm sure. I'm a nurse."

"Mrs. Lalaban," Dr. Jones said, "There's a difference between a nurse and a wife. I think you're being more of a wife in this situation."

"Don't tell me what I'm being," she said and walked away.

"Mom, let's go somewhere, maybe get something to eat."

"I want to stay with your father."

"It'll be just for a moment. I want to talk to you."

Belen followed Emerson to a vending machine. He put quarters in the machine and pressed some buttons. A bag of cookies fell out. He ripped the bag open and offered her some chocolate chip. She took one and put it into her mouth. Belen looked at her son and could tell that he'd been thinking, a weary expression on his face.

"Mom," Emerson said. "He's been asleep for twenty-four hours. I'm sure he'll wake up soon."

"Of course, he'll wake up."

They sat for several minutes.

"What if he doesn't?" Emerson said.

Belen got up and walked away.

⟿

MICHAEL EXITED LAX, called Emerson's home number, leaving a message on his machine. "I here," he said. He drove home, back to Shangri-La Apartments. His roommates were gone, working their respective routes for Taiwan Air.

He unpacked, placing the blue T-shirt he bought for Emerson on his bed. His phone rang.

"Herro."

"Hi." It was Emerson.

"How you holding?"

"Not so good. Can I see you? I need to get away from here for a while."

"Sure."

Michael placed the blue shirt in an expensive box from Crate and Barrel and the most gorgeous wrapping paper he could find at the Hallmark store. Half an hour later, Emerson arrived.

Michael opened the door to the most tired man he'd ever seen. Emerson leaned against the door frame for support. Michael had the insatiable need to care for him.

"You need rest," Michael said. "You need rest bad." He took Emerson's hand and led him to the couch. Emerson collapsed into it, sitting back with arms and legs splayed. Michael sat next to him, leaned over, and kissed him on the cheek.

"Kiss me again," Emerson said.

Michael kissed his lips, kissed his chin, kissed his neck. He unbuttoned Emerson's shirt, kissed his chest, kissed his stomach. He unbuckled Emerson's belt.

⌒

ON THE THIRD day that Jory did not wake, Belen sat by his bed-side, thinking.

Belen, dear . . .

Oh, hello.

Hello.

You know, I adore you, Heavenly Lady. You know I have always turned to you in my time of need and your voice has always been a comfort to me. Blessed Lady, I sometimes wondered if you understand me. If you've been there for me.

Of course, I've been there for you, dear.

When my son died, the grief was overwhelming.

Don't forget that my son died, too. I understand that kind of grief rather well.

But your Son was a God. My Jun was just an ordinary boy. My husband is an ordinary man. I am an ordinary woman.

Belen, I know your trials. Yes, you've suffered. We've all suffered. We make it through somehow. Mother Teresa said it herself. God is in the faces of the poor and starving. Suffering is ultimately a way to know God.

You treat suffering as a holy concept, something to strive for. In actuality, suffering is gruesome.

Belen—

Wait, Divine Mother, let me finish. Think back. Think back to when Jesus died and you held His body in your arms. Do you remember His flesh? Do you recall what it is like to touch skin? Remember the touch of skin? The little hairs that folded when your fingers caressed His arm. The warmth that was there—gone. Soft, lively skin that had turned dull like wax. Or trying to lift a head upon lifeless shoulders. Or grasping a hand that used to wave at you, but now only lays there like a piece of wood. To wonder, sometimes for years, where did it go? Where did all that life go? He was on his skateboard, then he was in the ground. He was at work delivering mail, and now he's in a hospital bed. That burst of life that enabled fingers to move and joints to bend—gone. Seeing life go like that, in an instant, is suffering. Suffering is painful and awful. It stains the clothes you wear and obscures the days ahead. And if you knew suffering, Blessed Mother, really knew it, then you would make it stop.

I can only provide comfort, dear. I have no control over what humans do to each other or what you do to yourselves, the awful things that you people do. I can comfort you.

I don't want comfort. I want understanding. I don't want to cry in your lap anymore. I want someone to say, Yes, living can be a tough thing. Yes, I agree with you, children and spouses shouldn't die too soon and screw the world—*pardon my language*—for making it so. *Please understand, Divine Mother, I'm not turning away from you. I will always pray to you, ask your indulgence, but for the philosophical things. Not the ordinary things, not the plain things, not the regular worries of someone like me.*

Belen, I must say that you're making my heart weep. You saying that someone like me won't understand the plight of the ordinary person makes me want to cry.

Then cry, Divine Mother. I do not mean to be disrespectful. Let the tears flow. Let it come from deep inside you. And not the pleasant tears, the small ones that drop from your eyes. Cry so hard that the black mascara you bought at the 99-cent store streaks and blackens your face. That the mucous from your nose slips into your mouth and mixes with your saliva, then bubbles from your lips. Your hairdo ravaged from fingers ripping hairs from your head. Your clothes wrinkled from tossing all night, all day, and all night again. Your armpits, your breath, your whole being reeking because you don't have the strength to wash. Your whole body, your whole being emulating the sorrow that you feel. Don't cry like a Lady, cry like a woman. Cry like that.

⌒

ON THE FOURTH day, Emerson met with Dr. Jones. Dr. Jones told him the likelihood of his father waking was nil.

"Did you tell my mom?"

"I tried, but she wouldn't listen."

Emerson thanked the doctor, got into his car, drove to Chinatown, and parked in a lot. He walked around, entered a restaurant with ducks hanging in the window, bought sweet and sour chicken, egg rolls, and rice. He walked around a bit more and went into a store that sold a variety of roots, mushrooms, seeds, dried foods, and something that claimed to be goat's tongue. He looked up and saw a wall filled with jars. The jars were clear with white caps. Inside of them were snakes, floating in some kind of oil. Some of the snakes looked like cobras with wide heads, some of them were yellow or black.

"Can I help you?" a woman in a white coat asked. She looked like a pharmacist.

"I'd like to buy one of those," Emerson said, pointing to the wall of snakes.

When he returned to the hospital with his brown bag of food, his mother said, "Look, Jory, Emerson came back from Chinatown with food." She picked up a fork and dug into a white box, pulling up sweet and sour chicken attached to the prongs. "It's delicious." She placed the fork near Jory's face.

"Mom, you know he can't eat it."

"I know he can't eat it. I'm bringing it to his nose so he can smell it."

"He probably can't smell it either."

Belen withdrew the fork. Silence. "Where did you get the food?"

"A restaurant Michael—a friend told me about."

"This is more than the two of us can eat. Maybe the nurses would like some."

As soon as she left, Emerson pulled a paper bag he kept hidden under his coat. He pulled out a jar and tried unscrewing the lid. It was packed tightly. He banged the lid lightly on the metal bars of his dad's bed.

He tried unscrewing the lid again and it twisted with a small pop. A stench invaded his nostrils, something rancid and bitter. He looked into the jar and saw the top of the snake's head floating.

He pulled the snake out, keeping most of its body just above the jar, letting the oil ooze down the snake's vertebrae, back into the bottle. He hadn't contemplated how he'd do this or if this was even going to work. All he knew was that his father believed in such things. It was an act of desperation. He understood that. Dr. Jones said there was almost no chance that his father would recover. But he had to try one last thing. Just one.

He looked at the snake and thought of cutting it into pieces, but his father wouldn't be able to chew it or swallow. Cutting it into pieces would take time, and his mother would be returning soon. He didn't want her to see him this way, a man with a snake in his hand.

He lifted the serpent and saw the moist scales, green and yellow in color. All together, the snake must have been no longer than nine inches, but in his mind, it might as well have been six feet long. He smelled it and it made his eyes water. He put his mouth to the snake's body, shut his eyes, and clenched it with his teeth.

He pulled the head away from him and felt it easily detach from the rest of the body. The lower part of the snake fell back into the jar. Emerson's mouth was filled with something vile and wet and meaty. He almost gagged, but he chewed. He pushed the meat back and forth with his tongue, rolling it around his teeth. His eyes teared.

As he chewed, he placed the head of the snake back into the jar, replacing the lid. His mouth seemed to burn and moisture dampened his cheeks. He put the bottle, carrying the cut-up snake under the hospital bed.

When he was sure that the meat in his mouth had been properly tenderized, he pulled it from his mouth by pinching it between his fingers. He bent down, and with his free hand, opened his father's jaw. He placed the meat onto his dad's tongue, closing his mouth, then massaging his jaw.

"Here, Dad, snake just for you. It'll make you strong. Wake up."

Here, with the most significant man in his life lying comatose, Emerson began to feel sorrow. He hadn't felt this way since Jun died. No one should have to feel this kind of loss twice in one lifetime. He continued to massage his father's jaw when he heard his mother say, "What are you doing?"

"Just trying to make him feel comfortable."

"Oh. Can you stay here for awhile? I need to go to church."

⁓

BELEN WORE HER modesty veil, looked around the church. She was alone. She felt truly alone.

JORY DREW A deep breath, smelling air. It was fresh. He inhaled one more time, and the freshness filled his lungs. There was something different about this inhalation. In the back of his throat a bitter flavor formed. It made him cough. He inhaled again and the flavor became more pronounced, more pungent. He knew the taste. Snake. Oh, the memories of snake.

The flavor rode up his throat and filled the cavities of his nose and mouth. He felt the insides of his mouth with his tongue, looking for a piece of meat he knew he did not eat. He sighed and the smell and taste of snake overwhelmed him, causing him to cough and cough and cough.

"Are you okay, Dad?"

Jory turned and saw a little boy. He knew the child immediately. "Jun." He ran toward the boy and picked him up. He held the child, kissing him all over his face. He inhaled his son's scent. Yes, it was him. "Jun, what are you doing here?"

The boy touched his forehead to Jory's forehead. "Dad, are you ready to go?"

MICHAEL STOOD AT the entrance of the hospital arguing with the woman at the front desk.

"I told you I a friend of Emerson. He expecting me."

"I'm sorry, sir, but only family is allowed to visit. Besides, I don't know if you're a member of the press or what. Can you call him?"

"He didn't have cell phone and I leave message for him at home two times. Can you get him? He know me."

"We don't have the staff to go get people. Until—"

"What's the matter?" a small woman said, appearing from nowhere.

"Mrs. Lalaban, this man claims to know your family. He'd like to visit."

Mrs. Lalaban looked him up and down.

"Remember me, pretty lady?" Michael said.

"I talked to you on the phone," she said. "You can come up with me."

⁓

EMERSON STUDIED HIS father's face. It was clear.

"Emerson?" his mother said. He turned.

"Mom, look."

"You have—"

"Mom," he said. "Look." He stood up, took hold of his mother's wrist, and pulled her to Jory's bedside. "Look, Mom. This is wonderful."

"What?" she said.

"Look."

"Is he moving?"

He put his hands on her shoulders and said, "Look at his face, his eyes."

"I don't see anything."

"He's been sleeping for four days. No dead dreams. They all came to fruition."

Emerson and his mother were quiet for a long time.

"Emerson, you have a friend outside."

Emerson slowly left the room and found Michael sitting in the lounge.

Michael stood and said, "Happy nowhere."

"Happy nowhere to you, too."

⁓

BELEN BEGAN TO wonder about Mother Teresa. She knew what it would take for Mother Teresa to gain sainthood. Mother Teresa would be investigated by the church. Once it was discovered that she had lived a devout life, she would be open for Public Worship and given the title of "Blessed." If the Blessed is prayed to and there is documented proof that she has provided miracles in a truly hopeless situation, say, restoring a blind person's sight, then she will be given the title of "Saint." Some people have waited for centuries to be promoted from Blessed to Saint.

If she wasn't going to pray to the Mother Mary, perhaps she could pray to Mother Teresa. She would fervently pray to the Mother of Charity. Yes! That's what she would do. This thought made her smile. Once Jory woke, Belen would call the Vatican and tell the Pope that a miracle had occurred due to prayers to Mother Teresa. In exchange, Mother Teresa, having performed a miracle on a hopeless case, would get closer to sainthood. She imagined calling the Vatican.

"Was your husband's case hopeless?" the Pope would ask.

"Yes, it was."

"Are you positively sure?"

"Positive. My husband was in a coma. There was clotting. I prayed to Mother Teresa and he woke up. Now can she become a saint?"

"But was it absolutely hopeless?"

"*Yes!*" she said aloud. "*Yes! Yes! Yes!* It was hopeless."

She opened up her purse, pulling out some aspirins to relieve a headache. She thought about their life, especially about the time Jory had conducted his first *Kanyao*, ridding a woman of her migraines. Jory fainted at the ceremony. She went into the house to get a glass of water. She pulled aspirin from her purse and crushed it with her shoe. She put it into the glass of water, stirring it with her finger to dissolve the powdered aspirin. She later had the woman drink the glass. She had complete faith in her husband's abilities, but there wasn't anything wrong with helping a little. She wanted to help Jory, make him a little happy. Looking at her husband, she wondered if Jory was happy at all.

"Emerson?" she whispered. She went to look for him. She stepped into the hallway and saw Emerson leaning into his friend. Emerson's face buried in Michael's torso. This friend, this Michael had his arms around Emerson, rocking him, rocking him, rocking him. His face in Emerson's hair.

She walked closer to them. Closer. closer still. She was only four feet away from the two men. They did not notice her, feel her come near. Of course not, she knew. When you're in love, no one else in the world exists. There is no sound, no calendar.

"Emerson?" she said. She noticed how he pulled away from Michael, shot away from him like the wrong side of a magnet, straightened his shirt, afraid to look at her. There was something familiar about that look. She had that same look when she tried hiding her relationship with Jory from her mother, her friends, her province.

"Mom . . . Michael was just . . . he . . . Is everything all right with Dad?"

"I want to talk to you about something."

~

WHEN HER MOTHER shot her father, Belen knew, it was the least Ermaline Dubabang could have done for a man she respected and had three children with. She thought of this on the fifth day when Jory did not regain conciousness. It became clear, he never would. Belen signed the appropriate papers to have the respiratory therapist dismantle the machines that helped Jory breathe. The machines would be dismantled the following day.

Belen thought about her mother, a flawed woman, but the strongest woman she'd known in her life. Right up there with the Blessed Virgin and Mother Teresa. What makes a person strong, rather than ordinary, she surmised, was graciously rising to the most remarkable challenges with dignity, while at the same time preserving the dignity of others.

Belen met the respiratory therapist who would dismantle the machines that kept Jory's breath fluid. The respiratory therapist seemed to be a competent, well-mannered man, but had no personal stake in the matter of letting her husband die.

"May I?" she asked. She explained her background as a nurse and her knowledge of the machines while working at A Place of Rest. She showed him a trial run, performing with great skill how the whole procedure would go.

"Thank you, Mrs. Lalaban," the respiratory therapist said. "But it wouldn't be ethical."

"Please," she said.

"We couldn't," said the attending nurse.

"No, we could all get sued, lose our license to practice by letting you do this," Dr. Jones said.

"You've seen me here every day for months," Belen said. "You all know what I've been through. Do you think I would be the type of person to sue? Believe me, that is the last thing I want to do. I've cared for my husband for decades, and I think I should be the one who should let him go. You can say one of you took Jory off life support. I won't say anything about it."

Dr. Jones said, "Mrs. Lalaban, it's not going to happen."

Belen provided a tight smile and said, "Fine."

Later that evening, Michael had gone home. Belen sat with Emerson watching Jory sleep. Belen said, "It's very quiet in the hospital this time of year. It's the holidays. Nurses get more money when you work the holidays."

"Oh?" Emerson said.

"The staff is probably tired and distracted. You know how Christmas and New Year's do that to people."

"Sure."

"Emerson, I have to dismantle the machines myself. I should be the one."

"Mom, I wish you could. The doctors said otherwise."

"I can do it without them knowing."

"Mom, we can get in trouble."

"Emerson, look at us. What more trouble can we get into?"

"What do we do?"

"There's an alarm that alerts the nurses that the patient isn't breathing. I'll turn off the alarm, then I'll dismantle the machines. I need you to stay calm."

Emerson nodded.

"You stand there," Belen instructed her son, choosing one side of the bed for him to stand. She took the other side. She performed her tasks methodically and at a comfortable pace, pressing switches, removing tubes, unplugging plugs. She kept calm, reminding herself that this was the last act of love she'd ever do for the man she'd loved dearly from the moment she saw him.

"Everything is turned off," she explained to her son, "now he'll breathe on his own for a little bit, then his breathing will slow, and then stop." She did not realize it, but she was crying. She only noticed when a tear fell from her face and onto her arm.

She saw Emerson bend down, his cheek pressed to Jory's hand. She held Jory's other hand, watching her husband's face. Emerson was right. Dead dreams were nowhere to be found.

⁓

JORY WATCHED THE SKY, and he laughed. Jun was nuzzled next to him.

"Do you want to dance?" The wife Belen asked her oldest child. He saw her husband step outside and walk around the house on Carondelet, pouring salt from a canister. The husband entered the house again, finding the youngest son on the ground, and pulled the toddler to his feet, guiding the babe to his wife and oldest son, dancing to music they had brought from the Philippines.

The Sky eventually froze, then fell, floating to the ground, the image of this newly American family wafting down. A corner of the image touched the sand, waving slightly. Jory approached, touched it. It felt fine, gossamer-like, yet firm like leather. He looked up and saw the barren universe, the Stars and the Moon— oh, the Moon, rounder and fuller than he'd ever seen it.

"Take it," Jun said.

"What?"

"Take it and tie it around yourself."

He tied the fine-yet-firm fabric around his waist. He opened his arms and Jun grabbed hold of him.

"This is the fun part," Jun said.

Jory felt the fabric tug a little, sway a bit. He found himself standing on tippy-toe as the Sky slowly lifted itself back into space. The ground soon left him.

With his oldest son in his arms, he flew.

JUNE
———

EMERSON

"*J*USTICE HAS BEEN served," Emerson heard the mayor say on the steps of the courthouse. The press conference was for family members to comment on William Baylor's life sentence. Emerson stood, with his mother by his side, looking at the cameras and the reporters below him, Rabbi Shultz and Sylvia Jacobs not too far away. He looked out onto the street, and saw it was lined with white mail trucks with blue eagles looking toward the sky.

"And now," the mayor said, "to talk about the horrible tragedy that struck his family is Emerson Lalaban."

Emerson stepped forward to flashing cameras, positioning himself to the podium with over a dozen microphones attached to it. He said, "We are pleased with the sentencing." Actually, Emerson wanted William to fry or be injected with poison. Thom Fielding presented the option of the death penalty, but his mother said she'd had enough of death. No more. She asked if there were

other options. Thom said this was a really good opportunity to
send shock waves into the white supremacist community, by having William Baylor, one of their heroes, denounce hate. After
much arguing, Emerson eventually went along with his mother's
decision. Another death isn't going to bring your father back, she
had said.

"Nothing will bring my father back," he said, looking at jour-
nalists scribbling on their notepads. "Nothing. Our lives will be
changed forever." He felt tears building up, but he would not show
it. He showed it to Michael and that was enough. His coworkers
Daisy Chan and Eric Mori were among the crowd. Their faces
calmed him. "My mother and I must continue with the business of living. We don't know how we're going to do that yet,
but I'm sure the answers will come." Emerson looked upward.

"Mrs. Lalaban, do you have anything to add?" a reporter asked.

His mother joined his side. The podium and microphones were
almost taller than she. Emerson stood behind her. She said, "I
want to thank everyone who sent letters. It really helped, knowing that there is kindness in the world." She inhaled, and
Emerson was in tune with her. He knew she was going to cry. He
took her hand, and she cried. He led her back. She collapsed into
him, weeping, using his body as support. He held onto her, while
cameras flashed.

At the end of the conference, she continued to hold onto him,
her arms tightly wrapped around him as they made their way to
a parking lot across the street. Emerson had never believed that
he would ever comfort this woman. Now, there was nothing he'd
rather do but care for her, love her.

Michael stood waiting, a door open to the Ford Galaxie.
Emerson's mother entered the car. Michael sat in the back seat.
Emerson was about to sit behind the wheel when he heard
Rrrrrrrrrrrrrrring. It was coming from Michael's cell phone.

"Michael," Emerson said, "I forgot to call into the office, can I use your cell?"

Rrrrrrrrrrrrrrrrring.

Emerson walked several yards away.

—Hi, Emerson said.

—How are you and Mom doing?

—Better, I guess. We found out that the state won't be pressing charges against me and mom for our stunt in the hospital. We were told that we were under "extreme duress" due to the situation and not thinking or acting properly. Fortunately, they kept that out of the news.

—Good. You'll be all right, you know.

—I hope so.

—'Course you will. Treat Michael right this time.

—Don't worry. I'm not going to fuck it up this time.

—I'll call when you need me.

—I know.

Emerson got back into the car. His boyfriend and his mother chatted about a new restaurant in Glendale, something he didn't particularly care about. Emerson had learned to tune out when Michael and his mother got to talking. They talked about some of the most frivolous things, like the weight that Caroline Kennedy had gained.

He drove home, turning on the radio. A Beatles song came on. "Mother Mary comes to me . . ."

"Turn that off!" Belen ordered.

Emerson pulled up to the house on Carondelet. The house wouldn't be sold. His father's life insurance money allowed his mother to assist with the mortgage.

"It is your father's last gift," his mother said.

He got out of the car. Michael followed, still talking with Belen. He held the door open, letting them enter first.

MICHAEL

*T*HE NEXT MORNING in Emerson's apartment, Michael sat up in bed and looked down at Emerson sleeping beside him. He always woke before Emerson. He got out of bed, yawned, scratched his head. He stepped outside to pick up the morning paper. He stood in his underwear, gazing at the *Times*. On the cover was a picture of Emerson and his mother on the steps of the courthouse, holding each other in a tight embrace. He went inside and read the article. It basically recapped the shooting and William Baylor's sentencing.

He turned the pages and read an article about the sorrows of a country in Asia. A royal family killed by one of their own. The king and queen refused to let their son marry the woman of his choice. The angered prince killed his family for denying him this privilege. *Pearls can lead such devastating lives sometimes,* he thought. *They should have let him marry her.*

He turned the page and read an article about the Pope's Ecclesia on Asia in response to the Asian Synod of 1998. According to the Pontiff, the third millennium would be about Christ's presence in Asia. The first millennium was dedicated to the Christian conversion in Europe. The second millennium was dedicated to the Christian conversion of the Americas and Africa. The focus of the third millennium would be on the Christian conversion of Asia. After all, Jesus was born in Asia. Jesus is Asian.

Michael smirked. He turned to the section that listed the movies, wondering what was opening this week.

BELEN

"*I* GIVE ONE hamburger for your son," Michael said.

Belen laughed. She waved her hand at Michael and laughed some more.

"Okay, two hamburgers. Emerson worth at reast two Big Macs."

Belen squealed. She watched Emerson roll his eyes and dismiss them as idiots. Emerson in his blue T-shirt put down a platter of grilled vegetables on the table. She did not expect to be so hearty when she invited them over for brunch—a word that Michael introduced her to. "Pearls eat brunch," he said. "They have brunch all the time."

Belen wiped the tears streaming from her face. She never thought she'd ever laugh this hard again.

"I throw in fries and Coke," Michael said.

When Emerson sat down she continued to laugh, but the tears

of joy on her face streamed differently. She kept smiling though to give the appearance that she was still happy over Michael's jokes. What made her tears turn from sweet to bitter was the very idea that she'd never thought of what she'd give for Emerson. Oh, this wasn't the Philippines anymore, and the trading of food or objects for children was a thing of the past, but still she wondered.

As she bit into a mushroom drenched in olive oil, she heard the trailing conversation.

"I got you," Michael said to Emerson. "All I pay is a happy meal."

"Do you want Emerson?" Belen said.

"Can we talk about something else?" Emerson said. "I think this joke has gone on a bit too long. *Takalajo.* Calling all spirits. Mom, do you want more juice?"

Belen continued, "If you want my son, it'll cost you." She thought of her mother Ermaline and took a deep breath. She watched Emerson fill her glass, set the pitcher down, and look away.

"It's a high price," Belen said, quite seriously. She saw Emerson push a bell pepper from one side of his plate to another. She watched Emerson put down his fork and rest his arms on the table. "I want to make sure my son goes for more than me."

"Name your price," Michael said, smiling.

She thought for a moment, looked down, then looked up to see Emerson staring at her. "Seven cows," she said.

"Seven cows?" Michael said. "That's a rot of hamburgers."

She continued, "That's only the beginning." Yes, it was. The beginning of something else. "My family was offered several acres of land for me. I want more. Give me the coast of California."

"Emerson is not worth Malibu!" Michael said.

"Yes, he is," she said quietly. In that tone, Michael and

Emerson knew to become silent. "I want Malibu and Santa Monica and Redondo. All the way up to Oregon."

The room was still. She drank her orange juice and looked squarely at Michael. "That is what I want. Seven cows and the coast of California. He is worth that much to me."

"Well, Michael?" Emerson said. "Are you willing to pay that much for me?"

"I cannot afford."

"Then he is still mine," Belen said.

"C'mon," Michael said, whining.

Emerson offered, "Perhaps liberal terms can be arranged? How 'bout it, Mom? Give the guy a break."

"Maybe," Belen said, swallowing the last drops of her orange juice, putting her glass down with a noticeable thud. "Just know that Emerson is worth that much to me."

"Thank you, Mom."

"I will not lower my price, but will respect my son's choice in partners, something that I was not given."

"I got a deal!" Michael said. "This is better than sale at Macy's men's store."

"*Takalajo,*" Emerson said again.

JORY

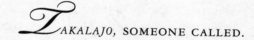*AKALAJO,* SOMEONE CALLED.

He heard.

And answered.

From places on high, he descended to that blue and white orb below, down to that patch of land between two oceans, lower still to the left edge, to the spread-out lights between water and desert, weighted to a house, with a table where three people have food to greet him.

The mother laughed, filling the room with sopranic notes. The son wore blue, a little bit of Sky draped around his body. The friend, strange and kindred, talked about shopping.

There is lightness again.

Takalajo, Emerson said again.

One more joined the quartet. Five in this house on Carondelet. The mother, the son, the friend, and two holy spirits—one big, one small.

THE LALABANS

*I*N JUNE OF 1971, after they had scraped up a down payment for the house, after they bought the Nova, a boxy brown car with no hub caps, after they bought the television, with green lines that disappeared only when you wiggled the antenna, and certainly after they bought the washer and dryer, Belen and Jory, but mostly Belen, decided they could splurge. They chose to spend their money on a Magnavox stereo with speakers two feet high. This was their fifth year in America, and it was decided that it was time to have music in their house.

When they assembled the Magnavox stereo, their boys Emerson, age two, and Jory Junior, nicknamed Jun-Jun, age four, were asleep in their bedroom. They planned to use the stereo the next morning when the boys woke. But Belen couldn't wait.

"You'll wake them," Jory said. "And you know Emerson doesn't sleep good."

Belen waved her husband away and ran to her bedroom. She wanted to hear music. She had gotten tired of relying on her television for entertainment. There was so much bad news relayed through that black box. She was tired of hearing of the Vietnam War. She was tired of hearing about the civil rights problems.

"Belen," Jory said, "if Emerson gets up. I will not put him to bed. You do it."

If Emerson gets up because of the music, she thought, *it would be worth the hassle of getting that child to sleep.* She wanted—needed—to hear melodies of something reminiscent, something wonderful.

"Of course, I'll put Emerson to bed," she said. Emerson! That difficult babe who bit her nipple when she nursed him, that babe who always needed to be carried. Jun-Jun began to walk when he was nine months old! And here was Emerson, already two, and still having trouble standing by himself. She carried that boy in her arms for well over a year, and when she tried to put him down, he grabbed locks of her hair in his tiny fists, refusing to let go.

She was willing to go through this, willing to hear her youngest son's wails, only if she heard music first. In her bedroom, Belen pulled out a suitcase that she kept in her closet. She went back into the living room and laid the suitcase on the sofa, then opened it. A smile came across her face as she carefully lifted out the packed items. She laid the first item on the floor and undid the wrapping, old black and white newspapers announcing the wedding between Senator Ferdinand Marcos to former beauty queen Imelda Romualdez. She crumpled up the newspaper and pulled out a long-playing record, *Elvis Presley's Greatest Hits.* On the record was a big picture of the King. She pulled out a second item, threw away the wrapping to reveal an album that read *Que Sera Sera,* sung by Doris Day. Another record was a soundtrack to a movie, *Love Is a Many-Splendored Thing,* with the actress Jennifer Jones dressed as a Chinese girl on the cover.

She pulled out one more record. This was her favorite. Her absolute favorite! It was a record of Filipina singing star Gloria Abanez. She sang slow, languid songs about love or longing or wishing or dreaming, but it was mostly about love.

"I can't believe you took those records with you," Jory said to Belen.

"I couldn't leave these behind," she said. And, yes, it was foolish to take records with her when they left the Philippines. She knew this as she packed her clothes, her photo albums. She knew this as she chose to leave more precious items, like Tabby, a teddy bear named after the actor Tab Hunter. But she couldn't leave her records!

She placed the Filipino love songs on the turntable, switched the play button, and waited for the song to begin. *"Napanaginipan Kita,"* she heard coming from the speakers. It was a song sung in Tagalog. "I dreamt of you," the song sang. She clasped her hands together, her shoulders rising to her ears, and yes, it was good to hear such romantic sounds again. *"Lagi Kitang Naaalala."* I always remember you. She closed her eyes, her head tilted upward, her lips mouthing the words of the song. Her whole body swayed.

She felt Jory reach around her, his arms embracing her, his pelvis pressed against her buttock. She laughed. She leaned her head back onto his shoulder. She turned around to kiss him, but stopped. She saw Jun-Jun and Emerson standing behind her husband. They were ten feet away, standing next to the entrance to their bedroom. Jun-Jun was yawning, wiping his eyes with his left hand. Jun-Jun's right hand was securely on Emerson's shoulder, keeping his younger brother steady on two legs.

At least Emerson isn't on all fours, she thought. *That boy is two years old! And he can't stand by himself yet?*

"Mama?" Jun-Jun said. The sheer sound of his voice, tired but curious, made her leave her husband to attend to the four-year-old.

"Yes, honey, did the music wake you?" She noticed again Jun-Jun's hand firmly holding onto Emerson's shoulder and felt sorry for him. Imagine! He had to hold his little brother up.

"Do you want to dance?" she asked her oldest, and before he could answer, she swept him up into her arms, letting Emerson fall back onto his butt; she heard the slight crinkle of diapers.

She was grateful Emerson was not crying. She used to have Emerson sleep in the same bed with her and Jory, but the babe cried so and thrashed in his sleep. He kept waking her. She would go to work the next morning exhausted and unfocused. Emerson's cries woke Jun-Jun, too, with the small boy wandering into his parent's room. She noticed Emerson calming down whenever he felt Jun-Jun near. It became apparent to her that Emerson should sleep in the same bed as her older son.

She danced with Jun-Jun in her arms, silently thanking him for being so good with Emerson. Jun-Jun giggled. *You like music, too,* Belen thought, *I knew you would.*

Jory watched his wife dance with their oldest son in her arms. He watched his youngest son sitting on the floor perplexed, trying to struggle with his stance. His wife was right, this house needed songs to fill the air. When he bought this home from a Japanese man who felt the neighborhood was going to hell (with Koreans moving onto the street), he inspected the grounds to make sure it was right.

This house—he came to know it as a 1920s California Townhouse—came with a thirty-year mortgage. What's thirty years when you're in your twenties? Jory could see himself spending the next thirty, forty, fifty years in this house. It was pleasant, with a small lawn—grass, it was always good have to have things grow in front of a home. There was a back yard made mostly of dirt, but that would change in time. But what made Jory go nuts about the place was that there was Sky. He could stand on the lawn or the back yard and see endless blue, not obscured by buildings or other rooftops or trees. There was Sky. He noted that the Sun would move directly over their home, not slightly in front or slightly behind, but right over their house.

And at night. At night. There He was, the Moon. He hovered in darkness like hope in a dying man's heart. Each night, each night, He turned and turned, revealing the burns that an angry God had given Him.

Jory and Belen invited neighbors, mostly other Filipinos, men and women from the mountains of Luzon, to join them for a house-warming. These men and women had heard of Jory and Belen's hardships and wanted to wish them well. (He did not invite his Koreans neighbors because they didn't speak English. He had a feeling they wouldn't come anyway.)

At their housewarming, they served rich cakes and chicken mar-inated in soy and vinegar, white rice and sweet rice, Coca-Cola and Sunny Delight orange juice. They served *lumpia,* Filipino eggrolls with crispy shells. They served three different kinds of noodle dishes: *pansit, palabok,* and spaghetti (they were, after all, in America now).

They all lifted Coors and Budweiser to the ceiling, toasting the Lalabans in their new home. Then Jory conducted his favorite rit-ual. He gathered all the children into the living room. The con-fused kids stood quietly while the adults stood around them. Jory pulled out a mound of coins and threw them into the air. The other adults followed, throwing metal and paper money onto the children, showering the young ones with wealth. The children laughed as silver coins and green paper fell on them, picking the money up as quickly as they could. Money and the laughter of children made Jory warm.

Belen, to her husband's chagrin, invited a priest to bless their home. Jory waited patiently as the priest made the sign of the cross, wishing well-being and happiness to the inhabitants of these walls. Jory rolled his eyes and couldn't wait for this man to leave. The priest eventually did but not before drinking three full glasses of wine. Belen shook the priest's hand, leaving a twenty-dollar donation in his palm. Jory did not shake the priest's hand, but simply nodded to him when the priest exited.

As day changed into evening, the people in their home left, went back to their houses down the street or across the way, got back on the freeway that took them to far away cities like Carson or Cerritos. With darkness around them, Jory poured salt onto his palm from a round box, a girl with an umbrella emblazoned on the cardboard canister. He stepped outside and sprinkled the salt around the circumference of their house, slapping his hands when he returned to the front steps. Then he called on Belen's ancestors to join them at this place.

In coming years, they would buy furniture from Sears-Roebuck, kitchen appliances from Montgomery Ward, and green shag carpet from Carpeteria. They became regulars at Vons Supermarket, with checkers asking them, "How are you doing today?" (They knew Jory because he delivered mail to the market.) Watching his wife dance with Jun-Jun to music he had danced to with Belen years ago, watching Emerson struggle with his footing, Jory was happy.

Years from now, if the Gods were kind, he would see this scene played out again. This time with his grandchildren. Jun-Jun and Emerson would be fully grown with lovely wives who would birth beautiful babies. He and Belen would be old and retired, expected to babysit at any given moment.

He approached the struggling Emerson on the floor, took his

son's little hands and pulled the child to his feet. "Walk with me, *sige?* Walk, okay?" Jory led his son, on unsteady legs, to the part of the house where the Magnavox was, playing songs in various Filipino languages: Tagalog, Illocano, or Cebuano. One song was in Ibaloi, with words like, *Pipiyanta ha, Pipiyanta ha . . .*